SONG OF THE UNSUNG MUSHROOM

Sarah Clarke Stuart

Connected Editions, Inc.

ISBN-13: 978-1-56178-096-9

Kindle: 978-1-56178-094-5
hardcover: 978-1-56178-095-2

Cover design by: Alexis Stuart

Connected Editions, 260 Underpass Road, #161, Brewster, MA 02631

https://connectededitions.com/

*To brothers and sisters everywhere,
especially Isaac and Alexis.*

WHAT THEY'RE SAYING ABOUT SONG OF THE UNSUNG MUSHROOM

"Sarah Clarke Stuart passionately explores how human diversity and self-discovery may break into new frontiers... and how fungi might actually be our friends."
-- David Brin, Hugo, Nebula, Locus Award-Winner; author of *Earth, Existence* and *The Postman*

"Haunting and fascinating! *Song of the Unsung Mushroom* is an intriguing exploration of identity, set within a unique science fiction mystery." -- Sarah Beth Durst, New York Times bestselling author of *The Spellshop*

"Glimmering with the excitement and danger of exploring a childhood world that never ends, *Song of the Unsung Mushroom* unearths the damp, soggy soil of the posthuman spirit." -- Roy Christopher, author of *The Medium Picture*

"*Song of the Unsung Mushroom* skillfully blends an aching portrayal of a big sister-little brother relationship with a fervent drive to investigate mysterious intelligences thriving in Florida's waterways." -- Rosemary Claire Smith, Sidewise Award Winner , "Apollo in Retrograde"

"*Song of the Unsung Mushroom* is an engaging blend of family dynamics and climate fiction, literary fiction style and science fiction tropes. It evokes lazy childhood summers even as weird scientists slowly work their way to the centre of the story. Highly recommended for SF fans who want something fresh and different." -- Ira Nayman, former editor of *Amazing Stories*

"*Song of the Unsung Mushroom* is a tale so unique it twists genres in startling ways. One of the joys of reading is picking up a book and sinking into a world of intrigue and discovery. Much rarer is finding a story so fresh and original that you know you've stumbled across something special." -- Bud Gundy, author, Emmy award-winning KQED producer, director, and on-air host

"Mind-bending and genre-twisting, *Song of the Unsung Mushroom* is a powerful tale about exploration and perilous discovery. Evocative of the Florida marshlands and inlets, and attentive to the ways that nature forms and transforms us, Sarah Clarke Stuart's novel raises crucial questions about our identities and our place(s) in the world." -- Michael Wiley, Shamus Award-Winner; author of *Monument Road*

"Sarah Clarke Stuart has written a novel that glimmers with beauty and depth. *Song of the Unsung Mushroom* is haunting and deeply original. Part family drama, part speculative wonder, it is always lyrical and alive. A truly original work that will linger long after the final page." -- Edwin Stepp, Award-Winning author and memoirist; co-producer: *Live Forever: The Ray Bradbury Odyssey*

"Against the wild, untamed beauty of North Florida's marshes and waterways, this luminous sci-fi tale flows with poetic, effortless prose, pulling you into a story so gripping you'll forget the world beyond its pages." -- Meghan Vickers, *Love Yourself to Health*

"Sarah Clarke Stuart's *Song of the Unsung Mushroom* is both lyrical sci-fi and Florida Gothic coming of age story. It evokes the poetic in the scientific and vice versa. Here, prophecy rises out of the swamps, intelligence flows through fungal networks, and siblings grow up amidst tragedy in an ecosystemic wonder much larger than any of us. *Song of the Unsung Mushroom* will pull you in and work miracles for you." -- Tim Gilmore, author of *The Mad Atlas of Virginia King* and *The Wilderness and Willie Browne*, and creator of JaxPsychoGeo.com

CONTENTS

ACKNOWLEDGEMENTS

This book would not have been possible without the inspiration of my two children, the support of my husband, Jonathan Oakes, and the encouragement and early editing work of Jen Hale. Thank you! I would also like to thank the Community Foundation of Northeast Florida for their generous grant, which supported the early stages of this book, as well as Florida State College at Jacksonville for the sabbatical that allowed me the time and focus to continue the novel. I'm especially grateful to Paul Levinson at Connected Editions for believing in this project and, with Tina Vozick, guiding it into print. Thank you also to Joe Coenraad, first fan and reader of this story. A final acknowledgement goes to my late father, Gary James Clarke, who passed away in 2024. Even as his memory began to decline, he never stopped reminding me how important it was to finish this project. Thank you, Dad!

EPIGRAPHS

"Every organism – including homo sapiens – is an assemblage of organic algorithms."

–-Yuval Noah Harrari, *Homo Deus*

"Once you are real, you can't be ugly, except to those who don't understand."

–-Skin Horse, *The Velveteen Rabbit*

PROLOGUE

The pointed finger of a live oak tree branch taps on the bedroom window, tap-tap-tapping the girl awake. The trees are growing too close to the windows. Someone needs to trim them before next hurricane season, Gran keeps saying.

The girl pushes herself up onto her elbows and looks around, recalibrating after being immersed in dreams, tuning into the frequency of waking life.

The bedroom is cheery and tame: pink curtains, a white wicker dresser, the closet with its door askew, floral dresses peeking out. A messy notebook lies on the desk, tendrils of torn pages falling from its spiral.

It's all so different from the earthy dreams still stuck beneath her fingernails, entangled in the root of her spine. She's always slow to cross that bridge from nighttime dreams to daytime dreams.

At night came visions of growth and connection, rot and decay. Nature doesn't know the difference between these things. Rot is growth. Decay is connection. Mycelium works its way through dead wood, transforms timber into mushrooms, and gives new life to creatures. This time, she'd dreamed that a pregnant bear ate the mushroom. The fungus would be transformed into energy for birthing cubs.

The girl always wakes with that same musty taste in her mouth and the memory of her naked feet planted into the earth somewhere in the middle of wilderness. She was sinking, she was eating, she was feeding her young, she was being consumed. Was she the bear? Was she the wood? Was she growing or dying? It wasn't clear...

There is no death. Only energy transformed.

She can hear the words of the pastor in her mind. The Healer. Was he planting these dreams in her head? Or was it *The Book of Instructions*? Last night, she fell asleep reading it. Now, she reaches for the paperback submerged in the folds of her blankets.

"Page 24: *Do not mistake the word 'death' as the opposite of life. Death does not oppose life. Death creates it, and life always strives towards death. It is a goal. But never the end. Cycling, recycling, clinging, letting go.*"

She climbs down from the top bunk of her bed, a single mattress she'd long outgrown. She can hear the morning noises coming from the kitchen downstairs. An animal mewling, a spoon clinking the side of a bowl, her brother's pubescent baritone, her grandfather's clipped tone.

Still in a haze, she can't find language–the name of her brother, the creature making noise, all of the labels of things. She does remember Gran. And the pastor, who some call The Healer.

Smells are easy, and so are textures and sounds. But making words out loud is so much more difficult than listening and feeling and smelling.

"I am...," she says to the image in the mirror. It's a start. Everything will come back in a matter of minutes. She's not going to panic this time.

Do not try to be a flower if you are a tree. Be the best tree in the forest, and let the flowers alone ...to be themselves.

"Claire!" Gunther shouts from below. "It's time. You have to drive me. I can't be late again."

All of it floods back at once: She's eighteen now. She drives to school every day in the green station wagon. She's not doing well in math. Because of that, she may not graduate from high school. She doesn't know what she will do after graduation anyway. But there's that place in the mountains she could go; the other kids at church were talking about it. Just for the summer.

At the window, she peers out at a dreary Florida sky. Across the yard, she can see the lake water lapping against the trees. Why is the water so high? And that's when she remembers it: her parents are dead.

Boom. She waits for the emotion to hit. She holds tight to the window sill and stares hard into the trees, looking for signs of wildlife in the grey morning.

But the weight of grief does not crush her this time. It's mostly a feeling of being untethered. Perhaps she belongs to no one. She can go anywhere she wants when high school is over.

The Book of Instructions keeps her going these days, and she has so many questions for the Healer, but Gran says there's only one book that a real Christian pastor would share with his congregants, and it's not that. Gran was suspicious of him from the beginning. She'll never allow her to go anywhere with him.

The girl continues to review the data she'll need in order to get through the day, in order to function at least for now.

There's a loud knock. And then another. Bam, bang, bam. A fist on her bedroom door. She recoils and covers her ears.

"Stop, Gunther!"

This was easy enough to say.

He continues to knock, now with both hands.

"Coming ... I'm coming," she says quietly. And he stops. But stays by the door.

Things are still hazy. Every morning these shadow-dreams stick to her brain, creating a cloud. Her friends tease her for being spacey. Her grandfather says "she's not all there these days."

But the truth is that she can't remember anything before the last few years, not even her parents' death. Her grandmother seems angry that the girl acts differently. But she can not remember how to be. What is it that Gran dislikes so much about her now? What has changed? Something is missing. Something big.

Her brother's footsteps recede.

She brushes her hair into a thick ponytail, rummages through the closet, and pulls out the same sweater and jeans from the day before. Gran will protest, so she runs directly out the front door without passing the kitchen.

As she moves faster, all the bits of data are now trickling back into her brain. This is good.

She can hear her grandfather bellowing at her from inside the house, and fear jumps through her body like electricity. This is something she has no trouble remembering– the fear of other people's anger. The fear of other people. This is what makes her most human.

PART I: GUNTHER

CHAPTER 1:
CANDLESTICK LANE

Gunther

Present Day 2007

Gunther Flynn sits on the front porch steps of his childhood home at 18 Candlestick Lane, a house once filled with the endless tides of a growing family: hugging and fighting and eating and singing and practicing and pushing and pulling each other—toward and away, toward and away.

The home is a simple farmhouse set on a lake that leads to an inlet that leads to the river. The raucous, frog-croaking night has transformed itself into a quiet morning, and the smell is both putrid and intoxicating to Gunther: fishy, briny marshland.

The tide must be low.

All morning, the water had been seeping out, ocean-bound, exposing the bottom-most life of the marshes and lakes with all their squiggling bugs and jagged oysters and schools of minnows and stick-leg birds. But it would return soon enough; just when it seemed like the tub was drained, the tide would turn, and the rivers and lakes would fill up once again. He wonders now if Claire had known something that he hadn't understood then -- how things that disappear might return in different forms.

He and Claire used to imagine that the knobbly cypress knees rising at the lake's edges were some kind of marshy fairytale creatures that would come to life at low tide after the sun went down. Swamp Hobbits. Were those creatures imaginary after all? Nothing is as certain or clear as it once was.

Gunther shifts on the steps, fidgeting with a loose scab of paint on the porch balustrade. His fingers itch to peel more of it, but Gran's voice rings in his head: *Get out the paint brush, Gunther. Don't leave things half-done.* The memory stings more than it should, and he drops the flake onto the ground. Gran had always insisted on keeping a fresh coat of paint on the house.

When he'd gotten the news, Gunther had imagined coming back to the house with Claire. Now it feels strange without Claire or Gran there. The house seems more neglected than he's ever seen it.

Inside, he hears Mack's shuffle and the creak of the stairs. Gunther tenses. He's not ready to face him yet.

Memories reach their long fingers up from the earth, out of the riverbeds, and make their way into his nerves and bones and bloodstream. As he stares into the overgrown ferns in the garden, an early one comes to life: Claire squatting close to the plant, choosing the fattest strands of fern for her makeshift wings.

Light streams through the pale, ripply leaves, and he can almost see her now: weaving the branches together, duct-taping them to the back of her shirt, jumping from the highest step, leaves streaming, taking flight. He recalls looking up into the sky and seeing her far above the earth, fern-winged and free ... but of course that could not have really happened.

The front door creaks open behind him. Gunther flinches, his thumb catching the edge of the porch rail.

"You've been sitting out here all morning," Mack says. Gunther doesn't turn, but he can hear the weight of the old man's body as he lowers himself into the rocking chair beside the door.

"Just thinking," Gunther replies. He doesn't look directly at Mack.

Mack grunts. "Shouldn't think too much. Makes a man weak without action in accordance."

Gunther clenches his jaw. Mack was always repeating rudimentary life lessons that made no sense. He suppresses an eye-roll and forces himself to stay quiet.

It used to be that Gunther and his sister were inseparable. It was Claire who taught him to build a treehouse and to catch fish with his bare hands and to breathe underwater. It was she who gave him a paddle and pushed him out in the canoe until he learned to row, and she who convinced him that a housecat could navigate the waterways just as well as a human captain at sea. She trained the cat herself, she said.

She was always braiding strands of fiction so tightly into the knot of reality that a young boy could not possibly pull them apart. There are people who can do that...undetectably: they interlace all those bits to make a bright picture, and the myths are the parts you want to believe the most. As Gunther got older he realized that she, as much as he, probably could not distinguish the truth from her fantasies. After all, she was not even three years older than him.

Mack shifts in his chair, and the wood groans under his weight. "You going to sit out here all day? Gran's not coming back, you know."

Gunther snaps his head toward Mack, finally looking at him straight on. He wants to say, You think I don't know that? But all he manages is, "No, I know."

The old man stares out at the yard, his face unreadable. "Never know with you kids these days. Always got your heads in the clouds."

Gunther stands abruptly, the wooden step creaking beneath

him. "I'm going inside."

Mack just rocks back and forth, muttering something under his breath that Gunther chooses not to hear.

Inside the house, the smell of woodsmoke and clean laundry is overwhelming, almost oppressive. Gunther moves to the fridge out of habit, though he knows there's nothing in there he wants. The shelves are mostly empty except for a half gallon of skim milk, a purplish apple, several containers of crusty-looking leftovers.

He's about to close it when Mack's voice drifts in from the porch. "You should find your sister."

"What?" Gunther slams the fridge door shut and grips the handle until his knuckles turn white. He doesn't answer. There's no point.

Looking out of the kitchen window, he can see the old canoe turned face down at the edge of the lake, what looks like little more than a retention pond right now. The tide must be really low.

He stares at the oak tree that held him tight for so many years; the highest branch, bent like a sling for sitting, was his sanctuary; he would search the water, long after Claire left. Even all these years later he is angry that Childhood Claire is no longer around. She would've been the strong one.

The year she turned 15, something must have changed. He knew it wasn't her age like the grownups said ("Naturally, a teenage girl is not going to want to climb trees with her little brother anymore, Gunther.") But Gunther recalls that it was something else altogether that made the brother and sister drift apart. The Claire who returned wasn't just different—it was as if someone had switched off a light behind her eyes.

Gran would often tell the story about that hurricane when Claire disappeared. Gunther was white-faced and shaking when he claimed that Claire had been kidnapped. He was sure of it. She was taken underwater and whisked away by some malevolent organization. He remembered the strange lights beneath the water's surface, the way the lake seemed alive with unnatural movement despite the storm. When Claire returned, her skin had a different scent -- earthy.

When she had returned that evening, Claire laughed at his story. But he knew his sister had changed, that something was terribly wrong. Her once-fiery eyes that sparkled with shards of yellow and red, now were devoid of life -- not warm, not even brown anymore, but steely -- almost grey. Adolescence, his grandmother had explained. It can do weird things.

Gunther's hand tightens on the edge of the counter as he stares out at the lake. He can hear Mack moving inside now, his heavy steps punctuated by the occasional grunt.

"Cain't believe the damn oak is still standing after all these hurricanes," Mack says, breaking the silence. He pronounces it with only two syllables--her-canes. "Shoulda tore up outta the ground by now. Ground's so wet all the time."

Gunther nods. He thinks about the roots of that tree, how they mirror the branches above, sprawling and tangled beneath the earth. A mirror image, his mother used to say. But now he wonders if it's more like people—roots tangled beyond comprehension, invisible to everyone, even ourselves.

He doesn't realize he's speaking out loud until Mack grunts in response. "What's that supposed to mean?"

Gunther shrugs. "Nothing." He stares out at the lake, remembering its secrets.

CHAPTER 2: THE OLD CANOE

1999

From the Atlantic Ocean, a seagull flew inland, following the St. Johns River around a bend and down a narrow inlet until it arrived at a flat body of water dotted around with houses, where two children could be seen at the edge of a lake: a dark-haired boy holding tight to the aluminum sides of a canoe as he sat perched at the bow, and a lanky girl wading in the shallows, the tips of her fingers securing the stern. She crouched and launched, swinging one long leg and then the next into the canoe. The boy braced himself for several seconds as the canoe surged forward, the water rippling quietly beneath them. He leaned into the bow, letting the cool spray of water fleck his face, and let out a "wheee" sound.

The seagull soared above them, releasing its unmistakable throaty laugh, triggering memories in each of them of long summer days at the beach.

A damp bouquet of late-May blooms -- jasmine, magnolia, ligustrum -- swirled in the morning breeze, and the back porch chimes clinked and tinkled.

At age 12, Claire's quick movements and curious energy made her seem scampery, like a squirrel darting between branches, her deep amber eyes always scanning for the next adventure. In contrast, her blue-eyed brother had wide features, a broad face, and moved through the world in big, fluid motions. She was two and a half years older but only slightly bigger.

From the moment Gunther came home from the hospital as an infant, snug in a lime-green sleeper, the siblings had a unique bond. Everybody said so. Claire had been small for her age, and as the baby grew in great gulps and lengths, soon enough they were the same density, Gunther all round and muscley and Claire feather-boned and long.

As with most families, things started out hopeful— safe, small, easy to manage. But over time, the threads begin to fray, catching on the rough edges of the outside world. It's hard to tell exactly when one begins tugging away from the others.

Gunther's first memory had a dark and gritty feel to it; a memory of the damp scent of mildew clinging to the car seats. The memory was steeped in unease, the kind that made his small body tense even as the rain pattered rhythmically on the car's roof. They were in a car, his father driving over the narrow red bridge at night, and it was raining. He and his sister were bundled under blankets, a worn out three-year old in blue footed pajamas, and a five-year old girl in a Strawberry Shortcake nightgown. Gunther remembers sitting and waiting for what seemed like hours in a dreary parking lot, waiting for their mother. He recalls the tight feeling in his chest, the anxiety about what would happen next, the deep longing for his mother. When she finally appeared outside the bar, a stranger lightly holding her arm, Gunther squeezed his eyes shut and buried his head under the blanket. His father got out, slammed the car door, and suddenly there were loud voices. Claire whimpered beside him and squeezed his hand.

Finally his mother was in the front seat— teary-eyed and still as a stone. After the ugly laughter and the shouting, her silence now was like a death. She was there but not there. She was buried somewhere beneath heavy makeup, unfamiliar clothes, and the sickly smoke that Gunther could smell even with his nose burrowed in the blankets. He wanted to reach out and touch her, but he was afraid it might not be her. She reached for him, but only the top of his head stuck out, so she tousled his hair. The familiar fingertips pressed on his scalp, and after several minutes he relaxed into a deep sleep.

There were several disappearing acts, as their father called them, but that was the one that stuck with him.

That version of Jessica didn't align with the mom he knew who would take them on exciting trail hikes, and teach them about plants and mushrooms and agree to adopt any baby animal that they happened upon. When Mom was good, she was great, but there are big gaps, times when she was just a shadow of herself. Dad was much more predictable.

But recently things had been getting better. Claire and Gunther had their canoe. Mom was going back to school, back to the university studies she had left long ago. She was in graduate school when Claire was born, and she had never finished.

Mom and Dad still sometimes fought about money. Dad would say, "I'm the one paying for all this. Must be nice to just do what you want, Jessica." It wasn't very nice, the tone he used, but maybe he was right. Mom wanted to be a mycologist--that's a mushroom scientist. Even to a young boy, it seemed like a frivolous expense of time. She could very well stay at home with the children and forage for mushrooms, Dad pointed out.

Before the canoe came along, there was no boat at the house, unless you counted that ancient fishing skiff sitting dormant for decades, weeds growing all around it. It was motorless and filled with holes--someone's long-ago target practice. The arrival of the canoe felt like a small miracle, something that breathed life into their otherwise ordinary days. It was their ticket to freedom. For Claire and Gunther, it symbolized possibilities they hadn't yet imagined.

The Flynn family had inherited the house from a great uncle who built it "with his bare hands" long before wealthier folks began developing subdivisions there. At one time, there had been a barn and a decent plot of land for goats and chickens, but since the expansion of the suburbs, the family sold their extra acreage to developers. Fortunately for the children, they still had a sliver of waterfront. Most of their neighbors had sturdy docks and motorized boats, but not the Flynns. There was never enough money for that kind of thing.

Gunther believed the canoe had belonged to a kind neighbor who passed away. They encountered him only once, on an unusually happy and peaceful day at home.

An old man and his wife were out on the lake fishing that day, not far from shore. The army green canoe appeared brand new and its aluminum rails shone silvery in the sun. Gunther was seven years old at the time, and he was splashing on the lake's edge, while Claire surveyed the waterscape from the sweetgum tree above. Mom was in good spirits -- working on the vegetable garden nearby.

Gunther loved watching the boats go by, especially when a motorboat came along and sent waves out to the shore for him to play in. The low growl of the engine and the slap of water against the hull thrilled him, making the lake feel alive with motion.

He was crouched over a fiddler crab, imitating its sideways walk, when he saw the man and woman and their fishing poles. When the man unhooked a shimmery fish and placed it in a red bucket, Gunther stood up and watched. Claire watched too, perched above like an egret on a branch.

"That's a catfish," the man said, loud enough so the children could hear. He was smiling, looking into his tacklebox, but he knew the children were listening. "But don't you worry about him," he continued, "He's got plenty of water in that bucket, and he's already forgotten about the hook. It was just a pinch."

Gunther wondered what made it a catfish; he imagined it should at least have pointy ears. But it just looked like a regular old fish. As though responding to Gunther's thoughts, the man held up the fish and grinned. "See there?" He held up the slippery creature and pointed to its snout. "The whiskers there -- ya know it's a catfish."

Then he said, "you kids want to hold the fishing pole? Here, have a go." He paddled to the shore and held out the green and silver pole, making eye contact with their mother, who had wandered over to the lakeside. She gave a nod, and Gunther stretched out an arm and grabbed the handle and reel.

"And ... some bait," he said, holding up something small and alive that Gunther and Claire couldn't quite see.

Gunther let the man hook the bait, and then he dunked the line into the water and waited. One little tug and the bait was gone. Gunther groaned when he saw the empty hook, but he wasn't discouraged. He looked to the man for more bait.

Not far away, their father, Josh, had been watching; he frowned and tipped his hat at the man.

"My turn!" piped up Claire, clambering down the trunk and jumping off the lowest branch. Jessica shushed her and motioned to Gunther to return the rod.

But the man smiled and put up his hands saying, "No, no it's yours now. Enjoy, kids!"

Josh joined them at the shoreline as he and Jessica exchanged looks.

The old man handed over a small jar of wriggling bait. He and the old woman smiled, as the whole family thanked them loudly. Gunther held the jar tight, peering inside at the tiny fish, and Claire held the pole, keeping her gaze on the old man and woman in the canoe for a long time as they paddled away.

***

Next they heard, the woman had passed away. A few months after that, her husband followed. One week later, the canoe and two oars showed up on shore, right in the backyard. There was no note or phone call. Mom and Dad made it clear that the children were required to knock on all the houses within two miles to see if someone had lost a boat. They posted fliers on telephone poles.

Not finding an owner, the canoe was taken out on its first journey on a crisp day in October. Gunther could still feel the crisp air on his face, the tingling excitement in his chest as they pushed off from the shore. Claire laughed, a bright sound that echoed across the water, as the canoe glided smoothly over the surface. He marveled at how vast the lake seemed from this new perspective— the world opening up like a story yet to be written. They were untethered, explorers venturing into the unknown, and the thrill of freedom made the moment unforgettable.

Gunther would remember that afternoon the rest of his life, even long after his other memories faded: the geese honking overhead, throwing shadows on the lake, the rounded hollow belly of their own little ship, an orange flotation vest stuffed under each seat. The children waved at their parents, separated by what seemed like miles of water, liberated for the first time in their young lives.

They spent the next 6 months learning to paddle and steer and fish, as their father kept watch from the backyard. Gunther remembers it this way, always: their father keeping watch outside, strong and worried, their presence a steadying force, while their mother moved slowly through the house, a hazy shape in the window — a reminder of something fragile, slipping further away. This dynamic stayed with him, shaping his need to protect others and fueling a quiet resentment toward the helplessness he'd felt as a child.

Dad warned them never to venture from the lake without permission but was never clear about what was out there. Gunther imagined treacherous waterfalls downstream. Mom laughed when he admitted this, showing him on a map where the gentle tides connected to the ocean. It was not like a mountain river, she told the children. It was connected to something bigger, flooding and ebbing according to the moon.

CHAPTER 3: DECAY

The Hybrid

By the time the video is found, it is damaged and much of the footage is missing. It is a VHS tape labeled "Experiment 2B: The Early Hybrids."

Much of it is just grainy security footage of research labs and offices, but there are a few scenes featuring interviews and lab experiments. These documentary-style shots appear to be the handiwork of a novice camera operator.

In the first discernible interview, the digital date at the bottom of the screen reads JAN. 29 1999. A long-legged man in a white lab coat is sitting next to an office desk. He is absentmindedly clicking a pen. A shaky caption reads: Dr. David Meehan: Head of Research, and under that, Location: Nest 33. A voice from behind the camera says, "okay -- rolling."

Dr. Meehan nods and pushes his glasses up onto the crook of his nose. His head is higher than the camera, so he shifts forward and down, pressing his palms onto his knees. He speaks directly into the lens.

"So first, I will say that this is not the kind of genetic cell replication we saw in Scotland a few years ago. At first, we considered building on that concept of somatic cell nuclear transfer process, but the cross-species and even cross-kingdom nature of what we do makes our procedure worlds away from basic cloning. We kind of leap-frogged over certain things, you might say. It's a little unorthodox, the way we do things here."

He chuckles. His British accent is slight but bewitching, and as another scientist enters the picture, he flashes a smile, leans back, and continues. She stands next to him, most of her face out of the picture.

"Our lovely assistant here has even contributed some of her own genetic material for this research, which, uh, can sometimes make things complicated. We don't normally do this. But she comes from a unique background. And it's turning out that her hybrids are the most robust -- a brilliant surprise for all of us." He pauses for a moment and then waves his hand in the direction of a chair nearby. The assistant sits down next to him as the camera zooms out slightly.

Off camera, someone says, "state your name and title," but Dr. Meehan sits up, his eyes flashing in the voice's direction.

"Uh, just your title, dear," he says to the woman. But before she can reply, he speaks for her: "This is Donor X and an esteemed scientist in training." He forces a smile.

The woman nods and smiles too, appearing unrattled. She is lean in the face, with dark eyes and honey-colored hair. A caption appears on the screen: "Donor X: Prototype/ First Genetic Lineage."

She sits up as tall as she can but is still dwarfed by her colleague. "Um, can I share some results, Dr. Meehan?" Her voice faulters, and it's clear that she is younger than she first appears.

"Yes, let's discuss the amazing potential we have growing here in the lab," he replies. "What are we working on today, dear?"

She looks at the camera and begins to speak, but the video cuts out and shows static for the next 30 seconds.

In the next scene, the same woman can be seen attending to some infants in a large, sterile-looking room. There is no sound. The date says, MAR. 2 1999. Rows of infant boxes are set up like a maternity ward, but only a few are occupied. Medical personnel mill about.

Then, another woman appears in the frame, and she begins talking. Her hair is pulled back in a severe ponytail, but her brown face is soft and beautiful, and her black eyes are animated with speech as she gestures to the infants and then to the equipment on the other side of the room. There is no caption on this one, and it is silent throughout the clip.

This is followed by several minutes of static until the sound cuts on again and a woman can be seen holding a baby wrapped in hospital swaddling. The woman's face is obscured, but she is slight and blonde like "Donor X" in the first scene. Then there is a close shot of the infant, its pale skin luminescent, and its dark eyes staring at the harsh lights above. The date is MAY 3 1999.

There is something on the child's forehead, appearing at first as a crust of blood. This time, there's sound, and several voices can be heard speaking at once. Urgent-- but quiet at first.

"It's happening again…we need to document it this time."

"Can you get a better shot? May I take a peek through the camera?" Unmistakably, Dr. Meehan's voice.

Next, there is a tighter shot of the baby's face who is squirming and squeezing its eyes shut in a pre-crying expression.

"Dr. Meehan! Please. We need to get her to surgery," a woman says.

"I agree, Dr. Meehan. Right now," says another voice.

The infant begins to cry—small yelps at first with long silences in between.

"We have the treatment in its system," he replies. "This will buy us some time."

"No. No!" shouts the first woman. "The mycobiont treatment is not working. I told you that yesterday!"

The baby is turning red as its cry grows into a full-throated, piercing screech.

"Okay, yes. We are headed to surgery. But...Quick shot of the species here .... Please, sir -- bring that camera in." Dr. Meehan's voice comes through cool and clear, in a tone that doesn't match the growing chaos around him.

The camera wobbles and then zooms back in on the child, its forehead wrinkled in fear as it continues to shriek. The mark just above the brow bone appears to be growing. It's not blood at all, but some sort of greyish-brown lump as though the baby has a large birth mark. But as the camera zooms, the image blurs.

The scene shifts unexpectedly and jolts toward the ground.

"Get off!" says the first woman. "Turn that thing off." The camera resets on her face. It is Donor X.

The woman looks directly into the camera, tears in her eyes, then she looks down at the infant, her mouth dropping open in fear. Ever so slightly, she recoils. The growth is expanding over the baby's forehead, moving up towards the head and across the temples.

The camera falters as the others huddle around the child. It continues to roll but unfocused and off-center. The voices and crying are cacophonous for the next several seconds.

And then there is a single scream from one of the women. Abruptly, the crying ceases, bringing with it a stone-cold silence. All that can be heard is the breathing of the cameraman.

"No! No," says a woman. "She's...she's disappearing. Do something, Dr. Meehan. Please! She's..."

Donor X is seen briefly at the edge of the shot, crumpled over the baby and squeezing it to her chest. But when she opens her arms, there is nothing there. Just a thick layer of dust, which tumbles out of the blanket, creating a puff that clouds the camera lens.

The video fuzzes out for a beat, and then the scientist in the ponytail is shown, looking calm and professional. It's the woman from the infant ward in the scene without sound. Now, the date says, JUN. 7 1999 and the caption reads, "Experiment 2B: Results with Dr. Das."

Others are standing around, gathered awkwardly for an announcement.

"The benefits of this technology will far outweigh any ethical concerns some detractors have raised in the past," says Dr. Das. Coils of light hair frame her dark face. She smiles warmly. "I don't think they understand the quick progress we will be able to make in human health, not to mention the incredible work we can do to fix the looming environmental crises."

The camera zooms out and other scientists are seen nodding in agreement. Donor X stands in the background, arms folded and looking away. The camera pans in the direction she is gazing, and a large window can be seen. On the other side is the infant ward, but all cribs appear empty now.

"There are losses, of course," continues Dr. Das. "There always are. But these small failures lead to future successes. And, in this case, we know exactly what needs to be more aligned next time. Namely, the rapid development of the specimen. We should have accounted for this: human development is far too slow to keep up with this particular species. This is a very exciting outcome though! It means we don't have to wait years to know how the technology will behave. Our test subjects simply need to be more developmentally mature at inception."

Dr. Meehan is now in the shot, smiling and nodding. "Absolutely," he adds, folding his hands. "And this last hybrid -- well, she is the most robust of them all. That was clearly the one. The secret formula. We just need to get the timing and development right next time. Here's to The Hybrid!"

The others clap timidly and nod, all except the small blonde woman in the back, whose arms are still crossed, eyes shifted downward.

"Come on in, everyone," says Dr. Meehan. "Gather in for a group shot, how 'bout it?"

Donor X drops her arms and moves forward hesitantly. She appears much thinner than the previous scenes --older too, although only six months have passed. The white lab coat is far too big for her narrow frame. She forces a smile as everyone arranges themselves for the picture, and the video fades into static once again.

CHAPTER 4: CREATURES
IN THE WATER

Gunther

1999

As they paddled through the water on this Tuesday morning in June, a white cat with black splotches peeked out from underneath the middle seat, letting out one loud yowl, and then another. The cat insisted on traveling with the two, but never failed to complain for the first 10 minutes of each trip.

"Cat," as he was first named when he started hanging around, was spotted -- like a dairy cow -- and he would yowl when he joined the family on long walks ... trailing behind them, imploring them at each crossroads to turn back. He had beautiful, prize-winning hind quarters, with fuzzy pantaloons and a squirrel tail, but in the front, there was a chunk of ear missing, evidence of his past life as a tomcat, and a bald spot around his neck where an atrocious collar must have been -- another past life.

It was only after Claire and Gunther discovered the cat's willingness to go boating that he finally earned a real name. One Saturday morning the big tomcat hopped in the canoe, and off they went. Thus, Cat became Captain.

Today they had a clear goal. A neighbor across the lake had reported an otter sighting. Their mother warned them that otters could carry rabies, but the idea of seeing an otter in real life was too much of a temptation. The neighbor may as well have announced she saw a unicorn handing out candy across the lake.

They made their own sandwiches that morning and filled a large Thermos with water and powdered Country Time lemonade.

When the children stopped paddling and the boat stood still, Captain lapped from the lake. Gunther rustled around in the tackle box where he had left two rolls of Smarties. Captain pounced on Gunther's rustling, as though there was live bait.

"Ouch," Gunther groaned.

Claire laughed loud enough to scare up a flock of Canadian geese that had been loitering nearby.

"You're so loud," Gunther said. But he was smiling into the sky. Happy to have the full attention of his sister, to be on an adventure with Captain, to be out of the watchful eye of Gran, who constantly shooed them away from video games and smelled like cigarettes. She was babysitting while Mom was at school, even though they were old enough to watch out for themselves, Gunther thought.

"Let's go," said Claire, waving her oar in the air. Slightly heavier, and better skilled at paddling, she always sat in the back, steering their journey, sometimes coaching Gunther on his form.

The canoe glided along the shore for a while, and then they turned directly north heading straight across the broadest part of the lake toward the haunted shack lot. It was the best spot to tie up in a neighborhood where most of the lakeside was private property. No one seemed to know who owned the rundown cabin, and so it was a perfect destination for Claire and Gunther: wooded, mysterious, and sheltered. There was a shed near the dock, partially open, with a rusted metal roof for shade.

The otters had been spotted at the Hadleys' lot next door. The Hadleys, a privately-schooled, Presbyterian family who had a pool and a trampoline and a sailboat, spent the summers in North Carolina, so Claire and Gunther needn't worry about that side. They were already gone for the summer. But they had to keep watch for the Whitehead brothers, Frank and Randy, who smoked and were both too big for their ages. They sometimes hung around the vacant lots in this area, leaving behind smoldering fires and empty beer bottles.

The lake was quiet, the gentle lapping of water against the canoe mixing with the faint rustle of leaves in the warm breeze. The sweetgum trees, bright with spring leaves, cast dappled shadows on the shore, their stillness a striking contrast to the hidden tension rippling beneath the surface. A great blue heron touched down on a nearby log jutting out into the water. It peered backward at the two humans in typical bird fashion, judgmental and haughty. Claire placed a finger over her lips. Hush. They had never seen one this close. It stretched its impossibly thin neck and fluffed out its feathers.

Captain pounced out of the boat, and darted straight at the giant bird, perhaps not realizing how huge it was until he got close. He cowered under a nearby bush as it showed the full span of its wings and flew away.

"Captain!" both kids shouted in unison.

Claire hopped out, right into the thigh-high water, while Gunther searched the water for evidence of otter life. He knew they liked to hang out among the trees at the water's edge, and this lakeside had no shortage of thick tree trunks, both alive and dead.

Gunther tied the boat to a leg of the dock and scrounged around the tackle box for more candy. Suddenly it was quiet. He looked around. No sign of Claire. A slight panic in the pit of his stomach. How could she have disappeared so fast?

He stepped into the wooded area, leaving their lunch bag in the boat. He could see the corner of the crumbling house in the distance. There's no way Claire went in that direction …?

But Gunther suddenly realized that's exactly where she went. In fact, that's why she wanted to come this way. She had said they came for the otters, but really she wanted someone to come with her to take a closer look at that haunted spot, the one that Gunther never even wanted to think about, much less go near.

There was a crackle in the bushes. And then another. And another.

Gunther froze. His pulse quickened, a hollow thrum echoing in his ears. He wanted to shout "Claire!" but no sound came out, his throat clenched tight as if even breathing would summon some hidden threat from the underbrush. His feet felt rooted to the ground, torn between retreating to the safety of the canoe and pressing forward into the unknown. He looked toward the crackling and saw a small grey bird flitting about, stuck in a large brambly spot. He exhaled loud, stepped once toward it, and the bird found an opening and flew away. Such a little thing to make so much noise.

In the distance, he heard Claire summoning him. She sounded excited.

She was much closer than he had imagined. Around the next corner there was a clearing and there was the old house. She was grinning, and in her hands she held a fishing net.

"Where were you? You left me by myself. You're not supposed to do that."

"I was right here…." She trailed off. "But look at this! We could catch an otter!"

"Let's go back," Gunther said, shielding his eyes from the sight of the dilapidated building. "You know I hate this place."

"Gunther, it's just an old house. There's no such thing as a thing being haunted. It's just a bunch of old wood and bricks. And there's probably all sorts of stuff in there!"

A splashing sound came from the lakeside, and they both started.

"What was that?"

Claire bunched up the net under her arm and headed down the trail, Gunther close behind.

At the lakeside, the canoe was teetering back and forth in the water, and the lunch bag was gone. The water rippled. The plastic bag was floating on top of the water.

"Gunther…" Claire pointed out to the end of the ripple in the water. They could just make out two marbly eyeballs peeking above the water's surface.

"Alligator!" they shouted in unison.

Gunther's jaw dropped open, and his fists balled up tight, nails digging into the skin.

"Let's go," he said. "We should go back home."

"Why? It's just an alligator. You know they are shy."

"Yes, if you don't feed them. We just fed them!"

Claire waved him away and started back down the trail to the shack. "Your fault. You left the food in the canoe."

Gunther stood still in protest, wanting to leave but not wanting to get near the water. He waited several minutes.

He noticed there was still a trail of crackers from their picnic floating in the water. He knew the alligator would return any minute. But just as he was about to run, a tiny hand reached out and snatched three crackers from the surface of the water.

Without turning his head, he whispered to his sister: "Otters! Otters, Claire! Otters!"

A pair of tiny brown hands, and then a slick head, popped above the surface. And then another head.

The fear from only moments ago was gone, and Gunther spun around and started down the trail to fetch Claire again. But as soon as he turned the corner, another predator blocked his path. Arms crossed, legs like trees, it was Frank. 13 years old, only a grade higher than Claire, but somehow twice the size. He grinned at Gunther with only his mouth, ice-grey eyes unmoving.

Just the week before on the bus, Gunther had stood up to Frank. Not intentionally of course. Frank's friends were teasing Claire, trying to get her to sit with them, an onslaught of mean-spirited flirtations. Claire paid them no attention as Gunther tried to push through to his usual spot next to her. These boys were not as big as Frank. Gunther pushed through a throng of them and gritted his teeth, inadvertently bumping his lunch box into someone the next aisle down. Not realizing that the someone was Frank.

"That's my seat… " Gunther told the boys, but then he trailed off as Frank slowly rose from his seated position where he had been pawing at a giggling girl.

"That's your seat?" Frank laughed, slowly looking around. He pointed to all of the seats in the front of the bus. "These are all my seats and you can sit in them only if I tell you. Your dumb sister can sit there. You can't. So that ain't your seat." Gunther stood there for several seconds in shock. Then he noticed the fire in Claire's eyes.

"Shut up Frank," she said. Quiet, but strong. She reached out and pulled Gunther toward her through the crowd of boys. They began rumbling, and Frank reached out to grab Gunther, but just then the bus door shut with a loud scrape and suctioning.

The bus driver didn't say a word but opened his eyes wide so the whites stood out fluorescent against the dark irises. He rose out of his seat, all six feet and five inches of him, and everyone stopped talking and took a seat wherever they could find one.

Now, Gunther stood face to face with Frank in the woods, far from any supervising adults. All he wanted was to get to Claire and tell her about the otters. He wished Frank would disappear.

"You're trespassin'," said Frank in a scratchy drawl. "This ain't your property."

"It's not yours either." Gunther's breaths were fast and shallow.

"My dad is friends with the property owner and he wants me to make sure nobody gits on it."

Gunther knew he was lying, but he didn't say so.

"We had to tie up our boat because..." Gunther weakly pointed toward the dock.

Then there were footsteps, more than one pair. Gunther suddenly felt chilled despite the humid weather, and he tried to stifle his shiver. There were deep voices.

"Frank! What are you doing? Get over here and help us." It was Frank's older brother, Randy...and Randy's friend, who looked like he had recently been released from prison according to Gunther's limited knowledge of that kind of thing.

"There's a trespasser," said Frank, locking his gaze on Gunther.

"What?" Randy's voice sounded hoarse and dangerous.

Gunther opened his mouth to protest as Randy approached.

"Haha. Hey buddy," Randy said to Gunther. He looked amused as though they'd found a baby rabbit tangled in a raccoon trap. "what's up?" He turned to his brother. "Frank, stop being a bully and come help us."

Randy, 15 years old, flicked his cigarette into the woods with a powerful thumb and forefinger. Gunther followed it with his eyes and then looked into Randy's face. He was smiling, but the cold eyes did not match his kind words.

Just then Claire appeared. She and Frank exchanged a hateful gaze for several seconds until Randy punched him in the arm hard. Frank winced.

"Don't pay any attention to Frank. You kids have fun." But his smile was menacing, and he seemed to look at Claire for too long.

Finally the boys turned away and disappeared into the woods, their raspy voices fading away; a grotesque laugh could be heard, and then, farther away, another.

"Stupid, oversized ...," muttered Claire still keeping watch where the boys had retreated.

At the lake's edge again, they spotted them, first one and then the next, and then there were half a dozen otters swimming in front of them, playing and snacking on Claire and Gunther's lunch.

Both children wondered now if there had never been an alligator at all --maybe they imagined it. They watched the slick, brown bodies dive and play and nibble, reminding them that in certain species, childhood can last forever.

***

When Claire and Gunther got home that afternoon, they were muddy and happy, but Gran was gone and Dad was cooking and ruminating aloud, which meant only one thing: Mom was under pillows and sheets, probably smelling of wine. Gunther skipped every other step up the stairs and tiptoed to his parents' room to listen. He held his breath for an entire minute, hoping to hear Mom humming or whispering. But there was only silence and an occasional shifting-in-sheets sound.

Dad was downstairs in the kitchen piecing together processed ingredients --cheeses and carbohydrates. He had that desperate, huffy energy about him. It was Mom's fault.

Gunther wanted to tell someone about the otters, but he knew Mom wasn't Mom right now. So he crept back downstairs and remained quiet throughout the meal. There was something much more gratifying about telling his mother a story, its meaning and magic out of proportion with the tale itself. But she had messed up again, and Dad wouldn't understand. He would only tell them all the reasons why they shouldn't have done what they did.

"Jessica has been good lately," Gunther heard Dad saying over the phone after dinner. "For the most part. Only the devil knows what set her off. It was probably Gran on the other end of the line. Josh defending Jessica once again. In any case, at least I have the full attention of the kids. When Jessica's around, they're always clamoring for her attention. Maybe I'll take off some time and get things tightened up around here."

This word, "clamor." It sounded like something annoying. Pests. "Clamoring for her attention."

Now Josh began to raise his voice: yes, Mom, I know it's a disease! I don't need you to tell us what to do. This is my family. And then noticing Gunther's shadow in the doorway, he lowered it: Okay, okay, I'll look into programs. I just don't know how spending time away from the kids would help her.

That night Gunther tiptoed to Claire's room and whispered, "What's gonna happen to Mom? What's wrong with her?"

Claire already had her ear to the thin wall between her bedroom and her parents', and she motioned for him to come over and listen.

"Jessie...what happened?" His father's baritone.

"Oh Josh. The kids. They want to take the kids. ...We have to all go...we have to stay together. I made a mistake. I made a promise. Just....just. Keep us all together, okay?"

She was slurring her words.

"All together. Okay. No one is going to take the kids, Jessie. Shhh. Just sleep."

CHAPTER 5: AWAKEN

The Hybrid

Location: Nest 33

2001

In the beginning, there are webs of light with stars at their intersections—pulsing white root systems against a curtain of black. Sometimes the root-stars coincide with the zip and boom of chaotic vibrations. Sometimes they do not. There is no pattern.

But one day, the vibrations separate themselves into distinct sounds and begin organizing into noises she can distinguish and remember–thud versus clink versus hum versus squeak. Some noises come from the inside, but the hums are always from the outside, and many of them are repeated in exactly the same way each time, such as "Claire" and "mother" and "grow."

Light pulses beneath her eyelids, twinkling and blotting and growing and shrinking. The temperature changes from cold ...to fear...to pleasure. She relaxes into this new sensation: mammalian warmth.

But every now and then there are awful tearing and breaking noises– threadlike ripping from within. This creates a bolt of discomfort disturbing her eternal nap. Then she hears a lot of humming from the outside, and finally: a pleasant sensation washing through her body. The temperature changes to just right, and she feels zipped up in her egg once again.

The hums from beyond the eggshell grow chirpy sometimes, and she can follow the patterns and create meaning now. The voices sound wet and rubbery, like octopus limbs painting pictures on her brain. Eight different hums at once. But there is one single voice she can hold onto. It sounds like safety. It is Mother, moving through the light out there, smelling of blossoms that the girl doesn't yet know the name of.

This is the day she realizes there is an opening beyond the stars and the roots and the black night, that there is something more to the hums and chirps. So she moves the flesh away from her eyes for the first time, and the universe rearranges itself to create order and meaning out of light and sound.

Several faces greet her, creatures with flashing eyes and white robes. The whites of their eyes match their clothing. It is the only thing the girl can focus on: that bright absence of color. Their eyes shift back and forth so fast, and the white space is aggressive.

But then there is Mother, with a soft brown face encircled by golden coils. She touches the top of the girl's head and says not to worry. Eventually, she will get used to this new system of light, assures Mother, with all of its shapes and lights and movement. She smooths the hybrid's forehead.

"It's a shock to be so new to the world," Mother says. "You will adapt. You will make sense of it all. Eventually. You have nothing to fear."

And that's when the hybrid remembers: she's been here before. But there is nothing more to this memory than a flash, a feeling that she's already done this: she's opened her eyes for the first time ... once before.

CHAPTER 6: SUMMERS AND DEATH

Gunther

1999-2001

Mom recovered from her "bad day" and life went on as usual. No one mentioned it -- not even Gran.

The summer palette changed from pale green to vibrant emerald and then withered into yellow. But the hot weather didn't bother Claire and Gunther.

In the canoe, they were safe. Dad said they reminded him of a pea pod. Three peas in a bean-shaped boat: Gunther, Claire, and Captain. Gunther liked to think of them that way, with the cat having equal status.

After that first otter discovery, they spent long days watching and feeding and swimming with them. Right up until the day the Hadleys returned home for a weekend, and Mrs. Hadley telephoned their mother to say, "... it's just that I worry, Jessica, the children are going to get rabies -- or worse." It was her nicest way of saying, "keep your children off our property." Then she put in an unsolicited recommendation for Claire: "a good summer camp for girls," which Claire begged Jessica not to send her to.

On another outing, the kids came to shore on a strangely unwooded, yet undeveloped lot. It was filled with huge piles of construction dirt, and yet no structure was visible. It was set high above the water, so they would have to climb the bluff if they wanted to investigate. But there were signs posted that said "Trespassers will be prosecuted," and that was enough to make Gunther use his paddle to push them away from the bluff before they even beached. He knew that the term "prosecute" didn't necessarily mean "execute," but they might as well not take the chance.

Nevertheless, by the next day Claire had convinced herself and Gunther that they should explore it. It was just too unusual not to. Most of the land around the lake had been taken over by houses, private property where purebred dogs barked at them from well-groomed yards. The Hadleys had ruined one of the last "free spaces" for them to play.

When they returned to the bluff, they still didn't see any sign of life. The children climbed the sandy slope up to the strange mounds of dirt. What they saw when they reached the top was better than they could have imagined: an archaeological dig.

"This must be that spot," Claire said, "the one mom and dad were talking about. Timucua … Indians."

"Native Americans," Gunther corrected.

"Native Floridians."

Gunther had a chilling thought: "Burial mounds?" He'd read about vengeful indigenous ghosts in an old cowboy story once, and the idea still haunted him.

Claire grinned and shrugged. Sometimes she delighted in the drama of Gunther's minor terrors.

They spent the afternoon hopping from plot to plot, hiding in the bushes every time they heard a noise or a far-off car engine. There wasn't much to see but a lot of holes in the ground, as the archaeologists brought their finds back to a lab for safekeeping.

But on their third visit, Claire found something! It was a pink arrowhead almost four inches long. Not in one of the carefully scooped-out holes, but off to the side near where they anchored the boat. The artifact was the color of Georgia clay and cool and heavy in her hand after she cleaned it off in the lake water. Gunther saw her holding it up to the sun, watching the light reflect off of the quartzy minerals, and he reminded her that she needed to leave it at the site.

"You could be persecuted if you take it," he told her. "Leave it here."

Claire laughed. "Prosecuted."

But she had agreed with him and placed it near one of the dig sites. Or at least that's how Gunther remembers it, so he was puzzled years later when he found it in her bedroom, hidden inside an old tackle box, long after she'd left home.

Their visits to the site came to a halt one day when they discovered an orange mesh fence installed around the property and over the holes. "Keep Out" signs dotted the lot.

Another time, they found a tiny island in an adjacent lake, which they entered through a tunnel under the road. At first, they were hoping to make it their own private hideaway, but it was filled with prickles and snakes. Besides, it was clear some teenagers had gotten to it. There was an old fire pit littered with beer bottles. Cigarette butts too. The thought of running into Frank and Randy Whitehead out there was enough to keep them from returning.

But the starkest memory of these middle years was one evening in July when the children encountered a glimpse of human death-- a brush with someone else's tragic end. Claire was 13 and Gunther was 11.

It was getting late. Sweating and shooing away horse flies, the kids struggled across the street with the canoe. They were trying to get home after crossing underneath the road, but they didn't get to the tunnel before the tide went out. So much water had gone out with the tide that the tunnel wasn't passable.

They carried the boat over their heads down the bank of the next waterway--finally at their own lake. Out of breath, they both flopped down on the shoreline, a quick rest before they would have to push off into the water again. Among the reeds and grass they didn't see the body at first. But they smelled it. Claire stood and looked around.

"Ewww, smells so bad," said Gunther.

When she spotted it, Claire covered her mouth with a hand and crouched down quickly as though hiding from the dead. Her eyes large, mouth still covered, she pointed and muffled a scream. Gunther stayed low, not wanting to see what Claire saw, terrified enough by the look on her face.

At the sound of the children's screams, a boater slowed down, and a startled family poured out of a nearby house. Claire and Gunther darted up the bank, abandoning their canoe. As they ran, Gunther couldn't help but turn and look, which caused him to trip.

He saw it now: the body of a girl, floating face down, long black hair like ribbons among the sawgrass. Her arms were splayed out at her sides as though she were trying to fly away, minnows casually nibbling at her fingers.

He lay there, helpless to the horrific image. Claire finally got him to his feet, and they ran toward the closest house. Minutes later, squad cars arrived on the street.

He would not easily forget that first encounter with death: the sunlight fading, the blue and red emergency lights incessant, the yellow police tape. The nauseating stink of death still in his nostrils.

***

Later that night, the children overheard their parents talking about the body.

"They say she was just 15 years old, dumped way up river, close to the city. I guess when the tide got so low…Can you imagine …?" Jessica trailed off.

"Mack says she was a prostitute," said Josh, dismissive.

"I bet that's not all Mack said, the old bigot. Besides, so what? She's somebody's daughter for godsakes. People say things like that so they can believe it will never happen to their own families."

"People didn't *say* anything," Josh said, his voice amping up. It didn't take much for him to get riled these days. He was always impatient lately, especially with Mom. "Mack is literally assigned to the case, Jessica. That child was a working girl."

"Josh! Shh … the kids are right upstairs …. Why do you have to get so angry anyway?"

In fact, the kids were not upstairs; they were listening in the next room over. Claire put her hand to her mouth. "Oh …."

It was clear she had heard something Gunther had not. "You know what they're talking about, right?" she asked her brother.

Gunther did not, but he pretended to. They tiptoed back to their bedrooms.

Alone in his bed that night, he was haunted by the sight of the veiny, water-bloated flesh. Lucky it was face down. When his eyes finally closed, he saw a beautiful mermaid in the lake. Long black hair and a green tail. But when it emerged from the water, the face was missing, a completely hollowed-out skull wrapped tight in terrifyingly blank skin. Claire must have had a similar dream because when Gunther awoke, she was sleeping at the foot of his bed, snuggled up to Captain.

Later, they would find out the body belonged to Khalilah Johnson, a girl just a few years older than Claire. They had all attended the same elementary school. When the fifth graders came to read to the first graders, Gunther and Khalilah were paired up. He remembered reading aloud for the first time in front of others in that classroom, maybe even sitting in Khalilah's lap. She had been patient with him, showing little Gunther how the letters formed words and the words formed sentences, and the sentences were built on top of each other, brick by brick, to make up whole stories. He had feared his first grade teacher, the stony Mrs. Grey who seemed to dislike children, but Khalilah had been sweet and smart and encouraging, helping Gunther's love of reading to blossom.

He would never be able to reconcile those two conflicting memories of this girl--the two Khalilahs.

***

Unfortunately, death would continue to follow Claire and Gunther that year, striking right at the heart of all childhood fear.

One night under a blanket fort, in the yellow glow of flashlights, they whispered to one another about an island they had spotted, a new adventure, if they could just get to it. They had seen it from the bridge; it was one of those river islands. But much, much bigger than the little island in the lake. They were sure they had seen huge treehouses built along the shoreline.

When they asked their mom, she said, with a wink, *now that is a very special place, kiddos. I'll tell you about it someday. But don't ever try to take the canoe there. Could be dangerous out on the big river.*

With just a slight cock of her head in her brother's direction, Claire indicated they would get to that island one day, one way or another.

Gunther wasn't so sure. It was his mother's reckless navigation of the world that likely shaped Gunther's timid nature. He was a careful soul from the very beginning, and he measured every sound and shape around him with great precision -- checking the conditions of danger like his father checked the weather. He knew: 'Could be dangerous,' were strong words coming from his mother. She didn't want them going there, but she was trying to be casual.

As they kneeled over the map that night, Gunther's finger followed the jagged blue line that illustrated waterways. The river, appearing so tame and cartoon-like, seemed an easy thing to conquer.

But of course a map never reveals the actual landscape of a journey--the sweat and hunger and mosquito-bitten path that really lies ahead. Such is the distorted perception of life: snuggled safe in the nest of childhood, the birds-eye view is simple and neatly-drawn, mapped out on the page like a comic strip or a math equation. But when dirt and rain and heartbreak muddies up the pathways, all seems lost, and much too often.

It was best Claire and Gunther didn't yet know this.

Captain purred beside them, cuddling himself into a cat-ball, one paw hugging his nose. Two rooms away, there was the routine clanking of dishes in the kitchen. Their mother was humming. All felt twinkly and cozy. Neither he nor his sister could know this would be one of the last times they would feel exactly like this. After all, how does a child know when the last bedtime story is being told? How can he know that this is the final Christmas he believes in Santa, or the last afternoon he climbs to the tippy top of the sweetgum tree?

A month later, Josh and Jessica left for an anniversary trip, what was supposed to be a five-day excursion. They departed from the dock at Mayport, happily waving their goodbyes to the children, and sailing into the Atlantic Ocean.

They lost touch with the mainland two days later.

CHAPTER 7: A FANCY BOAT

2001

They needed a vacation, Gunther remembered his parents saying. Time away from the kids. Or maybe that's what Gran said. Or was it the friend who suggested they go on a trip? The one who lent them the boat?

The night before their journey, Josh and Jessica brought the kids aboard for a little tour of the vessel. The couple who owned the boat was there, and Gunther overheard the wife talking to his mom. Jessica told her the plan: they would snorkel, they would fish, they would tie up at the docks at night, and for one night stay at a swanky hotel more than 200 miles south of home in a place called Jupiter Beach, which didn't sound like a real place to Gunther.

Swanky. Gunther would always remember that word in that context.

They both were good with boats, Jessica assured the woman. They were big on safety. She was talking very fast, he thought, and some of the things she said did not make any sense.

The friend's wife had a kind way about her. She and her husband were older and wealthy. Gunther was sitting next to his mother, playing with a roll of Snoopy stickers the woman had given him. In each sticker, Snoopy was playing a different sport –basketball Snoopy, golf Snoopy, football Snoopy. He peeled away a soccer Snoopy and tried to give it to his mother. But the sticker fell in between the hard plastic seats and when Gunther reached his hand to retrieve it, Snoopy stuck to the side, way down deep. He wanted to cry, but Claire looked over at him and frowned.

The women continued to talk, and the men played with the sound system, turning the music up louder and louder until it hurt Gunther's ears.

The older woman placed her hand over Jessica's and said, "you both deserve it. Please enjoy. You two are going to do great-- you're going to be fine." And then she turned to Gunther, "you want to drive the boat, little man?"

"My sticker …," he said, pointing, but the music was too loud.

"Oh me!" volunteered Claire. "I want to drive the boat!"

"Claire, don't be rude. You'll get a turn," said Jessica.

Gunther turned his attention to the shiny, chrome steering wheel.

Like their children, Josh and Jessica were strong swimmers and no strangers to navigating the water. Josh, especially, knew the ocean and understood the tides and the wind. He had been raised close to the spot where they departed, where the mouth of the St. Johns River opens wide into the ocean.

But the truth was that he hadn't operated a boat in years. They should have double-checked their VHF radio, people said. They should have hired a captain to help. Gunther and Claire heard all of the should'ves while eavesdropping on the grownups on those eerie afternoons following the disappearance of their parents. Strangers would visit the house bringing dishes of strange-smelling food and looking upon the children with pity.

When they first went missing, shock and disbelief were the initial responses; after that, some ill-spirited rumors of foul play. And then there was the jealous-spat angle, gossip about Jessica having an affair and Josh finally breaking. But Claire and Gunther were spared these comments until much later. It was commonly agreed that the children had enough on their plates of grief for now.

The Coast Guard searched for weeks, long enough to know that the missing couple could not have survived, and that the boat had likely capsized and been swallowed by the ocean, the bodies gone.

Gunther would never recover from the trauma of that sudden and final decision--stopping the search. Giving up on the two most important people in the entire world. How could they just stop looking?

There was a double funeral, a gloomy blur of a memory for both children, consisting of an unfamiliar minister, a mob of well-intentioned mourners, an inconsolable grandmother from California whom they had never met before in person, and an aching, bottomless longing to have the bodies of their parents in front of them, even if they were lifeless. They needed to see. They needed to touch.

For a long time, the kids forgot about that mysterious island and their plans to venture out to the river. Gran and Mack held them painfully close, not allowing them out of their sight. What had begun as a fun weekend with the grandparents babysitting while the parents vacationed, turned into an altered version of family -- instantaneous, confining, and mournful, with awkward gaps of generational misunderstandings.

The grandmother from California, Jessica's mother, left the day after the funeral, said she had to get back to her husband in LA. Apparently a third husband. The adults gossiped about this other grandmother endlessly, as though the root of all the Flynn family's problems must have originated somehow with her, her daughter, and their California-ness.

Before the tragedy, Gran had been planning to buy a blueberry farm and move out to the country with Mack who was semi-retired. They would open a U-pick farm and live out their days among happy families coming to harvest their own food. That's what she used to tell the children almost every time Gran came to visit, which was very frequent. Gunther couldn't remember a weekend or holiday without Gran around. But when Josh died, she and Mack sold their house and moved in with the children. And that was that--there was no more talk of a blueberry farm.

The overturned canoe sat lonely in the yard, dry and cracking in the sun. Every now and then, Captain would rub his chin against it and meow at the empty lawn, looking around for signs of human life. But the children stayed indoors, while Gran rifled around in old pictures and long-shelved notebooks.

Things were more bearable when neighbors and friends stopped by. They always brought platters of food and whispered sympathies. Claire and Gunther spent most of their time camped out on their parents' bed, aunts and cousins bringing them food and old friends paying their respects in the master bedroom. Who could bear to make the children leave, to strip the bed and scrub clean the floral, fading smell of the parents?

One day, Claire found a notebook in her mother's dresser and showed it to Gunther: sketches of plants and mushrooms and their underground networks. There were musings about the nature of the biological world, poetry inspired by photosynthesis and mycelial networks. There was one comment that stood out:

> *This kind of regeneration is unique to the salt islands of Northeast Florida, specifically Field Station #33 (Nest 33), far up the river in fresher waters. What is different about the soil here? What is different about the networks, both electrical (within each specimen) and interspecies -- animal to plant to fungus to animal, etc.?*

Claire stowed this notebook away in her own dresser drawer, and she and Gunther would study it each night, looking for meaning beyond the pages, searching most of all for a mention of their own names. Any kind of message from Mom.

CHAPTER 8: MACK AND GRAN

2002

It was six months before Claire and Gunther went out on the lake again; for a while it was difficult for Gunther even to imagine being in open water. But once they got back in the canoe, Captain by their side, they realized the briny waterways were more home to them now than their own house.

When Mack had moved in, he brought an energy that took up all the space in the home. At first, he made an attempt to be soft and kind to the children. But he was neither soft nor kind. His crude judgements, spoken or not, always reverberated off the walls. Claire never passed up the chance to challenge her step-grandfather, sometimes resulting in an all-out shouting match. When this happened, Gunther would cover his ears and hide in his room.

The first time Claire and Gunther returned to the lake, they spent the morning fishing far out on the inlet right at the mouth of the river. Grandpa Mack said it was a good spot and gave them special permission to be out there. By midday they had caught only one very small bass, which they threw back. Neither of them liked to fish much anyway, but Mack had been raised to believe that every child should know how to catch a fish and skin a deer.

"At least the boy!" Mack had raged at Gran one evening when she refused to force the kids to go hunting with him and his buddies the next morning. "When else is he gonna learn?"

"If they want to go, they can go. But I won't make them," Gran said in her quiet way, drying her hands on a dish towel. "That's that."

And that was that. Mack never invited them again, and they never asked. He would frequently grumble about how much time they spent doing nothin' but making friends with every goddamn fish and feather in the lake, but his grievances rose and fell like a roller coaster. The children were learning to ride them out.

Short-tempered but well-intentioned was how his friends described Mack, but Claire suspected that he was one of those police officers with a questionable record, and she never missed a chance to remind Gunther of that. At age 63 he was built like an ox, a towering figure with wide shoulders and huge fists. He shaved his head and had glittering blue eyes that perhaps Gran had fallen in love with so many years before, but when he was angry they made him look monstrous. He wasn't so much violent as he was unpredictable. You never knew what he would do or say.

After Josh and Jessica died, Mack hijacked Gran's dream of buying a farm, and he turned it into a rallying cry for how much he and Gran sacrificed and how they put off their retirement plans for these ingrates. It didn't matter that Gran always reminded him what she really wanted was to be near the grandchildren.

Once the shock of the deaths didn't sting so much, Claire began to clamor for some independence, any chance to get out of the house. She begged to start using the canoe again, which drove Gran over the edge with agitation.

"You want to take a boat out on the open water? Over my dead body." She would shake her head and tut, tut in shame. "You may just turn out to be as reckless as your mother."

Gran had started making comparisons between her daughter-in-law and granddaughter lately, and not in a good way.

"You're just hell bent on killing your old granny aren't you?" she said one night at the dinner table.

Claire reminded her grandmother that she was 14 now, and that she'd had more freedom when she was 12…when her parents were alive. Mack stewed in the background, threatening and dark. Claire and Gran bickered for several minutes, until Mack pounded his fist on the table.

Gunther jumped. Claire scowled. Everything was quiet for a moment.

Finally, he said: "She's not kidding, young lady. We won't tolerate disobedience. Your dad may have let your mama run all wild and hippie, but we are raising you to be a God-fearing woman." Then he cleared his throat, and put his hands back in his lap and said, "You'll thank us one day."

Gunther stared into his plate of fried chicken. He'd lost his appetite. He wished with all his might that Claire would not respond, that she would simply, say, yessir and be done with it. But he knew that would never happen.

Claire pounded her own fist on the table, and simply said, "No!" Then she stood up.

Mack's pallor turned bright red. His fingers gripped his bald head and ran down the sides of his face very slowly. Gran looked for a moment as if she were going to say something, but then she pretended to continue eating. Gunther's stomach turned.

"What did you say, girl?" Mack slowly rose out of his seat.

"You're not my father," Claire said quietly, and then turned.

Before Gunther knew what was happening, Claire was hollering and Gran was screaming, "No, Mack, don't touch her!"

But Mack had already pulled her by the wrist to face him, and struck her across the face. Hard.

"If they don't respect my words, they will have to respect my actions," Mack said in Gran's direction. Then he sat back down in his chair and finished his chicken.

Claire ran out to the holding-hands oak trees and hid high in the branches, Gunther not far behind. He was huffing and puffing when he got to her. Her face was wet with tears and her nose was bleeding.

She stared across the lake and said, "Let's take the boat out, as far away as we can."

"Um. Okay." He looked down at the canoe.

"Not now," she said. "Some day they're not paying attention. Soon as summer starts."

CHAPTER 9: THE RIVER

2002

Exactly eight months after the death of their parents, school was out for summer.

On the very first day, they took off in the canoe, planning to stay out as long as possible. Ever since the night he hit Claire, Mack (and Gran) had been making amends, approving requests that were previously shot down. In truth, Mack could care less if the kids spent all day out on the lake. He simply didn't want any talk-back.

Gran was out of town for the weekend.

It was the white-hot middle of the day, and sweat glistened on the back of Gunther's neck. They rowed closer to the shoreline to find some shade. It was lunchtime.

As Gunther looked off into the distance, past the inlet and into the wider channel of water, he thought how strange it was that all water is one continuous entity--all bodies being able to pour into one another if given the chance. Was it possible that the water he was now touching with his fingertips had touched their mother's body? He shivered at the thought of his parents at the bottom of the ocean somewhere, chewed to the skeleton by fish, exactly what would've happened to Khalilah Johnson's body had they not spotted it.

They were both quiet -- in a daze after the hustle of that last week of school. Everything felt difficult and awkward because Gran was doing it now.

As they ate their peanut butter and jelly sandwiches, a silvery bird fluttered overhead -- back and forth, round and round -- like a pleasant vulture. It dove daringly close toward the sandwich in Claire's hands. She broke off a crust corner and flicked it onto the water. But the bird, a leggy water fowl with yellow eyes, continued to swoop toward the children and ignored the bit of sandwich that the fish were already nibbling.

Wrapped around its ankle was a tiny tag. Captain sat at attention, tail twitching. Finally the strange bird landed, branch-like feet perching on the metal side. Captain hissed. Upon closer inspection this feathered thing looked less like prey and more like predator. But it was difficult to determine whether it was more owl or heron. One silver wing dangled longer than the other.

"It's hurt!" Claire said. "Maybe it can't get back to shore."

Gunther and Claire exchanged looks and then began to lean toward it, the canoe teetering to one side. The bird did not try to flit away, but swiveled its head to the right.

Gunther drew back. "What is it?"

Claire shrugged and said, "not an Ibis, like I thought," which made him back up even more. He thought that she knew every species of bird.

"What does its tag say?" Claire drew closer, not hesitating to reach out.

"Claire! Don't touch."

But she held out her hand and whistled softly. The bird was gentle, stepping lightly onto Claire's outstretched arm, bare but for the sprinkling of bright blonde hairs against sunny skin.

Gunther leaned forward now too, feeding off his sister's courage.

The bird screeched, high-pitched and predatory. Captain growled, not taking his eyes off the spectacle of girl and bird.

Gunther covered his ears. Claire stood stone-still so as not to frighten bird, beast, or brother.

She peered so close at the bird that Gunther worried it might decide to peck her on the head.

"If lost, return to the island near the bridge," she read aloud from the tag. On the other side of the tag were numbers and unfamiliar symbols, as though the bird had flown in from another continent.

Captain continued his meow-ish growl.

"Is it lost?" asked Gunther. Claire shrugged.

"Maybe it's tired," she said, watching as it hopped from her arm to a folded towel on the middle seat. "Something is definitely wrong with its wing."

Sure enough, it began to drowse, upright but eyes closed, every now and then taking note of the cat's position by cracking open an eye.

The quiet lake rippled around them. A mockingbird twittered from a far-off tree.

Without even discussing it, they began paddling toward the mouth of the river. They knew what they had to do.

Captain creeped over and placed one paw on the seat where the bird slept; he sniffed, mewed, and then backed down. If it wasn't going to flee, there was no use in pursuing it. He situated himself into a loaf underneath the seat and began to purr as the children made their way past the boundary that had never been crossed and into the wide river.

Leaving the safety of the inlet, Gunther remembered what he had seen when they drove over the bridge to soccer practice that one day almost a year ago: a green island far below the highway, and just to the north, right where the river came to its widest point, opening itself up like a yawn before closing into a narrow channel at the next town over. Standing around on the island were a band of young people— girls and boys who looked about his age. They were dressed in wet suits and getting ready to dive into the water. Or so he thought.

After their mother told them not to go there, they tried their father, but he had said, "It's just a dumping ground. They would never allow children to swim there. I don't think that's what you saw, Gunther."

But now they were going to find out exactly what was out there.

CHAPTER 10: NEST 33

As the river grew broader, the claustrophobia of the suburbs finally lifted, and Claire and Gunther took in the new landscape: the enormous pier in the distance and the city skyline, and the bridges, and a helicopter high above. In the lake and canals, the scenery had always been the same: fussily manicured properties and slick, unfriendly docks, sometimes a dog lunging and barking in the direction of the canoe.

Unfettered sawgrass grew on the banks. An anhinga was drying its spindly wings on a steel bar rising up from the river bottom. Smelling the closeness of the ocean, Claire and Gunther basked in the exhilaration of such raw life, the intermingled waters supporting the lives of dolphins and alligators alike.

They passed Hazzard's Bluff, the fabled cliff where a 200-year old house loomed above them. This is where, many years ago, a mayor's wife had hung herself, so the legend went. She still haunted the property, and the dock was just a skeleton of its old self. No boat dared to approach.

And then there was the unfolding mystery right here in the boat: this strange, Muppety bird allowing them to ferry it home. Was the island perhaps some kind of exotic zoo? Neither of them considered why there would be a bird with a note on it fluttering around their inlet, or how anyone would know it would reach the two of them.

Forty-five minutes later they encountered a current, and the winds picked up. It seemed that the closer they got to the island, the more difficult it was to paddle. Finally, Gunther stopped and groaned.

"We'll never make it." He crossed his arms as the oar clattered to the canoe bottom. The cat sprang up. The bird awoke and fluffed its wings, not looking so injured anymore.

"Gunther, we're almost there. Keep going."

Captain unfolded himself and began panting in the heat. Claire wiped the sweat from her face with her forearm and continued paddling.

A flock of gulls swooped toward the water's surface as if to find fish. But it was the wrong time for them to be hunting. It was far too hot right now.

The sound of so many seagulls reminded them they were far from home, and Gunther looked into his sister's face for any signs of danger, like an airline passenger gauging the level of peril by searching the faces of flight attendants. Maybe the tide really would sweep them out to the ocean.

Gran was out of town visiting her sister. Mack wouldn't even notice their absence for hours.

And then, he saw something. Like one fat footprint upon the water, and then another, and another, an outline of a beast from below was burbling and swimming alongside them.

Gunther shot out of his seat, standing straight up, and peering back into the water. The sudden movement jostled the canoe; Claire gripped the sides.

"Oh my gosh, it's a manatee!" he whispered, pointing, not letting his eyes off of it.

The manatee flopped one of its mighty fins and made a clapping sound on the water. Both children shrieked and laughed. Then the manatee spun around and splooshed out of the water as though it were a dolphin. It swam around to the back of the canoe and the children felt a bump underneath the boat. Both of them hung on tightly. Then another bump. And another and another.

The bird opened its eyes and let out an ear-piercing screech.

"It's pushing us!" Claire exclaimed. "It's helping us."

Gunther wasn't so sure, his knuckles a pale yellow as he hung tight to the sides of the canoe.

The bumping became more smooth and steady. It was clear they were moving quickly toward the island.

Claire smiled. "See?"

Without a sound, the bird swiveled its head, fluffed its feathers again, and took flight, making a beeline to the island. It didn't appear lost or hurt at all.

If lost, return to the island near the bridge.

They both relaxed a little, but exchanged nervous looks. The brambly-looking island stood in front of them, growing larger and larger as they coursed through the water. The great bridge arched high in the distance.

At first, the island he remembered as such a vibrant shade of green looked almost as drab as a nearby shipyard, which was all vacant lots and burned-out boats and industrial warehouses used to offload giant shipping containers. Was this island just a dumping ground for the shipyards? Maybe this wasn't the one he had seen from the bridge. They could see one modest dock and a slightly-trodden path. There were plastic grocery bags and glass bottles and various old fishing supplies strewn in the water, lazily bumping against the shore in a tangled mass.

Gunther wondered about this manatee, if it ever mistook trash for food. In school they had learned that some sea creatures will swallow plastic bags and then eventually die from intestinal injuries. But this manatee seemed far too intelligent to eat garbage.

Moments later, the entire landscape of the island began to change. As though an orange and rosy sun had risen exclusively over this small patch of land, the trees and plants and dock and path became animated with color. Everything else in their line of vision began to recede into a sepia tone, getting smaller and smaller as the island rose to a much bigger stature than it had appeared only moments before.

The children could now see it in great detail, and creatures hopping and climbing and slithering into view. An entire flock of those silver heron-owl things careened through the trees. The whole scene was as terrifying as it was magnificent, and Gunther drew back in awe. The cat growled softly from underneath Claire's seat.

By some strange trick of the light, the trees changed from grey and white trunks with pallid leaves, to deep browns and emerald greens, and the plants seemed to blossom out of nowhere. The colors were overwhelming. Mushrooms, the size of boulders, stood out in striking shades that neither Claire nor Gunther had seen except in picture books--pinks, yellows, and purples. The children were silent for several seconds, and then Gunther dug his paddle straight down into the sandy bottom of the river, trying to halt and reverse. But the momentum was too much, and before they knew it, the canoe was sliding directly into a smooth boat launch on a grassy beach.

They could see two adults--a man and a woman-- strolling down a path with a boy at their side who looked about Gunther's age. At the first sight of people, Claire and Gunther looked around for the injured bird they meant to return. It was as though they had imagined the whole thing.

The boy started skipping their way. Gunther was trying his best to put the boat in reverse, pushing and tugging his way with the paddle, but Claire counteracted his efforts by planting her oar in the meshy landing.

An official-looking sign that said something about research and national security was posted off to the left side. It said "Nest 33," and the local university's logo was printed at the top.

In his periphery he noticed another person-- a young woman-- standing over a bright object. Turning, Gunther saw the woman gently tapping on a large, spotted toadstool. As she rhythmically drummed, the mushroom changed colors! It was subtle at first, so Gunther figured he was imagining it, but when he noticed Claire gaping at it too, he knew right away: this was a special place. And then another realization: their mother must have known this island. *Now that's a special place, kiddos.* The memory of his mother winking at them in the rearview mirror in the car long ago--that image etched into his heart-- grew large and achy.

But other things--stories and various threads of memories-- began to weave themselves together to create a brighter understanding of what he now saw in front of him. The notebook, their mother's fascination with mushrooms, her unfinished studies, and why she came to Florida in the first place, all the way from California.

The water had turned crystal clear, revealing bright yellow fish and pink crabs and glittering schools of minnows.

When Claire and Gunther asked about this radical transformation later, they would only get the response, "people see what they want to see."

Seeing the kind look on the faces of the people approaching, Gunther began to relax, the warmth of the colors around them melting the anxiety that had gripped him only moments before. They both gaped as the island came to life around them.

As usual, Captain was the first to set foot on land. He darted after a spotted lizard and disappeared into a bush.

Claire scooted forward until she was close enough to nudge

Gunther. The manatee who was spluttering under the canoe came to the surface and splashed them out of their trance.

Giddy, Gunther swung one leg over the side of the canoe and took a deep breath.

The boy approached and held the canoe still for them. His face was round and golden and his eyes dark and intelligent.

Gunther stepped onto the island. The two boys stared at one another for a moment, and then pulled the canoe up the bank, as Claire stared up into the enormous trees. Gunther followed her gaze, wondering how he could have missed these gigantic sequoia-like trunks from the bridge.

"Welcome," said the woman. Captain was rubbing against her legs, so she knelt down and gently scratched the cat under his chin.

The woman's skin was the most vibrant shade of brown Gunther had ever seen, and she was tall, with shining black eyes and coils of curly blond hair hanging down her back. He had never seen such a person. She was as tall as their dad but as slender as Claire. The man by her side was even taller, but he was pale, exquisite-looking in his own way.

"We are happy to see you here. I am Dr. Das, and this is my husband, Dr. David Meehan. But you may call us Lana and David. This is our son, Jeremy."

"Where is this?" asked Claire. "I mean ... is this the place ...?"

Gunther could tell she couldn't say the words out loud, she couldn't say "where my mom..." to these strangers. They rarely said the words "mom" or "dad" out loud, even to each other.

The man laughed in a pleasant baritone in perfect harmony with the woman's chuckle.

She stepped forward as Claire began to explain about the bird.

"Yes, that's a silver water owl," said Lana. "Beautiful, right?"

Claire and Gunther waited for further explanation, but all they got was Jeremy's response, "we knew you'd come!"

Lana smiled at the siblings and offered to get them something to drink. "You must be thirsty from all that paddling."

Gunther wondered how she knew they had traveled a long way.

David pointed to a tree that appeared to have a roof on it, just a short distance across the island.

"See there? That's our building -- our treehouse. If you need a drink."

Claire and Gunther looked at one another, eyes wide. They'd been trying to build a treehouse for the last several months but only managed so far to nail boards to a tree for a ladder. They were waiting for Grandpa Mack to help them do the rest, but when Claire made a fuss about how long it was taking, Mack called her the B-word, and that was the end of that.

Gunther watched to see what Claire would do. She looked across the river toward home, and then in the other direction, far away towards the bridge in the distance.

"I don't know," said Claire.

"It's just a short walk, and you'll get to see what we do here," the woman said, pointing to a clearing in the distance. "Once you see the treehouse, we can better explain the island to you."

Gunther detected a slight accent in the woman's speech.

The siblings stared at each other for a moment.

Finally, Claire spoke, much more shyly than usual. "I'm Claire and he's my brother, er... Gunther."

The woman simply smiled and gave a pleasant bow. Jeremy and David followed suit, and they all turned and began walking.

Gunther got a better look at the treehouse now, a strange architecture built into a fat cluster of live oaks. He shrugged and they both fell in line with Jeremy behind Lana and her husband.

Gunther knew that if their mother were here, she would've done the same thing. *Well, we're already here. Let's check it out!* she would've said with a smile. But Gran-- if she knew what they were doing, she would never let them out of her sight again. And Mack would kill them if they found out.

But after months stranded inside the grieving house, Gunther felt like he was finally coming back to life.

Around the corner they came upon a tree-sized mushroom, a four-foot monster of a fungi. No wonder their mother said this was a special place.

"Go ahead," said Jeremy. "Look what happens when you touch it!" Gunther declined, knowing that some mushrooms could be deadly.

In contrast, Claire did not hesitate. She placed her fingers on the spongy tabletop of the yellow toadstool. To their amazement, the mushroom flesh behaved like human skin, changing colors where she applied pressure. It was as alive as they were.

"Wow!" the children said in unison.

Gunther peered under the cap of the mushroom to see the papery gills inside the umbrella. He sat beneath it, and leaned against the stem as though it was a tree.

"Careful," said Jeremy, "Sometimes the spores fall, and this one has an inky spore print. It can stain."

Gunther looked up into the strange pattern of the cap's underbelly and remembered his mother creating spore prints on white paper. *Aren't they amazing?* she would say. He can't remember what it was for, maybe just a Christmas craft.

But his father would never touch the mushrooms she brought home. He was the one who told Gunther, "don't ever pick those," when they came upon a mushroom in the woods. But it was because Dad didn't know, so he feared them, like many people do. *Mycophobia,* Mom called it.

When they caught up to the adults, David began explaining the nature of these mushrooms. He said that there are biological pathways under the earth--under their feet-- connecting the trees and helping them communicate with one another.

"But not just our big, colorful mushrooms here. All mycelium all over the world can do that-- the 'roots' of the mushrooms— they can *talk* to one another!"

Claire and Gunther looked at one another, remembering their mother; she talked just like that. At the time, they found it a little embarrassing, but now they would give anything to join her on a foray or listen to one of her "fun guy" jokes.

"And we can tap into it," added the woman, "But it's a very delicate system-- we must listen carefully. That's where the Listeners come in. You can see them over there."

Gunther wondered what she meant by "we." Were there others connected to this strange island?

In the distance they saw an open meadow--inexplicably at the center of this tiny island, an open field, bigger than two football stadiums maybe.

As they grew closer, they could see more people-- mostly young, not much older than Claire-- sitting and lying down in the grass wearing huge feathery headphones, hands planted on the ground, in complete quiet. In another context, they could have been teenagers lounging at a park, each plugged into her own music.

Gunther was struck by the silence. How could it be so quiet in the middle of a city, cars and ambulances and trains not far away? It didn't seem that they were anywhere near town anymore, and they had completely lost sight of the highway bridge.

Dr. Das, noticing Gunther's puzzled look, spoke directly to him in a quiet aside: "The density of the mycelial network here is unique. We believe it broadcasts complex signals- – think of it like bio-chemical camouflage. To most nervous systems, it registers as 'unremarkable,' even 'decay.' A deterrent. But clearly, your perception is filtering through that. Perhaps a compatible resonance." She smiled. Gunther did not understand her words but smiled in return. Somewhere deep inside, he felt a tiny zing of apprehension.

Dr. Meehan continued his lecture, explaining that mycelium was the network of threads underneath the ground and mushrooms were just the fruit. He stopped and pushed over a rotting log, pointing to the white lines of fungus growing underneath. The children scrunched their noses. The man smiled.

"This stuff grows in all directions as far as you can see." He pointed in several directions, "...but it's all underground." Claire and Gunther looked out into the distance, both wondering how the island looked so much smaller from the outside.

David continued, "Our research here...uh, we are basically listening to these mycorrhizal highways. And using them to transmit messages. But it's not just for communication, it's so much more than that. Difficult to explain all of it in one afternoon."

Gunther whispered "mycorrhizal symbiosis" to Claire as though it were a code word. They had read the words many times in their mother's notebook, but neither were clear on what it meant. As if reading their minds, David went on to explain that the origin of the word mycorrhiza was a combination of Latin words for "fungus" and "root."

"Mycelium and tree root communication pathways," he said. He crouched down and dug into the soil with the tips of his fingers.

"So ... what are they listening for?" asked Gunther.

"We listen to them trading carbon for nutrients...with the trees' roots."

Gunther must have looked unimpressed. Because David laughed and said, "Did you imagine they would actually speak? They don't have mouths, so they have to communicate in other ways. With hormones usually."

Gunther stared at the ground. Adults rarely spoke to him like this, so candid and yet so technical.

David continued talking -- about the trees now -- and everyone else walked in silence.

After a while, Gunther heard the words, ".... Hub trees -- or mother trees -- nurture younger ones in the understory...."

He and Claire looked at one another again. This was a superpower they had: always tuning in and out at the exact same moment. They were always on the same frequency.

"*Understory*!?" they said in unison

The woman smiled. "I know ... it's a lovely term isn't it? It means the younger, smaller trees. I like to think of it as the up-and-coming story versus the established story of the taller trees."

Not for the first time in his life Gunther wondered what trees would say if they could speak. So, finally feeling comfortable with their vibe, he ventured, "...and what is their story?"

The woman smiled again and said, "We're still learning. We use isotope tracers to detect what they are saying and to track their conversations."

Now they were walking among the Listeners in the meadow,

though the young men and women paid them no mind.

"We also help the trees and the mycelium connect and provide them with more nutrients. In exchange, they are stronger and will allow for our own information to be sent underground."

"*You* can send information through the ground? Through the mushrooms?" Claire asked.

Gunther wondered aloud how this was so different from the world wide web. At every opportunity, Gunther mentioned his knowledge of its existence, much to Claire's annoyance.

The man admitted that it was probably not all that different, except that it was completely secure and only used by their people, *those who have this island's best interest in mind*, and the larger environment's as well.

Their people? Gunther gave Claire a look, and they both checked to see their canoe far across the way. It was still there; they could see a silhouette of it teetering to one side, with Captain keeping watch nearby.

They were now entering that cluster of trees, a small forest along the opposite shoreline, oaks hanging heavy with Spanish moss.

David continued, ".... Older or injured mother trees tend to send great amounts of information to the younger seedlings -- they send messages before they die."

A sign stood next to the path; light brown and green, almost invisible among the woodsy backdrop. Gunther read, "Nest #33: Mycology and Animal Behavioral Husbandry." The logo was a tree with roots like electrical cords. On closer inspection, he could make out two eggs in a tiny bird's nest situated in the middle of the tree's crown.

The man completed his explanation by adding, "These 'stories' the mother trees tell actually do have a nurturing quality for the younger trees."

Gunther thought about his own mother and the stories she used to tell. When did Mom stop telling stories, stop tucking them into bed? It occurred to him that in the months before their deaths, Claire had started asking for a later bedtime and would stay up with Mom, while Gunther read to himself.

Finally, they arrived at the largest tree among them, long arching limbs reaching out and up, and some even sloping downward to reach the earth again; moss hung like drapes all around, and at the center of it all stood a grand treehouse. It was further away than it originally seemed. And much, much bigger.

It was more of a compound than a treehouse. It ran along the entire south end of the island, some parts perched in the trees and other sections on the ground. It was as large as Gunther's entire elementary school. Several large species of birds had made their homes directly above the treehouse.

"This is your home?" asked Claire.

"Home? Not exactly." Lana said with a soft laugh. "Well this is not just a house, dear. In fact this is an international hub."

Gunther didn't exactly know what the word hub meant but he knew enough to doubt there could be an international anything on this little island.

Claire looked just as dubious. Suddenly it felt like they had been there for days, and yet they just docked an hour ago. He whispered to his sister, "We need to go."

"I know. We will ... I just wanna see if maybe they knew Mom ...?"

"Why would they know Mom?"

Gunther had a lump in his throat now. Even whispering the word was hard.

"Gunther, whatever they are doing on this island, wouldn't

Mom have known about it…? Don't you remember it's why she came here in the first place?"

All Gunther had was a vague memory of his mother and father meeting at the local university after she won a scholarship and moved across the country from California, still a mysterious place to Gunther that Mack only referred to derogatively as "the Left Coast." He did not remember what she came to study or even if she finished college. His knowledge of his mother was muddied with her bouts of disappearing, which did not match up with his image of a university scholar. He remembered his dad saying on more than one occasion, "just because you're book smart doesn't mean you have any sense, Jessica."

"Don't say anything," pleaded Gunther. He didn't want them to know about their parents. He was tired of that sympathetic look from strangers.

"We need to figure out a way to come back here and stay for several hours without Gran finding out," whispered Claire.

Despite the fact that it looked like a Disney ride, they declined going into the treehouse. This was still a stranger's house.

Jeremy brought out cold bottles of water and lemonade packaged in strange resealable glass bottles with Chinese labeling. This was unsettling to both children, but they were so parched they couldn't refuse. They'd run out of water.

"I think we need to go home now," said Claire, peering again at the canoe.

Lana and David both nodded and looked at each other. Gunther froze. This felt like the moment in a movie when the children get kidnapped, never to be seen again.

But Lana gave them a reassuring look. "Can you fetch a cart so that we can drive them straight back?" she asked a young woman who had emerged from the ground floor of the building.

Somehow, the island seemed to have stretched itself, and now they were no longer in walking distance of the canoe.

In minutes, the young woman returned with what looked like a golf cart but appeared to have no metal or glass and was spongy to the touch. It didn't make any noise. Gunther wondered what the engine must look like. He imagined it was something soft but powerful, like the muscle of a giant snail. And just as Lana, promised, it delivered them back to their canoe.

****

As they paddled home that evening, they made a pact to never tell Gran and Mack they had ventured into the river. But they wished there was someone they could tell: the treehouse and the giant mushrooms and the mycelium listeners and everything Lana and David had explained. If only their mother were there, they could've told her.

Mom would've had an explanation for how the island had changed so dramatically when they arrived, how the mushrooms and trees behaved so differently than normal. Maybe it was like where she was from. She used to tell them about growing up in the California wilderness. "It had the most stunning and communicative trees in the world," she would say. "They talked to each other…and to me!"

But neither Gran nor Mack could ever know. They wouldn't be interested anyway, being the kind of people who were both incurious and fearful of everything. If they found out, Claire and Gunther would be on restrictions for sure. No canoe for a month. Or maybe two. And they couldn't spend an entire summer without the canoe!

They had promised the islanders they would return the next

day, but a summer storm kept the children inside until it was too late to go that far. They promised each other they would go the following day. But it was Sunday, so there was church and then a visit to Great Grandma in the nursing home, and then it rained again.

On Monday they sat on the porch steps waiting for Gran and Mack to leave for work.

Mack grumbled, "Goddamn always underfoot..." as the cat attempted to thread through his legs, almost causing Mack to tumble head first down the stairs, paperwork and all. Claire and Gunther laughed easily, giddy with their secret, and pleased at Captain's trick. Mack shot them a look: "I got one word for you kids: the pound." He wagged a finger at the cat.

Claire and Gunther grew red with stifled laughter, and Claire mouthed to Gunther, "that's two words."

"Grandpa, they don't call it a pound anymore," she said, all reckless. He turned to face her, seething, a large green vein popping out of his neck. Gunther grew cold in fear, but Claire continued smirking until Mack was gone. Captain jumped into her lap and rubbed his head under her chin.

Gunther gaped. His sister had never stood up to Mack like that.

"Good boy," she said, glaring at Mack's car until it disappeared down the canopy road.

They packed their gear and their lunches and set out for the island before the heat could set in.

That week -- the first full week of summer -- they spent every day on the island, usually getting soaked on their way back because of the afternoon summer storms. One time, Mack came home from work early and found them sludging in from the pouring rain, dripping wet, Captain yowling, bags and towels drenched.

As he assessed the mess, Mack's temper rose and he audibly

calculated their time out on the canoe. "You left at 9?" And then his fingers started going: 1, 2, 3, 4 ….

"You shouldn't be going so far that you can't get back before it storms. And why hasn't the dishwasher been emptied and the trash taken out? Where have you been all day? Is your grandmother going to have to take off more work and babysit you all summer?" Mack's outbursts toward them since the death of Josh and Jessica had been growing in frequency.

He was taken aback when both children rushed to give explanations and reassured Mack that it wouldn't happen again and that they would do their chores right away.

"Hmmph, well … just remember your grandmother would die of heartache if anything happened to you two. And it's my job …." He revved up and knitted his brow and dove into a long speech about duty and respecting your elders, while the children completed their chores as quickly as possible.

Sharing a secret of this magnitude made Gunther feel important. Claire frequently mentioned that the islanders were counting on them: Lana and David made it clear that they trusted the children to not disclose their location. There were more families who lived on the island--dozens of them. Children who didn't go to school. Parents working on a confidential project. There were people from all different parts of the world gathered there.

Claire and Gunther understood now that it wasn't just about mushroom-listeners and treehouses. David explained it this way: "we specialize in biological technology, with an emphasis on the biology. When people think of biotech, they usually think more about the 'tech' part. But for us, the natural machines of the biological world come first. Nature has the solutions already. We don't need to reinvent. We simply need to discover, and sometimes enhance what we find."

Claire was convinced that her mother must have worked

among these people at some point, but when Lana spoke to the children, she was vague about anyone else's involvement, even the university's. When Gunther asked if they were working for the government, David tilted his head and replied, "Not exactly, but in some ways it's bigger than that." It was all cryptic information about who or what they were connected to, and where Nests 1 through 32 might be, and whether there were even more Nests than that.

It was an endless source of mystery for the two children, a secret that strengthened their bond. But the day Claire started lying to him, that bond began to crumble.

CHAPTER 11: MOTHER

The Hybrid

From far away, the hybrid watches. She is allowed to now. Mother takes her by the hand and leads her down a long hallway, and upstairs to a room high in the trees. The hybrid sits down in a chair near the window as Mother points to the dock far in the distance.

"Watch us from here," says Mother. "That's where they will arrive. We will try to bring them close so that you can see."

The hybrid obeys. She sits all morning and waits. She longs to be out there in the grass with the others. *One day*, promised Mother. *Someday soon you will be free to go where you want. Just stay here and learn for now. Observe. You have so much to learn first. A whole life.*

Mother cracks open the window, and the hybrid can smell the heavy summer air: the wet wood and the fishing boats and the brackish water surrounding the island. Fragrant, fetid summer river. This was her most advanced sense, they keep saying. She felt proud at first -- a keen sense of smell sounded like a good thing. But they followed it up with, "We need to enhance vision and auditory."

We ... not she.

The hybrid is still a product that they need to tweak and program. Mother says she is human now; she is a girl. But that's not how they speak about her.

The hybrid knows that she is a girl though -- just like Claire. *The hybrid is a human girl now*, she tells herself as though she were one of the scientists. *I am the girl! Not the hybrid.*

She understands these kinds of things now. She's beginning to see what they see. There are groupings, categories, hierarchies; some things are better than others. Some things deserve priority. And the top priority is always humans. She must remember this– she matters only if she appears human. Otherwise, she might be discarded. Perhaps she had already been discarded before. And somehow came back. But these are thoughts she doesn't share with Mother. She wouldn't know how to express it anyway.

A few days later another doctor had agreed with the first, saying, "You're right. Her language is not where it should be."

Language. Such a soft and flexible word. An edible word … as though she can chew and swallow it. *Like "sandwich,"* thinks the girl. Bread and cheese and meat. This is the best way for her to learn words–through touch and smell and taste. They are right. Words are not a natural thing.

As she sits at the window, she can feel Claire's presence. Joy and energy mixed with a heavy sadness. Mother had taught her these words. She knows the feelings well now because she is always overcome with them when Claire is nearby. It's as though she is perfectly content and empty otherwise, but when the children come, Claire fills her up with a swirling tornado of emotion…even from far away. It is both thrilling and disturbing. But after they leave, it passes, and she is once again just a bit of biology, a happy plant swaying in the wind, waiting for Mother to tell her what to do next.

Her very first memory of being conscious was in the lab, behind a glass enclosure. She was not fully formed, but rapidly growing. Her arms and legs were fastened to her body and to the cocoon around her with fine mycelial threads that held her in a soft embrace. She grew so fast that it hurt, and the booming voices of the humans had been frightening.

And then there was the pain... and an unsettling wail rising from the pit of her own body. Those were the first sensations. After that, the soothing voice and face of the woman: Lana. Mother.

But then there was another memory, separate from this one, as though she had been a different child with a different mother. What was that? Perhaps bad programming? She already knew that's what Mother would say, so she did not mention it.

She didn't want to say anything that would remind Mother she was created and not born. She would do anything now to be seen as a human instead of a "hybrid."

A girl can not be so easily erased as a hybrid.

CHAPTER 12: THE MOUNTAIN

Gunther

It was the hottest day of the year, and they arrived at the island at the hottest time of the day. Jeremy asked his parents if he could take the children to The Pool. As long as Ovid joined them, they said. Ovid was Jeremy's older brother-- tall and moody and quiet at 16. He took after his mother, with golden-brown skin, yellow hair, and black eyes.

Claire and Gunther always wore their bathing suits when they went out in the canoe, but swimming in the lake at this point in the summer was not exactly refreshing. At best, you'd be swimming in bathwater temperatures and at worst there could be toxic algae blooming. A pool was just what they needed right now. Gunther wondered where a pool was. So far, everything they had seen was built up into the trees or raised up on stilts, which made sense; everything was so near the water.

The Zhou Sisters were just coming down the stairs of the main tree house. Sying and her twin were Gunther's age. They giggled every time they saw him. Claire would tease him about it. They also had their swimsuits on.

"We want to swim!" shouted Sying in a Mandarin-accented English.

Gunther remembered when he had first met the girls. Jeremy shouted "Sying! Sying ...!" across the field of Listeners. Sing! is what it sounded like. He had been struck by what seemed to be a command for him to *sing.* But then he saw the girl, shiny black hair down to her waist and a huge smile pointing directly at him. Her sister, though an identical twin, was not as beautiful, but Gunther couldn't explain why. The girls were orphans who came from the Chinese countryside, they had been told. But when and how did they get here? Gunther always wondered. How did all of these people get here?

As they walked through the woods, a towel draped over the shoulders of each child, Gunther realized they were about to encounter another "stretching" of the island, its unique ability to shapeshift and create larger spaces than could possibly be contained in such a small piece of land. But this time even the topography was changing-- they were coming up on foothills now, and in the near distance there was a small mountain!

Ovid was quiet as usual. Jeremy, on the other hand, talked incessantly. He was ten years old and gregarious. Claire and Gunther listened. They didn't ask as many questions now, realizing that each question led to a new question, and that everyone here, even the young children, gave highly technical responses about how the island worked, how it was different somehow than other parts of the world.

At age 12, Gunther was beginning to fancy himself a skeptic and a man of science, especially after the death of his parents, but he still held space for the possibility of flying reindeer and spell-casting witches and saviors and creators and all of those stories that most humans crave. This island world did not make sense, but he did not care. He wanted to believe.

They walked for almost 20 minutes, rounding the hill six or seven times, until finally they reached a landing where the ground was flat and a sparkling mountaintop lake could be seen. It reminded Gunther of a picture he had seen of the Austrian Alps in summertime.

"Behold, The Pool," said Ovid triumphantly, clearly appreciating the incredulous look on Claire's face.

Jeremy and the twins dropped their towels and ran as fast as they could to the lakeside. Claire and Gunther did not speak for several minutes, just taking in the unexpected scene.

"What...?" Claire finally managed to say. "How...?"

Ovid smiled shyly. "It's a spring!"

"A spring? In the middle of an island...on a mountain....in the middle of a river?"

"Huh. Yeah," he replied and shrugged. "Cold spring in the summer and hot in the winter."

It was 99 degrees that day and Gunther had been sweating since they left the house in the morning humidity. "Ahhh, how cool!" he finally proclaimed.

Claire walked to the edge of the spring, and waded in slowly, but kept her shirt on. She still didn't seem to believe it.

Ovid peeled off his shirt and joined the other kids. He splashed the younger kids and then darted away like an otter, faster than Gunther had ever seen anyone swim except in the Olympics. He disappeared underwater for a long time and when his head rose above the surface again, he had a huge grin on his face. Another head broke the surface of the water and nudged Ovid-- a manatee. And then there were dozens of them, floating all around the boy, some turned over, their glistening bellies pointed skyward. Gunther ran and splashed into the ice-cold waters.

Claire finally broke out of her trance and in a moment was swimming straight toward Ovid and the manatees.

She was a strong and fast swimmer ("part dolphin," as her father used to say), and so was Gunther, so they were impressed by Ovid's ability to hold his breath for four minutes underwater and to swim from one side of the spring to the other in less than a minute. Jeremy could do the same.

"Every child is taught how to do this at a young age," explained Ovid. "It's very important for everyone to know." He sounded a lot like his father. "After all, we live on this island completely surrounded by water." Casually he added "... and over a huge system of underwater caves."

Jeremy shot his brother a look that both Gunther and Claire noticed, but Ovid just smiled mysteriously and swam away.

Gunther recalled seeing the children in wetsuits that afternoon long ago, as he peered from the backseat of the car on the way to soccer practice. He had seen each child splash into the water, one by one, and disappear. For so long, he thought he had imagined it.

All afternoon, Ovid showed the other children how to swim with the manatees and talk to them and feed them. In the last several years he had quickly become the manatee expert of the island, learning about how they communicate and how they travel from the springs to the river and how they can help humans. He had been the one to train the manatee who came to get their boat that one day, he explained to Gunther.

Animal Behavioral Husbandry, Gunther remembered the sign saying.

Then there was the competition. It began as nothing unusual–just the typical one-upping that children do. But for Gunther it was just one of many tests throughout their childhood that would prove Claire's prowess over her brother.

Ovid timed the other children to see how long they could stay underwater. Jeremy was at a whopping three minutes, Sying and her sister stayed under for three and a half, but Gunther could only do a minute. Claire was under the water for so long that Ovid went down to check on her twice. Ovid, not one to gush, said, "That's incredible," which made Claire blush.

"You just have to not think about it," she said, looking at Gunther, as though admonishing him for performing so poorly. He hated when she tried to coach him. "Mind over matter." She tapped her temple.

Gunther stomped off. Claire never missed an opportunity to show off. She didn't have to rub it in.

***

That night at home after dinner in the living room, Claire peeked into Gunther's freshly-made blanket fort.

"I have something to show you," she said.

"Humph, I'm busy."

Gunther had his drawing notebook in front of him, trying to record everything they had seen that day in pencil drawings. Claire waited a few beats, watching his face as he drew.

She started humming, which made him lose his focus. "Claire!"

"What did I do?"

After a few moments he shrugged, realizing she had probably forgotten about the afternoon. Sometimes she was so thoughtless. He studied her face. Why was she such a showoff? Why couldn't she act like a big sister?

"What?" she said. "Stop being weird."

Finally, he scooted over to make room for her.

She held a flashlight lantern in one hand and a large canvas-covered book in the other. It was a photo history book of their town. All evening, she and Gunther pored over the pages about the waterways and small slivers of land that dotted the water near the shipyards. A whole chapter of fantastic names for bits of land: "Pirate's Point" and "Silver Goat Island" and "Alligator Isle." The author noted that when the large river island was first discovered, settlers noticed strange vegetation and creatures--very different from what was found on the mainland--but in the end, no one wanted to develop the land. "Once boaters and fishermen realized how hostile some of the plants could be, they decided it was better off left to itself. One developer characterized the islands as 'mushroom-infested wasteland.' " And later in the book, the author stated, "the unfamiliar and seemingly unwieldy wildlife made it such that no one wanted to claim it. Nothing could be built on the marshy patches of earth, so it became an unofficial dumping ground."

And that was it-- no mention of a small mountain or a spring, and definitely nothing about people living there or building a sprawling system of treehouses.

How could it be that this patch of land didn't even have a name yet? How had they been granted access to its lush, habitable side, and for others it appeared a brambly tangle of trees?

Claire and Gunther could hear murmurings from Mack and Gran in the other room and Captain mewing for his dinner. Things felt secure and cozy for the first time in a long time.

"But Mom knew about it, Gunther. I know she did. It was in her notebook."

"I don't know...was it the same island? Why wouldn't she have told us more about it?"

"I don't know ... but they definitely knew her."

Over the next several weeks, Claire and Gunther would tag along when Gran went to the library, always checking out books about the river, mushrooms, manatees, local history, Florida springs, and other objects of curiosity that sprung from their island adventures. Gran, a lifetime resident of the town, would never satisfactorily answer their questions about the strange island. She would always say, "What? Rubbish Island? What do you wanna know?" in a way that did not invite more questions.

CHAPTER 13: THE FIGHT

The summer's end was fast approaching, and Claire and Gunther found their days of long canoe rides increasingly disrupted by back-to-school shopping, teacher meet-and-greets, and church gatherings. Each morning Gunther could still hear the sound of his mother's voice right before he woke-- a phantom's voice– and Claire was sometimes found sleeping in her mother's dresses. But being out on the island made both kids feel strong again, as though they were a couple of normal children with very alive parents waiting for them back home.

One Saturday morning, Gunther woke early to the sound of footsteps and the creaking of the old farmhouse staircase. He lay awake staring up at the planets and stars hanging from the ceiling of his bedroom. When the back door scraped open, he knew it was her. Where was she going?

He tiptoed downstairs and into the kitchen in his footed pajamas that were too small. It was a gift from his mother the Christmas before.

From the kitchen window he could see the fog-morning lake, gum trees overhanging, looking fatigued from the long, seething summer. There was something about the subtle change in light this morning and something about the smells; it was not a change in temperature yet, but simply the desire of autumn approaching. It wanted to be fall, but summer held her heavy grip for as long as she could. The leaves, still secure on their branches, hinted at a turn in their color, just on the edges -- a thin, brown crisp.

Gunther watched Claire turn the canoe right side up and push it toward the lapping waters. But then, she must have heard him: the crackling from the back doorway, a slow, timid door-opening. She turned and faced him, looking bleary-eyed in the morning light.

"What are you doing?" he whispered. It was not even 7am.

As though awakening from a trance, Claire looked down at her feet -- bare -- and then at the canoe, half in and half out of the water.

A sharp meow came from behind Gunther, and Captain wound around the boy's legs and bounded through the tall backyard grass. In one graceful swoop, he jumped straight into the canoe, as though to halt it from going any farther.

Claire shrugged. "Nothing. Just getting ready, I guess." She nudged the canoe back up the bank, and sat in the grass.

Gunther joined her, pajamas wet in the morning dew. "Gran and Mack are sleeping. We can't leave yet."

"I know," said Claire shortly.

Gunther felt a chilly emotion coming off of Claire. This was something new.

And then, Gran from the back balcony: "Helloooo! What are you two doing up so early?"

They stood and waved, and then went inside, Captain following close behind.

Claire and Gunther sat silent at breakfast, skirting around the suggestion that they join Grandpa Mack at the grocery store. He excused them but not without a short lecture: "I don't know what you kids do out there all day in that canoe, but you should be prepared for it coming to an end. School starts, homework in the afternoons, and all your chores on top of it."

Gunther audibly sighed and looked over at Claire who was staring at her plate. He thought he saw tears in her eyes. He knew they were tears of anger; he was angry too at Mack trying to steal their last few days of joy. He stood back while she left the table, scrubbed her plate, and noisily jammed her things into a backpack. He followed her outside and they prepared the canoe.

For a good part of the trip, Claire and Gunther didn't speak. Gunther felt as though there had been a shouting match, but nothing had happened. He steered clear of aggravating her. A yellow notebook poked out of her backpack, the same notebook that had belonged to their mother. He wanted to ask her about it. She wasn't going to share it with Lana, was she?

As they rounded the corner out of the inlet, a strange creaking noise disrupted their silence. It was coming from the small tributary of water just off the main river. They had explored this little stream once before, and it was just a dead end.

Craning their necks to see beyond all the summer brush and foliage, they detected movement, a shadow of something large swaying with the water.

Falling into rhythm with each other, they paddled directly toward the noise.

Making their way under and around brush and brambles that had grown over the narrow waterway during the summer months, they came to a half-sunken sailboat, its mast squeaking in the sudden summer breeze.

"How long has this been here?" asked Claire, breaking her morning silence.

"Whoa!" Gunther said, "Look at all that stuff on deck!"

There were buckets and clothing and fishing nets and poles, all covered in a green film.

With the panache of a pirate, Claire jumped from canoe to boat in one swift motion.

"Hey!" Gunther grumbled, stabilizing himself. "You coulda told me first."

This also woke Captain, who'd been sleeping on the floor of the boat. He peeked over the side as Gunther held the canoe closer to the crumbling boat. The cat soundlessly jumped from boat to boat and followed Claire's lead, sniffing around the oddities left behind by unknown fishermen.

"What are you even doing?" asked Gunther. "That could sink any minute."

Claire just laughed. Gunther felt queasy. Claire's rapid emotional shifts were beginning to speed up lately, leaving him unstable.

When she peeked into the window of the tiny console, the boat groaned. She shifted her weight back. Captain leaped back into the canoe, and let out a meow as he watched her totter back and forth.

Claire finally said, "Okay, okay...but just let me get something."

She opened the door to the console, and crouched down, disappearing from Gunther's view.

"Claire ...." He looked around cautiously as though he was just noticing the surrounding jungle.

A clatter and clank from the groaning boat.

And then Claire emerged with a big grin on her face and one fist carefully curled closed. "Ready!"

Just as she spoke, something cracked beneath her and one leg slipped and she slid toward the sunken area of the ship.

Gunther shot up from his seat on the canoe. With one hand, he held onto the boat and with the other he reached for Claire.

"No, no, I've got it. Just hang on tight to the boat," Claire said, protecting something in her hand, while trying to pull herself up with knuckles on one hand and long fingers on the other.

She struggled for several minutes, and she wouldn't let go of whatever she was holding. Her foot was stuck.

Gunther turned white. He looked around, but there was no house or person in sight, only the deep prickly woods of pine and palm. There was nowhere even to beach, unless they were willing to plunge into a giant spider's web or a nest of water moccasins, or both. He was just about to start screaming for help, when Claire said, "Okay, I got it, I got it now."

After a lot of sloshing and cracking of boards, and scrapes and bangs, she did have it. She pulled herself up and lowered herself back into the canoe.

Captain was completely puffed out and panting hard. Gunther was also hyperventilating and holding on so tight that his hands ached.

Claire heaved a sigh of relief and sat down on the canoe bottom and began unlacing her soggy shoes. "Can you row in the back while I get situated?" she asked without looking at Gunther. "We should get out of here."

Gunther was stunned. He did what she asked, but tears of anger burned his eyes. Why did she always have to scare him? He quietly picked up his oar and moved to the back of the canoe.

He paddled them out of the tributary and into the open water. At that point, he turned the boat to the right instead of turning left.

"Hey where are you going?" Claire asked. "Wrong way."

"I want to go home," was all he said. She turned around to face him but he would not look at her.

"Gunther, we're supposed to meet Ovid and Jeremy ... remember?" And then, "You're not mad, are you?"

"Tell me what's in your hand," challenged Gunther.

Claire was silent for a moment just looking out into the distance in the direction of the island. She opened both of her hands. They were empty.

"Nothing. What do you mean?"

Gunther studied her.

She said, "Anyway…I can't believe that boat is actually here. I thought Ovid was just making up a story when he mentioned it."

"Ovid …. hmmph. What's going on? Why didn't you tell me you knew about it? Why did you go in there if you knew it was so unsafe?" But what Gunther really meant was, what are you not telling me?

"I didn't know … I mean, wasn't sure."

This wasn't like Claire. She knew how to spin a tale, but she was never uncertain about the details like this.

In the end, Gunther gave in and they went to the island. He knew it would probably be the last summer visit.

That was the day that Gunther saw Claire crossing the field of Listeners. Or that's what he thought he saw. She was dressed in a white gown and her movements were very strange– languid, not like Claire at all. He watched her take a seat on the ground next to another girl. It had to be her. But Gunther knew that Claire had just been at his side, dressed in normal clothes and talking to him in the intense way she did whenever she had a secret.

She had been telling him about the shipwrecked sailboat; she said that the boat had belonged to a family who used to visit the island, and that only Lana knew who took the boat and crashed it there. Claire didn't finish her story before she went bouncing off with Lana. And now here she was sitting out in a field dressed in white.

When Gunther finally decided to move toward the girl who looked like Claire, he could hear his sister's voice behind him. It was time to leave.

Lana was speaking his name too. He turned and saw them. They were walking to the canoe together. Claire was in normal clothing, moving quickly and nervously as usual. He swung his head back in the other direction. The girl in the white gown was still there, but of course it wasn't Claire. He was mistaken.

Gunther was still walking toward the dock, still a good distance away when he saw Claire pull something out of her backpack. Lana was with her. Was it the notebook? It was too far to tell. But later when he asked Claire about this, she denied it.

"What'd you give her?" he demanded

"I didn't give her anything. I showed her something. None of your business. NYB." This was another first-- her shutting down a conversation like this. Gunther decided not to mention the girl in white. Maybe she knew already; maybe she didn't want him to know.

That night Gunther built a fort as usual, but he posted a sign that said: "Keep Out--this means you." He expected to hear Claire say, "Hey what's this?... let me in!" He expected her to come and explain everything to him, to reassure him and get excited about the next visit to the island. But she didn't even come out of her room after dinner. She never saw the fort or the note.

So when Gran called him for bedtime, he pulled the blanket fort down around himself, making the chairs clatter over and a lamp crash.

Gran and Mack rushed into the living room, but not Claire. Gran uncovered her grandson, and found his face wet with tears. She interrupted Mack's outburst, "... what the devil?!" and motioned for him to leave. This one, she would take care of.

For 30 minutes, Gunther and Gran sat amid the disarray, and he wept in her arms. She cried a little too. Not once did she question him. Of course, of course. *You poor sweet boy*, is all she could say. Gunther had been ready to tell on Claire -- to tell Gran all about the island and the boat and the notebook and the strange people. But it felt as though this would betray Mom somehow. All he could do now was go limp in his grandmother's arms and weep.

CHAPTER 14: BROTHER

The Hybrid

She is so close now. She watches the brother and sister as they argue. The boy seems angry. The sister, Claire, looks nervous.

The girl tries to mimic Claire's speech. Language is improving now, and her hearing is becoming her best sense. "Stop it, Gunther," she practices in a soft voice. "Stahhhh-ppp."

Faster, Mother had coached her. *More energy. Claire is intense. Think of the mice in the lab.*

Intense: this is a new word for the girl. It's like a flurry of ants marching in all directions when she accidentally disrupted their mound one time. The girl could hear the ants' anger and confusion. Intense. *Nnnn-tintssss!*

She can't imagine how to move in jerks and jumps, and speak so crisp and loud as Claire. "We still have plenty of time," she'd heard David say to Mother. "She'll get there."

After Claire and Gunther leave, she walks outside. But without supervision. Mother has been allowing her to spend time in the fields with the Listeners. But she is not allowed out when

Claire and Gunther are on the island. And the girl thinks they were gone. So she strolls over to the field and sits down among the Listeners just as she had been told.

But then she sees them. Oh! They are still on the island. A flutter of excitement rises from her gut. She can see him across the way–the brother–and he sees her. They lock eyes for just a moment. In this moment she longs to go to him. To run over and speak the words she'd been practicing. It's the first time she'd ever ached to be close to a human–besides Mother.

She is beginning to remember things–impossible experiences that could never have fit into her short life. *Mem-er-eeezzzz,* Mother says slowly. Not simply implanted memories. She is *becoming* Claire, as the genetic code continues to lock in.

The girl can hear them talking about her– the team. How she might never be able to interact normally. But this! She wants to be near her brother. She has a brother. She feels she knows him already. But just as they catch each other's attention, a young woman beside her pulls her toward the grass, tugs at her gown and hisses something harsh. She cannot understand the words, but she knows that she has done something bad. She will be punished. She is not supposed to interact with Claire or Gunther. Not yet.

"Just stay down and be still. Stay low!" says the other Listener when she sees her bewildered expression. The girl is happy to do so. Low down in the grass, close to the earth, quiet. This is where she wants to be anyway. The woman shields her from Gunther's view. The moment passes.

Later, David reprimands her: "Never go outside without one of us guiding you! What were you thinking?" The girl shrinks in fear and confusion. She is escorted back to the lab and left to sleep in her chamber for the next several days.

He intended it as a punishment, but she's relieved to be once again connected in her cocoon, the endless network of mycelial threads that embed themselves so neatly into the pores of her skin. She drinks it in and dreams for days. An underground dream. Pulsating but silent, in her egg of life.

CHAPTER 15: RESTRICTIONS

Gunther

Fall 2002

Once school started, they couldn't visit as often-- Claire started high school and Gunther joined the track team. They were at separate schools for the first time since Gunther started kindergarten.

So when the first Saturday track meet was rained out after a long overnight storm, they snuck away to the island.

But it wasn't the same as their summer visits. Claire went off on a hike with Ovid. Gunther stayed with the little kids in the swimming area on the river beach. And that's when Gunther began to realize there was something even more strange about the island people than he first thought, and it confirmed that Claire definitely knew more than she was sharing.

He and Jeremy had been fishing for almost an hour, the younger boy jabbering away and Gunther occasionally muttering "uh-huh" and "oh?" Gunther looked up at the sound of a voice in a nearby tree, and thought he was mistaken. It was Jeremy -- somehow now sitting in an oak tree 20 feet away. But in his periphery, baiting a hook right beside him, Jeremy still chattered on.

"Jeremy ...?"

Spooked by Gunther's tone, the Jeremy beside him fell silent and followed his gaze.

"Do you have another brother..?"

The boy did not reply at first.

"Jeremy …. Hullo …?"

Jeremy looked all around, then opened and closed his mouth a few times before finally whispering, "Ummm. Kind of …"

The other Jeremy climbed down from the tree when he noticed they were staring at him.

"Hi, I'm Jeremy. Nice to meet you," he said to Gunther. His eyes looked grey-ish and vacant; something was odd about his movements, but he held out his hand, and Gunther shook a perfectly warm and human hand.

Gunther looked across the beach at Sying, her silky black hair glistening in the sun. She wore a bright pink swimsuit and pigtails. Her sister wore a long braid and a blue swimsuit. They were identical, but Gunther could always tell who Sying was because she would do all the talking and smiling and eye contact. It occurred to Gunther just then, that he didn't even know her sister's name, that she seemed not so much a sister as a shadow, copying everything that Sying did. Gunther just figured the twin was shy. She would simply giggle and cover her mouth. Sying's twin was just like this boy standing in front of him. Something was not right.

When Gunther told Claire about it on their way home, Claire did not seem surprised. She didn't even seem curious. What was going on?

"I know," was all she said. "I have met Jeremy II. He's kind of like a clone."

"Kind of …? A clone …?" What else did she know?

She had no explanation for the whole thing, just as Jeremy had very little to say about it. This was more than Gunther could take.

"How can he have a clone? There's no clones of people. That's impossible."

"Gunther, it's just his brother, okay? Don't worry about it. He's perfectly normal."

Gunther stopped paddling.

"Come on," said Claire, "we're going to be late. I had to beg Gran to let us out today."

Gunther held his oar across his lap. "This makes no sense. Why didn't we know about Jeremy's other brother before? What's his name? Why do you know so much more than I do?"

"Haha. In general? Because I'm awesome," said Claire, with an unfocused skyward gaze. He had turned around in his seat to face her.

Gunther's face grew dark. "You know what I mean. Why do they tell you everything? Are you going there without me?"

"Gunther I don't really know much of anything about Jeremy's hybrid or whatever. Look, there was a sheep cloned a few years ago. You know that. Doesn't it make sense that humans can be cloned now too? If anyone could pull it off it's these ... people."

Gunther's brow wrinkled. "Who even are these people, though? Why are they doing weird science stuff on an island in our river and no one knows about it?"

"Mom knew about it. Dad knew."

"What do you mean? How do you know?! Why didn't they tell us?!"

Gunther's eyes were growing big and threatening to water, but Claire didn't need to see his face to know that he was about to cry. His voice reaches that distinct pitch and warbles with a certain texture. It's how all siblings meet at the very beginning: that first squall of companionship and rivalry.

"Why are you crying?"

Gunther turned bright pink and yelped, "I'm not crying! ... Stop it!" and then he faced forward– away from her– and began paddling furiously, tears streaking his face.

After several minutes, Claire carefully picked up one last thread of the conversation: "Anyway, when would I have time to go to the island alone, huh?"

Gunther did not reply.

Claire waited a long while. Neither of them spoke or paddled. They had made it back to the lake, and the water was still.

"Lana knew Mom," Claire blurted. "Okay? They worked on this project together and they figured out to basically grow an animal...even grow a human in a lab. But they aren't really human ... is the thing."

Gunther sniffed and wiped his eyes. "Whatdya mean? Like they're robots or something?"

"No they are fully biological."

"What does that mean?"

"They are made of human and plant material, well actually not plant...did you know mushrooms are in their own kingdom, separate from plants?"

"I know, Mom told us that like a hundred million times. So you're saying Jeremy's twin is a mushroom ...?"

Claire laughed. Gunther frowned. This surely had to be a lie. It was one of the first times that Gunther began to doubt Claire and all of the myths she had built all around him. The flying ferns, the talking animals. This--of all things -- could not be true. It was time for him to grow up, just as Mack had been saying.

"Not a mushroom exactly, but a certain kind of fungus that grows alongside human cells to make it develop really quickly, so they can make people out of nothing, just like that." She snapped her fingers.

Symbiosis, Lana had explained. Super-symbiosis, actually. Fungal hyphae can sometimes grow rapidly, overnight even. This specific kind of fungus mimics animal cells and "reads" human DNA. By accident Lana and her team stumbled upon a way to grow what looked like an exact clone, but really was a hybrid of both fungus and human. Jessica had been there when it happened. In fact, she was *instrumental*, Lana had added.

Gunther tried very hard to keep up with his sister's explanation. The memory of Mom swirled around him. The dubious nature of her ideas, her studies, her character. Now here she was again, resurrected in Claire. He wanted to believe all of it. He was desperate to believe– to be a part of whatever this was.

They were quiet for a moment. The canoe was almost touching land, and they were in shouting distance of Gran. Gunther lowered his voice.

"But why wouldn't Mom tell us?" He paused and splashed the paddle in the water. And then the acknowledgement of a spooky notion: ".... So they're *not* humans?"

"Part human, I guess."

"I don't believe it...at least Dad would've told us...." The tone of his voice ascended into a question.

"Mom was going to tell us...that's what Lana said. She was gonna let us go to the island and everything...but I guess she was just waiting for the right time."

"So ... were you really on a hike with Ovid just then? Where did you go?"

"Of course I was on a hike," she whispered and then put a finger to her lips. They were in the yard now. Claire turned the canoe over and walked toward the house, Captain at her heels.

"So then .... Where did you guys go?"

But by now Claire was done talking. She had shared as much as she was willing.

"NYB," she replied. Then she dropped the oars at the back door and went inside.

"What does that meeeean?" Gunther muttered miserably. "Claire!... We're not done cleaning up. You need to help! Claire!"

But she was already upstairs.

"What the goddamn hell?!" Mack was outside now, looking as though he'd been roused from a hard nap. "What's all the goddamn hollerin?" he shouted. His face was red, and his monstrous blue eyes popped.

***

After that, Claire and Gunther visited the island only twice, both visits ending with fights, and the final one with Mack's proclamation that he was going to haul "that piece-of-shit-boat to the dump" if they ever crossed him again or went beyond the threshold of the lake. They didn't bother to ask what they had done to "cross him." It could be anything and they better not question it. Mack wasn't the kind of person you asked for clarification.

Gunther would learn later that one of Mack's buddies from the police department had spotted the children far out on the river when they were on their way back from the island. After Mack got the call, he demanded that Gran reign in the children's excursions. He didn't say where they had been spotted, but he told her he was worried. In truth, Mack was embarrassed at the lack of control they had over the grandchildren.

Mack appealed to Gran's ambition for her grandchildren to succeed at school, saying that Claire needed to apply herself and Gunther needed to make friends his own age. "A 13-year old boy!" Mack exclaimed, "He needs to learn to be a boy with boys! Tell that girl she can stop babysitting and let 'im grow up."

"He's twelve," Gran corrected quietly. "No one said anything about babysitting. The kids like each other. They need each other, especially with all that's happened."

Mack grunted.

"What exactly are you trying to prove?" asked Gran, exasperated, but she went along with the new restrictions: no canoe rides unless the adults were home, and unsupervised boat rides could not be longer than an hour. That wasn't enough time to get to the island and back.

Gunther knew Claire was hiding something more from him. She didn't know that he had seen her with Ovid and Jeremy high up in the treehouse together, looking excited, laughing loud, together, without him. And then there was Lana and the other scientists taking Claire down into the underground "tunnels." The truth is, he was too scared to go down into the tunnel ways, and he could've joined the other kids in the treehouse that day. Claire pointed this out to him, but Gunther couldn't shake the feeling of being excluded, of Claire leaving him behind. And what about the girl that looked like Claire? Had he just imagined that? She didn't have an answer for that one.

As an early birthday present, Claire received a standup paddleboard, a mode of transportation all her own. It was like a surfboard but for flat water, and it was the new thing among her high school friends who lived at the beach. She told Gran and Gunther all about it, but never considered asking for one.

So it was a shocking extravagance when Mack came home with it one day. Claire even hugged Mack. But Gunther had a theory: this was Mack's way of separating them.

And sure enough, Claire was so stunned by the generous offering, that she ignored Gunther's entreaties to go to the island again and spent the afternoon learning to balance on the board. She offered for Gunther to take turns, but he refused.

The canoe sat by the house, unused for weeks.

At school, Michael Hadley began talking to Claire in her Spanish class. He was a sophomore, and he lived with his mother and stepdad across the lake. Gunther overheard Claire talking to her friend about him one day. Gunther was on the balcony unbeknownst to the girls down below in the yard. Claire was giggly.

Their families didn't have much in common so the kids didn't know each other well, but they'd grown up across the lake from one another. Claire had seen Michael out there on a small motorboat. She knew that he fished Sunday mornings with his stepdad and that the family had a pool.

Michael offered to take Claire out on the boat and teach her how to fish.

One Saturday afternoon, Claire and Gran were outside in the garden, and Gunther was up in the tree. He was the first to see Michael's motorboat coming toward their property. In the boat were Michael and his friends and lots and lots of beer in the cooler, which Gran could not see. A barefooted Michael stepped into the shallows and came up on land to shake hands with Mack and sweet-talk Gran into letting Claire join them. They were allowed to trawl around the lake looking for fishing spots, but Gran would not allow the boat out of her sight while her granddaughter was on it.

At the last minute, Gunther was allowed to join them too. For the first time in his life, he got seasick while they were out— it was probably the smell of beer. He was angry that Michael treated him like a baby and held hands with his sister.

This did not seem like the same Claire that went to the island with him.

CHAPTER 16: A PROPOSAL

But the next day, Claire was back to her normal self. It rained from dawn to dusk, and Gunther spent all morning playing video games. Mack was out of town on a hunting trip, and Gran would be at church until 3:00.

When Mack wasn't at home, Claire seemed to grow bigger and stronger. She became the Claire that she used to be, the one who came alive when they were on the island. Even Gran seemed more fun when Mack was away.

Claire came downstairs and stood between Gunther and the TV.

"Hey, what's the deal?" cried Gunther, trying to see around his sister.

"I need to tell you something."

"Right now? Hey stop Claire! My high score…"

She stepped aside but she had already done damage. His player was dead.

Gunther threw the controller at Claire.

"Hey! Ouch."

Gunther was silent.

"What the hell, Gunther?"

"What the hullll, Gungffer?!" Gunther mimicked.

"I'm ready to tell you something … about the island … but never mind if you don't want to listen …." Claire left the room and went into the kitchen.

He could hear her rummaging through the fridge.

"Why don't you tell your beer-drinking boyfriend?" he shouted.

No answer.

He sat dazed in front of the screen, video game colors in his eyes and the repetitive digital melody in his ears.

"What? .... Claire!" He was shouting now, but still staring at the TV. "What is it?"

She strolled back in, two cheese sticks in her hand. She peeled away one and tossed it to Gunther. He caught it in the air and lay back in his overstuffed bean bag chair.

"Gunther, here's the thing. Mom and Dad totally knew about the island."

"Dad did ...?"

"Well, I think so ...."

"Okay ...."

"Well the thing is, Mom was working with these people ... a lot. Through school. Through her classes at the university."

Gunther felt the familiar pit in his stomach -- that dull ache he felt when someone brought up Mom and Dad. But now it was worse. He could tell that Claire was going to tell him something scary. He could sense her excitement, which, in his eyes, usually meant danger.

"How? I mean, what ...?"

Claire looked around and listened, checking to make sure they were actually alone. Gunther kept his eyes on Claire as though she might disappear.

"Well ... you know how Mom graduated from high school super young?"

Gunther nodded.

"She went to some special camp in Oregon after that, for like gifted kids or whatever. Some farm."

Claire continued explaining it to Gunther the best she could. She had gleaned bits and pieces from the notebooks, evidence of their mother's other life. And any questions she had, Lana was able to fill in the answers.

"So, based on the work she did at that camp...which wasn't really a summer camp because it lasted all year, she got recruited to the university to work with this special group of scientists. So when she enrolled in college, that's when she met Lana! Can you believe it? Apparently, Lana was like a PhD student already by then. She says Mom was really smart, and everyone loved her. It was really sad that she just kinda dropped out after a while."

She paused for a long time. "....I guess that's when I came along -- when she got pregnant. When we came along."

Gunther thought about all of the arguments their parents used to have about Mom going to school.

"... But Mom was working on that cool project. That fungus that can hijack a mammal's nervous system and mimic human growth."

Gunther made a face. "Not like, the zombie fungus?" He shuddered, remembering his mother showing him a page from a book where a mushroom bloomed through the head of a carpenter ant after the fungus had taken over its body. The idea had haunted him for months.

"Kind of the same idea ... but no, not that! The patients control what the fungus is doing. Lana says that in people with neurological ...? ... or psychological ...?... problems, one of those--the fungus could act like this biocomputer where the patient could control the fungus, and the fungus would tell the muscles and neurons and synapses what to do. It can cure diseases!"

Now Claire was really excited, but Gunther was lost. And she reminded him of Mom again ... in a bad way.

"What does this have to do with anything? Why are they here, still? They're definitely not university people. I mean not from here. And what about the clones? Did Mom have something to do with that?"

"I mean ... I don't know. It seemed like she kinda dropped out or something way back then -- you remember how she was. But the point is she did help to make some of the stuff that's happening on that island. Isn't that cool? And apparently, she was going to go back there and bring us and maybe have us go to that camp and start studying with them before we even go to college."

"So why didn't we know? And why didn't they just say that right away?"

"They wanted us to discover it all organically and figure out what we are drawn to... at least that's what they said."

"What we're drawn to ...?"

Gunther knew there was something Claire wasn't telling him. Something big she was saving. He still hadn't mentioned the time he thought he saw her on the island. The twin of her.

"I don't know, I think they just wanted us to enjoy it without bringing up our parents' death or whatever."

"And Dad? Did they know him?"

"Lana says she met him a few times. I guess he didn't like Mom working so much for them."

"But anyway...here's the thing: they want us to join them. Me and you. Like, full time." She must've been holding this back for a while now.

"Join them?"

"Yeah, she said I'm almost old enough to give my consent to

live there as long as they provide an education ...."

"What about me?"

"Yes, they're working on that. We can both go. Oh! Wouldn't it be awesome?"

Gunther felt chilled and giddy. He fed off of Claire's energy, always.

"Ummm. I guess. What about Gran?"

"We'll have to get them to come talk to Gran. I'm sure Lana could convince her, don't you think?"

It occurred to Gunther, maybe for the first time, that Lana and the island people lived in the same universe as Gran and Mack. Up until then, Gunther felt like the island was more like a video game than real life. It was as though they were completely immersed in fiction when they were there. But here was Claire inviting Lana and David over to their house, to talk to their grandparents ... to ask .... to ask what exactly?

"Gran will never say yes," he said. Captain was curled in his lap, purring. He stroked the animal's whiskers.

"Gunther, think about it. Gran would love it. They wouldn't have to, ya know, take care of us anymore. She could do her blueberry farm and Mack wouldn't be bossing us around anymore, and they could visit whenever they wanted."

"I don't know." Gunther looked around. Sometimes, he thought he couldn't stand one more day looking around at the walls and furniture that reminded him of Mom and Dad. Sometimes he wondered why they hadn't just moved to Gran's place. But now, faced with an option, he couldn't imagine leaving.

"Weren't they very clear about not telling the outside world about them?" asked Gunther.

"But this is a special case. I mean, right? Gran would have to know …?"

It was unusual to see Claire unsure of herself, asking Gunther his opinion.

"She's not going to agree," he said. "And then what if Mack tells on them or something?"

Claire knitted her brow. "Well they're not doing anything illegal … I mean I'm not sure why they have to be so secret anyway."

Looking back on this conversation, Gunther would wonder how authentic Claire was being with him. Had she really been that naive? She must have known. She must have had a more complicated understanding of how it was all going to go down. Or was it that simple for her?

She stood up suddenly and crossed her arms. "Well I'm going," she said. "Sooner or later, I'm going to figure out how to join them. I don't want to live here in this shithole with that old bully any longer."

Gunther looked up, surprised by the unexpected profanity spoken aloud in the same house where Gran lived. The cat sprang off his lap.

All was quiet in the house. Claire turned on the TV and switched channels for several minutes.

"Can you mute that for a second?" he asked. He had been gathering up his courage and he needed to focus. "Okay," he finally said. "Okay, I want to go too."

She dropped the remote and clapped her hands together. "Great! We'll tell Lana next time."

And that was that. It was decided.

He would turn this moment over in his mind for years to come: she must've known that he didn't mean it. He hadn't acted confident enough. She must have looked at his scrawny twelve year old body and decided for herself that he wasn't big enough or strong enough to go with her. Whatever it was, Gunther would wonder for a long time what she had known, what she didn't know, and whether she really wanted him to come.

She didn't mention it again, and they never returned to the island. At least not together.

CHAPTER 17: DECEPTION

The Hybrid

One afternoon the girl is taken into a dark room where several children are seated in a circle. Their eyes are closed and they seem to be in a deep trance, as though asleep but sitting straight up, cross-legged.

The girl feels flutters in her stomach. She'd never been this close to so many young people at once. She knows they will not be interacting with her or even aware of her presence, but she is able to gaze on their silky hair and smell the sweet human perspiration and feel the vibration of their youthful energy. Like a human in the presence of a forest of beautiful trees, the girl appreciates this collection of fleshy organisms.

And then there is Claire. And her brother. *Their* brother

She sits directly across from Claire, their knees almost touching, and she can feel electrical impulses as she draws closer. The girl looks up at Mother. The electricity is overwhelming, but Mother said it was normal. Lana nods in reassurance and the girl stays grounded in her position, a mirror image of Claire's hay-colored hair and golden skin, deep set eyes and skinny arms.

When she touches Claire's fingertips, the girl is immediately transported into Claire's perspective, drawn deep into her meditative state. She is swimming in a lake on a mountaintop, and all the other children are there with her. There are manatees, and Ovid is timing the kids to see how long they can hold their breath underwater. The girl feels Claire's sense of anxiety–something about how her bathing suit fits–and the excitement…a mammalian attraction to the tall boy, oxytocin and testosterone and progesterone running through her body. They had told her about these powerful sensations. They told her to simply feel them and know what they are, even if they caused discomfort. The experience would make her more human, they said. And more human is good.

But then the scene goes fuzzy, and darkness clouds the girl's vision. With a shock, she realizes Claire's awareness has returned to the darkened room, and her eyes are open. The girl opens her own eyes and there they are, face to face: Claire and her hybrid clone. The girl feels dissociated from her own body. Which body belongs to her? Was she the original Claire or just the copy? For a moment, she doesn't know. But then she notices Claire pulling her fingers away and forcing her eyes closed again. She's balling up into herself. She doesn't want to see.

Mother urges the girl in a severe whisper: "get up, let's go!" This isn't supposed to happen. The kids never fall out of the trance.

Has she done something wrong? the girl wants to know, as she tries to keep up with Lana's long stride.

"No, you didn't do anything wrong, my dear. It's Claire. She's much stronger than we thought. You need to be strong too."

"Yes, Mother," says the girl obediently. *Yes*, the girl thinks to herself, *she will try her best. Anything to become human.*

CHAPTER 18: THE HURRICANE

Gunther

They followed the track of Hurricane Grace across the Atlantic, turning from storm to tropical depression to hurricane. For three days, he and Claire watched the report on TV: the swirling red dot aiming itself toward Candlestick Lane, getting closer and closer with each passing hour. With giddy anticipation, they waited for the sweet sound of the anchor on television to announce, "countywide school closures after the governor declares a state of emergency."

But the nature of Claire's excitement was not in tune with his. Gunther knew something was off, something was different. Maybe it was just the tension between them lately. Hurricanes had a tendency to bring out whatever chaos was lurking beneath the surface. Gunther remembers the time when they found Mom outside during a hurricane years before. She said she had gone outside to meditate in the yard, and then found a squirrel in distress, and then three baby squirrels fell dead out of the tree. She was sobbing over the little nest of squirrels as the storm raged around her and the giant oak branches whipped back and forth above her, threatening to break at any moment. Dad had to force her back inside. Gran had been there that day. She shook her head and said, "God in heaven, what is she thinking? What kind of mother does that ... and during a storm?"

The morning before Hurricane Grace made landfall, both televisions were blaring, and Grandpa Mack was out on the front porch with his radio to his ear. It was a Tuesday, but school had been closed since the Friday before. It was going to be a big one, they said. There were evacuations for some. Most everyone in town lived in low-lying areas. Families were encouraged to stock up on water and canned goods. Fill the bathtubs with water in case the water supply is compromised. Gunther knew the drill. Every kid in Florida knew it.

Gran was at the foot of the stairs, dressed in a floral blouse and jeans, prepared to face the mobs at the store, to squabble over non-perishables and bottled water. She wanted Claire to accompany her but the girl had disappeared somewhere. Gunther woke to the sounds of Gran calling her name and then Grandpa Mack and Gran arguing.

"This is all you, Emily, this is your fault. You're too soft." He sneered. "That girl. You've always let her get away with murder....and now look, she can't even bother to help an old woman."

"Hmph," Gran replied, "I'm her grandmother. That's what grandmas are for ... I was supposed to spoil her."

"It was Josh and Jessica too .... It was all of you. I told you from the beginning ...."

"Don't you dare .... don't you say one more word, Mister. How dare you say his name with that tone."

With that, Gran slammed the door.

Gunther suspected Claire was listening, probably curled up by the attic window, waiting for the voices to quiet. It did not occur to him that Claire was really gone. It was only 8:00 in the morning.

But later that morning, when he went outside to escape Mack's grumpy mumblings and confusing insults-- "stand up straight, son. You look like your grandmother walking like that"-- he saw the paddleboard was missing. At first he thought someone had stolen it or it had washed away in brisk pre-storm waves, but then he noticed the paddle was gone and exactly one life vest was missing from the pegs in the laundry room.

But Claire would never risk going out in these conditions, at least not for very long. If she went anywhere, it was probably to save a turtle or something. She would be back soon. But, boy, would she be in trouble.

Just then he heard the clunk of Grandpa Mack's boots.

"Son!" Mack shouted. The wind picked up just then and all Gunther could hear was the air whipping past his ears, but the old man continued shouting.

Gunther felt dizzy as he tried concentrating on the commands Mack threw into the wind.

"Wha...?"

"We told y'all. Get your crappy boat and things up to the house, pronto. Anything that ain't nailed down."

Gunther's head swelled with the thick air and low clouds, the buzz of pre-hurricane life. Frogs were croaking at the wrong time of day. Crows cawed chaotically, and blimp-like clouds cast thick shadows on the ground.

Maybe that's what happened -- Claire already brought her board to the garage, thought Gunther, as he dragged the canoe across the thick St. Augustine grass. It was itchy on his bare feet, and he was sweating in the late September heat.

He was feeling nostalgic for hurricanes' past, especially the time when his parents and Claire evacuated to Tallahassee years ago and they were all together and safe, packed in the small, two-door sedan. It took all day to drive 160 miles because everyone in town was going west too, fleeing their oceanside and riverside homelands, if just for the stormy weekend.

Back inside the house, Gunther ran back up to his room before Mack could snag him. As he shut the door, a pink note flitted onto the floor. It was written in Claire's bubbly letters: "I'll be back soon. Don't let Gran worry. Don't tell."

He held onto that note for a long time, imbuing meaning into it that would seem silly to him years later. She's going to check on the island. She's going to help them prepare for the storm …? She's going to see Ovid ….

It only took a few minutes for his relief to give way to anger. Why didn't she bring him? He crumpled the note in his fist, shoved it deep into his pocket.

Later that day, when Gran and Mack were finally worried enough to involve the police, and the neighbors had been alerted, and Gunther had been interrogated, he finally showed the note to Gran.

"That's all I know," he shouted and burst into angry tears, enraged by his sister's carelessness. How could she leave during a hurricane warning? Among the panic and preparation for hurricanes, Gunther and Claire used to always have each other, and they would make it exciting, building their own little nests in the hallway in case the winds got too strong near the windows.

Noon turned into evening, and Gran and Gunther sat quietly at the dinner table. Mack, who was now semi-retired, had recruited everyone with a badge to form a search party. Normally, a teenaged child is not considered missing for at least 12 hours but Mack created an urgency and made others' rally around it. The impending storm added to the frenzy, and pretty soon the whole town was on the lookout.

At 7:00pm a police woman came to the door to get an official report. Apparently Mack had bypassed all paperwork in his haste. The policewoman especially wanted to speak to Gunther because "you know her best, sweetheart, and you might be able to guess where she paddled off to."

To Gran she spoke grimly: "They can't keep search boats out on the water overnight in that storm."

Gunther sat on the couch in the family room, staring at cartoons, with the volume turned all the way down. Every 30 seconds or so he peered out the back window, hoping to see a flash of her yellow hair in the distance.

Mack came in after a while and tried to be comforting in his awkward way. "Anything you need, Buddy? Your sister will be back -- you know that. Haha. She's a tough one -- you and I both know! Don't we, Buddy? Tough girl ... real tough ...."

Gunther tried to recall a time when Grandpa Mack actually referred to him by his real name. It was always "son" or "little man" or "buddy," or when he was really angry, "boy".

Gunther sunk himself deep into the couch at the farthest corner away from Mack.

Gran came in and squeezed Gunther's shoulder. She was mostly quiet, a tear streaming down her powdery face every now and then.

Finally the call came in. It was Claire's voice on the other end of the line.

Gran leaned on Gunther for support, and crumpled in relief. Mack growled and appeared to brush away a tear.

It turned out that Claire had paddled across the lake to Michael's house. His parents were out of town, and could not be reached when the neighbors spread the alert. Michael wasn't in the house when the search party came.

Apparently, Claire had wanted to see Michael before the hurricane lockdown. It was only supposed to be for a few early morning hours, but she lost track of time and by the time she was ready to go back, the current was too much. As she paddled away, Michael saw her struggling to keep the board going in the right direction. She was swept toward the river. He had managed to get his boat out but not in time to help her.

She lost the board and the paddle, and the Coast Guard found her clutching a life vest, Michael's little skiff bobbing in the choppy waters almost a mile away. They had to rescue him too.

 "I tried to tell her. I tried to tell her," Michael kept saying when they arrived at the station to bring Claire home.

Both kids were wrapped in blankets, Claire shivering, eyes downcast. Gunther watched from the backseat of the car, and when she finally fixed her gaze on him, it was a stranger's expression. Her eyes looked metallic, like robotic irises closing over the pupils when the light shone in her face and they asked her questions. When she got in the car next to Gunther, she barely looked at him. Not like her at all. He squirmed away and stared out the window at the flimsy pines bending in the storm winds.

Mack said, "C'mon, be nice to your sister. She's really been through it."

Gran said, "Blessed be God in heaven."

Claire's eyes drooped and she fell into a deep sleep.

***

The next morning, the storm had passed. The damage was minimal-- a branch here and there, a neighbor's flooded garage, some discombobulated wild animals.

"See I told ya there's no need to evacuate," said Mack to no one in particular. "Just a buncha overexcited reporters... trying to sell us bottled water and godknowswhat."

Gunther had almost forgotten the previous day's drama, a

heavy night's sleep wiping the slate blank. A new dawn. A calm day. He ran to Claire's room, excited to assess the aftermath of the storm, a tradition of theirs that she wouldn't want to miss. But when he got there, the door was locked and when he knocked the voice was unfamiliar -- bored and uninterested in Gunther's call to action.

He went outside by himself, first to the front yard where a stunned possum was wandering around the garden in broad daylight. Gunther jumped in her path and could almost reach out and touch her before she scampered under the house.

In the backyard, Grandpa Mack stood over a large osprey lying still in the grass. He was trying to figure out what to do with the body when Gunther joined him and noticed the bird was still breathing.

"It's alive! Claire will know what to do!" said Gunther. "Keep watch!" he said, running back to the house.

But when he went to retrieve her, the door was still locked. Silence.

By the time Gunther finally persuaded her to come look, Gran had wrapped the black and white bird in a sheet and moved it to a spot on the balcony, "where at least it won't get snatched by a dog."

"It's just in shock," explained Gran. "It probably got knocked out of the sky. What do you think, Claire Bear?"

Gunther and Gran looked into Claire's sleepy face.

"Oh. Yes I guess," was all she said, but nothing about her bird books, nothing about osprey mothers and osprey nests and raptor behavior. She wasn't even looking at the bird.

They both followed her gaze over the trees and then all three stared out at the lake for a long time. The world had refreshed itself-- all was still. An alligator bellowed in the distance, the deep throated roar of a reptile engine. And then the lake was completely silent, finally resting after a long torturous night.

From then on, there were strict prohibitions on the children. Under no circumstances were they allowed on the water without an adult. Claire was on restrictions for a month. No friends, no Michael.

And her new paddleboard was gone, swept away by an unforgiving force of nature, just like their parents' boat.

But Claire didn't seem to mind. She had little interest in going out, and no interest at all in canoeing or tree climbing. Gunther was anxious to get back to the island somehow, but when he mentioned it to Claire, she acted as though she didn't know what he was talking about. She remembered an island, but when he started talking about the people who lived there, Claire just said, "Don't be silly, Gunther. Of course we were just pretending," and "We can't. It's too dangerous." This was the first time Gunther remembered Claire saying that something was too dangerous.

Gunther continued talking to her about the treehouse and the mushrooms, Ovid and Jeremy, Lana and David, but Claire never added to the conversation or even acknowledged that they were anything more than figments of their imagination. In her newly-acquired manner of brushing him aside, she would close her eyes for several seconds, take a long breath, and say "I can't play with you right now, Gunther."

So, Gunther learned to keep quiet. Claire must have lost her memory in the storm. He tried to convince Gran that she had a concussion, but there was no evidence, and no one else knew about the island anyway. "She remembers exactly what happened that day, Gunther. And her noggin seems to be doing better than ever," said Gran tapping her temple with a ring finger. In fact, it did appear Claire's brain was just fine that term -- she made straight A's for the first time ever.

Gunther also noticed that her teeth -- which always had a

slight gap in the front-- seemed to be straighter and whiter, and that she began wearing makeup and dresses and jewelry.

But Captain must have known. His loyalty suddenly switched from Claire to Gunther; instead of trotting around at the girl's heels, he stayed close to Gunther. In fact, the cat kept entirely clear of Claire, always galloping off when she came into the room. But the strangest part was that Claire didn't even seem to care.

CHAPTER 19: TRUST

The Hybrid

After the girl is escorted by boat to the house at 6:30am, she stands in the backyard with the paddleboard for a moment, assessing the home she knows but doesn't know, trying to understand who exactly she is now. The team wanted to make it look like she'd gone on an early paddling trip, in case anyone had been awake to notice. She is now Claire, they told her, for all intents and purposes, though her hybrid file name was claire.0 and many of the team members just called her "the Hybrid."

The unfamiliar clothes, Claire's old t-shirt and shorts, cling to her skin, the humidity like a second layer of clothing. She skims the yard with her eyes-- the rusted swing set, an under-inflated football, a metal cat food dish filled with rainwater, the garden of overgrown weeds marked with handwritten popsicle stick signs: tomatoes, peppers, okra.

The black and white cat appears from under the house. The girl bends down and tries to coax it toward her as she's seen people do in television shows, but Captain isn't fooled. This was no Claire. The team warned her: animals and small children may not recognize her as the same person, but everyone else will.

She is most nervous about encountering Gunther. That one time she caught his attention. He must have suspected something. Why couldn't they just tell him? Claire has told him too much already, Mother had said. Just deny everything. Your life depends on it.

A familiar tug coaxes her toward the trees. She notices two huge oaks nearby, a cheerful pair of trees clinging to one another with their arm-like branches. She can hear the sound of the networks beneath her feet. The mycelial threads are woven into the plants' roots beneath the soil, and they continuously talk to another. David said that noise would stop fairly soon. She won't have to hear it anymore. But this thought makes the girl sad.

It isn't actually sound anyway. That's what they don't understand. It's more like a vibration and a smell all mixed together; there is no word for it in any human language. But even so, she is still trying to translate her mycobiont sensations into words that she can share with humans. There had been moments of sheer frustration when she just stopped attempting to communicate. It wasn't until the real Claire showed up on the island, and she saw her mirror reflection for the first time, that she truly understood what she was supposed to do. She had wanted so much to be like Claire, to experience all the feelings and sights that Claire experienced. But now, she feels the tug of that other part of her– something underneath -- dark, cold, and wild.

She takes a deep breath and prepares to enter the house. Just then she hears a boat's motor puttering in the distance. It grows closer. A tall boy– almost a man– is driving the boat. His brown summer skin and wavy blond hair give him a warm and toasted look. He looks surprised to see Claire standing there. The boat swerves and bucks, as though he's just learning to operate it, but upon further inspection claire.0 can see that he is impaired in some way. Perhaps fatigued? He stops at the lake's edge and switches off the motor, as he squints through the trees at Claire.

"Hey!" he puts a hand up.

His eyes are red and his hair mussed and salty. He tests his breath in his hand and peers at himself in the boat mirror. She doesn't move, but stands there with a vacant smile, probably for far too long.

He motions for her to come close, and so she does. She wades ankle-deep into the water and listens to him talk. Apparently, he has been out all night long, partying at a friend's house down the river. He is not supposed to have the boat out, but his parents are out of town for the weekend. He's talking very fast. She feels the buzzing of the networks underneath her feet, beneath the water's sand. Perhaps this is what it feels like to be a cypress tree.

"Claire? Ha ha. Earth to Claire! You going paddling?"

"No. Uhhh. Just going in...inside."

"Ooookay." He raises his eyebrows.

She backs up, out of the water, listening for the voice she's supposed to hear over the radio network. She's supposed to get instructions from the island. They told her Claire would be with her the whole time, but the connection isn't there yet. She's supposed to activate a receiver somewhere near the house. She scans the yard once again.

It's not that she can't do it on her own; she knows the characters, she knows the story. Essentially, she is Claire. This is her purpose– to be a stand-in. She knows everything Claire knows, the memories were programmed into her long-term memory; she was just having trouble accessing them. And they promised they would guide her at first. She's only been alone for 10 minutes. But where are they? She taps her temple. The messages should be firing directly into her brain. It had worked on the test run earlier.

"You alright there?" Michael asks. He looks up at the sky and then glances toward his house across the way. "Hey uh, remember we were gonna get together today. Hurricane party?" A goofy smile, with a pinch of danger.

The hybrid tries to remember. She knows that Claire promised something to Michael. A date? Was it supposed to be today?

"Oh!" she says. This is her first interaction with anyone outside of the island. She doesn't want to mess it up. She remembers Claire liked Michael. They were "going together." But what does that mean? "Yes, that's right. I can't wait."

"Okay. So ...?" He bows deeply and waves a hand at his boat. "What's wrong with now? Let's do this."

She puts up a finger as she had seen people do and says, "Okay. Just one minute."

She turns away and whispers, "Hello? Where are you guys? Am I supposed to go with Michael?"

She looks down at her forearms with horror and sees the mycelial threads, white and pearly, poking through her human follicles. She scratches at them and they fall away. What if Michael saw? Mother promised her she would soon learn to control this.

If you can't get in touch with us, just do what Claire would normally do, they had instructed.

But she doesn't know. She doesn't have instincts in the way someone with years of human experience would have. Right now, she has to rely on others around her to guide her. They had taught her about trust– who to trust and who not to trust, but she couldn't remember what they said about Michael. In this new world, every person she encounters will be new, and they all appear so similar to one another.

So, hearing nothing on the other end of the line, she follows Michael onto his boat.

She insists on bringing the paddleboard with her. He shakes his head, and mutters "sure, sure," as she hoists it up and over the boat's side.

"Uh, don't forget your paddle," he says.

As she fetches the paddle, she takes one long look at the house. She doesn't want to go in there yet anyway. What if they don't believe she's Claire? What if she gets in trouble with this Mack person? Memories of fear and disgust rattle through her brain even though she's never encountered the man herself. Regarding Michael, she has fluttery feelings that could be fear as well, but the sensations are a lot more pleasant.

So she moves toward the pleasure and away from the fear, just like any creature would do.

***

It would take the girl a long time to remember what really happened that day. There was a struggle, and afterward her body hurt. But she was so new at life that she didn't know what things were supposed to feel like. It was like her insides, between her legs, had been gouged out, so it was confusing when she found all of her body parts intact. Her fingertips were curiously painful that next day, and all she wanted to do was sleep.

After she was rescued from the water, she stayed in her room those first few days. She was terrified of course, not only about what others would do to her, but also about how she should act and whether they would notice something was not quite right. She stayed away from Gunther the most because he was the one who constantly called it to everyone's attention. But just like the team told her back at the Nest, no one would question it, no one that mattered, that is.

She had been instructed never to talk about the island or the other Claire, and to always refer to herself as Claire. What she did not know is that she was programmed to slowly forget the fact that she was a hybrid. She would forget much more quickly than the team had planned, perhaps because of the trauma. Blocking out unpleasant events came natural to her apparently, and eventually she moved forward with only a twinge of feeling different. In this way, she squeezed herself into human life, and molded herself into a proper teenage girl. She became Claire.

But the dreams of mycelial growth and decaying life and the tunnels and wild plants of the island would continue to haunt and delight her for years to come. Sometimes she could even tune into the real Claire. The girl would allow Claire to peek into her old home. This of course was simply a dream too, and when she mentioned it to the school therapist once, he calmly told her it was just a part of her dissociative disorder. So much trauma, he had said, shaking his head. Of course you've split into more than one person, my dear. Let's put you back together.

And so the girl continued into womanhood, making a great effort to be the one, true Claire Eliza Flynn.

CHAPTER 20: LOSING CLAIRE

Gunther

Downtown Jacksonville

The day they tagged along with Grandpa Mack downtown was the day Gunther knew once and for all that Claire was not the same person.

Both children had always loved a visit to the city, with its haunting blocks of quiet, old buildings deteriorating in the wake of suburban sprawl and urban flight. There was still a shining gem, a small vibrant center of town that glowed with bookstores, street musicians, and museums, and the wide, twinkling river flowing slow and steady through it all.

It used to be that on outings like these, Claire and Gunther would lollygag behind their mother, talking to pigeons and peeking in store windows, always together. Now, Claire kept pace with Grandpa Mack and did not seem to notice their surroundings at all. She listened placidly as he explained something about the city's homeless problem and the danger of "vagrants".

At the next street corner Gunther could see an orange traffic cone balanced atop a yellow fire hydrant, sitting just so: the hydrant resembled a small yellow man with short muscly arms wearing a large party hat. Gunther smiled, knowing that's how Claire would have characterized it. She was always making things come to life like that. "Look--a little man with a hat!" she would say and make eye contact with Gunther, one hand over her mouth to stifle a giggle.

But today, it was just a plain old fire hydrant and was passed by without comment. That was the moment he realized she had ceased seeing all the magical, absurd, and curious things that no one else saw, whether it was a teacher with outrageous false eyelashes or the squirrel in the backyard who seemed to develop a romantic attachment with the turtle statue in the garden. But just as she had been since the day of the hurricane, Claire was vacant and quiet. This was not Claire.

For a long while after this, Gunther continued to notice these bits of curiosity all by himself, but Claire never acknowledged them anymore, never made them come to life. And after a few years, he stopped noticing too. When there's no longer someone to share it with, you can lose your ability to see.

That same day in town, they encountered Jamie, the homeless woman. One time upon seeing Jamie, their mother had given them a correction Gunther would never forget: "Don't say she's 'crazy,' sweetheart. She's probably schizophrenic and simply doesn't get the medication she needs." Jessica had always had a gift for upholding the smallest shreds of dignity in the lives of people who needed it most.

But that day, Mack just said, "keep your eyes down. Don't look at the loony in the face," as he shuffled the children around the woman pushing a grocery cart and yelling profanities and saying, "Chil'ren of the devil," but never looking directly at the family.

She held a small sign that read, "Death is just the beginning." Claire and Gunther studied Mack for a moment and then exchanged knowing looks.

The woman turned and looked Mack straight in the eye and whispered, "White Devil."

Fortunately, for her and for the children, Mack was losing his hearing and didn't react. He was unpredictable, and if he felt attacked, he might put his hand on his gun or even call for backup.

But Gunther and his sister had sharp auditory powers and could hear everything she said: "This land will snag yo' ass one of these days. You stole, you stole it all. But she rise and haunt you, one day! Rise and haunt you! She got caves under the water, tunnels, hear me?!..a dungeon for you, White Devil."

The children's eyes glittered with horror, but they kept walking, faces averted as instructed.

She continued in a seething whisper, words that made no sense to Gunther at the time: *We're all just bags of meat gettin' sucked dry by the vampire of the devil economy and the fools who run it. Immiseration! Immiseration! They feed us just enough to keep us alive. Just enough water to keep us conscious.*

Jamie was something of a Marxist, Gunther would conclude many years later in his college philosophy course. But on this day, against the backdrop of Grandpa Mack's loathing, Gunther shuddered at her shocking epithets and the thought of Claire not being Claire. In the car on the way home, Gunther expected they would have a lively debate about Jamie, or at least Claire would say something interesting.

"So sad," was all she said.

"Sad, my foot," Mack replied. "That woman doesn't even *want* to help herself. She's just looking for handouts."

Jamie had not asked them for anything, nor had she ever asked for any handouts, in all the times they encountered her with Mom in previous years. Gunther expected Claire would point this out to Mack, but instead she gave him a weak nod of agreement.

For the first time in his life, Gunther felt completely alone in the world.

As a last ditch effort, Gunther took the canoe out that

afternoon without permission. He tried to find the island, but without Claire, it was impossible to navigate and too far to travel. He got lost for such a long while that he thought something magical might happen. Maybe that strange bird would come find him. But then he saw the tumble-down dock where they had played with the otters so many years before. He hadn't really gone anywhere.

As he paddled home that day, he began stitching together a theory about what had really happened the day of the hurricane. He pitched it to anyone who would listen: Claire had been taken, he told them. The people from the island rescued the real Claire from the storm and replaced her with another version of Claire.... somehow. Of course he couldn't explain this part, couldn't make them understand that there was even a possibility this kind of cloning could exist.

After all, who was going to listen to a 12 year old boy traumatized by the loss of his parents, a mother and father drowned in the ocean? As the result of his grief, he was making up stories about his sister being taken by some mysterious river people. Of course, no one faulted him for this.

Claire settled into high school and did what she was supposed to do, drifting deeply beneath the cover of youthful vanity and hyperfeminine dreams– the teen magazines and perfume and hair dye and long showers and prom nights. Gunther sometimes smelled cigarette smoke being puffed out of her window when Gran and Mack were away. Then she would spray the entire upstairs floor with body spray as though it masked the smell. It would always give him a headache. He would threaten to tell on her, and then he and Claire would argue.

After a while, Gunther began to forget that Claire wasn't Claire. She had simply grown up–and the island became a distant memory. None of that could have been real anyway. Mom's old notebooks were just the silly scribblings of a drunk, as Mack pointed out one time when Gran found them in Claire's room.

Most notably, Claire had stopped bringing home turtles and bugs and baby squirrels, and she never went out on the lake or river again. She had developed a fear of open water. Of course, no one faulted her for this.

And so it went: their childhood companionship dissolved altogether as Claire climbed into young adulthood. The canoe was tossed aside and left to crack and wither through the seasons. Mack purchased a small motorboat and taught Gunther to become a proper fisherman. Things began to settle into place, the way Gran and Mack had always imagined, in a world where boys are boys and there are no magical islands. Even Gunther's memories of Mom began to fade, in a way that made everything more bearable.

CHAPTER 21: A FUNERAL

Gunther

Present Day 2007

The morning of the funeral Mack reminds Gunther, "this house belongs to you kids. You'll need to sort it out. Only the devil knows where your sister is."

"It's fine, Grandpa. I told you, I'll find her. We want you to stay here in the house if that's what you want." Gunther is learning to be soft with Mack, realizing that he's lost without Gran.

Gunther now sits at the kitchen table with Mack and two neighbors, old friends of the family--two elderly women--one tall and one very short. They are making final arrangements for the funeral. Mack appears almost catatonic as the ladies chatter away. Gunther listens and nods and stares out the window at the canoe. The pulse of the cicadas can be heard through the back screen porch. The summer is descending, harsh and unrelenting.

Gunther stands and leaves the table without excusing himself, as though drawn to the hypnotic call. He needs to be in the yard, near the water. His face is upturned at the sprawling branches of the water oaks. For hours each day they used to play there, in the two giant trees that held hands, as Claire used to say, the arms winding around each other in a wooden prayer.

What could she be thinking? Gunther wonders, and then out loud he says, "Where the fuck are you?" not realizing anyone is around.

The taller of the two ladies is quietly smoking a cigarette on the patio, and she reveals a playful grin when Gunther turns bright red. She puts out the butt with her shoe and joins Gunther in the yard.

Sidling up close to him she whispers, "She left that boyfriend of hers … and that clinic … and joined some kind of cult. It was a secret between her and your grandma."

Gunther stands there for a moment in shock shaking his head. Great, now he has to track her down.

The back door opens, and he and the woman turn to see Beth at the doorway.

Gunther crumbles in relief. As a girlfriend, Beth is not so much inspirational as she is reliable. She has rock-like qualities, that kind of person you want around for emergencies and funerals and potlucks and difficult toddlers and all the other menial tasks of life. This is why Gunther thinks it's best to link his life to hers even though they are very young. And today he is gratified by his choice.

As they gather around the table again, a call comes in from Claire: She might not make it to the funeral. She's not talking to Ken, her boyfriend, so she doesn't have a car. She's broke. And so on.

Everyone watches Gunther as he responds with, "uh-huh, uh,-huh, ummm, … but Claire..?" Beth makes a big huffing noise, exasperated for Gunther's sake.

How could she? whispers Beth, shaking her head as she watches Gunther's expression teeter on the brink.

"We will move the date, then. You need to be here for this," Gunther tries to sound authoritative as he locks eyes with Beth.

"Let me talk to her," Beth mouths, holding an invisible phone to her ear. She will take care of this.

Beth talks. A lot. Claire seems to say very little. Beth hangs up the phone looking more smug than usual. Claire is coming.

But when she doesn't show up the next day, and Ken doesn't answer the phone, Gunther isn't surprised. She lied to Beth. Sometimes Claire seems like an illusion, as though she has erased most of herself and there are just rubbed-out pencil marks to show what she used to be. He can never quite grasp if she's ever telling the truth.

"Should we call the police?" he asks.

Mack reminds him that it's just another one of her disappearing acts; she doesn't want to be found. "Just a waste of police force. Just more paperwork for some poor rookie."

Beth is certain she said the right things. In any case, why should Gunther be responsible for his older sister? Why were they the ones stuck with making the funeral arrangements? Claire should be the one doing all of this. *Claire's the eldest*, she reminds Gunther.

That evening in the backyard, as they watch the lake turn topaz in the setting sun, Gunther consoles Beth. The truth is that Claire probably never intended to come, and nothing Beth said was going to change that.

"Yeah, I'm sorry, Gunther. I'm sorry she's like that." And then with a flourish of generosity, she adds, "It really is lovely here on the lake. I see how you and Claire must've had a fun childhood here. Why you love it so much."

Gunther squeezes her hand hard in gratitude. He hasn't cried yet, but he feels it coming.

A night heron watches the two humans with one red eye. A small memory drifts around in Gunther's head like a moth caught indoors: Claire used to call these little herons "Muppet-birds," with their huge heads and round eyes. He remembers that look in her eye when she would get unusually close to a wild bird, as though she was going to grab it. She was always capturing bugs and butterflies and baby birds, anything that could fly– she wanted to inspect them close up. Maybe she had a sharp hunting instinct, or maybe she just always wanted to have wings of her own. This particular memory turns Gunther's grief into a palpable thing, as though he is carrying it in his hands. His temples begin to pound.

***

The next morning, he receives a text from an unfamiliar number: "This is Claire…using a friend's phone. I'm okay. But I'm sorry I can't make it. I'm sorry for everything, Gunther. I'm the worst."

Everything. The worst. She always speaks hyperbole when she's decided she can't do something, when she's decided to give up. She's gone again; she won't "come through" at the last minute, as he keeps reassuring Mack.

So, on the day of the funeral, when Claire actually shows up to the church, looking healthy and alert, eyes sparkling with tears, Beth's mouth falls open, Gunther stumbles over the kneeler in the church pew, and Grandpa Mack rolls his eyes.

"Nice of her to show up … after you and Mack took care of everything." Beth squeezes Gunther's arm in support, but it feels as though she's desperately pulling him, some unnamed fear gripping her as the entire mood of the church shifts under the spell of Claire's energy.

After the ceremony is over and everyone has gone home, Gunther finally gets a chance to see his sister up close, and he knows that something is wrong. Or not wrong. Something is weirdly familiar.

Claire has returned, he thinks irrationally, and he is suddenly a little boy again. This isn't the same woman who was planning on missing her own grandmother's funeral. There is something in her eyes that tells him this is her, as though her soul had flown out of her body years before, leaving her vacant and aimless. Now, this spiritual energy has returned, and it's led her home to Candlestick Lane.

Illustration by Daria Likhodedova

PART II: CLAIRE

CHAPTER 22: GONE

Claire

Fall 2004

On the morning of her 17th birthday, Claire woke up in a windowless room with a bitter smell lingering in her sinuses. Artificial sunlight beamed down onto a cylindrical hydroponic garden, and a maroon curtain hung down from the ceiling, hospital-like, on two sides. The other sides were concrete walls, covered in thick beige paint.

Her mouth was dry and her tongue felt thick. She tried to sit up, but her arms and legs were like sandbags, the kind that she and Gunther used to slog from the garage to the house to seal all the doors before a hurricane. That was their job.

Claire's heart began pounding and her palms dampened.

The hurricane.

Gunther.

It's been two years now.

They had promised. Nothing bad would happen to her or her brother. That was so long ago now. But -- what room was this? The ceilings were too high. This couldn't be the treehouse room, could it? That tunnel system must be much larger than she imagined.

Her heart raced even faster when she heard a door whoosh open on the other side of the curtain. Trying to sit up felt like she was pulling herself out of a hole. That's when she noticed the nauseating tug of an IV in her hand.

Suddenly there was a face at the curtain--wide and pale, yet feminine, with large pink lips and grey-blonde hair. Happy Birthday, it said. All sweet and mom-ish, but with something cold around the edges. Maybe it was the British accent.

"My birthday's not until next week." The words were difficult to push out of her brain and into her mouth.

Now the face was beside her bed, peering over bifocals at a machine. Pressing buttons, the green light of a computer illuminating her face. Then the woman gave a pleasant sigh and turned to Claire to help her lie back down.

"Your birthday is today, Claire. I think you missed some days. You've been mostly asleep during your travels."

Travels ....

"Have I ... was I injured?" Claire looked at the back of her hand with the IV and then scanned the rest of her body. All parts were in place, unscathed.

The large, white face loomed over Claire and smiled without using its eyes. A hand appeared and smoothed Claire's forehead, gently pushing her eyelids closed. Like an exhausted baby, the girl resisted for a moment, tried sitting back up, and then pulled in a long, ragged breath. In less than 30 seconds, she had surrendered to sleep.

CHAPTER 23: REMEMBERING CANDLESTICK LANE

In her favorite memories, Claire is immersed in water. She has no memory of a time when she couldn't swim. Her father used to say she had gills instead of lungs.

Claire's earliest memory of her mother shimmered with water -- a ferry ride from Mayport to Fort George--just the two of them. Gunther stayed behind with their father, while Claire and Jessica had something of a mother-daughter outing, their first and only one as far as Claire can remember. She was so excited that they would ride a "fairy" and was only slightly disappointed when they arrived at the dock and Jessica pointed at the large ship bobbing in the small waves of the river and said "ferry." It smelled of shrimp and gasoline when they rolled down the car windows.

Jessica tossed her head back in laughter when Claire told her she had been counting on a "fairy ride." And this is what had made Claire most happy. Her mother's good mood.

"No, sweetie, it's a car ferry! See ... we drive our car onto the ship, and then we get to park it and walk around on deck."

The car rolled over the ramp and onto the boat, Claire strapped in her car seat in the back. A man in a uniform tapped at the window. Winked twice--once at her, once at her mother. Took their ticket. Claire was very young, maybe three and a half -- so it's a fuzzy dream-memory. But she remembers one thing for sure: when the ferry left the dock and the horn blared its thunderous honk, her mother lifted her from her car seat and held her high above her head. Claire squinted out across the glittery bay and saw the islands beyond, filled with pine trees and water oaks, puffy clouds floating above them. She beamed into her mother's face, sun-kissed and shining. Then, they were running together, to the helm of the ship, Jessica pointing and speaking in a soft, excited voice, a voice just for Claire.

After a year of the new baby, and cranky parents, this day of undiluted attention from her mother was intoxicating. The boat, the salty air, and on the other side of the river, the ruins of an old plantation with giant oaks and a wild orange tree in the woods. As they walked hand in hand down the wooded trail, her mother said, "see the tall tree with the dark, dark leaves? That's an orange tree growing wild on its own out there." She explained that it was planted many decades earlier, for a home that no longer stands. A wild orange tree. Something so domestic and tame; a fruit that belongs in an orchard under the careful watch of the farmer. But this had become something different -- singular and wild, with gem-green leaves, twisted, thorny branches reaching skyward. Claire recalls the longing to climb it and touch the fruit, but her mother said the wild ones are far too bitter.

There weren't many good days like that with Mom, but Claire kept each one safe in her memory, storing them away like rare coins. There was something wrong on the inside, Dad would say, and Claire suspected something bad happened to her mother when she was very little. Jessica went through long spells of silence when she would just sit outside barefoot by the vegetable plants and bury her hands in loose dirt as if she were gardening.

But when Jessica was doing well, she had lots to say, bits of this and that to teach her children: the Timucuan people used to fish on this riverbank; enslaved Americans lived in those tabby cottages over there; the white water birds with fluffy feathers are called snowy egrets; a live oyster with its razor-sharp edges can easily slice a little toe off; lavender oil keeps away the mosquitoes; don't ever eat the yellow berries; dark berries and red berries are usually safe; the woods are filled with edible mushrooms, but just not this one; poison ivy has three leaves, not five. And so on.

Looking back on it, Claire realized that it was probably her father who taught her half of those things, but it was always her mother she remembered, squatting down in the mud, holding out a flower or a bug for the children to examine. From a very early age, Claire mimicked her mother's best behavior and used her little brother as a way to practice being mom and teacher.

Claire liked to think she had a good mother, but the truth is that Jessica spent much of their childhood either shut away in her bedroom or out walking alone...or doing godknowswhat as their grandmother would say. So Claire took it upon herself to compensate for her mother's deficits, especially when it came to her little brother. She comforted Gunther as a small child when he whimpered for Mommy. She was brave for him when bigger kids tried to bully them at school. She would always protect him, even when she wasn't sure how she would protect herself. Or at least that was how she remembered it.

She came to believe that building a fantasy world would shield both her and Gunther against the drab reality of grownup life. She remembered one time in particular when pretending became a serious matter, and she confused herself about what was real.

It was a vivid memory. The velvet body squirmed on the wet pavement, soggy and bruised. Hands on hips, 9-year-old Claire bent over and examined it as evidence: proof of a magical world. Gunther stood close by and watched.

It twitched. The antennae were plant-like, further confirmation this was not an ordinary creature. How could an animal have ferns for feelers? If an insect can have plant parts, can a tree have human parts? It all seemed feasible. The edges of Claire's little world began to unfurl as she explained her theory to Gunther.

He peered over her shoulder, tiptoed and wide-eyed.

"Ohh! It's dying," he said, watching as it folded itself, one wing onto the other. "Leave it alone." He did not have the stomach for such things.

"We're not bothering it by looking."

Gunther turned away. Claire crouched closer. All was silent but a far-off crow's warning.

After several minutes, the body was motionless, and Gunther returned to inspect the corpse. They looked in awe at the creamy colors, the vivid spots, the furry body, but mostly, its enormity. The wing-span was wider than a grown man's hand.

The tops of their heads were touching now. Hands on knees, squatting low, Gunther whispered, "What do you think it is?"

"Something like a fairy."

Once Claire tapped into a theory, a bit of calculation that she had foraged from deep in her imagination, it all became clear so fast. There was no doubt in her voice: "But not exactly a fairy. It's called a ... a Flutter ... Root. A FlutterRoot. Grows in the ground at first like a plant-- see these leafy things...? And then.. when it blooms, it makes wings, not flowers."

Its floralness was at once apparent to both children.

Claire's understanding of the natural world was irrefutable. She was 9 and Gunther 7. She spun explanations spontaneously, and once they were spoken aloud, they lived on forever. After this encounter, Claire and Gunther would speak of FlutterRoots as though they were cardinals or snails. Just another fact about the natural world.

At some point later in life, Claire would learn that this type of insect was a giant silk moth called a cecropia, a species that never, ever eats and only survives for two weeks as an adult.

Magical in its own way.

But at that moment, in the quiet morning backyard of their childhood, they were witnessing the death of something akin to a fairy.

Another time, they discovered spongy cascades of shaggy pony hair on the dead trees in the woods nearby, and although Gunther assumed at first it was some kind of mushroom, Claire made her case: they were tiny Pegasus-type creatures that would ball up and attach themselves to wood whenever humans came around. When they came to life--usually only at dusk -- they were small horses -- furry, winged, and translucently-white.

"If you catch them at the corner of your eye, you might see them flying, but you can never look directly at them," Claire explained. "If they know you're looking, they'll stop."

Gunther held tight to his skepticism longer than usual, so she continued. "Look. At the side of your eye." she explained. "It's called peripheral vision -- you can see them buzzing in the air."

"Purrifurral," repeated Gunther, pointing his head forward, his eyes rolling back and forth, corner to corner.

Her logic made sense. She must be right about how they hid from humans. When you looked directly at them, there they were again, sitting perfectly still. If people knew what they really were, they would take them to a lab and chop them up to study them, she said. But the Mushroom Ponies were too smart for that. To further her argument, she told him to think of hummingbirds --they're hard to pin down, too.

Perhaps if Gunther scoured the internet he could prove his sister wrong, and she wouldn't make up such theories. But they didn't have a computer until later. Cell phones were rare, and many families still weren't connected to the internet. In the Flynn house, the Internet connection was too slow to even bother. For home-grown research, they still relied on the set of encyclopedias from their father's childhood.

So, unless her fantastical explanations frightened him, Claire's storytelling went largely unchecked. If they were scary, like the time she told him the wizard head carved into the top of the walking stick came to life at night and stole his Halloween candy from the bedroom, Gunther would go directly to a parent for fact-checking. So Claire skewed her stories toward the pleasant and scientific-ish.

In the end, Claire knew that the hard facts were not the point anyway. Being able to see the science and the myth all at once, like the optical rabbit-duck trick of holding both images in your mind, was the most useful lens for viewing the world. But maintaining focus is a tricky thing. And illusions are hypnotic.

The day they saw the otters for the first time, she shielded Gunther from reality in a different way. She didn't let on that she was scared of the bully brothers, Randy and Frank. Randy, who was in high school, acted nice but had mean eyes and said creepy things. She couldn't quite read what kind of danger he presented, but whatever it was made her feel sick to her stomach. That day, she'd found a knife in the haunted shed, and she would've used it if she had to. But she never told Gunther.

Claire used to consider herself very brave.

But after their parents died, Claire began feeling different. Almost breakable. She felt fragile, like the tiny snails she would rescue from the summer sidewalks, their thin shells barely holding everything together. Claire felt it was her duty to save such careless creatures, including the earthworms that seemed to catapult themselves onto the sidewalk at the beginning of a very hot day. With long, delicate fingers she would place them in the grass. After Mom and Dad were gone, she began to imagine how easily a little snail family could get crunched underfoot, with only that eggshell armor. And yet they always forged on anyway, right out of the cool grass and onto the hot pavement. This wasn't valor--it was stupid innocence. Perhaps she had never been brave in the first place.

She was only fourteen years old when they died, and it wasn't fair.

It certainly was not fair at all, the therapist had agreed. The children's grief therapist, an obese woman who walked with a cane and smelled of cheap dryer sheets, paid the children a visit every two weeks and forced them to play ridiculous games with blocks. She assured Claire that it was okay to be angry; she acknowledged the injustice of it all. But at some point, Claire would need to put that aside and move forward. Everyone faces unfairness at some point in their lives.

One day, the woman came with a gift for Claire, a pink Hello Kitty notebook with a squishy cover, and suggested Claire start keeping a journal. In the pages, she should express her feelings openly without judgment, said the lady. Claire wrote a total of eight words: "I'm not six years old, you fat hog." But she never showed it to anyone and insisted she had nothing to say, nothing to write. It was not a lie. She only wanted to know how people could move on with their lives when she and her brother had been left motherless. But she couldn't express in words how unfathomable it was that life just continued on without Josh and Jessica Flynn in it. Writing wasn't going to make it any less shocking.

Shortly after the deaths, Claire began squirreling away unwashed items of her mother's clothing before Gran got to them. A coral dress. A smoke-grey robe. The favorite blue T-shirt with a whale printed on the front. The girl could not bear the thought of that smell being gone forever. She also found her mother's journal, which she spent countless evenings trying to decipher, looking for clues about who her mother really had been. But it was just a raggedy spiral notebook for a college Biology course. Hardly a heartfelt journal. Only one page mentioned Claire, but it didn't make any sense and only strengthened the case that her mother had been mentally unstable, a narrative Grandpa Mack liked to promote any chance he got. She read it aloud to Gunther once: "Mycobeasts. Mycomen? Fetal DNA. Can they grow the Hybrid in a lab? Can I rescind consent?" At the bottom it read, "Claire Eliza Flynn." That was it. Gunther shook his head. She could tell Mack's comments were starting to rub off on him.

"What if Mom was part of something…dangerous?" she asked Gunther. "What if that's why…"

Gunther just shook his head again, not ready to talk about Mom. He was quiet for a long time after the deaths.

That first day they journeyed to the island, Claire briefly considered turning around. They weren't allowed in the river. It was 2:00 in the afternoon, and it was already going to take them an hour to paddle home from where they were. It could take another hour to get to the island, and the river might get choppy. She remembered the island was at a place in the waterway so broad that it scarcely resembled a river. She could hear Gran's voice in her head telling her to protect her little brother. But as they rounded the bend, and passed the great bluff, and inched closer to something new and possibly magical, Claire couldn't stop herself from guiding them farther away from home.

CHAPTER 24: THE ISLAND

Summer 2002

On the island, Claire felt awkward at first-- childish in her cutoff shorts and flip flops, with river muck between her toes. In those years, it was always hard to know how to act; people had started treating her differently. She was still a kid, but the outline of a young woman was now discernible.

As their canoe approached the island and she saw it change from grey and foggy to intense greens and yellows and blues, she knew that this is where she belonged. She felt shy as the family approached their canoe that first day, but then Dr. Das had said, "call me Lana," and squeezed Claire's hand for a long time.

And from the moment that Dr. Meehan -- David -- began talking about trees and mushrooms, Claire realized this was the place. This was the subject of so much speculation in her mother's notebooks. As she sat on the ground with the others and touched the carpet of grass beneath her, Claire felt a sudden surge of energy, as though touching the fingertips of her mother's spirit. She imagined Jessica here as a very young woman, not much older than herself, cataloging critters and identifying birds and studying these strange mushrooms that did things Claire had never seen before.

Whenever they were on the island, the outside world didn't matter to her-- not Gran, not Mack or school or anything. No one could touch them. High school, 10 long weeks away, seemed like a tiny speck on the horizon. She just wanted to stay there forever. Back at home, the only things her friends wanted to do was stay indoors and listen to music and play with lotions and makeup. They never even wanted to climb trees or swim anymore. They said the humidity messed up their hair… and forget about getting near the gross river water. *Everyone goes to the beach now*, she was informed. One of the meaner girls even said, *Don't be a river rat, Claire. People can SEE you out there*, as though canoeing was somehow a scandal now. So, she stopped talking to her friends about it.

One day, several weeks into the summer, when she and Gunther arrived on the island, Claire asked Lana, "What is this?" and thrust a yellow sheet of paper at Lana. It was a note that had been hiding in the pocket of her mother's notebook. Something new she'd found in the artifacts of her mother's life.

"Where did you get this?" It was a whisper. And then Lana mouthed the words as she read. Claire watched her face carefully.

The legible part of the note said, *SubRez is activating biocomputers, using living network-based organisms to measure and communicate with the health of the planet. In the salt islands of North Florida, the team is using large-scale fungal systems to act as an alert system to tell us when the environment is in danger of falling ill.*

After that, the handwriting got too messy to read. At the bottom was Lana's name.

Claire stood with her hands on her hips.

Lana's eyes narrowed for a second -- a micro-expression -- but then she smiled and her brow smoothed and she said, "you and I, we need to have a little meeting. I know you're ready to hear more. I promise we will tell you. We have a lot to tell you."

Claire's stomach filled with butterflies: it felt as though the world was about to open up. She would finally discover what her mother had been doing; they might even know why her parents had died–what happened to them.

***

The day they went swimming in the spring and Claire held her breath for five minutes, Ovid asked Claire, "Did your mom teach you that? How to hold your breath? Or were you born like that?"

They were standing on a balcony at the treehouse. Mosquitoes buzzed around her ears.

Claire looked carefully at Ovid's face. She swatted a juicy bug that landed on her thigh. It left a splotch of blood.

"My mom is dead."

"I know. I'm sorry. I was just curious…"

"Did you know my mom?"

"I mean I just know about how she…"

Just then Lana called up to the two of them. She had been listening.

"Claire. Uhh …. Your brother is waiting for you!"

Claire squinted into the distance. Gunther was sitting on the overturned canoe with Captain at his feet.

"You know about how she what …?" Claire asked Ovid.

He shrugged. "Ya know …."

Just then, Lana came upstairs and stood by the open door and summoned Claire out. The intention seemed playful at first. But she said in a pinched tone to her son: "Ovid, I'll be the one to talk to Claire about this."

Claire and Ovid maintained eye contact while Lana all but dragged her away.

"This could be a sensitive subject, dear, with your mom just passed. Let's talk about it next time you come."

***

Something was strange about the people on the island, Gunther kept telling Claire.

"But they knew Mom," she reminded him, "and they're so nice and so smart, and they feed us grilled cheese sandwiches and popsicles and brownies with M&M's. Come on, Gunther. I mean, how bad could they be?" She was trying to get Gunther to smile.

Gunther said, "yeah but ..." every time they had this conversation.

But he couldn't deny they had liked Mom.

They all said she had been special. And it seemed that ever since the death of their parents, Mom's name had been dragged through the mud. She suspected Gran even blamed Mom for the deaths somehow. But these people-- they knew the truth. Mom had not been crazy; she had been working on something important.

"Right, Gunther? Don't you see? Dad and the others just didn't want us to know."

Gunther shrugged and said, "Yeah, I guess so..."

They were sitting in the grass in the backyard, whispering to one another so that Mack, who was busy grilling hamburgers nearby, did not hear.

She studied Gunther for a moment, and then blurted out what Ovid had told her: they have ideas about the future and about our generation's part in it. The whole rest of the world seemed so doomy and gloomy regarding the future, but this group, and others like them around the world--they are going to make things better. And we get to be involved if we want. They'll teach us.

Gunther's eyes grew wide with curiosity...or was it fear? She could see that look in his clear eyes, the blue dread in his pallid color, revealing his urge to run to Gran and tell her everything.

She grabbed Gunther's hand and stared into his face. They both peered over at Mack for a moment. Claire slowly shook her head. Gunther shrugged and shook her hand away. He would not tell.

But still, the more Claire got to know about the organization, which reached far beyond the island and out into the world, the less she told Gunther.

One day, Ovid revealed new information. What they really wanted was for Claire to join them the way her mother had planned on joining them. Claire wasn't sure what he meant by that, but he kept talking, more than she had ever heard him talk before. Their goals were nothing less than saving the world. She could be part of an underground university, part of a movement for the next generation to save themselves and save all biological life from the brink of destruction. There were Nests all over the world, and linked to each Nest was a local university or research facility. The global network of all these Nests and research labs was called SubRez, short for Subterranean Resistance.

Her mind swam.

"No way," she said to Ovid. "How ...? What are they doing here on this little island then? I mean ... here of all places."

She studied Ovid's face. Sometimes those dark eyes were like one-way mirrors in which she could only see her own reflection, but other times they would deepen and open up to her. Like right now.

He tucked a wavy lock of hair behind his ear. "This place

is...ecologically interesting. That's what my dad says. Honestly, it's not my favorite place we've worked...It's too hot. Too many gnats and mosquitoes."

"How many places have you ... uh worked? And don't you go to school or anything?"

"School is part of work, for all of us .... Lotsa places." He looked off into the distance, his dark eyes closing off to her again. "Anyway, you'll see ... if you join us. You'll get to travel, too. Probably go to Finland ... maybe China."

Aside from beach destinations in Florida, Claire had traveled to Georgia, the Carolinas, and Washington D.C. And once the family flew to California. That was it. The places Ovid mentioned were a puzzling combination of countries, but nonetheless she felt dizzy with excitement at the prospect of traveling to another country -- any country. Excited and panicked. It was a serious decision, one she couldn't make without Gran's consent. What if she said no?

CHAPTER 25: DISCOVERING CLAIRE.0

Claire

High school had already been looming, dull and uninspiring, but once Ovid told her about what the organization was really about, 9th grade may as well have been a prison camp in comparison. Even going back to church activities or hanging out with friends seemed tedious. Suddenly, no one she knew was interesting anymore. Only the island people.

So by the time school started, Claire decided she would do it, with or without Gran's blessing. One afternoon, a week after 9th grade started, she told Lana and the rest of the team that she was ready, as long as Gunther could come too, as long as she could start telling him about all of this. *No more secrets.*

High school was as terrible as she had imagined, and she knew it would just get worse. She'd been put in remedial English and she had no one to sit with at lunch. And anyway, what teenager wouldn't want to escape forever to a utopian island and leave a clone in her place so that no one would come looking for her?

That was the actual plan. They had developed a full-grown hybrid of Claire. They were calling her claire.0, and Claire's job would be to "train" the clone to be just like her. Part of it would be a matter of programming and part would be Claire just spending time with her. Lana explained that her mother had already given consent to create and develop claire.0. They had the legal paperwork to prove it.

This was the life her mother had hoped for, Claire began to think; maybe this was what she had meant by providing a better, more intellectually stimulating and holistic place to raise children. Claire remembered Mom complaining to Dad about how their town was full of dead ends and hicks. She seemed to have unending plans to move someplace that would make them happier. Dad said, "Stop with the fantasies, Jessica. We can't even pay for health insurance right now."

But this island – this is what had given Jessica hope that life was better somewhere else. This is where real life was.

***

The first time she encountered claire.0, Claire felt a little wave of nausea. It was her but not her. It was a blank slate of Claire, like a 14-year-old newborn baby.

"I don't know," she told Lana. "I'm not sure if I can do this. It's too weird."

But Lana squeezed her hand and said, "You are making history, Claire! I know it's strange, but sometimes you just have to push through those feelings of hesitancy and do what's best."

Mack had doubled down on restrictions, claiming he was going to send her off to a boarding school if she crossed him again. Not only that, but the boy she liked, Michael, was beginning to pressure her into doing things she didn't want to do. She liked his attention, but she hated how he acted sometimes. It was the alcohol. The one time she had tried drinking beer with him, she almost threw up. It smelled like bile and depression, and a bitter memory of her mother surfaced with the aftertaste. She hated remembering her mother like that. She wanted to remember her mother as an equal to Lana and David, another scientist on this magical island.

Claire ended up confessing all of this to Lana, and Lana assured her that she would never have to deal with that again. "I can understand why you would want to leave all of that behind," she told Claire. "There are better options for a smart girl like you. You shouldn't have to tolerate bullies like Mack...and Michael, well, he just sounds like trouble, if I'm being honest."

Claire wasn't sure how to respond. *How did Lana know all of this?*

"The entire culture is toxic, Claire," David added with conviction. "You are saving yourself from it by joining us. Nothing is safe in modern-day America. Your peers, for starters -- but also the foundation of society: your school and the economy and healthcare -- everything is broken. You need to be here with us, making the future better for everyone. You'll see. It will all work out for you."

Yes, she knew everything was going to be okay once she and Gunther began living on the island. If only she could bring it up without scaring him. If he was spooked, he would run straight to Gran, maybe even to Mack.

***

That first session with claire.0 felt both strange and natural. The hybrid was like a life-size doll made in Claire's image, but grown in a lab by scientists like a plant, and programmed by scientists like a robot. When Claire entered the room where they were keeping her, she was flooded with a surge of new sensations, a flush of foreign thoughts and feelings. It was like having an external mind enter her brain and mix with all her own thoughts.

Lana told her, "It will feel like there's a whole lot of noise in your head, meaning you're going to hear her thoughts to a certain degree, but once you adjust and get on the same wavelength, it will begin to feel less invasive. Your minds will blend together. Just breathe into it. And you will eventually calibrate to her frequency, just like your eyes adjusting to bright light."

Claire didn't like the idea of her thoughts blending with someone else's, but she had to remind herself that this was basically her. The only thoughts that claire.0 had were the memories of her short history here on the island, and she was shocked to "see" how much she had watched Claire and Gunther before they knew anything. This gave her pause more than anything, but she pushed down the feeling of hesitation.

They sat together in the quiet room, candles illuminating their matching faces. Claire tried to just focus on her breath, the way she had learned in 5th grade. One of her favorite teachers, Mrs. Ray, had been into yoga and meditation, so she taught her students how to meditate as a way to stay focused in the classroom. Now Claire sat in front of her newly-formed twin and tried to stay calm.

She could feel the presence of another mind all of the sudden, a mind that experienced the world in a very different way. It felt too intense to stare at claire.0 in the face, so they both kept their eyes closed. Claire could feel the non-human parts of the hybrid weave into her psyche, a primal sensation of wanting to take cover, of feeling exposed and vulnerable. Claire recognized this emotion well; it was the feeling of being a 6th grader for the first time in a big, huge middle school where some kids were bigger than the teachers. It was the feeling of helplessness when Mack's giant hand came down hard on her brother's arm when he innocently reached across the table for the butter at the dinner table. A fear of others. But the hybrid's emotion was raw and unapologetic. Claire could see she was not practiced at controlling her emotions. The girl was visibly trembling. Claire took her hand. She was surprised at how human it felt.

They each had a piece of paper with a list of questions that claire.0 was supposed to ask Claire. Claire was instructed not to say anything until the session was over. "Just think about the answer," David had instructed. "And we can clarify answers out loud after the session is over."

He wanted Claire to simply program things into claire.0, thoughts and feelings that the rest of the team could never access. Things they weren't able to know about Claire, such as the complicated love she felt for her family, the grief of losing her parents, the particular brand of anxiety she harbored about growing up, the fear of impending womanhood, the melancholy of a childhood's end, and all of the microscopic memories and impressions that make up the totality of Claire's life, those tiny emotional twists and turns that no one ever sees.

Claire.0 asked the questions, and Claire responded by thinking and feeling her answers inside her body, so that the hybrid could have the sensation of each emotion and how the responses made her feel.

"What is your earliest memory of Mom?" claire.0 asked. She was supposed to refer to Claire's family as her own.

That day on the ferry with Mom flashed across her mind, and she was overcome with grief. The hybrid immediately began to sob. She couldn't control herself at all, thought Claire. How would she survive in the world?

"What do you fear most?" claire.0 continued after a few minutes. Claire opened her eyes and saw the hybrid's face glistening with tears. She didn't yet know to wipe them away.

She closed her eyes again and thought about her strongest fear.

Claire didn't want to scare the hybrid too much, but she couldn't help feeling all throughout her body the terrifying sensation of being locked in a small elevator that one time in Great Grandma's nursing home building. The stink of antiseptics and ancient smell of the elderly man standing too close intensified her anxiety.

The hybrid began shaking.

"It's called claustrophobia," Claire said out loud. And then from the shadows came a "Shhhushhh."

But by then claire.0 had opened her eyes and was shaking her head.

"No more, please. No more. I don't like it."

"Did I do something wrong?" asked Claire, looking at Lana who'd come to comfort claire.0.

"No, nothing, Claire. You're doing just fine. But you have to understand that Claire here–this Claire–hasn't experienced anything yet. She's like a baby. We will have to go slow. It's okay. We will continue with some easier questions."

Claire nodded and closed her eyes again. She took three deep breaths and tried clearing her mind to calm claire.0. Then she imagined Captain snuggled into her lap, purring loud. This had a powerful effect on both of them, and they sighed deeply in unison.

After this session, there were three more sessions, and claire.0 seemed to get stronger and stronger. She developed a lot more quickly than Claire imagined possible. By mid-September, she was fully functional and Claire-like. The team felt confident she would be ready to go out in the world.

***

When Lana declared that Gunther wasn't ready and they would have to wait for Gunther's own hybrid to develop, Claire crossed her arms and said she wasn't going. Not without her brother. She asked Lana why they couldn't just tell Gran about it. Get her permission.

"Claire, you haven't told your grandmother about this, have you?" David asked the following week, under somewhat formal circumstances.

He and Lana and three other researchers sat across the table from Claire in one of the underground "bubbles" that had been carved out underneath the island, underneath the river. They had called a meeting.

It was then that she really wanted to tell Gunther. But she didn't. Would it all have turned out differently if she had? If Gran and Mack and the authorities had been informed?

When she and Gunther arrived that day, Ovid was there to greet them at the dock, and he quickly ushered Claire away to have a meeting with the adults, while Jeremy drew Gunther's attention to the beach where all the kids were playing.

Claire followed Ovid into the building, down a cold hallway to an elevator, its door opening from the top and bottom like a mouth. From the corner of her eye, she noticed Ovid staring at her as they rode an elevator down to meet Lana and David. The compartment was partly translucent and they could see right into the soil and water and rock around them as they moved through river and earth, and down under the aquifer. Claire placed her hand on the thick see-through plastic. She smiled with shy eyes and glanced over at the boy. Ovid seemed to enjoy her shock at the journey down into the earth. This was only the second time the two of them had been alone. His eyes were large black pools, brimming with something dangerous.

Guards stood outside the elevator and up and down the hallways. It was the first time Claire encountered any kind of law enforcement among the island people. She moved stiffly down the hallway.

In the meeting room, there were four men seated at the table, one of them David, and then there was Lana, the head researcher at Nest 33. Claire had seen the others around the treehouse before--two engineers and one doctor, an accomplished group. David had his PhD in forest pathology and mycology, Ovid told her once. Lana was a paleoclimatologist.

Apparently, Claire's mother was going to be the head mycologist of this group, back when she was an undergrad. So, when she dropped out, Lana wasn't happy.

Claire had just learned this fact weeks before. She now wondered exactly what they really thought of her mother. Had she let them down? Had they only wanted her for the hybrid program and the consent to use her genetic material? This was an ongoing debate in Claire's mind: had her mother been a genius or a guinea pig?

Now at the table, Ovid gone, Claire reassured everyone in the room she had not said a word to anyone, including her grandmother.

But then she added: "I just don't understand why we couldn't just tell her though…"

In a monotone voice, one of the engineers blurted, "Because if she knows, it could ruin everything, for you, for the hybrid. We wouldn't be able to do the experiment. It would make things… a lot more difficult for us." He seemed impatient.

"So how about … we just wait? I can wait for Gunther." In truth, Claire didn't want to wait another day, and she certainly didn't want to endanger her chances of joining, but she couldn't just leave him.

"No dear, you don't have to wait. We will go forward as planned." That was Lana, very matter of fact.

"Gunther's hybrid will be ready in no time, and we'll get him right over when it's ready," David said. He sounded calm and completely sure of himself.

Claire fidgeted with the rubber bracelets on her wrists. One said *Hope*. Another said *Washington DC*. The hot pink one said *Miami Zoo*. Souvenirs from trips with her parents. She looked toward the door. Ovid had been excused from this meeting. Was he lingering outside?

"But we have to go *together*, both at the same time." She could sense her voice sounded weak.

She pulled at the bracelets, round and round her wrist, until one of them snapped. Claire watched as it landed near the doctor's chair. He bent down and handed it back to her. He made eye contact with her, and she noticed a sadness in his kind, blue eyes. Vaguely Claire remembered her mother's drunken words that night she and Gunther eavesdropped from her room. *We have to stay together. All ... together, okay?*

"I totally understand," said Lana. "You're such a good big sister. Yes, we'll do what we can. But, hey, you can get started here whenever you want. We're all ready for you, and if you get here before Gunther, you can get things all ready for him. How does that sound?"

That sounded great as far as Claire was concerned. Besides, she was tired of trying to keep things together, to constantly watch out for her brother. She really wanted to, but it wasn't like she was some kind of hero. She wasn't a Harry Potter or even a Hermione. She was just a regular kid. She wanted to be brave for her brother, but she also needed to do her own thing. When would she get a chance like this again? According to Lana, never.

She nodded. "Yeah ... I guess. But when? When will he come?"

It did not even occur to Claire that perhaps Gunther would choose not to come. It also did not occur to her that these adults were lying to her, not until it was too late. Sometimes we want things too much to question them. We suspect that if we dig too deep, something dark may reveal itself, and then we would have to re-evaluate everything. Claire did not want to re-evaluate.

"Very soon," assured Lana.

Claire stared down at her hands and realized she would have to lie to Gunther once again. She was beginning to understand that when you make your plans in secret, the lies become big and sharp and inflexible. You have to keep lying in order not to hurt anyone.

And then, one day, you find yourself alone. Secrets can push people away from one another just as they can bring them closer. It all depends on what side of the secret you land on.

She now knew that she and Gunther were on separate sides of that wall.

CHAPTER 26:
LEAVING HOME

Although it was September, the summer cicadas were deafening. In this part of the world, summer doesn't end until the final big hurricane of the season blows through, usually in late October. But even then, there were many Halloweens when Gunther and Claire sweated through fur and mask and full-length costumes in their determination to be a certain character. Claire realized with a pang that this Halloween would be different.

This year, everything would be different.

Leaving the house that morning long before sunrise, Claire felt like a thief. She always knew she might leave home prematurely -- probably go to college at a young age like her mom -- but not in the middle of the night without fanfare or family. And she never imagined she'd be pushing off into dark waters on a single vessel, taking only the clothes on her back. All of her things needed to stay at the house so that the hybrid would be able to slip into her life, undetected.

A small boat met Claire out on the water. It was marked with a red and gold flag and manned by two agents. She did not truly believe it, until the 27-foot boat rounded into the inlet and turned off its motor. They raised the flag, just like Lana said they would do, but no one made a sound. The boat sloshed in the morning waters like a toy boat in the bathtub. They eased their way over to Claire and her paddleboard.

The quiet of the morning was eerie. She recognized the boat's captain as one of the scientists on the island. He was rugged for a lab guy--a fisherman with an unkempt beard. He waved,

"

all friendly. The other man was lowering a ladder at the back of the boat. He motioned for Claire to come around. The hybrid was there; Claire had seen the silhouette of her own body from a distance, like watching a video of herself shot far away. She swallowed hard, swallowing down all of the fear, all of the hesitation. No time for that now.

She knew the plan: claire.0 would take the paddleboard back to the house. Out here in the wide inlet, far from any residence, was a perfect spot to make the exchange. Even if someone happened to see them, among the morning fog, all they would see is boaters trying out a paddle board.

Originally, the plan was supposed to happen the following day, but now with the hurricane coming, they needed to get Claire to the island and get everything locked down before the storm hit. It was supposed to be a simple swapping of bodies. Both Claires understood and had fully consented, as much as a fifteen-year-old girl and her brand-new-to-life twin self can give consent.

Claire's greatest regret was not being able to tell Gunther anything. Not one word. The hybrid had also been coached: If anyone doubts you, do not give in or give up any details. We can't take the chance.

As Claire stepped onto the boat, the two men hurried the hybrid onto the paddleboard. Claire locked eyes with claire.0 just for a moment, and then she was gone, headed for a home that Claire may never see again. The quick and quiet nature of the transaction felt anticlimactic to Claire after all the stress that had gone into making the decision.

Later that morning on the island, she could hear the cooing of the doves low in the woods. It was still early. Marsh rabbits hopped away as she and the others crossed the field in the early morning dew. It was strange to be here without Gunther; he would have chased the rabbits.

Most of the island was still, but a tech crew, including Ovid and Lana, had been up for hours, preparing for the big transition: Operation Mycobiont. It was the first time they would release a human-fungal hybrid into the world like this -- all by itself. Claire still found it incredible that, of all places in the world, they were doing it here, almost in her backyard, with her own genetic material.

Somehow the reality of leaving home for good had not registered until that morning. It was too much to grasp all at once-- leaving the only place she had called home. But ever since she'd been told the truth of her parents' death, Claire knew she must go. Any hesitation disappeared. If only she could've told Gunther before she left.

It had been a brief exchange but Lana was very clear: "We have reason to believe that your parents, well at least your mother, was targeted ... by an agency working against us. We don't know much more than that. She wouldn't let us protect her."

When Claire pressed for details, Lana reminded her that it was only speculation.

"I suppose it could've been an accident, but Claire, you need to understand that some of our technology is extremely powerful. In the wrong hands, it could be used in terrible ways. They may have been after information. Her information. Do you understand what I'm saying?"

Claire nodded but wasn't sure. She thought of the tattered notebooks her mother left behind. *That* information?

Lana promised that once she was fully trained, they would tell her more, and she could even continue her mother's research. Most of the recruits from around the world had been orphaned, or they were volunteered by their families. With Claire, it was different. Jessica would have consented, Lana explained. In fact, she had been on the verge of bringing the whole family in before she died.

That afternoon, while they were in lockdown for the hurricane, and waiting to hear from the hybrid, Lana told both Claire and Ovid more about Claire's mother. They sat in the rec room, away from the windows, Ovid next to Claire, both cross legged on the floor. Lana was on the floor too, her back against a cushion.

They watched as the trees swayed in the large picture windows across the room. Claire's uniform shirt felt too small, and the buttons wouldn't lie flat on her chest. She smoothed it down and tried pulling in her ribs, sucking in her stomach while she kept watch in her periphery for signs of Ovid's attention. She wasn't accustomed to wearing button down shirts, or the khaki pants that everyone on the island seemed to wear.

Ovid was slightly slouched, staring at his hands, gaze shifting toward Claire now and then.

"We've actually been dabbling in hybrids or what they called mycobeasts ever since Jessica -- your mom -- worked on the island as a student. When Jessica got pregnant, she volunteered DNA from the fetus. These cells eventually became your hybrid clone--a mycobiont. Apparently, Jessica never told anyone outside of the organization about the details of her research, not even your dad."

"Why would she keep it a secret from him?"

"I'm not sure. It was a huge deal ... in fact, the original plan was that both of her children were going to be a part of this community. Both you and Gunther."

Claire felt a twinge of guilt. But Gunther was going to be fine for now. He would never have to know anything was different.

"These other children you see around here? Many of them have come to do the same thing you are doing. Their parents volunteered them."

"Yeah, except there's no one with a hybrid replacing them...," interrupted Ovid.

Claire had noticed that she would see new children, and then the next day they would be gone. Ovid told her that they move on to other Nests.

Claire soaked it all in, all of this new information about her mother. How important she was.

"But what happened? Why did she stop?"

"I guess she just really struggled as a new mother and wife and young student way back when..." She trailed off, and then as an afterthought: "... and then later on, her other issues were troubling to many of us here. At one point they considered not involving her at all."

Claire wondered who "they" were, but the way Lana characterized her mom was not unusual-- it was that same tone other adults took when they spoke of her mother. Such a waste. Such a shame. Claire hugged herself in the cold air conditioning. But she knew what they meant.

Lana continued in a more upbeat tone: "... but in the last couple of years it looked like she might return to the program. Not even a year ago, I remember one afternoon she came to the island to see how far the hybrid program had come. She looked so alive, so beautiful ...."

Claire felt her whole body smiling. Just to think of her mother– here in this place, beautiful, sober, for all the world to love. *Why wouldn't she have told us?* Claire wondered. It was not fair that Jessica hadn't shared this world with her, and with the family.

Lana paused and folded her hands -- a moment of reverence. She smiled with great empathy.

"While she was here, we spent some time together locating her original cell donation, and we started a project based on your genetic material, Claire. Your mother signed some of the preliminary paperwork, and for a while we were talking about getting you on board right away. That was the plan–she just needed to convince your father. But anyway...your clone developed quickly and successfully, without any irregularities, but by then ... well, it was too late."

Claire shifted and stretched out her legs. Those notebooks. There was nothing crazy about them.

Lana pulled a wireless computer out of her satchel and scooted over next to Claire. She opened it and clicked around as she continued talking. Claire had never seen such a sleek-looking foldable computer in real life.

"After their deaths, we weren't sure what to do about the whole thing, because at the same time, your mycobiont -- the genetic combo with human DNA from your mom's pregnancy -- was turning out to be the most vigorous and intelligent specimen they had ever grown in the lab! But we needed you in order to activate it and feed it neurological information. And we knew your grandmother would never allow it."

Claire wanted to ask how she knew that. *How did she know anything about Gran?*

The trees outside began swaying so hard that they bowed close to the water–towering oaks that suddenly resembled twigs in the pre-hurricane winds. Claire's eyes widened.

"Don't worry," Lana assured. "These buildings may look like tree houses, but they are tornado and earthquake resistant, made with military-strength framing and foundation, and windowpanes thicker than my hand. They can certainly handle a little tropical storm like this."

Lana began clicking through images of the hybrid on the screen. Claire could hardly believe what she was seeing. A body blooming in a test tube, being nourished through both mycelial networks and human bloodstreams, until it took on a form that resembled a girl. The dates at the bottom of each photo illustrated its rapid growth: February, March, April, May … from infant to teen in four short months.

"Wait … so this is really…? … how she grew?"

It was like *The Matrix*, but with a lot less machinery. It was plant-like, but with a mammalian bloom.

"Yep," replied Lana. "The mushroom that we use to help her grow is part of her DNA. That's the element that makes the fetus grow so rapidly. From a few cells to a fully formed young adult in a matter of months. And then she stops aging–just like that!" Lana snapped her fingers.

"Wow," Claire replied. "So, she won't get any older?"

"Well, as far as we know, her growth patterns beyond her 'birth' will mimic the growth of the original human template–you, in this case. As long as she stays in close contact. But to be honest, this is all so new that we don't know what the full lifespan of a hybrid could be."

Claire thought a moment. "So how did she become … me … so quickly?"

"So when you got here, we began scanning you right away for the information we needed, and running tests…as you know. But we also had what your mother provided, don't forget."

Claire studied Lana. What did she mean by "scanning right away"? They began that first day? No, Claire hadn't known that. She knew about the "scans" but not until that day in the darkened room with the other children.

That was when she had first started lying to Gunther. The day they went swimming at the spring on the mountain, they had all been given a special tea and told to sit in a circle in the glassed-in yoga dome, air conditioning blasting from beneath. They held hands and Lana's voice guided them through a "hike" up a mountain and to the spring.

In reality they did not go anywhere. They never went

swimming. In reality there was no mountain on the island. It was a shared meditative experience, a powerful narrative that made all of them see and remember the same exact things. That explained the seemingly magical stretching of the island.

Claire had broken through the spell once, enough to figure out what was going on, but she enjoyed it so much that she allowed herself to fall right back under its spell. That was why she could hold her breath underwater for so long. Because she understood that it was all an illusion. There was no water.

She never mentioned it to Gunther because she didn't want to spook him. She didn't want there to be any reason for them not to return. If Gunther knew, he would definitely report it to Gran, and Gran would proclaim it was something evil -- witchcraft.

Even Claire had to admit now, it was pretty scary. What else had they given them? She studied Ovid closely. He seemed to be perfectly healthy and mentally normal. They must be doing something right having all these kids here, something even better than what Claire and Gunther were accustomed to. Their methods are simply unorthodox. That's what she imagined her mother would say.

But the thing that would've disturbed Gunther the most about that day was the moment she opened her eyes and saw her doppelganger sitting directly in front of her, cross-legged, knees and hands touching her own. At the time, Claire assumed it was just a hallucination, a side effect of the tea (unlike the other children she remembered drinking the tea) but at the next visit, Claire learned the truth, more information to conceal from Gunther. The hybrid had been scanning her for neurological information.

Now seemed like a good time to mention this to Lana, to inquire about the tea. "What *was* it? Was it okay to give children?"

Lana just laughed it off as though it was a ridiculous question, and said that some of the most enlightened native Mexican tribes did it for hundreds of years. Then she lavished Claire with praise: "but no one ever breaks through when we do that meditation, not with that dosage. Your mind is strong, Claire. The fact that you woke up, even just for a moment, and that you remember the tea … is remarkable. You're definitely a special young lady. No doubt."

Claire's attention returned to the screen in front of them. She gazed at the image of the hybrid, all curled and fetus-like but with the long, awkward limbs of a teenager. The body was enclosed in a semi-translucent egg of goo. It was a strange and embarrassing sight, and she blushed when she noticed Ovid looking over her shoulder.

"So how will we … or I … stay in contact with her long-term?" she asked Lana.

"Well, she will be the first to survive far away from her human template. This is an experiment…but we do have a theoretical mode of communication that she may be able to use."

"Far away? Theoretical …?"

"What I mean," Lana quickly interrupted, "is that all the others stay with their hybrids for long periods. We're not even sure what will happen when they get separated. But with you, we already know claire.0 can survive on her own…without you nearby. And there are new ideas for communication that we'll discuss later. Exciting stuff that involves using sporeways for messaging."

Someone was calling Ovid out in the hallway. He was needed in the radio room. Claire watched his tall, narrow form as he sauntered out the door.

The wind screeethed against the sides of the building. Branches tumbled out of the trees and splashed into the river. Lana and Claire were both quiet for several moments as they witnessed the storm.

Lana stood and offered a hand to Claire. "I have more to show you in my office. Come on. We have some time."

While they continued to wait for the Hybrid to touch base, Claire sat in Lana's office and watched old video clips of SubRez's history.

"With every new generation comes hope, but if that generation is mired in the sickness of consumerism and media distraction and an unrelenting hunger for more, a systemic wasting of all resources, how will they know what to even hope for, what to strive for?" This was a spokesperson for the group in one of the rare media interviews that SubRez had agreed to.

Claire felt a bubbling-up of anxiety as she continued watching. Who were these people ...really? She was beginning to realize she had no idea. The man on the screen reminded Claire of a charismatic preacher she had once seen at Gran's church.

"We train representatives from all over the world, from each and every country, big and small. Children and teens, with the support of their families, of course. We only choose the best and brightest, but we are inclusive when it comes to race, nationality, and religion. We want every region to be equally represented."

Lana filled in the gaps: apparently, this had been a big push with her own (and Jessica's) generation, with the international camp, and the university program--but it hadn't panned out as predicted, and now they were rebooting it.

"After we learned lots of hard lessons ... mind you ...," David added from across the hall.

Claire came to attention at the sound of his voice. She was sitting in a beanbag chair, her knees folded into her chest – she didn't realize anyone else was in earshot. He was now in the office, watching the TV over her shoulder.

David, an Englishman by birth, had a worn-down London accent after years of living in the States. He had been with the organization for decades now, and had seen the ups and downs of its evolution. Claire noted that up close, under the light of the fluorescent bulbs, he looked a lot older than Lana.

"But now," he said, "We are much bigger and have a much greater reach. We're gaining ground in the global race to save the wild– to save the world." She turned to look at him. His green eyes seemed to fog over for a moment.

A billionaire entrepreneur had been pumping it full of money for years, he said, and now they had bases in dozens of countries, all in environmentally-interesting "Nests," as they called them.

"All building materials are organic and native to the area," explained the man on TV. The program looked like it was from a regional news station, maybe something out of Miami. "All of the Nests contribute to the progress of SubRez's biotechnology research," he continued. "Florida has the most unique and diverse collection of springs, including subterranean rivers with openings called karst windows, holes where you can see down into the mysterious underground waterway. And then there are the river islands of Northeast Florida: this area is ground zero for fungal biocomputers, using special types of mushrooms found only in subtropical zones with major aquifers and exorbitant rainfall."

When the newscaster pressed the representative for details on the rumors floating around about "mycobeasts" or animal cloning, he denied the viability of such experiments. "It could never work … for many reasons," he said. "Though these speculations are not completely unfounded," he admitted, "they are based on purely theoretical research. The fungal hybrids are still fiction."

Claire looked at Lana who was watching her carefully.

"Press pause," she said. "I need to clarify."

Claire fumbled with the remote.

"Obviously, SubRez does not want the general public getting any ideas that we are doing anything dodgy."

Claire nodded.

It was astonishing to Claire that there had been any media coverage at all about this area, specifically about the tiny islands of the St. Johns River and intracoastal. Why had she never heard of it? For so long this island felt like a secret only she and Gunther knew about.

David was back, now standing at the office door. His glasses dangled from his hand. He began to prattle on again, justifying their actions in the most reasonable of phrases:

"You can see why we settled on fungal cloning versus regular human cloning, right?"

Claire raised her eyebrows.

"Well, first of all, the specimens are much stronger, much more resilient, and grow much faster than if we were working with human material only. What we are talking about here, Claire, is Artificial Intelligence that is fully biological but only partially human. And of course there are no mechanical parts like a robot, and fewer legal issues than a fully human clone. Mushroom people aren't really people. And with the special *Sapien Fungus*, we can easily control the clone, from the inside, through mycelial networks and spore networks...and 'donors'...like yourself." He made air quotes.

Lana added, "We can program them like computers, but they can be independent and continue growing and developing on their own."

She put a hand on David's shoulder, a nod toward Claire's

glazed-over look. Then she sat down close to the girl.

"You know ... your mom was instrumental in helping identify that Sapien Fungus."

"Really?" Claire thought of the notebooks.

"Yep. In fact, our engineering team had been developing biotech with different mushrooms for years, species that no other institution even knows about. And then she found it, the fungus that behaved like human flesh. When your mother donated her cells--your cells-- to the cause, she had just made that discovery about the chitin of that particular mushroom. We use it in nanotechnology and biotech to make artificial skin and other fibers. She came in at just the right time. Your mom was both the scientist and the guinea pig! She's in good company--some of the most extraordinary and eccentric scientists in history have done this."

"Chitin...."

"That's what the cell walls of mushrooms are made of."

"And butterfly wings ... and moths ...." Claire was making connections now. Mimicking things her mother used to say. Those bits and pieces of useless data, coming together. She realized with some regret that she'd never really thought of her mother as a proper scientist at all, not until the last few weeks. Dad had never taken her seriously, about much of anything.

But also, as she suspected, a lab rat, herself.

Claire thought of the rats they used in the labs here. How many of them were clones?

"These are the big players now." David pointed to a map. "That's what blue means: major biotech innovations --very important Nests."

Claire saw there were only three: one in China, one in the Appalachian Mountains, and one here in Northeast Florida, right under their noses all these years.

"All these Nests," continued Lana, "These are also homes to massive cave systems like the one underneath here, a system of dry caves adjacent to the river and springs. They used to be filled with water. These make perfect places for an organization like ours to conceal our research. And now with the mycelium networks--we're learning how to simply go through the ground and into the soil, not just under it."

Claire nodded but did not understand. She'd always been taught that there was just a giant aquifer beneath the ground in Florida.

Lana continued, "At times, we have to use hydrostatic displacement chambers to push the water out and create pressurized dry spaces below the water table. The mycelial networks actually help in this way. We've bioengineered the root systems to reinforce the tunnel walls."

Claire studied the maps and photos strewn out over the table and on the computers. All was quiet for several minutes. It was too much to take in at once, and yet it all felt familiar, as if she had known some of these things all along, that they had been there just beneath the surface. Or perhaps she had absorbed some of these ideas as a small child, listening to Mom before she could understand the words, before she was even out of the womb.

As though reading her thoughts, David said, "All of our research is field research--our schools and 'colleges' are built into nature. Even sometimes built right into the family home."

Claire thought of her brother. Gunther would be the only snag in this whole transition; if anyone could distinguish between Claire and the hybrid it would be him. It could be the snag to unravel everything. But they couldn't turn back now ... could they? Did she know too much?

It was clear they were trying to distract her. She had asked several times to peek into her home, to see if everyone was okay. There were some cameras set up, they said; they could show her. But Lana said more than once, "not yet, dear."

CHAPTER 27: MAKING CONTACT

Over the loudspeaker, Ovid and his parents were called to the radio room. Claire was told to stay put for the time being.

In his casual way, Ovid said, "found this for you to read," and handed her a book. "Be right back." Then he shut the door.

She listened as their voices receded down the hallway, and then she opened the book to a random page. *If we could plug into the mycelial networks and interpret the signals they use to process information, we could learn more about what was happening in an ecosystem.*

Claire peered out of the office window, into the empty hallway. No sound. She could not stop wondering why they shut the door behind them when they left, but she did not dare try the doorknob. Not yet.

Instead, she poked around Lana's desk, looking for signs of her mother, signs to solve the puzzle of the past and the puzzle of her own future. She saw a diagram of a maze, the kind used for lab rats, but this one was labeled, "*Physarum polycephalum.*"

She remembered Mom talking about how slime molds could solve mazes; it had seemed almost a magical notion at the time. And then there was the nightmarish tale of the zombie fungus. The *Ophiocordyceps Unilateralis* can take control of a carpenter ant's body and act like a prosthetic organ, almost like a parasitic artificial intelligence, forcing the carpenter ant to bite into the vein of a leaf. She made a note to herself to ask Lana about that when they returned. The power they had over claire.0–was it similar? Was she just a zombie that they were controlling?

Still, everything was silent. Too quiet.

Where was everyone?

After five minutes of biting her nails, Claire finally tried the doorknob. It didn't budge. A sick feeling began to take over, something in the pit of her stomach that had been there for a while but had not been acknowledged–until now. Why would they lock her in?

But just as the feeling began to grow into panic, she heard voices coming her way and then Lana and David were back in the office and the door was open; she was free to move around. They seemed casual and relaxed, no sign of trying to keep Claire against her will.

"Everything okay?" asked Lana. "You look pale ... I mean besides all of ... everything. I know this must be overwhelming for you." She gave a small chuckle.

Claire studied her and then decided not to mention the door being locked. Maybe it had been unintentional.

"Yeah, it's okay." she said. "Just, you know, big change."

Lana patted her on the shoulder and nodded in empathy. "You just let me know if you need anything, mm-kay?"

Just then, an alarm sounded, a piercing blare for 30 harsh seconds. Claire covered her ears.

Then, static over the loudspeaker; it was the sound of the open line to the hybrid. Two voices whispered over the dead air. Claire could hear them clearly: "We can't let this go on for much longer. We're completely losing control of the situation."

Then a loud crackle and screech on the radio. Claire's body shook with the sound. Half a dozen tech team members ran past the office. Lana followed and Claire did not leave her side this time. No one tried stopping her. They seemed to forget her presence momentarily, and Claire had to rush to keep pace with them.

One of the assistants flagged down Lana. "Dr. Meehan ...." He was out of breath.

"Dr. Das," Lana corrected. Meehan was her husband's last name. Once, she had explained to Claire that she and her family were trying to live in a "post-patriarchal world," but not everyone had caught up, and she had to remind them sometimes. Even among SubRez colleagues.

"Right. Sorry, Dr. Das." He gave a microscopic bow. "But ... uh ...." He peered at Claire. "Umm ... we're getting a message."

In the radio room, three men sat in front of computers, all madly typing, searching for the message.

"What do you mean? Why isn't it live?" demanded Lana. "Why can't we hear her?"

"We're trying to understand, Dr. Das," said one of the engineers. "Looks like this came over the air ... three hours ago ...? She was close to the black box, but not enough to activate it."

The hybrid was supposed to make contact with the team within minutes of being dropped off, but she'd only managed a short plea for guidance.

It did not activate the box, but, now, hours later they deciphered it: "Hey! Helloo?? Am I supposed to go with Michael?!"

***

They had known there'd be a delay between the time that claire.0 arrived, and when she would find the receiver that Claire had planted beneath the house. Up until then, they knew it was going to be a very glitchy connection, so they would give her a couple of hours, just in case Gran and Mack confronted her. Claire had warned the hybrid that she might have to endure a scolding.

Claire already told the team that it was very likely that if the hybrid got in trouble with Mack she might be sent to her room all day. They shouldn't panic if she couldn't get to the receiver right away.

But after six hours they could no longer just sit there. A hurricane was coming and they needed to know what happened. Claire suggested that maybe the whole family evacuated before she could activate the box, but once they translated the comment about Michael, they knew: she really *was* missing.

They sent out a team to investigate. Ovid was demanding that he be included but his father said he was underage and he was not permitted to join the small crew of "officers" charged with locating the hybrid.

"Why would she go somewhere with Michael at 6:30 in the morning?" demanded Ovid of Claire when they were alone in the supply room. All of the "active duty" adults were at their stations, and all the children and the others were secured in the underground rooms for the evening, special storm rooms with plenty of cots and no windows. Claire and Ovid had stayed behind to collect extra blankets and pillows and other supplies they would need for the night.

He acted as though it was a purely investigative inquiry, but they both knew his feelings for Claire somehow extended to the hybrid, complicating the simple adolescent attraction they had for one another.

Claire just shrugged. She was feeling too overwhelmed to speak now. As the hours wore on, she worried about Gunther and Gran, and slowly realized the hybrid was not ready to fill her shoes. But she couldn't go back now.

"Aren't you worried about where she went?" Ovid continued the interrogation. "Would you have gone with Michael at 6:00 in the morning? I mean, what was he doing out there? That's just weird."

"Yes, it's weird. And maybe I would have. So what?"

Her face grew hot, and she felt like she might cry so she turned away and said, "Can you just stop? Why are you accusing me of something she did?"

Her voice was high and strained, and immediately Lana appeared around the corner, clearly unsettled. She shot her son a look, and put her arm around Claire, which triggered a sob in the girl. She shrugged off Lana and stomped away.

***

Another hour passed, and then a message came in over the radio. The team was at the house: "We don't see her paddle or her board. It's not at the house. But no canoe either."

By then Claire was in the radio room, mic'ed up and ready to talk to the team on the ground.

"They cleared the yard for the storm," Claire told them, remembering how they would prepare for hurricanes. Sometimes it completely flooded the property and anything in the yard would get washed away.

"Go to the house across the lake," Claire instructed. "Spanish tile roof. Two-story. There's a pool. And a big dock. See if the paddleboard is there."

"Roger that ...." Then a lot of static. "It's looking bad out here though. Do you really think she would have gone out on the lake again?" Claire was already growing tired of the subtle judgments, as though claire.0's bad choices were a reflection of

Claire's character. As though she could control claire.0.

By the time the SubRez agents arrived at Michael's house, no one was there. They searched the property inside and out and finally ran out to the dock. The winds whirled, and the sky darkened. The agents called 911.

They had spotted Michael in the distance, struggling with the boat. There was no sign of the hybrid anymore. They couldn't get involved with local authorities.

Claire could feel the others staring at her. She knew there was nothing else to do, but eavesdrop -- listen to the emergency services over the radio.

They probably thought she was as distressed as they were at the thought of losing the hybrid. But secretly Claire was beginning to wish claire.0 really would disappear. She was having second thoughts. Ashamed but hoping, she listened for a confirmation of what they were all thinking: the hybrid was not strong enough to survive. Bad choices, weak constitution, inability to problem-solve. Whatever it was, they all assumed she was long gone. Drowned. Body pulled out with the tide.

CHAPTER 28: LOSING GUNTHER

Now they could hear confusing commands shouted over the dispatch between the police department and the Coast Guard. David and Lana, who usually spoke with calm and intention, now argued in sharp whispers.

Claire just wanted to go home now. This was a mistake.

All of the interesting ideas she had learned about SubRez and her mother were beginning to feel sinister, as though the setting sun was throwing deep shadows on it, like a beautiful statue transforming into a beast at night. Who cares if the hybrid was lost? It wasn't her; it wasn't even a human. Even if claire.0 turned up, they would know right away. It would never fool Gunther.

Finally, long after dark, they heard the news: "positive identification --14-year old girl. No injuries. Hypothermia and disorientation. Returning to family after medic check." Everyone sighed in relief. Claire and Ovid held eye contact for several seconds.

And then Claire turned away, so no one could see, and began to cry.

All she wanted to do was call her grandmother and Gunther. They must have been terrified. This wasn't like Claire at all. Yes, she could be impulsive, but she would never have gone to Michael's house like that. Gran must be so disappointed in her.

Everyone but the engineers filed out of the radio room. In a daze, Claire followed, trying to dry her tears. She didn't know what to do with herself, so she joined Ovid and Jeremy in the rec room. She didn't want to raise anyone's suspicion. She slid against the wall next to the boys and hugged her knees to her chest.

The older boy spoke. "You okay?"

"It's just ... they're so close by -- my family -- but I can't even call my grandma."

Ovid put an arm around her, but it felt more awkward than comforting.

"Sorry," said Jeremy.

It seemed like there should be something she could do, but no one was permitted outside the buildings or even above ground because of the storm, and no one, especially her, was permitted to make any calls. The tiny ball of panic rolling around deep inside of her, grew a little. She wanted to take comfort in Ovid, but she was beginning to feel that even he was hiding something from her.

As the hurricane passed through the town that night, the winds slowed, and it was downgraded to a tropical storm. But over the warm river waters, it kicked up for one, final seven-minute spectacle. A huge waterspout formed and danced down the river toward the island. Everyone watched on TV and computer screens, broadcasting from the main station. There were several cameras pointed in all directions around the island.

Claire watched as the water tornado bucked and spun. While everyone else held their breaths and rubbed their necks, hoping that it would dissipate before crashing into the island, Claire looked longingly down the dark corridor of water and into the past, remembering crouching underneath the window with Gunther during hurricanes. They would dare each other to pop their heads up and peer out the window at the trees bending and swaying underneath the mighty winds, the water droplets pelting the window pane. He would have loved to see a waterspout so close. Had he seen it?

What was he doing now?

***

They told her she was going to enter into a quarantine of sorts, a place she could "detox from the outside world," but because of the hurricane, it had been delayed until they could establish a decent line of communication with the hybrid.

Claire still had time. She could change her mind, couldn't she? She could leave if she wanted ....

The storm passed with minimal destruction-- the waterspout turned out to be all bark-- and after almost an entire day of waiting, Claire finally heard her own voice on the other end of the line.

"Hello? Hello? Mother?"

Lana stood over the radio controls and held a small mic to her mouth.

"Yes, dear. We are here."

She motioned Claire back into the radio room so that she could listen.

She sat down and placed giant headphones over her ears, the kind she had seen the Listeners wearing. Now, she was a Listener.

"I activated the receiver below the house," said claire.0. "I did it."

"Good, now go back up to the bedroom. Claire's bedroom. Your bedroom."

"Yes, Mother."

Lana looked distressed. She replied, "No, I am Lana, remember. Your mother is dead, please...please, dear, let's not forget!"

"Yes, Lana."

And then the hybrid was silent, and only the noises of wind could be heard.

Several minutes later, Claire could hear the girl tiptoeing back up the stairs. It was 5am.

She kept the headphones on into the wee morning hours. The sounds of the house were in stereo-- the clattering of pots and pans, Mack hollering from the yard, Gunther knocking at her old bedroom door-- and the homesickness became overwhelming. And Captain! She could hear him mewling, begging for the canned cat food. Did he at least know that there was an imposter? With a sinking feeling, Claire realized she had been so eager to escape the pain of missing her parents that she hadn't even noticed how much she loved all the other parts of home.

Claire knew she could not share this with the team.

But Gunther would know that this wasn't Claire. He would say something, and they would find her, and everything would return to normal. Right?

Over the special radio system, the team could hear not only sounds, but sometimes they could hear claire.0's thoughts, which Claire found embarrassing, and then terrifying. What if they knew about her doubts? What would they do to her? She had to keep those fears under wraps, pushed way deep down.

But she also found that with this strange myco-neural communication system, she had some control over the hybrid's words, actions, and behavior, if necessary. Once she got through the quarantine and some basic training, she would learn how to control it better, she'd learn more about the mycelial networks and the "sporeways," and eventually become an expert. That was the plan.

"I'm sure it's weird to hear your own voice like that," said Lana shortly after Claire returned to the radio room.

She must have noticed Claire's demeanor.

Claire shrugged. "She doesn't really say things I would say."

"She's learning. You can coach her. It will get easier, I promise."

Claire just wanted to hear Gunther's voice again, but the hybrid had shut herself in her room.

There were so many things claire.0 didn't understand: the importance of their post-hurricane hikes or how Gunther liked his peanut butter sandwiches (with honey, no crusts) or how to stand up to Mack. And did she even know how to steer a canoe? What if she messed up things with Michael? Claire knew she had to let go, that it was not her life anymore, at least it would not be for a long time, but in the meantime the hybrid was going to mess it up.

"Well!" said Lana later that morning. "It's all coming along. You must be so relieved."

She seemed to study Claire for a moment, and then she set down a drink in front of her, an ice-cold glass of lemonade. Claire was parched and drank it greedily.

She nodded, tried to smile, and said, "Thank you, Lana."

"The sound and the radio waves are good, and we have a clear channel to the hybrid. You can begin your official training. We'll set you up in the quarantine wing of the facility."

Claire took a big breath. Somehow she was going to let go of control of that world, of the hybrid. She would no longer be able to control what "Claire Flynn" would be like … and any notion this whole thing could be undone.

She could not be concerned anymore about what was happening at home, Lana reminded her. That was not her world anymore.

But by then Claire had collapsed into herself, barely hiding her disappointment that the hybrid had survived.

"Ummm, Lana? Can I ask you something?"

Lana turned around. David turned around. It seemed the whole team was suddenly looking at her. And then the room began to roar. Had someone turned on a giant fan? A blender? She stared into the faces around, searching for an explanation. But the edges of her vision were growing fuzzy.

She looked toward the door -- she had to leave the room, the building, the island. But her brain was foggy and her limbs were heavy. She was exhausted from staying up all night– and now, she couldn't remember if she had eaten. As the woozy feeling descended over her like a dark, wool blanket, panic rose in her throat. There was a bitter taste now. The lemonade glass sat perched on the desk nearby, filled only with ice now. She reached for it and tried to speak, but nothing came out.

Lana said something about Claire looking pale. She helped her to a couch in the corner and covered her with a blanket.

"Just sleep now, hon. It's all done. You did it."

CHAPTER 29: LOSING CLAIRE.0

Claire dreamed that her shadow had been torn away from her, like in Peter Pan. She needed to sew it back on. Except this shadow was made of flesh and bone and was dying from the detachment. There was a lot of blood. Peter Pan was there to help … but then he turned evil, fangs shining at the corners of his mouth.

She woke up with a start … in a puddle of her own blood. She could see Lana across the room gesturing to others, calling out orders. What had happened?

A young woman stood over her. "Hi Claire. My name is Nicky. Let's get you cleaned up."

Claire pulled away. What had they done to her? She could see now that there was real blood on her hand. She wanted to run, she wanted to push this woman away, but when she realized it was her pants, wet with her own blood, hot tears of embarrassment rolled down her face. They hadn't done anything to her. It was just her period. That and the sleep deprivation.

Nicky covered her in a robe and guided her down a long hallway to the dorms. But Claire could hardly walk. Her arms and legs felt too heavy. What was wrong with her? Maybe there was something in the lemonade after all. Claire couldn't hold a clear conviction.

In a dorm room, Nicky gave her a fluffy towel, a new uniform, and a wooden bathroom caddy full of toiletries. Claire noted the strange white labels with plain black type font: "Shampoo–

ORGANIC," "Soap–GOAT MILK," "Toothpaste–ORGANIC."

Nicky, quiet and freckled, seemed very kind. She was gentle and empathetic, as she led Claire to her captivity. It dawned on Claire too slowly, what was really happening.

Nicky had tricked her. They had all tricked her.

She said she would wait while Claire took a shower, but moments after she turned on the water, Claire knew. She felt, rather than heard, the sound of a lock. It clanked in her body, like a tiny iron gate being twisted into the corner of her gut. Claire ran to the bedroom door and pounded with all her strength. She pleaded with Nicky– "I need to go home! Please take me back. I need to talk to Lana!"

No reply – not a sound. A minute passed. Claire banged on the door once again.

And then a response, short and curt: "She's very busy right now. Someone will come to your room when they are done." The voice was low and unfamiliar. A man.

Someone? Didn't Lana know she needed her?

She was so shocked by the voice that she didn't even reply; she just sunk down onto the floor, engulfed in the oversized hospital robe, her face beaded with shower mist. And then, a very real cramping feeling brought her down even more, folding her into a fetal curl on the cool, tile floor.

***

This time when she woke up, Claire was alert. Back from the dead. No longer in slow motion. She sat bolt upright in bed when she heard someone knocking on the door. But how did she get in bed?

Then a key was turning. Her heart raced. The same male voice from the other side of the door.

"All decent in there?"

"What? No -- I mean, where is Lana?"

Claire looked down -- she was fully dressed in a SubRez uniform, her hair was partially wet from the shower she barely remembered taking.

One foot was tingling, taking its time waking up. It felt stuck, almost paralyzed. The tingling rose to her ankle and calf. Claire panicked and shook her leg as hard as she could.

It was stuck. Her leg was bound to the bed. Not in chains, but with a soft, yet indestructible material. Or at least it felt that way as Claire tugged and tore at it. It was strong but soft as the sheets, something to bind her invisibly, comfortably, as she slept.

Claire looked around the room, barren but for the bed she was on and the wooden caddy, which she could not reach from where she sat, locked to the bed.

She searched her memory, trying to recall when this had happened. Did Nicky do this?

"Hello...?" said the voice, gruff and impatient, a tone very different from David or any of the other men she'd met here. Was she still ... here? She looked around. It was the same room where Nicky had left her.

"I'm stuck," said Claire. "Help me."

A red-headed man entered the room, tall and skinny, a gun on his side that he was touching lightly with one hand. A gun. It did not fit into this world. Not at all.

His bright hair was buzzed short. As he approached, Claire realized he was more boy than man– maybe 18 or 19. He could have been Nicky's brother with the pale freckles and meek face. But it was clear he was overcompensating for his slight features with the powerful baritone voice. When he spoke again, it boomed in Claire's ears.

"Stuck! Ha–right. Come on get up." With great speed he unhooked the binding from the bedpost and linked it around her other foot, so that her legs could move, but only so much. He offered her an arm, but Claire didn't move.

As the shock of the situation wore off, she realized that her entire body ached. A headache wound its way into her shoulders and down her spine. She wanted to cry out. Her right arm had a deep bruise that she felt into the bone.

Her body remembered something. But her mind did not.

So, she did the only thing she could do at that moment. She took the guard's hand and stood.

"Uh … get your stuff," he said a little more gently. "I'm taking you to your quarantine room."

Claire heard someone moving at the doorway, shuffling around.

"Lana …?" she said, hopeful.

A man cleared his throat in response.

There were two of them– two unfamiliar male guards.

".... and shoes," the first guard said. "Put 'em on."

He seemed to be growing unsure of himself, even though Claire was not resisting. Tethered to herself now, she sidestepped across the room, gathering the few things she now owned: the caddy, three uniform outfits, one pair of boots, and one pair of slides. Then she tied her tennis shoes and followed him into the hallway. The other man looked like a carbon copy of the first, except in darker colors, as though he were drawn with more ink.

It was less of a "wing" as they kept referring to it, and more of a completely separate building, Claire noted, as they exited the main "house" where she'd spent the last two days. Or had it been three?

The second guard did not follow them outside.

Claire quickly learned that the binding at her ankles allowed her to stretch just enough to keep a normal walking pace. She concentrated on her feet as they moved down the pathway. The guard said his name was Sean.

Her shoulders sagged in relief the moment they were outside. At least they were still on the island, still in the September heat of North Florida. Everything smelled and felt wonderfully familiar. A mockingbird chirped. Barbeque smoke wafted through the air from a passing boat. She squinted into the sunny waters of the river. There was still hope -- there were people out there, not too far away.

But then the pathway wound downward, spiraling into a hallway in the ground, a surprising topographical feature in the flat Florida island-scape. Minutes later she was locked in the room where she would spend the better part of two years. But there was no way she could conceive of such a thing at this point. There was hope and sunshine and Gunther wasn't far away. She still remembered the feeling of choice, of choosing to paddle to shore on a whim, simply because she and Gunther wanted an adventure. She could still see his face– his trusting eyes and unswerving devotion. And even as her faith was beginning to falter, she still held tight to the notion that the island people had her best interest in mind, even as this gruff guard silently led her to a chamber of solitary confinement. The use of force was unnecessary. She would have willingly walked to her doom if Lana had asked. She was still under the spell.

CHAPTER 30: REPROGRAM

The Hybrid

The first week was unbearable. The hybrid didn't belong. That's what she kept telling Lana. She wanted Claire to come back–to help her. Where was Claire? Lana reminded her -- you are a human girl now, not a hybrid.

I am a human girl, she repeated. *I am Claire.*

"We have someone for you to talk to," Lana said. "A psychologist." They explained she would need a little counseling for her transition, and that it needed to be a professional. Claire could not help her right now.

"I don't want to talk to anyone but Claire," whispered claire.0. She always whispered now, afraid of who might be listening.

She was lying on her bed and clutching a stuffed toy, the grey lamb that Claire carried around for years as a small child. It seemed a mysterious thing that such an inanimate piece of cloth could be soothing to a mammal, claire.0 had thought when Claire first told her about Lamb-Lamb. But now she understood, and she clung to the raggedy toy as though it were a tiny mother.

"Claire will be back online in a week or so. You remember-- she needs some training."

This wasn't how it was supposed to be, at least the girl didn't think so. It's not how Mother had explained it. She felt all alone, and the only person who could understand was Claire; she was the only one who could tell her what to do next. The girl began to feel paralyzed with anxiety.

She remembered learning the word *ang-zigh-etty*. It sounded tight and buzzy. Now, it felt horrible, as though someone were holding her down, closing a hand over her throat just enough to feel depleted of oxygen, but not enough to kill her. Lana said it was normal, that most people living in the "normal world" have this anxious feeling.

She tried to stop thinking so much, but soon realized that was impossible. They could probably read her thoughts. And somehow, she could listen in on them whether she wanted or not, as though she had dozens of voices in her head. If anyone knew what her mind sounded like, they would think she was going crazy.

"Turn up the endorphins," David instructed the team. "Balance the hormones. Something's out of whack."

The girl knew what they were doing. She could hear them. David didn't bother hiding their strategy. What could claire.0 do anyway? She was simply a biocomputer. Right? That's what Ovid had told her. She was a less human copy of a real girl. Or maybe she wasn't human at all. They had explained to her what she was but it didn't make sense now.

Lana had always praised her for being such a vibrant hybrid, the most successful model yet made. This used to make claire.0 feel so proud. She was doing well, better than any other. Before she even realized what this meant, she was motivated by their encouragement. Now she realized that it was all a game for them–just a silly experiment. And she hadn't done anything to prove her value–it wasn't based on any merit of her own. It was their own scientific prowess that they praised.

Now that she thought about it, she realized they barely considered what they were doing as they planned her "birth." Just a four-month experiment that may or may not have worked. They could always destroy it and replicate it.

But now she was a fully sentient being with all the thoughts and dreams and desires and worries of the girl who'd been living for 15 years. She had the body of Claire and the mind of Claire, so wasn't she Claire?

But there was one difference: because of her connection with the lab, they could change claire.0's mind in an instant. And so she did what any 15 year old would do who feels like her independence is being quashed. She threatened to run away. She rebelled and stopped talking to the team altogether.

But she forgot to turn off the receiver. She forgot it was there-- she was programmed not to remember certain things such as this.

In response to her resistance, they tweaked her brain waves until she became compliant and content. She would never know. She just woke up the next day feeling happier, feeling determined to fit into the world, and she began to forget her own past.

In time, she would forget that she was born in a lab. After all, it would sound crazy if she told anyone. As the thoughts and memories of Claire crowded her own very short history, claire.0 became Claire, a happier, simpler version of Claire.

CHAPTER 31: LETTERS TO GUNTHER

Claire

Dec 15, 2002

Dear Gunther,

You'll probably never see this letter, but I have to record what is happening to me. I need to believe that one day you will read these words.

There's no paper or pen to write on, so I'm using this old computer, and I'm storing this on the floppy disk that I found in the back of a desk drawer. I have no idea if this thing will be able to save anything on its hard drive anyway.

It's been at least three months since they locked me down here, and I'm guessing you all are getting ready for Christmas. I can't think about that too much, or I will die of sadness.

By the way, I'm really sorry for leaving. You were right to be afraid of these people. I can't say everything here, but basically you were right to be scared. They tricked us– and mostly they tricked me. I feel so stupid.

I'm sure that you are confused right now and I wish so badly that I could talk to you, but the best I can do is to try and talk through her– the hybrid. I wonder if you are starting to believe that she is me.

Every so often a pair of guards comes in and they take me to a lab down the hallway where they hook me up to a weird machine. I was terrified at first because they use these tentacle-like things that attach to my skin, behind my ears and all along my spine. But it allows me to close my eyes and see into the world of claire.0– into your world– and talk to her. Once I realized that it's not painful or anything, and that I get to see you, I began looking forward to it. But I never know when they're coming back for me. Maybe never. I miss you guys so much– even Mack if you can believe it!

Hug Captain for me.

Claire

January 2003

Happy birthday, Gunther! I don't know what the date is anymore, but if I missed Christmas, then I missed your birthday too. I'm sure it's the new year by now.

I think they forgot about me.

Anyway, I can't believe you're a teenager now. I bet you're growing a lot. Pretty soon you'll be taller than me, I'm sure!

I'm feeling okay today, but most days are awful. Gunther, I hate to scare you but I really don't know if I'll ever get out. To think that no one even knows I'm missing. It kind of makes me feel crazy. But you know what? I'm going to be okay. I can just feel it. Pretty soon, they will do something dumb, and I'll find an escape ... or the hybrid will tell someone and you guys will come find me. Right?

Love,

Claire

January 2003

I think it's only been a few days, but who knows anymore. They're probably playing some tricks on my mind, too, and speeding up the passage of time. What if they put me in a time machine????

Anyway, just kidding about the time machine…I just don't understand what they want from me. They haven't told me anything. I "programmed" the hybrid for them or whatever, and I thought I would have a lot more sessions with her, but now I'm beginning to wonder. When will Lana come back for me?

All I can hope for is that their stupid experiment fails. I mean, how will they explain it to the police when the hybrid just crumples and dies and begins disintegrating on the spot? That's what I heard these mushroom-people do. They are hyper-biodegradable, and they just kind of disappear when they "die." When that happens, they'll have to take me home.

Is Captain okay? I miss him.

Signed,

Claire Eliza Flynn

Spring 2003

Dear Gunther,

I have no idea what month it is, but I know it's springtime because there are ducklings! Somehow a duck found a tunnel into this hole in the ground where I'm living and she built a nest right outside my cell. It's in this little nook, and no one has noticed it yet. I saw it once when they took me to the lab. But last night, the little guys must have hatched. I heard the peeping, so I know the babies are there. Can you believe that?

Love,

Claire

Summer 2003

Dear Gunther,

I can hear what's going on at home through this device they keep hooking me up to. I've talked to claire.0 through the strange radio signal, but I'm only allowed to say what they tell me what to say. I wish so much I could speak with you. Sometimes I fall asleep in the machine for what seems like days. They want me to be in a dream state when I speak to her. I'm guessing it's so that they can hypnotize me into brainwashing her.

I'm so confused these days, and I'm still not sure how much time has passed. They won't tell me the date. But I overheard Lana say something about us first coming to the island a year ago. That makes me unbelievably sad. I can't account for all that time. All I know is that I'm determined to make it back home, Gunther. I don't know how, but I'm getting out of here.

Your sister,

Claire

Fall 2003

Dear Gunther,

It doesn't sound like claire.0 is doing very well. She doesn't even know who she is anymore. They say that's good– that she is supposed to think she is me, but I wish I could talk to her and tell her she's not crazy. I also wish she would stop messing up my life. I'm coming back as soon as I can. I don't know how, but I'm not going to let them keep me here.

Love,

The Real Claire

2004?

Dear Gunther,

They've cut off our signal to her, so it's just one way now. I really can't talk to her at all anymore. Apparently she doesn't need any more input from me. That's what Ovid said.

By the way, when I was in the machine last week, I heard Mack yelling at you. It sounds like it was a bad fight. I'm so sorry, Gunther. I wish I could be there to help you stand up to him. He's such a bully, and the hybrid is terrified of him. I can tell by the signals she sends out. They make me feel queasy with anxiety. I've never felt like that before. I think it's contagious because now that I know how it feels, fear comes more easily to me.

Give Captain a hug. The hybrid doesn't seem to like him, but I miss him so much.

I miss everything.

Claire

????

Dear Gunther,

I haven't been outside for more than a year now (close to two?), and they say I'm getting out tomorrow. I can't believe it. But I'm also afraid it may not happen. I know I must have that Stockholm syndrome thing or something because I'm not even thinking about escaping. I don't care anymore. I just want to see the sun!

I'm probably going to lose this disk with all my letters on it, but I don't know where I could possibly stash it.

I'm coming home as soon as I can. Tell Gran.

Your sister,

The Real Claire Eliza Flynn

CHAPTER 32: THAT BOAT

Claire

September 2004

Finally, the day arrived when they led her out of the cell and up the spiral stairs and out of the underground bunker. The sun was so bright; it burned her skin. She had asked dozens of times if they were done with claire.0 and if she would be going home, but no one gave her an answer. The only information she caught was when Lana vaguely told one of the assistants that they were moving on to the next phase. Claire wasn't allowed to speak directly to Lana anymore. Not since they had locked her up. At first she had yelled at Lana and David, "why did you trick me? Why did you lie to us?"

That's when they began referring to her as "unstable" and "a risk to herself and others." Once Claire learned that they would not engage and would not come near her if she spoke like that, she stopped trying. But she had already done the damage

She had wondered a thousand times if things would have been different if she hadn't yelled. It reminded her of how Gran used to say she made things twice as hard on herself for being stubborn and impatient. It had to come to this, she thought. Well now she had learned to stay quiet. To wait. While in the bunker she focused on listening as carefully as she could, trying to find clues, anything that would show her a crack in their plans.

Outside, she was flanked by two of Lana's assistants. One of them held a bag with items from her cell, including the computer disk wrapped deep in the stuffing of a pillow. They walked her across the yard, not far from the water. Over the last year Claire had lost so much weight, it would have appeared ridiculous for her to be shackled and guarded. It was clear she had no strength to escape.

They had to walk past the main dock, a much larger dock than the one where she and Gunther arrived. This one housed several boats, each one bigger than the next. There were six in all. Were they new? She wondered why she had never noticed them before.

The rays of sunshine were reanimating her mind and body. But it was all happening too quickly.

On this side of the island she could almost taste the salty air of the ocean. The mouth of the river, that led to the ocean's belly, was just around the next bend. Claire felt that tug of hope pulling at her heart as she watched the cars in the distance, passing by over the bridge.

She recognized one of the assistants from their sessions in the lab. She knew his name was Rob, but just like everyone else, he treated her with such cold detachment that she began to start feeling like she was the hybrid. He must have noticed her staring at the distant cars because he hurried her along.

Then there was a man's voice coming from the boats. "Hello? Rob, is that you?"

It was the guy who had been on the little boat that brought Claire to the island. It seemed so long ago, but that was definitely him. His beard had gotten even bushier and his face was sunburned. It looked almost as though he lived outdoors and slept on the deck of the boat. He was waving both hands. Claire's heart relaxed just a little.

"Hey, man," replied the assistant.

"Need your help real quick ... if you don't mind," said the

boatman.

Rob shook his head and pointed at Claire. "We got duty. Strict orders. Be back later though."

"It'll just be real quick. C'mon. Like 5 minutes."

The other assistant shrugged his shoulders at Rob, and then they both steered her to the dock.

She followed Rob down a dock, the other assistant behind her. The dock seemed to grow bigger and grander the further they walked. "Wow," Claire whispered.

The boatman held out his hand and pulled her up onto the deck. She peered around warily wondering now if this was all part of some plan. Suddenly, she realized maybe they would be taking her home! Her heart swelled so suddenly that she felt dizzy, but she immediately scolded herself for having hope.

Still, she couldn't help looking around the wide-open waters and thinking of escape. That's when Claire noticed the boatman was armed. The assistants probably were too. But she realized her brain was slowly prickling to life again.

So, she listened. And waited.

Rob was the island's best mechanic apparently. He and the man bumbled around on the control pad while Claire and the other assistant sat down.

It was warm on the deck and her legs dangled over the water. Hands propping her up behind her, she leaned back and closed her eyes. The sun's heat burned but it gave her energy.

"Hey … uh, no way." It was Rob's voice–loud and gruff. "Get her over here." He pointed to a seat behind them. She realized with a shock that his hand was on a holstered gun at his back pocket. It must have been hidden under the jacket he just took off.

He pointed at a cushioned bench that doubled as a large cooler.

Claire was at full attention. Until now, the only guns she'd ever seen in real life were Mack's hunting rifles. She wondered if they began using guns over the course of the time she was underground, or if she had just never noticed them before.

Five minutes turned into 10 and then into 20. By then, Claire had a full-blown plan for escape, even though she knew she couldn't move fast enough. She wasn't even sure if she would be strong enough to swim. That made her sad.

Just then, Rob shouted out a curse and something small and hard pelted her leg and fell into a crack in the seat next to her.

She sat up with a jolt. Rob looked at her squarely for a moment and then offered a lame apology.

"A little help?" he said and pointed to the seat.

"Uh … yeah." Claire reached her hand down the crack of the seat but felt nothing. She peered into it, and saw a number of lost items -- a screw, a pair of sunglasses, a cocktail straw.

On the inner wall she noticed a child's cartoon sticker. It was quite worn, but she could make out the shape of Snoopy – just like the ones Gunther used to have. He carried that roll of stickers around after the death of their parents like a little kid. It seemed very babyish, but Gran said that's what happens sometimes. Grief makes us all feel like babies sometimes.

And then it hit her. This boat. This was the same boat that her parents took on their death cruise. That older couple– they must have been connected to SubRez somehow. She tried to scan her memory and conjure up their faces, but no luck. Who were those people? How did this boat get here? It was supposed to be wrecked, at the bottom of the ocean somewhere, along with Mom and Dad. Claire's stomach began to churn and her vision grew bleary for a moment.

"Hey there," said Rob. "Earth to the prisoner. We're looking for a little grey knob. Popped off. Just like this one."

The prisoner.

He held up something small and indistinct. Her nausea grew. Maybe it was the sun, or being crouched over like this. She tried to remember what that boat looked like. Could it be a coincidence?

"Yeah. I got it," she said, trying to act calm. She pulled out the knob and brought it to the guard.

Her nausea grew, sending her a message without words. But she was so tired now, all she wanted to do was lie down. She sat down on the bench again and continued staring into the crack of the seat. When she pulled away the cushion she could see the image clearly: a faded Snoopy holding a soccer ball.

One minute later she was vomiting into the water, over the stern of the ship. She almost didn't make it.

The assistant yelped in protest and almost tackled her before he realized what was happening.

"Better get her inside," Rob told Boatman. "Sorry, man. I'll have to fix this later."

But now Claire could see it all so clearly. These people were capable of so much more than she ever imagined. The fact that they had even kept her around for this long was a miracle. A deeply-tethered instinct of survival began to grow inside of her.

As she sat, head hanging in her hands, tasting the bile in her throat, she could hear them whispering. The assistant handed her a towel.

The two assistants stood aside and whispered. That's when she remembered overhearing a guard when she was waking up in her cell one day. It was one of these guys: "She doesn't realize she's just one of their 'multipliers' or whatever. She's been fully replaced here. Her clone is complete. They can take her away now."

Claire was doing her best to look as weak and pathetic as possible as she continued to hunch over the side of the boat. The guard walked a few steps farther away. If there was any chance at all, it was now.

She pretended to vomit again, but actually she was unlacing her shoes. Quietly she pulled them off and then made huge heaving sounds as she launched herself as far from the boat as possible. As she hit the water, she could already hear the men yelling and running on the deck above her.

Her feet found the bottom of the lake and with all of her power she pushed, and her body bolted through the water, away from the island.

Within moments the island sirens were screeching and there were three guards pursuing her underwater. Not the skinny lab assistants, but muscled giants who sped toward her like crocodiles. A small motorboat came careening around the island, stopping her head on.

A net appeared beneath her as though arising from the lake floor, and she was scooped out of the water like a goldfish.

Lana stood far off watching the whole scene unfold. Once on land, Claire made a weak noise in her direction, but Lana didn't move.

The underwater guards were drying themselves off with towels from the boat. Claire was handcuffed and handed over to them. Someone roughly slung a towel around her and they all marched into the closest building. Rob followed behind sheepishly, carrying her bag. Claire sensed Lana was instructing from far behind but she couldn't be sure she was coming.

The air conditioning blew through the vent directly above, and she shivered in her wet clothes. Claire hoped she would see someone she recognized, anyone from the short time she'd spent on the island before her capture, but mostly Ovid. What had he thought of all this? She had spent months loathing him and feeling so hurt and betrayed that he'd been part of the scheme. But, like many of her ruminations, her feelings about Ovid had dwindled to a low flicker, a spark that would surely die soon and forever.

Her hopes of seeing familiar faces were dashed. The building was hollow. There would be no faces at all.

They led her down a hallway and into a dark room.

One guard shoved her into the room and slammed the door. She heard two locks scrape against the door.

She couldn't shake that spine-tingling feeling that she had on the boat. Suddenly her entire life seemed darkened by SubRez's shadow. And what did that guy mean by, "she's been fully replaced?"

Seeing that faded little sticker was a vivid reminder that she might never see Gunther again. Or at least not as a boy. *He must be 14 years old now.* She knew that he would change dramatically over the next two years. If only she could have swum faster.

She looked around in the dim light, and realized she was in a mostly empty broom closet. Clearly, they were improvising.

She couldn't stop the shaking, and she wasn't sure whether it was actually cold or if it was just the shock of what she had done. And what they might do to her.

But one thing was clear: she felt awake and alive for the first time in a long time. She now knew she was going to have to fight for her life. The rush of the water around her body as she fell in, made her remember that she could fight. And seeing the boat where her parents were last seen gave her hope. Were they *alive*?

She must have fallen asleep at some point that afternoon because the next thing she knew, she was back in the underground bunker, but this time in a small animal cage, with a blanket covering it. Someone was shaking the crate and there was an earsplitting scream, monstrous and disturbing. The blanket fell off as the shaking continued and Claire was screaming now too. Looking around she saw the bunker was filled with icicles, as though it had turned into a frozen cave. Two enormous white paws were gripping the cage, and she realized the sound was coming from this yeti-type monster.

She woke with a start, surprised that she was still in the broom closet. An alarm was sounding, and Claire was covered in goosebumps and feeling feverish. She could hear someone running down the hallway. And then there was a sudden banging on the door. It didn't make sense. Why would someone be trying to get in?

"Claire … Claire. It's me." A hurried whisper.

Claire's mind swam. Who could this be? Was it a trick? She remained silent.

"Claire, I found your disk. I read your letters. And I'm so sorry… about all this…I would have helped. But they told me you were dangerous. That I shouldn't talk to you. My parents lied to me…about so much stuff. I'm sorry."

"Ovid?"

"Claire! Yes, you're in there! Yes, it's me, Ovid! I don't have time, Claire…I just needed you to know."

"Know what?"

"Know that I know … and that I'm going to try to get out."

Claire was on her feet now, ear pressed against the door.

"Open the door! Please …."

"I'm trying, but there's no way without the key. Claire…if I don't leave now, I don't know what they will do with me. I was already planning on leaving. Then I saw what happened to you

-- they made me search your bag. They don't know I'm running away."

"Ovid. Please help me. They're going to kill me."

The alarm continued to sound.

Ovid was quiet for a moment.

"Ovid?" Her mind was filled with questions that she couldn't articulate right now. Through chattering teeth, she managed to utter something: "That boat. My parents…"

"Listen, Claire. I'm going to get you out of here. Just stay here as long as you possibly can. I'll figure something out. Don't let them take you … even if you have to play dead or something. They … they want to send you away."

"Away? Away where?"

"There's no time …."

"Ovid, can you tell me what happened to claire.0? Do you know anything about my family? Gunther?"

He shoved an envelope under the door. In it, there was a single document — what looked like an official report. At the top it said, "Hybrid File 108".

"That's all I could grab, Claire. I'm sorry. It's a recent report. Not much there."

Claire could hear shouting down the hallway, and heavy footfalls.

"The guards are here! I'm going to escape through the back exit. I'm going to find you a way out."

"Ovid! Please…"

But he was gone. She could hear the guards shouting at him, and then one yelled, "Secure the perimeter! Lock all exits! Now." They were close now, and Claire moved away from the door and fell into a heap at the back of the closet. She was exhausted and overcome with fever. It wouldn't be hard to play dead.

The door scraped open and she braced for an attack of some sort. She kept her eyes shut tight.

As she lay motionless, she remembered the words of that guard: She's been fully replaced. Time seemed to stand still as she calculated her value to these people. What would she need to do to convince them of her potential benefit? What did she need to demonstrate in order to stay alive?

But as someone approached, she demonstrated absolutely nothing. *Play dead.*

She expected the musky odor of sweaty male guards, but suddenly a familiar scent wafted over her. Lavender. A quiet composed presence was in the room. Lana drew a breath in as she touched Claire's forehead with the back of her hand. Claire imagined herself snapping at her like a dog, chomping down on her wrist bone with her teeth. But the gesture had somehow immobilized her. The smallest bit of human touch made her submit fully to the fiery illness that was overcoming her body. She could not even raise her hand to swat Lana away.

"I know this is very distressing for you, dear," Lana cooed.

Claire regressed to the girl she had been almost two years before when she discovered what was happening. She whispered, "I need to go home. I changed my mind."

With great effort she opened her eyes. Lana was calm and smiling. She almost looked amused. It did not make any sense -- why wasn't she going after her son?

"I'm sorry -- you can't go home now."

Then, in a harder tone she reminded Claire, "You already agreed to all of this. You agreed to come here and allow the hybrid to replace you. No one forced you. You signed a contract. We should not have to guard you like this." Her black eyes were like gems, glimmering with resolve.

That's when Claire noticed two large men at the door, standing with their backs facing Claire and Lana, like a pair of military dogs, silent and inhuman.

"You lied to me. You betrayed me," Claire whispered. She was too frightened to say what she really wanted to say: you killed my parents.

Lana quickly retorted, "no, it was you who betrayed us– just now. Abandoning your promise. Your contractual agreement. Now … we'll have to take appropriate measures."

Lana held Claire's hand and drew the girl close to her, in a terrifying embrace. The woman smelled of clean sweat and lavender oil, a fragrant calm. Claire had never felt so tired.

Then Lana whispered, "I will miss you, Claire. But now you'll have the opportunity to do great things for us."

Claire found her strength for a moment, and struggled out of Lana's embrace and cried, "no!" but the woman pulled away and stood up, and the last thing Claire remembers is feeling a tightening around her arms and chest and seeing Lana's treacherous smile at the doorway.

CHAPTER 33: NO EXIT

She woke up that night on an airplane. Ovid had never come for her.

She was groggy and nauseous in a reclined airplane seat, a belt too tight against her hips, the metal clasp digging into bone. Her fingers searched around for it, and then unclapped the big metal cover. It snapped back on her pinky finger. She moaned inside of her throat. She could not speak.

She could not turn her head or see over the seat, but an unfamiliar man sat nearby. He appeared to be wearing medical scrubs. He had a heavy face and bushy brows. Was she in some sort of clinic? A hospital in the sky. She drifted in and out of dreams; she could see herself as a large building with wings. Then, she saw a doctor at the gates of heaven, a cartoon of an afterlife.

But she couldn't be dead. She had to get home.

Each time she awoke, she felt something cold being fed into her veins through an IV in her hand.

She'd only traveled by plane once before, back when her parents were alive and everything was normal. She remembered it with an ache; she and Gunther were so giddy. Gate C4 at the Jacksonville airport. The feeling of rising into the sky, gazing down at the winding river and the intricate network of estuaries and creeks and marshland below. They bent and twisted like mycelial threads. It had been strange to see such a familiar landscape from above like that: from lake to river, the river spilling into the ocean, the sun melting pink into the clouds.

But this plane was smaller and much, much louder. No flight attendants that she could see. No one to tell that she was a prisoner. She managed to peek out of a window and thought she saw an expanse of ocean. "Mom," she cried, but so softly that no one could hear her over the noise of the plane's engine. Her stomach tumbled with nausea.

The next time she awoke, she was in a high-ceilinged room with maroon curtains, a quarantine space similar to that first night she stayed on the island, locked in a room on the main level.

But now, the British woman told her, she was in the original Training Tower. Nest 33 was not equipped with the kind of facility she would need for her "education." Nor did it have the necessary security.

"But where!?" Claire demanded, still feeling hoarse and weak.

"Shhhh," said the lady in a soothing tone. "Not far. We're in North Carolina."

Only later would she learn how far into the wilderness she had been taken, too far to leave on foot. Few roads, none of them paved.

She thought of the day long ago with Ovid, looking at the interactive map of all of the significant locations in SubRez, and the place called Slickrock Wilderness in North Carolina. At the time she thought it sounded fun, like that Sliding Rock place in the mountains. But he said it was a training facility for young people: "an education center, supposedly better than any college or university." His explanation carried with it a false air of reverence, as though he were just parroting the words.

Ovid.

She barely remembered his face, but she could still hear his panicked voice through the broom closet door. He had been duped too. His own parents had tricked him. For some reason this was very reassuring to her, and the fact that he knew–that someone knew–she was alive and she wasn't crazy. She was the real Claire. She wondered if he had actually escaped. What would his parents do to him for disobeying orders?

Everything was fine at home, the pale woman with a British accent told her. She wore a crisp white shirt and name tag that said, "Mary Anne." She seemed to know all about Claire and the hybrid.

When she saw Claire wake up in a panic, she put a palm on the girl's forehead and said, "Just rest. Don't worry. Your people are helping the hybrid get through it. And your family is okay. All you need to do is rest up and focus on your training. No distractions here."

It was a shock to hear someone mention her family. What did this woman know?

But what did she mean by "your people?" The same people who shipped her off when all she had wanted was to go home?

"Who'er you?" Claire could hardly speak. She still had the dregs of a fever.

"My name is Mary Anne, but most everyone here calls me Dr. Mary. I'm here to make sure you get well, Claire."

Claire wished she was still dreaming. She slept for another night and day, and after her fever subsided and she was eating solid food, she was instructed to shower and dress in new clothes. There was a locker room with a closet filled with clothing, mostly white, flowing shirts and pants. Different from starched uniforms on the island. But everything was too big, like the standard one-size fits all hospital scrubs and gowns. And Claire had grown so thin; she barely recognized her angular body.

Mary knocked at the door.

"Well, hello Claire. Are you ready?"

Although she had managed to shower and change, she was now curled up on the floor, trying to fall asleep again. When she opened her eyes, the mirror in front of her showed the image of a rumpled and bleary-eyed ghost. It was just a bad dream, right?

But when she saw Dr. Mary's furrowed expression, reality began setting in. She had been shipped off like an animal. They had never intended on keeping her there, close to home. They had just needed her to activate the hybrid.

"I want to go home." Her voice was still thick.

"I know," said Mary. She simply patted Claire on the back and pulled her up into a seated position. Claire shrugged her off and got to her feet by herself.

She followed Mary down a long hallway.

It led them to another room, and Mary nudged her through the door.

"You can call me whenever you need me," was the last thing she said to Claire. The door locked behind her.

Claire stood rigid and looked around at the cavernous room.

"Don't know how you would call," said a voice. "No phones in this room. You bring a cell phone or something?" Then, a chuckle.

She turned and saw a tall boy with a cherubic face and dark skin.

A hazy memory of the plane: this boy had been on the plane with her. He looked younger than Claire but taller. The soft coils of his hair gave him an angelic aura. He spoke with a southern accent and a touch of urban slang. He was from home, she could tell.

Now she remembered. There had been a woman on the plane

speaking to the nurse in scrubs: "They chose one boy and one girl from this Nest. The Florida river island is Nest 33, and these two are Malik and Claire."

The Florida river island, a strange way to characterize where they were from.

"Hi. I'm Malik." He grinned and sat down across the room from her.

There were games and a ping pong table and several tables and chairs. Claire glimpsed a mirror next to her, a small decorative thing that only reflected the top of her face. Her eyes were rimmed with red and the dark irises were deep and fiery. Until this moment she never realized that they were truly her mother's eyes, as everyone always said. This was how they often looked in her mother's face: dark and pink and restless.

Malik's smile disappeared when he saw the savage expression on her face. He looked down at his lap. After sighing and shifting for a few minutes, Claire nodded and tried a smile.

"Play chess?" he asked.

"I'm not supposed to be here," she said in reply.

He shrugged, looking cool. But she knew that she scared him. He was careful with his body, slow in his actions, as though he were confronted with a wild animal. She probably looked crazy, and she was fine with him thinking that. It was one way to protect oneself, she was learning.

Claire eyed him. "You're from...the St. Johns?"

"The river? Uh, yeah I guess."

"The island. Were you there?" she asked.

"Not for long."

They were quiet for several minutes.

"They kidnapped me," she said.

Malik shrugged. She wondered what they had done to him.

"Ummm. I don't know," he said as though her statement had been a question.

His eyes shifted back and forth like he was looking for an escape. He wound one long arm around another and folded his hands backwards. She could see black nail polish lavishly painted on the wide ovals of his fingernails.

She narrowed her eyes.

With a hesitant voice he began to explain: "I...I uh am new too. But I wanted to leave home. My mama's dead ... my brothers, they don't care."

"My mom's dead too. And my dad." She surprised herself by saying this. He looked surprised too.

"Oh ... I'm sorry."

"I'm sorry ... for you too."

She relaxed a little. He unwound his arms.

"But my brother," she said. "I left him." Tears welled up, also a surprise.

It was subtle, but she could see Malik back away, up against the wall.

"Umm. Sorry ...," he said. And then, "what's his name?"

She turned her head away and decided not to respond. She couldn't think about it.

Instead, she said, "What are we even doing here?"

This could be her jailer for all she knew. Maybe Malik was in on this, just like Ovid had been. She narrowed her eyes again and curled into a ball with her back against the opposite wall, nose on her knees.

"Quarantine. Preparing to train."

"Yeah, right. Quarantine. I already did that." She rolled her eyes. "I thought I was supposed to stay in Florida."

"Everyone is supposed to spend a year here … in training …?" He folded his arms and knees into himself too, mirroring Claire.

She became aware that he was focusing on pronunciation. She was suddenly uncomfortable that he was uncomfortable with her. She had friends who spoke with the same grammar as Malik. They would code switch, changing fluidly for white teachers and friends. Here, within the walls of a possibly hostile operation, it felt strange. For all she knew they could be in a foreign country. But Claire and Malik, they were from the same place.

Her senses shifted. An aroma of food wafted under the door. Unfamiliar food. She ached for the smell of home, the smell of the changing tide, the flushing in and out of the river. Here, there was not even a window to the outside. They could be anywhere.

"But not me -- I wasn't supposed to. I had a special project. No one ever said I would have to leave. They lied. They're liars."

And then looking around at the small cameras in each corner of the room she shouted, "You can hear me, can't you? They lied! Let me out of here. I need to go home … right now!"

Malik winced at her voice. His expression darkened, and he turned his back to her and started a game of chess by himself. She felt a hollowing in of herself, an emptying regret.

Only minutes later, the door opened, and Claire stood up, ready to bolt. Four more young people walked in, two girls and two boys. They seemed to all know one another. The tall, dark-haired girls started playing ping pong. The chubby boy sat down across from Malik's chess game. The blond boy found a book and began reading.

The door began to close with no sign of personnel. She felt awkward standing there, gaping at the others, but they barely seemed to notice. As the door swung shut, she rushed over to catch it, but too late.

Claire banged on the door until she grew tired. Then she slumped back against the wall, hugging her knees again.

The new kids took their cues from Malik, and no one tried to engage with Claire. They seemed to know who she was: the girl from Nest 33, the one with the clone.

Hours passed and Claire found a mat in the corner and a thin blanket.

The dark-haired girls were from Pakistan, the chubby boy was from China, and the other boy was from South Africa. Claire pretended to be asleep on the mat while gathering this information. They asked Malik questions about her, but he said he just met her. Their English was very good.

"But you're from the same village?" one of the boys asked Malik. "You didn't know each other before?"

"It's a big village."

Claire almost smiled, thinking of their rambling suburban city, the strip malls and hard edges and empty downtown. It was no village.

Then they asked him what Florida was like and if he had ever seen an alligator and if they lived close to Miami and why they had been chosen. Malik obliged: Florida was okay but too hot, and also he had never lived or visited anywhere else in his entire life; yes, he'd seen plenty of alligators; no, their town was 300 miles from Miami; and no, he did not know why he had been chosen. He figured it had something to do with gifted testing in school and his IQ. A team of psychologists had done a second evaluation, and then someone came to the school to meet with him and the principal. Some official from the government. Or so he'd thought.

Then the group began discussing IQ scores, but the numbers and the tests varied from country to country, so they finally let it go--that foothold they had always held on to in order to feel a little superior to others. Claire realized that she didn't know her IQ. She must be different from these people. No one had ever described her as gifted.

After that, dinner arrived. It was wheeled in on a large cart and smelled of turkey dressing. There was no meat on the menu though; this was a fully vegetarian facility. Claire's appetite roared to life. She opened her eyes and looked around.

She sat at the table with the others and tried not to gobble her food. There was that animal feeling again. Like a beaten dog, she kept her eyes low and only mumbled when spoken to.

When two identical Chinese girls entered the room and joined them at the table, Claire thought of Sying and her twin from the island, the orphaned girls who were about Gunther's age. There had been something very strange about them, or at least something off about the twin, Gunther said. She'd never gotten a chance to tell him what he probably suspected, that yes, the sister was a hybrid, although a feeble one. She had died within months of being "born," Claire learned by reading the document from when Ovid found her in the closet. "Showing symptoms similar to Sying hybrid who failed within 6 months." They were concerned about the fate of claire.0. Maybe that's why they hadn't killed her. They weren't absolutely sure she'd been "successfully replaced."

Claire had already suspected she was not the only one with a hybrid clone. There were lots of them. But if that was the case, why did these "twins" get to be together?

After dinner, Malik brought over a pack of playing cards, and distracted her by teaching her how to play Blackjack. Claire realized that even though he was scared of her, they seemed to be the only two from the US. By the time they were done, she realized she was smiling more than she had in two years. Even laughing some.

"How old are you?" asked Malik. "I'm 15 and a half."

"17. It was my birthday … recently. I think."

Malik sucked his teeth. "Ouch. Well … happy birthday."

"I got a paddle board for my birthday. Two years ago …. But it's gone now … and so am I."

He was looking at his fingernails, peeling the black paint. His neck was long and slender so that when he hung his head, he resembled a baby giraffe, curly-topped and cow-eyed.

He looked at her sideways, as though he had an idea. He pulled the headphones away from his ears, and looked around the room. With a small glint in his eye, he suggested they find a way out.

"Not that I want to…you know, just in case these people have it in for us."

"Ha, ya think?" Her sarcasm was biting, and he leaned back and put his headphones back on.

Claire glared at him and crossed her arms. "I guess you don't even believe me, do you? They will never let us out of here."

But her spirits were brightened in a very small way. Maybe Malik was an ally. She hadn't known friendship in so long -- it was hard to tell.

CHAPTER 34: VIOLENCE

The Hybrid

2005

One day she heard static in her ears. It sounded like a bad phone connection. She thought it was just in her dream, but when she woke up and went downstairs for breakfast it was still there.

She shook her head and covered her ears as she sat at the breakfast table.

"What's wrong now?" Mack asked. His voice was measured. Apparently, he'd been making efforts to connect with the kids. The comment was neutral compared to his usual tone. The girl had learned quickly how to avoid conflict– something Claire had failed to do– and she cowered in the face of Mack's vein-popping rants. But this morning she was too distracted to be vigilant.

She came to attention when she noticed his piercing blue eyes threatening from across the table. They were watery, which made his gaze even more menacing, as though a sea monster were lurking underneath. He did not say, "snap out of it, girl!" like usual, but he may as well have.

"I … I … erm." She looked up at Gran who stood over her with a bowl of cereal. "I'm congested."

Hopefully, Mack would not respond with one of his homemade remedies. In his mind, there was always a straightforward solution. Sometimes it was just "suck it up and it will go away," but much of the time he had some sort of hackneyed fix. His solutions were designed to end "pointless chattering." If someone had ever told him that sometimes children need to simply talk it out, he had not listened.

But this time it was Gran who offered the solution: "peppermint tea. I'll put the kettle on. It will clear you right up."

By this time, the girl had forgotten who she really was. *What* she was. She didn't remember she was something else than just Claire, the girl with dead parents. But she felt deep down somehow, she wanted to be different from her peers, different from all people, in fact. She had to be.

She especially began to believe this when they saw the news story about that mass shooting on TV, not far from their own town. It was unthinkable– and afterward the gunman turned the gun on himself. What creature would destroy its own species, its own tribe, its own body?

She identified much more closely with animals. They were only violent when necessary.

But when they learned that the gunman was none other than Randy Whitehead, Frank's brother from across the lake, the girl was physically ill. For days.

After that, bouts of anxiety would rise up in her chest and sit there at the base of her brain, paralyzing her ability to make decisions. She stopped leaving the house. She homeschooled for the rest of the year and when friends would call, she made excuses.

Before this all happened, she'd been reading *The Book of Instructions* and contemplating doing the youth trip in the mountains with the pastor from church. His name was Richard but some people called him The Healer. Others called him the hippie pastor, but in a derogatory manner. The church had hired him as an assistant youth pastor the year before, but the families of the church were complaining that he was too progressive for their taste. Many of the teens were being drawn into his New Age bullshit, they complained.

Claire liked his gentle approach and his enthusiasm for saving the environment and talking about the importance of nature in his sermons. Also, he seemed familiar somehow. He would coordinate weekend trips to the cold springs or the beach, always something outdoorsy. Gunther tagged along sometimes, but Mack's sway over the boy extended to his opinion of this man, and Gunther began opting out.

And Gran worried that the man had unsavory intentions.

It didn't matter now though because Claire could hardly leave the house. Pastor Richard called many times, and even made two house calls to check on her, but Gran turned him away. Claire was focused on school and couldn't be bothered.

Everyone had said how proud they were of her– losing her parents right before high school and yet still flourishing as a student. She remembered one teacher singing her praises and quietly telling her grandmother that it seemed, "Claire has gotten through unscathed."

But suddenly it didn't feel like she had gotten through anything. The ending of high school was simply a reminder that she was going to be all alone in the world. The approach of adulthood just felt like a reminder of her orphanhood.

By the time summer came along, she began to feel detached from reality. What was reality anyway? She wanted to ask the Healer some of these questions, and go away to the mountains like her mother had. But she wasn't allowed to go, said Gran. They wouldn't give her the car, and she needed to get ready for college.

But she needed to know: Was any of this real? Had she ever been real?

CHAPTER 35: A MIRACLE
IN QUARANTINE

Claire

The Training Tower

The physician spoke little English, but he met with each recruit individually, checking pulses and heartbeats, and trying to ask questions. But when Claire saw that he was also distributing medication, she refused to let him near her. Why was everyone else okay with this?

Finally, Dr. Mary came in and announced that everyone would be escorted to their rooms. Some people would get roommates and some would not. Claire would not.

In fact, after that evening, Claire would not see her peers for weeks. This was for her own safety, Mary would tell her.

As she was led down the longest corridor she had ever seen in her life, flanked again by two guards, Dr. Mary told her in a cool tone, "You will require an extended solo quarantine due to your outbursts and other behavioral signifiers."

Behavioral signifiers? She knew what extended solo quarantine meant. Solitary confinement; alone for a long time.

The room consisted of a cot and a desk and a bathroom stall, barely two feet from the cot. But it was much better than anything in Nest 33, especially the underground cell. It was a way keep out any distractions or ideological "viruses." That's how Dr. Mary explained it. Apparently the first solitary confinement had not broken her spirit enough.

Still, Claire protested, pointing out she had already been in quarantine. "For a long time," she added.

"And how long has it been since you tried to make an escape?" Mary asked. "Hmm?" She said this without a trace of bitterness, and then explained in a cool tone, "When there's an escape we always need to re-quarantine. You never know what may have caused it."

Claire remained quiet, wondering what she knew, and what exactly they knew in Nest 33. She'd never revealed what she suspected about her parents being killed. She didn't want to say it out loud anyway.

"Also ... maybe you should've been friendlier to the other recruits," Mary suggested as she bid her goodnight. "It will be a long time before you see them again."

No light came in. The two windows were shuttered tight. She kicked the door and screamed, "this is illegal! You can't ... you can't do this! They're going to know! They're gonna come for me! That stupid clone is going to die, and then what are you gonna do?"

None of the other rooms near her were occupied. Dead silence.

She finally crumpled to the floor, and the tears came. No one would be looking for her. She should've known from everything Lana and Ovid had told her when she first came to the island. This is the way they operated. At the time, it seemed clever. Now it just seemed evil. She cried herself to sleep.

The next morning as she lay in the darkness–without windows or lamps– she vowed not to fall apart; she would never become what they wanted her to be. She began to protect her future self, spinning strands of silk around her, like a cocoon. It was the space she needed for secret growth, a supernatural kind of melting and healing and spinning back together.

Dr. Mary would visit every now and then, and the guards would bring meals.

The quarantine was extended … and then extended again, until three months had passed, and she realized that she was not going to be leaving for a long time. She kept a close watch on her cocoon, on the hard shell she had built around her heart, but she began to act in ways that pleased them. Behavioral signifiers.

After four months, her room was set up with a workstation and a computer for her studies only. She had access to "the internet," but what came in and out was highly regulated and censored. They allowed her to spend three hours a day on it, and then it would automatically shut off. All of the information was SubRez-related. Brainwashing, she had to remind herself.

The Training Tower was near a "geological anomaly," a deep and winding cave system, and it served as a symbol of the group's mission. Subterranean Resistance. She learned that the Tower served as an educational research facility for young people from all over the world.

***

And then one day a new icon appeared on the computer desktop: it read, Biology 101. She clicked on it and a video started: it was one of their SubRez Biology professors lecturing. She was so starved of human interaction by then, so eager to see anyone's face and to hear anything but SubRez indoctrination that she drank in the content of the course greedily. She completed one course after the next in quick succession.

One day, a guard came in and opened the shutters with a special tool. Then he revealed a secret door hidden behind the desk and behind the wall, but it was still heavily armored and locked up tight. Another guard came in and actually spoke directly to her. She would be able to access the outdoors soon. Claire's heart softened ever so slightly, and a sense of hope reawakened. She could feel the cold air from the outside coming through. She could hear construction noises outside. When she peeked through the small window, she saw a large crew building a high metal fence all around, sinking huge posts and concrete in the ground and creating a small enclosure of nature around her little door. By the end of the day it was done, and they had topped off the 10-foot walls with razor wire.

Seeing those people working outside had left her with a sense of longing she couldn't shake. They were covered in masks and safety helmets, and bundled up against the early spring cold, but she didn't care who they were. She needed to see a person, to talk to someone, anyone.

The garden had been a special request by Mary apparently. But the ground was frozen solid, so the word "garden," seemed like a stretch. Even indoors, Claire knew: winter would stick around much longer than she was accustomed to.

***

One day Dr. Mary and her ill-mannered assistant, Lev, came to Claire's room bearing gifts: seeds and cuttings of plants. Claire had been studying botany and biology in her online "classes" and doing quite well. There was nothing else to do anyway, and she was not yet allowed to start studying with the other students. She would require a longer quarantine period than most, Mary had said.

They placed the plant things in front of her like a sacred offering.

Claire did not budge.

"What's this?"

The lush, green leaves called to her– the smell alone was intoxicating, but she would not let Mary have the satisfaction of a reaction from her. She had continued spinning her cocoon, creating her own quarantine space in her heart where the brainwashing could not enter.

"Claire," Mary began. "We need your help."

Claire scoffed. "Yeah right."

"In truth, we want you to be able to contribute, dear. It will help you as well. But we can't take the chance of letting you out and about with the others...not yet. Here, you can grow plants in the privacy of your own little yard. You can grow food."

Claire bit down on her raw fingernails. She couldn't help glancing at the door to the garden. She longed for it to open.

"What am I supposed to do with this? Haven't you noticed this isn't exactly gardening weather?"

Lev spoke now, and Claire detected a Russian accent: "We see you're doing well in the science classes...er you can do this, no?"

But she suspected it was one of their experiments. Psychological. Sociopathic. They didn't need her gardening skills. They probably had some high-tech food production operation for the facility.

But they had the key to her small outdoor space, and she wanted to finally feel the outside air on her skin, no matter how cold.

The key shone bright in Dr. Mary's hand. "Want to take a little stroll?" she asked.

Mary gave Lev the key and he opened the door and unbolted the high lock that Claire could not reach. He and Mary walked outside. Claire couldn't help but follow them.

"Will you start a garden out here, Claire? Please?" Mary asked.

Claire looked at the barren spot where she was standing, in her ankle-length parka and leather gloves. There was a light snowfall. Claire couldn't figure her out. Was she serious?

"Not unless I can call my family," she replied. She folded her arms, but she knew she had no leverage.

Mary smiled and shook her head as though Claire had said something very funny.

Lev shook his head in disdain and said, "Suit yourself, girl. You're not doing yourself no favors."

After they left, Claire held the plantlings close to her nose and deeply inhaled. Her entire body relaxed, and she felt some life return to her body. Maybe she wouldn't die in here after all.

She filled up the shallow sink in her bathroom stall with water, and situated the cuttings in there, propping them up the best she could.

What Claire had not mentioned to anyone was that since her failed escape back in Florida, and the subsequent illness that overtook her, she started getting signals from claire.0, the Hybrid. Mostly in the form of dreams, but they were incredibly detailed. At first, she thought they were just fever dreams, but as she had emerged from her illness and they continued to haunt her, she realized she was watching her family in real time, she began paying close attention.

At times the visions were disturbing, since the hybrid did not seem to be doing well. But Claire could see Gunther, watch as he grew taller and listen as his voice changed. By night, these dreams kept the flame of hope alive in her. Maybe this was why she stopped caring as much about getting out and being around the others. The longer she was alone, the more powerful the connection to home had become.

But Dr. Mary told her that the other students were progressing, and she was being left behind. According to Mary there were hundreds of recruits there, kids just like her. If she would just cooperate and show some sense of loyalty, she could come out and begin a proper training program. She was keeping close to home when all of those other kids had been cut off from their old lives. Sometimes she even had full conversations with the hybrid, and could feel the strange plant-like biological powers surging through her own body. She knew there was something more to it, but she had no connection to the outside world, to any kind of biological network.

This is why solitary confinement can be lethal, thought Claire. Humans, just like all animals, need to plug into other connective systems, whether that's neural pathways through touch or the root systems of plants or the bacteria that keeps the gut healthy.

But Claire was starved for outdoor life, plant and animal life. Of course Dr. Mary knew that when she brought her the plants. She probably even knew that as Claire lay in bed, she could smell the chlorophyll in the newly snipped stems of the plants sitting in her bathroom. She wondered where they had grown. What wonderfully warm greenhouse had they been grown in?

She got out of bed and walked over to the plants, touching their leaves and inhaling their scent. And suddenly she could see it: she knew the life history of each of the plants that lay before her. The vision overwhelmed her as though she had lived it too: being a seed covered in dirt, nurtured with minerals and sun and water. Sprouting and poking above ground, getting taller and filling with starch, being pulled from the roots—the whole thing. As she fell asleep on the floor in front of them, the lessons she learned in Microbiology began to weave into her mind, and she continued the story for the plants herself as she dreamed.

The next morning she woke up to a full garden sprouting out of the sink. At first, she wondered if she'd been in a coma, but she checked the date and time on her computer, she knew -- she had done this. Somehow her mind had pulled these little plants into an accelerated growing phase overnight. The rapid way that mushrooms can expand.

She was delighted with herself but when Dr. Mary and Lev came to visit, she tried to act like it was no big deal.

Dr. Mary looked pensive as she perused the strange garden, lightly stroking the long strands of rosemary. She sat down on the bed, one hand on her chin, and stared at Claire.

"They said you were capable of this ... but I had no idea you could do it in your sleep."

"I didn't do anything," Claire replied. But she was smiling.

Mary and Lev exchanged glances. What did they know about her? She did not understand it yet, but she knew somehow she had become more valuable to them.

The energy in the room shifted. Claire breathed in the fragrant smells of basil and thyme.

In that moment she also realized the danger she faced. Something was different about her and they wanted to take it from her. It was something even more than just growing plants or activating her clone. There was a reason for this tight security, and it wasn't her "attitude" as they claimed.

She asked Mary, "Did you know I could do this?"

"Everyone here is gifted in some way, and you have a magical sway over the natural world. So, yes. we knew." She seemed to be holding something back. "What matters now is you know you can contribute." Mary eyed Lev as she said this. "We wanted you to see what you were capable of."

Claire searched the woman's face for more information, but Dr. Mary just clapped her hands.

"Okay," Mary said. "Now let's get this mess out of here ... and you can play around with it outside."

In the days that followed Claire spent hours each day outside. As long as they would let her, which seemed to vary day to day. Just to keep her guessing. But the days were growing longer and with it, Claire's hope was growing.

A greenhouse was built and Claire arranged the new plants so that they would receive whatever northwestern sunlight might make its way into the tiny plot of land. They grew despite the cold night -- brilliant colors and fragrant flowers leaping out of the bleak landscape.

In April there were flowers and tomatoes. In May there were so many vegetables that she began getting visitors, agents of the organization she'd never met before. They would congratulate her and admire her garden, but they treated her as though she were an alien.

Claire had more than earned her freedom from solitary confinement. She was now out and about when she wanted to be.

CHAPTER 36: THE HEALER

Spring 2005

Claire was granted a little more freedom each week. Perhaps they concluded that she was no longer a threat to other students, no longer harboring a virus of "disinformation."

The training is different for each student, Dr. Mary explained to Claire one evening about the SubRez students.

"It's not like high school, or any school, really. There are no classes until you genuinely-- and organically-- discover your path. Like you have! Each trainee has to figure out her purpose, while working odd jobs to support the other students and keep up the facility. This can make for a long training process sometimes, but, even so, many of the students finish by age 20, and become full-time professional members of society, sometimes within the organization and sometimes outside of the company."

Claire's expression darkened. She was sitting over a cup of peppermint tea, breathing in deeply. She was allowed in the dormitory kitchen now, rather than eating alone. But her feeling of isolation did not dissipate as quickly as she'd imagined. She had become accustomed to interacting only with the plants and the visions from home, as well as the occasional visit from Dr. Mary, a woman whose intent was impossible to determine.

Mary now spoke to her from the doorway of the kitchen. It seemed everyone was afraid to get too close to Claire.

Mary made a "May I?" gesture and Claire gave a nod. The woman sat down at the table and folded her flowing skirt onto itself over her knees.

"So, once I'm graduated I can go anywhere I want? Not just work for SubRez?" Claire tilted her head in doubt.

"Yes, really -- that's actually how it works out...for most students."

"Then why would you train them, if they don't stay with the group? What do you get out of it?"

Dr. Mary laughed, clear and lovely, but Claire maintained her somber composure.

"It's why we do what we do. Not so that we can stay self-contained, but so that we can actually make a change ... out there in the world."

Claire hung her head and said nothing. She was tired of this kind of talk.

"So, if I finish my training by age 18, let's say, and I want to go work somewhere far away from here, you'll let me?"

Now Dr. Mary looked serious. "Claire. Oh dear." She laid a plump hand over the girl's long fingers. "We are not the bad guys. I know right now it seems like it ...?

"Seems?? You kidnapped me." She pulled away her hand.

Two girls and a boy were gathered in the hall outside, brushing past the doorway every now and then, their chipper laughter and guffaws echoing. Mary stood and shut the door.

"Claire, no one was kidnapped. You volunteered. You do remember that right? You signed paperwork."

"I never agreed to leave. And I'm just a minor. I doubt my signature is legal."

Mary raised an eyebrow. "I understand that, I really do. But you realize you couldn't have stayed. It was impossible. There can't be two of you in one place, not for very long."

Claire looked in the woman's bright green eyes, trying to detect some smidge of malevolence, but nothing revealed itself.

"Claire, we had to remove you from the situation. Once a hybrid takes over, there's really no going back. It would be dangerous for everyone involved. And traumatic for Gunther."

Claire stiffened. "Gunther was supposed to be in on this. Why didn't he ever come?" For a brief moment, Claire wondered if maybe they kidnapped him too. What if the visions she was seeing were just some kind of signals they were generating and sending into her brain?

Mary looked genuinely sad for Claire. She shook her head. "I believe they misjudged when it came to your brother. I'm sorry, Claire. We won't be able to bring him at all. Your mother, she didn't offer his DNA."

Claire felt some sense of relief, but somewhere deep inside, this information made her wither in grief. She knew of course that she would never see Gunther here, but to hear the confirmation out loud made it too real. She pushed her teacup away, and with her head buried in her arms, she wept into the table. Mary put an arm over her, which Claire shrugged away. But the woman sat close by for the better part of an hour with Claire. When they both stood up, Claire surprised herself by allowing Mary to embrace her. It was the closest thing she was going to get to comfort ... the closest thing to Gran. Her body sagged and some relief washed over her.

***

A few days later, she woke to a knock at the door, which was silly since she didn't have the means to open her own door. Whoever knocked had already decided they were coming in.

Her permission was irrelevant.

But she approached the door as though she were going to open it. She could hear the noises of the other students preparing for the day. Faucets and shouts and hurried footsteps and slamming doors.

"Knock, knock," came a voice behind the door. It was a serene and pleasing thing, the voice of the so-called Healer. Claire realized with surprise that she was happy to hear him.

"You can come in," said Claire.

The Healer slowly opened the door. He wore loose-fitting clothing, monk-style, and he introduced himself as Richard. His peaceful brown eyes had a calming effect on most people he encountered, and Claire was no different.

"Mary recommended we have a session together. What would you like to do? Perhaps some meditation in the outside garden?"

Outside garden? Claire had only been permitted in her tiny yard and in the hallway to and from the kitchen. It was a bleak day, overcast and muggy, but she shivered with excitement.

As her mood brightened, she pulled a rain jacket over her regular white uniform.

"Wear the boots," he suggested, "We will use the walking stones for our meditation today, but it might get muddy." Then he peered down the hallway and seemed to be gesturing to someone. He turned back to Claire and said, "I will have to meet you out there. The guards will come for you in ten minutes."

While she waited, she took a closer look at what everyone called *The Book of Instructions* or simply, "the *Book*." When she first arrived, he had led a brief service for the newcomers and handed out a slim volume titled *The Book of Instructions*. It was composed of bytes and books, he said. The "byte" was the first line of each chapter, and the book (or chapter) explained the "sound byte" in depth.

In the introduction the authors emphasized how the byte would always be an oversimplification of the idea. They were transparent about that part–a byte would never do justice to the longer book. You have to know the book in depth to really be a good follower. There was a brief section on breathing techniques at the beginning, something that had helped her get through the first few days of quarantine. Other than that, the book had sat unread on her bedside table.

Claire perused it now, in case The Healer quizzed her.

> *The shadow in me respects the shadow in you, and the light in me shines with the light in you. There is no darkness without light, nor light without darkness- and there are countless shades of illumination in between.*
>
> *Die every day and imagine yourself descending into the ground....*

Then there was a whole chapter on the art of being yourself:

> *Embrace your natural form. Do not try to be wood if you are fungus. Do not try to be flesh if you are mushroom. Do not try to be a flower if you are a tree. Instead, be the best tree in the forest.*

And the one about the many selves:

> *There are at least three selves: your present moment self (with no memory). Your narrating self (story you tell about yourself), and your external narrator (what the world says about you to you and to others). When*

someone dies, the internal narrator dies right away, the external narrator may live on for a little bit, but it is the present-moment visceral self that lives forever, in the soil, in the trees, in the rest of the world for as long as life on earth is sustained.

And more bits about death:

There is no death, at least not in the way we use the word death, as though there is finality and a useless lump of a body. Instead, we should look at death as not only "part of life," as people say, but as the other side of the same coin—inseparable. Decay is growth—it is the tail end of the growth cycle and the beginning of another life. We may still use the word "death," but we must not mistake it for the opposite of life. It is life, and life is it.

It was unclear who had written it. Or when.

Outside, in a labyrinthine garden, Claire found Richard. Now, in the outdoor light she saw him better. Small but muscled, with a tanned face and greying hair in a ponytail.

As she approached, she noticed the plants seemed to perk up and change from gold to green. She was beginning to understand the impact she had on plant life. Something must have happened when she and the hybrid exchanged energy. What else could it be? Unless … perhaps she never noticed before.

Claire was still escorted by the two guards. Richard waved them away, and they backed away awkwardly until they were outside the gate. Claire made a face in their direction and one of them snarled at her.

"Let's try to focus our energy away from that, Claire." He cleared his throat. "The high security here is necessary...."

Another pale cough. "But it doesn't exactly lend itself to a peaceful mindset." Then he smiled.

"Why is it necessary?"

"Hmm ... well it kind of depends on the person. They still think you're a flight risk right now when you're outside. Perhaps we can change that ... if your spirit is willing."

Claire studied his face just as she had studied Mary's the night before. But unlike Mary, Claire didn't question Richard's good nature. Still, she wanted to know what motivated him to be here. What motivated anyone to be here? Why had everyone bought into this? Didn't they realize what they had done to her? Maybe this is what they all meant by calling this "quarantine." It was brainwashing. Isolating newcomers so that they don't spread their "virus" of the outside world.

Richard folded his hands prayerlike and placed them on his sternum. "Let's begin with something simple."

"Something? .... I don't need healing, do I?"

"Do you? Only you would know that, Claire."

Claire rolled her eyes.

"I just mean, uh, let's begin our session with a simple meditation ... and then we can just talk ... if you like."

Claire grumbled but placed her hands at her heart, mirroring Richard. Still morning, it was cool enough to see her breath, and she followed his instructions, breathing in for a count of 4 and out for a count of 8. They were sitting on a garden bench made of marble.

"Close your eyes."

But she could not help peering around. After all, she had not seen the sky in months.

Richard continued, "Imagine yourself as an inert, dry seed, a pod of potential life sitting atop the sandy ground. No rain. No good soil. But eventually you will be blown to a place where you can express new life."

He was now reading from *The Book of Instructions*:

> *A dry seed is non-life, but also a rotting corpse is non-life. None of it is death. It's just the underbelly of life, the darker, more fragile side. Neither is good nor bad.*

He continued: "Listen. Close your eyes. Let's be still for a moment and just listen."

When her eyes shut, the sounds around her came to life. The bird sounds and the rustling of the trees roared to life. Claire had a sensation of relaxing but waking all at the same time. Coming to life, but very slowly. She was thawing.

Richard continued reading:

> *Humans are not individuals .... They are 'dividuals,' parts of a whole and an assemblage of parts. Each being is just an expression of the whole, a piece of the larger organism -- the species, the kingdom, the earth, the solar system, the galaxy, the universe.*

As the sun rose higher above them, Claire suggested they lie in a patch of sunlight in the yellow grass. Richard relented even though they were not supposed to leave the stone pathway. Perhaps he realized that Claire was suffering from a lack of sunlight.

Lying in the sun, although it was cool on the ground, she felt again as though something inside of her was thawing, and under the soothing instructions from Richard, she was able to truly move into a still space, somewhere far beneath her surface.

Richard urged her to feel the blood flowing through her veins the same way water moves through creek beds.

And that was the thing that set Claire off, spinning into a world in which her own body was a river and the emotions and thoughts flowing through her were ships and canoes and kayaks and swimmers. She had a flash of her mother and then Gunther's face, and she must have cried out, because she heard Richard say, "It's alright. You're okay. You are here with me. Listen to the sounds around you. And gently place your hands face down on the grass in order to ground yourself."

Palms down, she pushed her hands flat onto earth, putting pressure on the blades of grass and feeling grit between her fingers. And then, like a jab into her temple, a bright yellow image pierced itself into her mind's eye. She saw the Hybrid's face in her mirror at home and heard its voice as clear as the birds twittering around her. She could feel the girl moving through the house, the cat underfoot, Gunther and Gran looking up at her from the table. She could see the cereal bowls -- oatmeal with steamed apples and berries. She could smell the brackish air coming off the lake through the screen door. It was pleasant and painful all at once. And then it was simply cold and she found herself shaking uncontrollably.

With great effort, Claire pulled her hands away from the ground, to make the images go away. She felt her body convulsing.

When she came to, several faces were gathered over her, including Dr. Mary's. Richard was holding her hand. Their terrified expressions made Claire writhe with anxiety. She squeezed her eyes shut again, wanting to see what she had seen, to smell it -- but the voices brought her back to reality.

Panic sounded strange in Richard's voice: "It was just a gentle meditation. I don't understand what happened ...."

"Claire. Claire, listen to my voice," said Mary. "Can you nod your head for me?"

Claire moved her head and then opened her eyes again. The clouds loomed overhead in grey wrinkles.

"May have been a seizure," someone said. "Just give her space. Let's all back up."

That man from the plane, the bushy-browed male nurse, put a compress over her forehead, and wrapped her in a blanket. He held her head in a large hand and said she was burning up. The other faces dispersed. The clouds cracked open just enough for a sliver of sunshine to fall across the man's pleasant brown face.

Dr. Mary and Richard huddled together about ten feet away, murmuring. Claire couldn't hear what they were saying, but Richard's body language showed submission. Was he actually getting in trouble? Farther down the path, she could see Malik pacing awkwardly, peering in her direction.

She stayed in bed for 24 hours, and then after that, all seemed well. Her cold, her attitude, her fear -- it had all been exorcised within that one meditation and fever dream. Maybe this was a good thing. Or maybe Richard had put something in her food. She thought back to the previous morning. She hadn't had anything to eat or drink since the night before.

She overheard Richard and Mary whispering outside of her door--something strange had happened, something dangerous.

"It's the hybrid," said Mary. "She can see the hybrid. Don't ever do that again with her."

"But Mary Anne," he replied.

"Don't call me that," she snapped, more clipped and British than ever. She could be ice cold, Claire had noticed.

CHAPTER 37: OUT OF QUARANTINE

Summer 2005

Lev would serve as Claire's mentor now that Claire was out of solitary confinement. His English was heavily accented and sometimes she could not understand his commands. She realized soon enough that this was no mentorship; it was a guard and prisoner relationship. He knew nothing that she wanted to learn. But she was happy to move about more freely now.

On multiple occasions she had tried to convince Dr. Mary she was ready for a job too, ready to be apprenticed like some of the others.

One day she was standing in the foyer of the Tower, not far from the double doors. She could see Malik outside on the front lawn. He worked the grounds now. Lev was walking toward her. He had asked her to stay there while he went to get something.

He handed her a book, and told her to study it. There would be a quiz before she could "level up" to apprentice.

Claire made a face. "Another book?"

As usual he said nothing in reply– just sent her back to the rec room and locked the door. It was empty now since all of the students were in classes or doing jobs, but it was better than the same old four walls of her tiny bedroom.

She settled into a large bean bag chair near a beam of sunlight that fell on the carpet and warmed her feet.

She opened the book, which was dog-eared and well-studied; a history of sorts. Not like *The Book of Instructions*, which was more of a manual on how to conduct oneself.

Co-authored by the founders of the organization, it was designed for new recruits. The purposes of the organization were far-reaching and ambitious:

> *SubRez's mission is to create an entirely new nation, one that is not constrained by geography or background or ethnicity but that unites the world by having a presence in all countries. We're teaching the next generation to be self-redemptive by planting our mission in the minds of the young ... and by having representatives all over the planet working in cooperation with one another. We are discovering innovative solutions to global issues such as natural disasters, agricultural obstacles, economic disparity, food distribution, etc. to solve problems that could never be solved by disparate countries or only a few global leaders.*

Some of the text was tedious and scientific, some whimsical and far-fetched:

> *We use the most cutting edge biotechnology and natural, holistic therapies for healing the wild– untamed nature that needs space to reawaken and re-expand.*

The rec room door opened.

"Hey Claire...."

"Hmmm?" She looked up. It was Malik. She couldn't help but smile. She was glad to see someone besides Lev. Anyone, really.

But especially Malik, a voice from home.

"You studying for the test?" He looked around. "I'm surprised they let you in here. Haven't seen you in here since … that first day."

Claire had encountered him many times in the cafeteria since she'd been granted more freedom to move about. He was always kind to her, but since their arrival, he'd made a lot of friends, and there was always a group with him. This made Claire feel even more isolated.

She nodded and showed him the book.

In *Jeopardy* style, he pretended to quiz her: "untamed nature that needs space to re-awaken and expand for 200 points."

She frowned. "Wha?"

He waited a few beats and then whispered the words, "What is *the wild*?"

She cracked a smile.

He took the book out of her hands and read aloud in an official-sounding voice: "We believe that sustainable practices for the environment can also work to heal the wounds of fascism, slavery, and oppression that continue to plague humankind. Most importantly we are trying to preserve the wild and use it as technology, rather than against technology. We will need to change hearts and minds, and our greatest tools will be the youngest of them."

"Ew," said Claire, pretending to vomit, "Youngest minds."

They both laughed. The door swung open and they came to attention. It was Lev.

Malik pretended to stay focused on the book: "Er…Like any major movement, it has proven to be as problematic as it is well-intentioned," Malik continued reading, "but we are implementing changes the world has never seen before."

Lev nodded and stood by as Malik continued to read.

Claire listened to the ambitious and far-sweeping mission of SubRez. Now that its dark side had been revealed to her, the words sounded hollow at best. At worst, sinister.

He handed back the book and said, "I know it seems like a lot, but just listen to what they have to say. And memorize that vocab, girl! You gotta get past this level! Or you're gonna get left behind. You only get a couple chances...."

She flipped to the back of the book where there were hundreds of terms.

"What? Are they kidding?"

Lev cleared his throat as he jotted something in a notebook. Then he looked up at Malik and cleared his throat again.

Malik nodded and looked at his watch. "Gotta go, Claire. I can study with you later...um, if they let me." He peered at Lev. "I'm doing some workshop thing this afternoon. A kind of computer programming I've never seen before."

It was becoming clear Malik would be specializing in software and networking. Like Claire, he had a gift. In fact, he had several gifts.

Claire and Malik held each other's gaze for a moment, and then she said, "Thank you, Malik."

He nodded. "See ya round."

Lev opened the door for him and followed him out. "I'll come back for you in a few minutes," he told Claire.

Claire continued reading, remembering some of this from what Lana told her back in Florida: "These mushrooms, and their underground systems, are constantly reporting changes in soil quality, water purity, air pollution, etc. in a much more accurate and efficient way than mechanical man-made computers could ever do. We had it all wrong:

it's not about building artificial machines; it's about using nature's machines..... Are these fungal systems capable of cognition? Yes! It's a different kind of brain, but intelligent nonetheless...."

After a long while, Claire began to doze off, the sunlight beam now on her head.

She was awakened by Dr. Mary.

"How do you like the book?" she asked. "I can see you're riveted." She laughed.

Claire had not seen Dr. Mary in weeks, and was surprised that she felt happy to see her.

"Actually, some parts are pretty cool," Claire said. And she really meant it. When she mentioned the slime mold maze and connected it to her memory of the zombie fungus, Dr. Mary brightened.

"Yes, Claire! It's a lot like that -- very similar properties."

Claire brushed away her dark thoughts and began filling up with something warm– was it a little pride?

"Hey. I want to show you something," Mary pointed up. "It's on the next floor...has anyone shown you the labs yet?"

Of course no one had shown her anything. Mary knew very well Claire hadn't been allowed anywhere. She was still thinking about the greenhouse that must be on site somewhere. The place where those plants were cultivated in some artificially warm environment.

She followed Dr. Mary down the hallway and into a mirrored elevator. On the next floor they walked by an entire row of lab classrooms. All the lights were off except for the room at the end where there was a dim glow. Claire could smell the formaldehyde.

It was quiet as they entered; a man sat hunched over his work at a desk with a reading lamp on. He nodded at them. By the time Mary flicked on the overhead lights, Claire had already made her way over to the glass enclosures that housed various creatures and plants.

In the dark, it had appeared that the biome in front of her contained only plants, but in the light she could now see the horrific scene of hundreds of ants frozen or paralyzed, many of them just zombified corpses with mushrooms blooming out of their heads. Claire had never seen this fungus in real life, but her mother had shown her pictures. The idea of it was all the more creepy knowing that these ants were alive and conscious when the fungus took over and controlled their bodies.

The man stood up from his desk and folded his glasses into a front pocket. His white lab coat was too short for his long arms. His kind eyes and frizzy grey hair reminded her of a favorite teacher from 7th grade--Mr. Bucholz, tall and skinny and smart.

She looked back at the ant enclosure, as he spoke with a soft Canadian lilt: "I know -- the scene is pretty brutal, eh? Our special fungus -- what some call the Sapien Mushroom -- works with similar mechanisms, but we would never use it to puppeteer or destroy the host."

Destroy the host. Claire noted his detached tone. She thought of claire.0.

He tapped on another enclosure and motioned for her to come see. Inside were three identical mice, all with electrodes on their tiny mouse heads, devices similar to the feathery headphones worn by the Listeners in the field.

"Instead ...," he paused and opened the cage and placed his arm near a mouse, allowing it to hop on, "... instead we use it to give the animal new intelligence. Stronger characteristics. Hyphae can wind their way through body cavities, from head to legs and enmesh their muscle fibers and coordinate between the brain in the mycelial network. This is an amazing feat in terms of its pharmacological implications. For people with psychological issues or neurological disorders. It's much more fine-tuned than the drugs that are available now."

He sounded a lot like the textbook she had just been reading, a lot like Lana and Dr. Mary. This must be what it's like to work at a university, thought Claire, a work-camp type of university. She thought of her Mom. She must have known about the Training Tower.

Claire watched the twitching mouse face, all whiskered and red-eyed.

"And now, we've even figured out how to create a kind of fungal network in the air, among invisible spores." The man turned toward Dr. Mary, smiling. He was very proud of his work, Claire could tell.

"You're a mycologist, aren't you?" Claire asked.

"I am." He had a pleasant smile.

She wanted to ask him about her mother, but the way he looked at her -- she got a strong sense that he knew exactly who she was, and that he was only going to reveal what Dr. Mary and the others let him reveal. It was no use to ask.

She tapped on the glass of the next little habitat. It was filled with tiny monkeys. All identical. They appeared to be playing follow the leader, in which the first monkey in line was clearly the most vibrant and strong, and the others just weaker copies of the first. The last two biomes were dark and Claire tried to switch their lights on but they remained dark.

"What's in those?" she asked.

The scientist's face seemed to go blank, and he glanced at Mary who clapped her hands in a gesture that indicated they were all done looking at the creatures.

"Well!" she said, ignoring Claire's question. "Shall we get you back to your studies?"

As they walked back together, Mary let Claire make her case for working the grounds, like Malik.

Claire explained to Mary that she needed to feel the ground–more ground–under her feet. She could help with the outside gardens and food production.

"I've shown you what my purpose is, haven't I?"

Dr. Mary nodded. "Yes, you have a gift, Claire. It's most extraordinary. But there's so much more to what you can do, if only you knew."

Claire wasn't sure what she meant.

"I don't think you understand yet the extent of your gift. The Hybrid is a testament. It's not something you're even in control of … not yet. It's in your genetic material. It's why you're here. We can help you harness powers you didn't even know you had."

Claire wanted to ask her a hundred questions, but she just nodded. This was the first time anyone here had explicitly mentioned the hybrid.

Then Mary looked at her sideways and added, "But I have a feeling you're beginning to understand."

***

The next day, Claire joined a small group of students in the rec room for an orientation of sorts. They sat on floor cushions and listened to Dr. Mary and an official Tower Trainer describe the program, starting with the whole spiel about finding one's purpose organically. Claire did not roll her eyes this time.

"I want to be crystal clear on this point: our goal is a united one, and it is no less than changing the habits of humankind, changing the mechanisms of how all people operate in their daily lives. What is most important is that we are doing it together, always supporting one another."

Claire pretended to get excited about what she would be doing in the future, but deep down, all she wanted was to shake the other recruits. She looked around at the international band of kids -- all so eager, all glowing with a motivation she didn't have. She felt damaged compared to them, even though the first thing Malik said when they first talked was that everyone here must have their own story–their own traumas.

"No one got here because they had a happy home life, Claire. I mean, think about it."

The following Monday, Malik was waiting at the large wooden double doors, when a security guard escorted Claire outside to move gravel for the garden beds. This would be her first job. Malik had left quarantine long before her and already progressed to logistics and facility management.

She was relieved to see him.

"Malik!"

"Hi Claire." He was reserved but polite. They must have said something to him after their encounter in the rec room. Perhaps, he wasn't supposed to be alone with her.

"I'm allowed to work outside now!" she told him.

Yes, he knew. The logistics chief had told him to pay special attention to the comings and goings through this entrance and the yard outside.

Claire studied him. When she tried to catch his gaze, he averted his eyes.

She looked around at the summer landscape -- the sky, the evergreens, and the mountains in the distance. Every cell in her body was jolted awake.

Those first few weeks she happily swept the porches and steps and walkways--anything to be outside. This world was so different from home, so crisp and dry. It was beautiful in a very different way.

As she stood in the walkway, looking as far into the horizon as she could, she vowed to work hard. She saw how much freedom was given to Malik and she was determined to rise to his level. Eventually they would trust her. And once they loosened their defenses, she would find a way out.

In the back of her mind a plan was organizing itself, but she would have to bide her time.

CHAPTER 38: NO SANCTUARY

In the fall, classes began again.

Claire actually liked what they were learning when she got to attend classes. She had not anticipated she would be so interested in the research they got to do. She had always been a mediocre student, and she had no idea about her ability to connect with plants. On some level she wondered whether they had imbued certain powers in her or if the abilities were inherent. Was she actually gifted, or was it the program? Or was it claire.0?

As long as she stayed vigilant and did not get brainwashed like the others.

Besides, what they were learning in the classroom now had little to do with ideology. It was the real thing: botany, ecology, and mycology, just like her mom's studies.

Over the next several weeks, Claire's enthusiasm for the research began to grow, and things she never cared about seemed more relevant than ever. For instance, mushrooms can eat plastic (polyurethane) and petroleum. There was one teacher who claimed that climate change can be completely reversed. If mushrooms are used effectively, they can help trees absorb CO_2 at a much faster rate than any other method.

***

One morning in class, Claire noticed a set of twins–girls with fire-colored hair. And then another set of twins. Identical. And then at lunchtime a third set of twins. She did not dare ask about it lest she raise an alarm that she knew something. She didn't even know what she knew. She just had a feeling.

Dr. Mary had mentioned claire.0 that one time, but otherwise she always seemed to shut down every time Claire asked a question that had to do with the hybrid technology. And she was forbidden to talk to others about her experience with claire.0.

But of course, Claire knew how the technology worked. She just didn't understand how claire.0 could continue operating just fine without Claire being there to "feed" her more genetic information. Lana and David had been very specific about this point. In order for the hybrid to work, Claire had to interact with her and even be physically connected with her before the clone could go off on her own. Perhaps they discovered that was not how it worked, at least not for claire.0. Was Claire's hybrid different from these clones?

She must have been staring at the redheaded twins in class that afternoon because one of them approached her and said, "do we know you?" Not in a rude way. Just neutral. The girl didn't even seem curious–rather it was as though she was obligated to ask.

Her sister was looking on.

"No, I don't think so," replied Claire. "I was just spacing out. Sorry. Your hair is beautiful–both of yours." She nodded at the other twin. "I guess it caught my eye."

"Uh-huh. Okay." The girl looked back at her sister who was approaching.

The second girl said, "My name is Cheyenne, and this is May," she said. "Don't be weird, May-May."

She smiled but didn't extend her hand. Almost imperceptibly, she looked Claire up and down. Claire shivered.

"And you're … Claire, right?"

"Oh! Yes, I'm Claire. Sorry." Awkward pause. She studied their grey eyes–blank and unfocused.

She looked at the other set of twins across the room, dark-skinned girls. They had the same steely eyes, which sparkled in a peculiar way in their brown faces.

As she sat down with her lunch tray that day, Claire saw the third set of twins–Korean boys with dark grey eyes. That's when Claire remembered: the hybrid's eyes did not match her own. They were close enough, but not exactly brown–they had the same silver sheen that all of these twins shared. How had she not noticed it before? How did Gran and Gunther not notice that claire.0 was different?

Looking into the twins' faces, Claire had a vivid memory all of a sudden: that afternoon on the island when she and the other children were served psilocybin tea and hypnotized into thinking they were on a hike. All but her. She'd woken up from the trance to see claire.0 in front of her. Now, she had a clear picture of the Hybrid's face, so like her own, but so vacant-eyed. She remembered shivering at how empty it was–there was no understanding there. No experience, no soul.

But it was the tea that stood out in Claire's mind now. It had to have been some kind of psilocybin mushrooms. They had given them poisoned tea so they would hallucinate! She remembered Lana dismissing this point when she brought it up. Laughing, even.

Then there was that drugged feeling when she woke up on the plane, and afterwards in the quarantine quarters. It was a different poison for sure—more of an anesthetic. Clearly these people had no problem drugging their recruits when necessary. With horror, she realized that the last few weeks she'd been feeling foggy, and that she was ever-so-slowly loosening her resolve to escape.

Claire looked down at her bottled drink, a sparkling fruit juice that they manufactured right here on site. No logo. It was given to her with her midday meal. Every day. She hadn't questioned it. And what about the bottled water sent to her room? Where did it come from?

From that moment on, she only drank water from the faucet. How could she have been so stupid?

***

That night, Claire visited Richard in the Temple House. It was neither a temple nor a church, but a simple wooden building. Its purpose was to provide sanctuary to any recruit or employee, to provide a place of peace–that's how the trainers had described it.

SubRez encouraged non-religious spirituality. Breathwork and visualization, mostly. Physical health for mental benefits. It was all laid out in *The Book of Instructions*.

Richard was at his desk under the glow of a lamp. Claire could see several copies of The Book on the shelf behind him. He looked at her with a smile on his lips, but there was also a sad wrinkle between his brows. They had not talked since the incident in the garden. He gave a slight bow and folded his hands like always.

"How may I help?"

Claire looked around the small interior. There were yoga mats and cushions and a few church pews. There was a stage but no altars. A few candles were lit in the corners. It smelled like a church.

She wanted to tell him what she knew, that they were poisoning her, that they were drugging everyone. He seemed trustworthy. But as she stood before him, she realized he was not as powerful as she hoped. Perhaps he was even weak. He probably already knew what she was going to say, he probably even had found a way of justifying it with some line from that stupid book.

But maybe she could still get his help…

"Ummm. Er … I need to do that meditation again. The one where I become 'grounded' or whatever."

Richard nodded his head forward and looked at his hands as though he knew this were coming.

"You know I can't do that with you.…"

"Please… I need to see what I saw before. Those visions." Claire looked behind her at the door.

Richard held up his hands. "I can't. We can't talk about this."

"You don't even need to do it with me. Just show me."

"Does Dr. Mary know that you are here?"

"Um … I don't.…" Claire didn't realize she needed Mary's permission. She thought she was past that.

Richard's jaw clenched and he squeezed his hands together. "Claire, I can't. Please go now. Please."

Claire turned, bewildered. Richard wasn't even willing to have a conversation with her. Why did he seem scared? How could you be a religious leader if you feared the people you were supposed to lead?

She faced the entrance and realized the door had already been opened. It was being held for her to exit. Outside in the black night, a large man stood behind it, waiting for her. His face was neutral, and he nodded at her. She shrugged in response.

As she retreated, she turned to take one last look at Richard: his brown eyes shone with fear. Or was it regret? He longed to tell her something. What was it?

Richard disappeared behind the door as the large man closed it, almost gently. Then, the guard did something unthinkable. He pulled out a large set of keys and locked it from the outside.

CHAPTER 39: LEAVING CAPTIVITY

Winter 2006

"You've changed your attitude," Malik remarked one day. "You're doing real good, girl." He raised his hand for a high five.

She smiled and gave his hand a slap.

It was working. She even had Malik fooled. Ever since she stopped drinking anything that could be contaminated, she had been overcompensating. Her mind was clear and her spirit was angry. So she covered it up by appearing extra compliant. No one was going to grant her freedom. She would have to steal it. And that meant being sneaky and acting the part.

"So have you."

"Naw...."

"You're in charge of all this!" Claire spread her hands open indicating the entire south yard. It was true, they had charged Malik with several acres of the campus.

"This ain't my thing though. Why are they doing this to us? I mean -- you shoveling rocks? I thought they recruited us for our brains or whatever. This isn't what I signed up for. I ain't no janitor and don't intend to ever be one."

Of course they were using them for free labor, thought Claire. Only two classes per day, and the rest of the time they had to work. They probably had no intention of granting degrees. They probably weren't even qualified. But she stuck to the script. She was almost to the finish line.

"They're testing us, you know that. This is all part of the process. It won't last. That's what Mary says," Claire reminded him.

Claire was surprised at how candid Malik was with her now. It seemed that he was finally questioning SubRez's benevolence. But was he just testing her? After all, he knew as much as she did. The supervisors reminded them every night at dinner: "you all are finding your purpose and we are helping you do that. In the meantime, you are learning to help the group as a whole. All of these skills are important."

Claire reminded Malik of this, too.

"I know that. I just feel like if they keep me here much longer, they'll figure this is all I can do."

Claire looked at him and smiled.

"Just hang in there," she said with a light punch to the arm.

For the next several weeks, Claire and Malik ate lunch every day together. Eventually Claire confided her suspicion that they had been drugging her–once again. And probably many of the other kids. Malik said he didn't think they would do that, not on a daily basis.

But later, she noticed he stopped drinking the packaged drinks too.

She would talk to him about home, and how she missed the beach and the river and Gunther and Gran and her cat.

Malik would mostly listen. His memories of their hometown were mired in hunger and fights at home. Somehow, he had made it to age 14 without getting sucked into the streets, he told her.

"But I woulda been by now -- no doubt," he told her.

Most of the neighborhood kids started selling drugs by 8th

grade. It's the only way, he said. The last year of Claire's life at home had not been easy, but when she heard Malik talk about his mother's neglect and his sister's violent death, she realized she had been sheltered. She understood why he never wanted to return, why he was perfectly happy being a part of SubRez.

He was supposed to have a whole new life. But now that promise was starting to sour.

***

It was March when Claire finally revealed her escape plan to Malik.

"I want to go with you," he said without hesitation.

Claire was surprised. She'd been nervous to tell him because she was sure he would try to talk her out of it. But she needed his help.

"Malik, there's nothing you need to get back to. They aren't exactly holding you against your will. Why would you leave? You told me yourself: this is your only way out."

"But they don't respect me. They still haven't given me my program. They're just using me. This is bullshit. May as well stay in the hood if carrying out menial tasks for a shady organization is what they had planned for me."

"Don't be so dramatic. You even said so yourself– everyone has to go through this. They're still giving you the education you want. You wouldn't have that back home."

Malik rubbed his chin, and looked up at the pale sky. "I don't know." She knew what he must be thinking: what if SubRez really is doing bad things? By extension, so is he.

In the end, he didn't go with her. It was too hard to walk away from that– a group who depended on him and trusted him. A family, Dr. Mary had told him.

But he facilitated Claire's exit.

He gave her all of the codes she would need to turn off the security alarms. They mapped out all of the cameras hidden in trees and high up on the building and way out near the woods. The campus, after all, appeared perfectly open, as though residents could come and go as they please, but just because there are no physical barriers doesn't mean there is freedom.

***

The day she left, she had permission to start her shift early -- 5am -- before anyone else was awake. Dr. Mary almost trusted her now. That's what she said, but it was mostly the elaborate camera system that Mary trusted.

On the morning of her escape, she began her duties as always, performing for the security cameras so as not to alarm the watchers.

She brought only a backpack stuffed underneath a huge jacket. It was incredibly chilly early in the morning, so no one would suspect the extra "layers" of clothing. She slipped outside through an unwatched door and got to the space where they had shifted the cameras away. She marched right off the property and into the thick woods beyond. It was 5:35am.

CHAPTER 40: LOOKING
IN THE MIRROR

Once she was deep in the woods and had gained some elevation, she felt safe. At the top of the first mountain there were still patches of spring snow that sparkled in the beams of rising sun. The fragrant pines made her nostalgic for North Florida, except that these woods were nothing like the brambly scrub pine forests from home. This was more like a European fairy tale forest, where the tree canopy was high and the floor was clear of shrubs and bugs.

She walked and walked until she could no longer stand, and her feet were blistered. Since leaving Florida, she had grown … and so had her feet. Her shoes were too small.

At a clearing, Claire drowsed in the sun for an hour. She dreamed of Gunther and of claire.0.

Or was it real? It seemed that she could really see them through hundreds of miles of separation. She could see what they were doing. But she was the Hybrid and Gunther was accusing her of stealing his piggy bank. Captain meowed at the door. They were all alone in the house. Claire felt paralyzed, as though she could not respond, could not defend herself. Why would she steal money from him?

When she woke up, she ate a small snack even though she was so hungry she could've eaten all the food in the bag. She thought of Frodo and Sam on their journey to Mordor, eating lembas bread. Conserve for tomorrow, she told herself.

The way forward was a little more difficult to navigate. The branches were lower and there were prickly plants that would grab at her ankles and clothing. Every so often she opened the coarsely-drawn map. At the facility, they did not have access to information in the outside world, but Malik had managed to piece together their location well enough to know which direction would bring her to a town, or at least a little civilization.

Once it grew too dark to trudge any farther, she found a safe-looking cluster of trees to sleep for the night. As she settled in, she noticed a mushroom nearby -- fly agaric --the most recognizable one in the world, red with white spots. Super Mario's mushroom, a Disney mushroom … and was it in Alice in Wonderland too? As she closed her eyes she thought of how strange Alice's adventures were, such a terrifying story for children. She thought of how mushrooms were always feared in folklore; they were associated with witches and poisonous brews.

She now knew the potent powers of these toadstools. She was inextricably linked to them. Because of SubRez. They had taken good scientific research of the natural world and turned it into something nefarious, something her mother would never support. Mind control and worse. Much, much worse, Claire now knew.

The next morning, after walking for many miles, Claire saw the bell tower of a church, and then the rooftops of a set of modest buildings. As she drew closer, she could smell and hear the buzzing of civilization. Relief settled into her entire body, and suddenly she felt sharp pangs of hunger. Woodsmoke wafted into her nostrils, making her nostalgic for the campfires she and her family used to make in the backyard.

Before she reached the first house, a ramshackle farm cottage, two young women spotted her on the path and approached. They looked like sisters -- they were just girls, really, probably from the town.

Claire looked around in all directions, but the landscape was quiet and still; it was a wholesome shade of gold, powdered here and there with patches of snow. No sign of security guards or the conspicuous SubRez trucks.

The sisters were dressed in old-fashioned dresses like characters from *Little House on the Prairie*. And that's when Claire knew: something was not right.

She began to run before they even got close enough that she could see their faces, so when they caught up with her and practically muzzled her, muffling her screams, she almost fainted at the shock of it.

Not only were they twins, they were her twins. The girls looked exactly like claire.0 in doll dresses. More hybrids. The expressions on their faces were icy. These were the SubRez guards she had been on the lookout for. Hiding in plain sight.

One girl put her hand over Claire's mouth and the other shushed Claire with a finger over her lips in the exact same way she used to do with Gunther. Claire bit down hard on the girl's fingers, but as she did so she felt the pain herself. They both yelped.

The other twin had a tight hold on Claire's elbow, and she knocked her to the ground from behind. Claire continued to howl until the gag was pulled so tight, her jaw would ache for days.

"You can quit your yowling, no one's around," said one twin in a strange accent. She didn't sound like Claire.

"Also, you may have noticed," said the other. "If you hurt either of us, you hurt yourself."

This was the perfect security measure -- resisting your captor inflicts pain on yourself.

Claire screamed deep in her throat, a moan of grief. She could see the girls were disturbed by it, but they continued marching her across the field.

The twins dragged Claire into the farmhouse where an entire family -- two boys, two girls, a mom and dad -- had been bound and gagged. An officer from SubRez was there. He had a gun. The girls had guns in the pockets of their dresses, which they drew in a synchronized motion.

Seeing her doppelganger was alarming by itself. But to see two clones of herself in long dresses wielding pistols, was too much, and she couldn't help but laugh-- the absurdity of it filled her with dread, but laughing was the only available response. It sounded more like a bark through the gag.

The guard kicked her, snatched her from the girls, and pulled Claire toward the door.

"Thank you," the officer said roughly to the terrified family.

The mother's blue eyes glittered with fear above her gag. One child quietly wept in the corner.

The guard motioned for the girls to release the family.

With a rough palm, he grabbed hold of Claire's wrists and forced her to walk toward a barn where two giant pickup trucks were parked. There were more SubRez personnel in the trucks, all armed.

Before the twins got into the truck, they tied Claire's knees together and shackled her to a bar. Unnecessarily.

"Come on, come on! Let's get out of here," yelled the head guard. He was driving, and he motioned to the other truck to go. Claire looked back and glimpsed the faces of the children in the farmhouse window.

On the drive back, she stared at the twins sitting next to her, completely stone-faced. They were her, weren't they? Maybe she was delirious. How was it possible they had more clones of her?

If only she could reach Gunther somehow before they locked

her away again. That's the first thing she was going to do when she found someone. But the longer she was away, the more likely their bond would be lost forever; he may have already forgotten who the real Claire was.

Sleep overtook her and again she dreamed that she was the hybrid, that she was back at home. This time she was alone in the bathroom, staring at herself in the mirror. The mirror turned to liquid, and she was drowning in her own image.

When they arrived back at the training tower, Claire expected to see Dr. Mary first thing. And Lev.

No one greeted them, and they drove around the building to a wing of the facility she and the others had not been allowed to enter. It was cordoned off on the inside and there were rumors that Dr. Mary kept the most top-secret experiments locked away in there.

Now they were entering from the outside -- an actual drawbridge that she and Malik had assumed did not work anymore. No one had seen it open, and the moat was always overgrown. It was by far the creepiest corner of the sprawling facility, a building with farmhouse architecture in some spots and high-modern features in others. It was unclear when the whole thing was built.

Claire's stomach flipped as they crossed over the drawbridge and into a surprisingly clean interior. Where were they taking her?

But no one spoke to her.

After parking the truck, the driver turned around and said, "blindfold her."

Claire was still gagged but she tried to speak anyway. Where was Dr. Mary? The twins translated. They knew what she was thinking.

"No Dr. Mary" replied the driver. "Not today. You're a danger to the organization. You don't get to talk to nobody."

Under his breath he whispered to the guard beside him, "Mary is stupid for keeping her alive."

The guard shushed him, "the girl can hear everything!"

After that, everything went black. She tried not to panic when they led her to an elevator that was clearly small and unventilated.

They went down, down, down into the earth. The elevator clanked and chugged as it descended what must have been 10 floors beneath the ground.

Several minutes later she was in a small cell, all alone. Here she was again -- a caged animal. Except this time there was no bed, no accommodation at all. She could smell the deep, frozen earth and knew that behind the thin walls there was tangled underground life ready to reach right through and snatch her by the arms. No sunlight. No life. Just cold, grey earth and roots on the other side of the wall.

Was it true, what the guards had said? They couldn't kill her now, could they? After they'd seen what she could do with the plants? What would happen to the hybrid if she died?

She shivered as a rat scurried beneath the doorway. At least she hoped it was just a rat.

The hours crawled by, and no one came. She dozed in and out of sleep, shivering, her stomach gnawing at her.

And then finally, the chugging of the ancient elevator, moving its way back down.

It was Dr. Mary.

Claire could not hide her hunger when she realized Mary had food. She smelled it before she saw it. Ham and cheese on a baguette. Mary drew it from her bag, and Claire's stomach gurgled.

She ate as slowly as she could bear.

Mary was quiet and the guards stayed back. Claire felt self-conscious, but she dared not speak.

When Dr. Mary started asking questions, Claire just shook her head.

She refused to say anything until someone would tell her about the clones. "What are those twins? Why do they look like me?"

Beneath Mary's accommodating smile and polite British manner, Claire saw something creeping and treacherous. The green eyes had turned on her; they were different somehow -- closed off and reptilian.

Regardless, Mary explained with surprising transparency: "It was helpful to have them for this exact situation. It was an easier way of locating you and coaxing you back. After all, we always trust those who look like ourselves, don't we? Maybe to our own demise sometimes..."

Claire shuddered. "I was not coaxed. They had guns. Tell me what they are. How did you make them?" But she knew that Dr. Mary would not explain the whole truth.

"I'm sorry, my dear. We certainly don't mean to frighten you ... unless it's absolutely necessary."

This comment sent a shiver down Claire's spine.

And with that, Mary stood up, walked out, and addressed the guards in whispers. A blanket was handed to Dr. Mary and she gave it to Claire. It was thick and soft, and Claire was immediately grateful for the warmth. She had never been so cold in her life.

"Wrap yourself in that tonight. You need to be warm. Eat well and sleep well. You will need your strength."

Claire could not help but sink into the warmth of the blanket.

Mary turned and shut the prison door behind her.

As she drifted in and out of sleep, terrible fairytale images floated through her consciousness. The evil witch, Mary, had sent her henchmen to make sure she ate the poison apple. They were trying to fatten her up to be eaten. But by what? No one was coming to the rescue. The bond between Hansel and Gretel had long been severed. She had betrayed Gunther. No one was coming.

The familiar feeling of being drugged descended upon her quickly this time. But this was not any kind of suggestive psychedelic. This was deeper, euphoric, and had its own distinct smell: decaying leaves and deep earth.

This is how she would die, she thought. Uneventful, quiet. She was tranquil beyond her own understanding. Was this a drug or was she just at death's door. And that's when the ground began to shift.

She felt them before she saw them, white tendrils rising from the floor beneath her, capturing her foot and ankle, then another ankle, and then around her torso and up the spine, so quickly that movement was impossible. It was too many all at once. And yet she felt a full-bodied deep sense of peace.

PART III: FAMILY

CHAPTER 41: O CAPTAIN!

Gunther

Candlestick Lane

After Claire left home, she and Gunther stopped talking. But by then, he knew Claire would never be the same.

Anyway, he had his own problems: a dark spot began to cloud his psyche, and he couldn't seem to shake it. Everything felt dim and confusing. His parents were long dead, and his sister was irreversibly changed.

No one could give him a clear sense of direction, and he became untethered. High school would be over soon, and he realized his friends would just drift apart -- letting go, breaking apart, and drifting out to sea.

There was also the incomprehensible idea that Claire deliberately abandoned him and been replaced with a clone-- the one thing he was careful never to face head on, lest he fall into that crack in reality and never regain his balance. He refused to let anyone know how precarious his sanity actually was.

One time, Claire brought her boyfriend home to visit. By then Gunther was a senior in high school. Gran acted nervous as she prepared dinner that evening. Mack was unusually well-mannered. Ken, the boyfriend, was all but mute.

"That's a fine truck you've got there, son," Mack said as they sat around the dinner table.

"Yessir," replied Ken and continued chewing his pork chop.

Gran wasn't a great cook, and the pork chops were always too dry.

Gunther had nothing to contribute to the conversation. He could hardly believe this was his sister's boyfriend.

"Gran," said Claire, "I was thinking Ken and I could take the canoe out for a little ride after dinner. I could show him the lake."

Gunther felt a tiny jolt of jealousy. Where did that come from?

Claire always addressed Gran directly for things like this. She avoided talking to Mack whenever possible, even now.

Ken looked up, surprised.

Mack let out a condescending chortle.

"Ken doesn't want to ride in that crumbly old thing," said Mack.

Claire blushed.

Mack had his own idea: "Why don't I take him out on the little fishing boat I just got? How about it, son? First thing in the morning?"

"Yessir," said Ken. He seemed to be blushing too.

Claire glared at Mack, pushed herself away from the table and left the room. Ken made a move to follow her but took one look at Mack and stayed frozen in his seat.

Gunther wanted to go after Claire too. But he couldn't do that anymore.

"Go on," said Gran to Ken. She could see that he was conflicted about whether to stay at the table.

"Yes m'am," he said, eyes downcast as he rose from the table. He avoided Mack's stare.

After Ken was gone, Mack said, "that's a proper young man. Good kid."

Gran glared at Mack.

That was the only time Gunther met Ken. It seemed so strange that Claire was with this dull man who was much closer to 30 than 20. It didn't seem real to Gunther. But at the time, nothing seemed all that real to him. He was beginning to feel untethered.

The existential crisis continued until he met a girl named Beth. Even at such a young age, Beth had things figured out. She took a very straightforward, practical approach to the world. Things were black and white. She was popular, cute, and organized. And she rescued Gunther from the brink, ensuring he would not follow in the footsteps of his mother, the addict, or his sister, the ragdoll. She found Gunther sad and mysterious, and concluded that what he actually needed was to re-create himself, far from the shadow of his hometown and tragic family. She alone would help him.

In fact, had it not been for her, Gunther surely would have missed his college application deadlines and let his grades continue slipping. Instead, he graduated at the top of the class at age 17 and landed a considerable university scholarship.

Claire returned home once again for Gunther's high school graduation, but this time without Ken. She was there at Gran's request. But the whole weekend became about Claire, Gunther's graduation just a backdrop for her meltdown.

Apparently, on the morning of graduation, Gran had started a conversation with Claire about her future, and Claire cried and then disappeared all afternoon. When Gunther was supposed to be getting ready for the ceremony, he was instead searching for his sister.

She quietly reappeared just in time, got in the car, and dozed through the graduation. She nodded onto Beth's shoulder in the car on the way home. Beth smiled through it. Gunther pinched his sister awake several times.

"Gunther! Stop." Her speech was slurred, her eyes vacant.

At dinner she was alert, but quiet.

The next morning she hugged everyone, vaguely apologized, and asked Gunther to drive her to the airport. On the way there, he asked a few cautious questions -- "how's your job hunt?" "how's Ken?" "will you be finishing your degree?" -- and she accused him of interrogating her. It ended with a bland argument and another weepy apology.

Gunther knew that the whole ordeal would create a lasting impression on Beth.

***

"I'm sorry about my sister," Gunther said the next day. "I think she's going through a hard time."

"It's okay," Beth said.

"Honestly, I don't know what the hell is wrong with her. She hasn't been the same ... in like years. Ever since..." He trailed off, not wanting to admit his ludicrous suspicion.

Beth and Gunther were at a classmate's house, celebrating with their peers the weekend after graduation. The parents were gone and there was a lot of beer. They were both tipsy, Gunther delving into a dark mood from the alcohol, and Beth taking on a dramatic air. The music was loud in the house, so Beth and Gunther went outside in the backyard and sat at the edge of the pool. The crickets sang high and persistent in the background, invisible musicians of the night.

Beth shook her head. "I get it. I guess she's been through a lot."

Gunther looked up, surprised.

"Ummm. There's something you should know about Claire," said Beth.

The hair on Gunther's neck stood up and prickled down his arms. How would she know something Gunther didn't?

"About my sister?"

"I heard it from a friend who was in Claire's grade...I have a feeling you don't know."

"Heard what?"

"If I say, you can't let her know it was me...Promise? She probably just wants to forget..."

"Beth ...."

"You have to promise."

"Okay. Fine. I promise. What is it?"

He can't imagine what Beth could know.

"I don't know how to say it .... I mean did you know Michael Hadley ... uh like forced himself on Claire back when she was a freshman?"

"What? Of course not. No ... I think you heard wrong. Must've been someone else."

Gunther did not want to hear this. But it was too late.

Apparently, the day of the hurricane, Michael forced Claire into having sex when she went to his house. She went along with it at first, but ultimately, she pushed him away and ran out the back door. He got angry– maybe scared she would tell, chased her down, dragged her back into the house. Everyone knew. The boys called her a cock tease.

Gunther shook his head. No, he did not want to hear any more. Not about his sister. And that spoiled prick Michael Hadley...

Beth continued anyway. After it had happened, she said, Claire didn't know what to do -- didn't want to return home. That's why she was gone so long that day of the hurricane.

Obviously, she felt so ashamed. "Gunther …. Gunther? Are you okay? I'm sorry for telling you this … it's just that. Maybe it will help you understand…?"

He had pulled his legs out of the water and folded them into his chest.

Beth tried to touch him, but he pulled away. She continued talking, pulling all the pieces together for Gunther. Based on what she knew from Gunther's side of things and all of the rumors, she created a feasible theory. The sexual assault by itself would have been traumatic enough, but the danger of the storm, the public search party, and the fact that her parents had died only months before, forever changed her.

Of course she changed after that, Beth reasoned. Of course she couldn't have confided in her twelve year old brother. She didn't report it to anyone; she had no mother to go to.

This is not what Gunther expected to hear.

"And wasn't she also in the school during the shooting two years ago? I'm sure that didn't help," Beth added. "Gosh, I can't imagine. It's so awful. I don't blame her at all. I feel so sad for her." She sounded far too fascinated for Gunther to believe she felt bad.

This is why college didn't work out for Claire. At least that was Beth's assessment, her sweeping story of a ruined girl. There was no room for doubt.

"Stop," he said.

She folded her hands in her lap and nodded.

"When were you going to tell me this?"

"At first, I didn't even realize she was your sister. I knew the story but…."

"God! How? How would you know this? Who else knows? The whole fucking school?"

Beth stood. He almost never lost his temper in front of her. She looked stunned.

He peered at the house, bright with drunk faces, so many young, reckless bodies intentionally bumping around, shoving into one another. He hated them.

Still balled up at the edge of the pool, Gunther leaned so far forward that he splashed into it. He could hear Beth's voice through the water, a high screech of an alarm, but he stayed underwater. It felt good.

His mind was spinning with alcohol and rage. He remembered now how delusional Claire sounded those days before the hurricane. It was pure innocence, still playing pretend with him about the island people. She had said they offered her a job and training and a place to live. They had a clone of Claire; it would replace her so that no one would ever tell the difference. She wanted to get away from Grandpa Mack. She wanted him to come too. Had she realized she was just pretending at the time? Or did she really believe her own stories? He grieved for her now, that younger Claire, an inescapable anguish and regret. He always thought of her as so capable and grown up compared to him, but she had been such a kid. So innocent. This all made sense now. No wonder she became such a different person so suddenly.

***

The suspicion of Claire being someone else never disappeared altogether. There was always a sliver of hope that the real Claire was somewhere else, alive and well, sailing around the world or ziplining in Costa Rica. Anything but this ugly little life she had made for herself.

But things just got worse, and less than a year after Claire visited for the graduation, Ken checked her into a drug rehab clinic. He said it was prescription drugs.

When Gunther heard this, the nagging suspicion that Claire wasn't really Claire reared its head once again. At least someone was noticing it now; something was really wrong.

It all came flooding back. The sliver of doubt grew. This isn't who she was. He couldn't imagine her locked up in some blank-walled rehab ward. The Claire he knew was a mighty forest huntress, barefooted, with a baby squirrel in her pocket and a crown of leaves in her hair, climbing trees and catching fish with her bare hands.

The one time he spoke to her on the phone, he wanted to tell her, you don't belong there, but all he said was, "why do you keep trying to hurt yourself?" because that's what Gran kept wondering aloud.

The call did not end well.

"You have no idea who I am," she shouted at Gunther. "You never did."

And that was that.

It was the last time he spoke with Claire until Gran's funeral.

***

The summer after graduation, Gunther moved into a dorm, as early as the university would take him. A few months later, Captain died quietly at the foot of Gran's bed. "One minute he was purring, and the next he was not," Gran explained to Gunther over the phone. His black and white body had grown cold quickly, and Mack buried him in the backyard next to the holding-hands tree, so he would have a forever view of the lake. "First time in a long time I saw Mack shed a tear," Gran said. The old man and the cat had become close companions over the years.

Gunther cried himself to sleep that night, a silent weeping --

for Claire, for Captain, for their river-faring trio.

SARAH CLARKE STUART

CHAPTER 42: A BLANK ARMY

Claire

The Training Tower

Claire jolted awake at the metal clang of the cell door opening. But when she opened her eyes, there was only darkness. She heard muffled voices coming through the blanket that she had wrapped herself in. But when she tried moving, she realized it wasn't a blanket at all. She was held in place by threads, hundreds of them it seemed as she wiggled the tips of her fingers and only heard footsteps and dull sounds.

As panic arose in her chest, it was immediately quelled by a voice: "*Shh,*" it said, and she felt rather than heard the next words: *Stay very still and they will leave you be. We will free you. But first, we must wait. We will help you wait, help you relax.*

Claire was frozen in fear.

But it lasted only for a moment. She remembered Richard's words telling her to just breathe. She exhaled a long breath, something he had taught her to help her relax before taking action.

As she continued the breathwork, her head cleared. The first message that came to her, something from deep inside, was to trust the voice that was holding her. To not scream, to not let the guards know where she was. This system had pulled her down into the earth somehow and was intentionally hiding her from SubRez. It was a benevolent force, cradling her, trying to warn her that danger was near. At least, that's what she wanted to think.

She could hear the guards above tap on the walls as Dr. Mary yelled at them.

Claire continued the slow breathing, and she felt herself dozing in and out, until the soft voice of the mycelium rocked her into a deep sleep.

The next time she was conscious, she found herself back on the floor of the cell and shivering hard. She had never been so cold in her life, and as she pulled the blanket around her, she began to wonder if trusting a fungal life form that had very different needs from her own mammalian body had been wise. Had it taken something from her? Would she ever stop shaking? Would she ever return to a normal temperature?

That's when she noticed the door had been left wide open. She only had the strength to crawl toward the door, but once she peeked her head out and realized it was absolutely silent, energy surged through her. She pulled herself up to a standing position and leaned on the doorframe.

No one was around. The elevator was nearby. But the guards were probably waiting right there at the top. There had to be some other exit, she thought, looking up and down the long cave-like hallways.

She could feel warmth coming from the elevator shaft, so she stood near it wrapped in the blanket, thawing out. It seemed she had been entombed for years, but she had to wake up her brain and find a way out. The only lighting she had were scattered motion-activated strip lights on the floor. But her eyes had adapted to the dark, as though she were evolving into some deep-sea fish.

She thought the hallway was more like a tunnel as she ventured carefully away from the elevator, listening for any sign of life.

It became so dark that she was about to turn around when she felt a door on the wall. It opened easily, and a greenish glow appeared at the floor of yet another door.

All was quiet as she tiptoed through the room. The air became cold again. As she opened the next door, the entire building seemed to open up, a ceiling as high as three or four stories.

The walls were gone, leaving just a thin layer of clear plastic holding the frozen soil back. The bright white of roots and mycelium showed through, and in places they had tunneled right through the plastic.

Her head was thrown back in awe and she had to cover her mouth for fear she would scream.

It was a huge cave-like hall, a vast space filled with bodies as far as she could see. Not dead ones. Very much alive, but with blank expressions and meaningless movements. They wobbled around like plants blowing in a breeze, but there was no breeze down there.

Claire felt her knees buckling. She wanted to run but she couldn't move.

The bodies were languid and graceful, like an underwater garden of zombies. At first it seemed they were chained to the wall, but upon closer inspection Claire realized there were fleshy threads attached to their hands and feet. The ends were connected to the sloping walls all around them. Every being was covered with what appeared to be a film of white threads.

She finally began to move, but instead of running away, her body was carrying her forward. The shock was still there, but her fear was gone. *You are safe.* It was the same voice she'd heard when she was hiding in the floor.

As she got closer, she began to recognize a face–and then all of the faces at once. They were her. An army of Claires. This is what SubRez had been doing all this time, growing hundreds of them, using her as an unlimited human resource. A prisoner without consent.

She backed away, but as she did so, all of the bodies responded to her and took a step back as well. They mimicked Claire's body language as though mocking her. Their heads were covered in caps of mycelium–no hair yet. In fact, none of them were "done." *Base models,* thought Claire.

It was colder than ever, deep underground without insulation, and now Claire was shaking uncontrollably again.

CHAPTER 43: SEARCHING

The Hybrid

2006-2007

According to Mack, she had become a bad girl.

So, she tried fixing herself by becoming something else entirely. Her rebellions were sad, quiet, and meaningless– there was no one there to witness them after she left home. Everyone she met at college seemed wrapped up in their own chaos.

It was only when she took that trip to the mountains one weekend, that she felt okay: at peace … and possibly *free*.

The mountain air breathed something new into her and the wilderness felt so liberating that she confused her joy with an infatuation for the first man she saw: Ken, the group's tour guide and local mountain man. The autumn foliage and the pungent smell of the forest life all around was wrapped up in an attraction to him.

By this time she had stopped her weekly phone calls home to Gran.

So, when she decided to move in with him, she didn't even tell anyone. She packed up her dorm while her roommate was gone and didn't even leave a note.

They moved in together into a tiny apartment at the edge of a suburban forest -- a poor substitute for the wilderness, but it would have to do. It turned out Ken had been living a transient life for years, a combination of couch-surfing and camping wherever he got work. But they scraped together enough for a deposit in a dingy motel-turned condo. Claire was hopeful and happy to be away from the crowded dorm.

What she didn't realize is that isolation would drive her to self-destruction.

One day, she had a *mental break.* That's what Ken called it, at least. But she knew it wasn't the first time she'd experienced such a thing. The only difference is that this time she couldn't hide it like she did from her dorm mate. He could hear her talking to the voice in her head. *Who the fuck are you talking to?* he demanded. She was embarrassed and told Ken it would never happen again.

But one morning, when she was lying alone in bed, she heard the voice calling from far away. It was early in the morning, but Ken had already left for work. She wandered outside to a grassy area behind the apartments. She was barefoot. There were woods beyond the grass, and she just wanted to look into the trees and think.

"I'm trapped. Please help me," the voice said. It almost sounded like her mother. "They locked me up in a dungeon, and I can't move or speak. I can't communicate with anyone but you, Claire. You have to listen. You *have* to help me. Tell Gunther. Please."

Claire had heard this voice before, the first time many years ago after the hurricane, but of course she never told anyone. And then there were those strange dreams she would have in high school about the woods and the roots and the mushrooms.

And now the voice was back. Usually, it was in the mornings right at the edge of her dreaming mind. And she always had the sudden impulse to go outdoors. In the dorm she had been too self-conscious, and the spell would be broken. That morning, no one was around; no one saw her wander into the woods.

"Claire!" It was loud now. She had the urge to plant her hands into the ground, and then, her entire body. She wanted all the flesh to be touching the ground, reaching into the earth.

"Help me, please!" The voice grew louder, and Claire had visions of that island in the lake back home, that place Gunther always wanted to go back to. But what did that have to do with this voice? Or Gunther?

After that, she must have blacked out. Hours later, a neighbor found her wandering in the woods, disoriented and naked, screaming her own name, repeating, "Where are you? Claire! Where are you?"

She had to beg and plead with Ken not to send her home to Gran.

Ken told her, "You gotta promise not to ever leave this apartment without me unless you tell me–each and every time, Claire. I can't babysit you. Who's going to make money if I have to stay here with you?"

"I know, I know," said Claire. "I promise that will never happen again."

But the voice didn't stop. So, she learned to dim it. Back in the dorm, alcohol had helped turn down the voice. So, she began drinking her boyfriend's hard liquor. And then, when she began seeing a doctor at Ken's request, she discovered prescription medications. The combination made the voice go away altogether. For a little while.

On New Year's Day of 2006, she got the call about Gran's diagnosis. *Cancer.* She was going to fight it, Mack said. She would be okay. But maybe Claire could come? Mack sounded different, softer. She couldn't remember him ever politely asking anything of her. He had always demanded it or said nothing at all. She would come, she promised.

But Gran's mortality scared her, and by April, Claire still hadn't gone to visit.

***

She sat all day watching nature documentaries and re-runs of *Party of Five*, daydreaming that she had a family like that to return to. Once, when she couldn't get a refill of the prescription, she ran off into the woods again and Ken didn't find her until early the next morning.

They hadn't been together a full year yet when Ken dropped her in the lobby of a rehab clinic, just a few miles from that spot in the mountains where Claire had fallen in love with him. He didn't know if that's what she needed or not, but she refused to go home.

Somewhere deep inside she knew that being hospitalized could be dangerous, that she couldn't trust doctors, and that there was something she had to hide. But when she told Ken this, he took it as a sign that she was even more deeply troubled than he first thought.

As her body slowly detoxed from the substances, she realized that her own thoughts and jumbled memories were exactly what needed to be kept secret. Without the drugs, they began rising to the surface again. Her past was muddled, and what she remembered didn't line up with reality.

Gran called her in rehab and said the chemo was working. She wasn't dying after all.

Claire began to sob. "I'm so sorry, Gran. I meant to come, I really did ..."

"You will, my dear. Just get better yourself. And now, you have plenty of time. I'm going to be okay!"

Inside a cozy, book-lined office, a therapist asked about her childhood home. Thus far, Claire had barely spoken because she was afraid of what she would reveal. But this woman seemed kind; she genuinely wanted to help Claire.

"There were webs of light, with stars at their intersections," said Claire.

"The house?"

"The childhood. It was … uh, safe."

"Can you elaborate, Claire? What else was there?"

"I'm not Claire," she blurted.

"Okay, well then who are you? I'd like to meet you." She gave a genuine smile, not condescending or impatient.

Claire looked at the therapist carefully: the dark owl eyes, the moon-shaped face, the youthful skin and curly dark hair. She was a very soothing-looking person. But what would she say if Claire revealed the absurd thoughts that began to plague her? She couldn't say that she had been manufactured like a doll, that her creators had abandoned her, that they had cruelly plugged her into this horrible world to save Claire from a life of sadness and fear. That the real Claire had escaped this awful life.

But if she told her all that, she might be held against her will, taken to a government hospital and studied. Or at least that's what the voice in her head was saying. Or worse: something called *SubRez* might take her.

Where had she gotten these ideas anyway? Her boyfriend had wanted to know. On her bad days, she would speak them aloud to him. Now, Claire wasn't sure of anything. Sometimes the voice felt so real. So normal.

But to the therapist she said, "I *am* Claire. I'm just … I don't remember much about my childhood. We played in the woods a lot I guess …? My parents died when I was 14 … boating accident."

"That must have been unbearably painful," said the therapist.

"I don't remember," said Claire. "I mean I know it happened, but it's almost like I watched it on TV or something. I honestly don't remember the experience of it."

The therapist nodded in sympathy. "Disassociation. I understand. When you've disassociated from your body, it's hard to retain memories."

Claire glared at her. *No*, she wanted to scream. *She was never in that body*. And now, her own body was betraying her.

"I'm afraid I won't live very long," Claire said quietly. "I wasn't designed like other people; I mean I'm not like other people. I just won't be able to keep living."

The therapist touched Claire's hand. "You will if you want, Claire. We can help."

Claire shook her head and began to cry.

Apparently, this was progress. The therapist handed her a box of tissues, smiled, and said she would report back to the head nurse.

The rehab team and a visiting psychiatrist agreed that Claire's breakdown stemmed from repressing the death of her parents and being cut off from her childhood. She needed to be treated for trauma, not so much addiction.

"You need a real retreat, a place that feels like home … maybe something close to the woods and the water," said the therapist. Her dark eyes sparkled with excitement.

Claire remembered the Healer telling her something similar back when she was in high school. He kept telling her to "stay grounded" and "listen to your natural energy." Her friends had said it was creepy, their relationship, so she pushed him away. Now, she regretted falling out of touch with him. The last time they spoke, she'd been very rude. He had come to her dorm to see how she was doing, and when Gran and Mack found out, they forced her to file a restraining order.

"There's something not right about that man," Gran had said.

"You and I both know that, Claire. What would he want with an eighteen year-old girl? Huh? Whatdya think?"

"Use your head," said Mack. "For once. You're gonna get yourself killed if you just let anybody into your dorm room."

But now that Claire actually knew what an older man might want from an 18-year-old girl, she realized that the Healer was a different kind of person altogether. He didn't want anything from her. In fact, he was like the mother and father she no longer had. A real parent, looking out for her ... but from afar.

But why?

Now, in the sterile four walls of the clinic, Claire smiled at the therapist, and the woman brightened.

Claire said, "Yes, I want to find a place like that. It sounds nice."

"Great! Take a look at these here ...." She presented a folder of pamphlets -- woodsy cabins and countryside cottages with streams flowing past.

Claire looked through them politely but shook her head.

"I appreciate it but, could you ... um ...? Could you help me find someone? I think he knows of the perfect place. But I need to find his number."

The rehab residents weren't allowed access to a computer or a phone during their first few weeks.

The therapist cocked her head and studied Claire for a few beats. She was determined to connect with Claire. She raised an eyebrow.

"His first name is Richard, but unfortunately I don't even know his last name." Now Claire felt silly. "He sometimes goes by the name, The Healer. I knew him from my church."

The woman's eyes grew wide. "I don't know, Claire."

Claire racked her brain—where was that retreat he'd always

talked about? Somewhere in the mountains of North Carolina?

"Wait -- no, he's legitimate. He even runs a retreat center, just like you're talking about."

Claire knew that if he actually had a retreat, it was probably nothing like the ones the therapist had in mind, but it didn't matter. She had to find him. There had been some connections to a Native American tribe or something, but it had never been clear.

"I'll need more to go on...," the therapist said.

"Oh. It was a reservation!" She began to remember. "It's a Cherokee reservation or something like that, in North Carolina ...? He's Native American. So...his retreat center is kinda based on that ... or that's where he's from at least."

The woman looked skeptical still, but Claire knew she would do it. Claire's instincts about people were very keen...when she wasn't under the influence.

Maybe there was another way, another future for her.

The Healer would help her.

CHAPTER 44: THE GROWING LAB

Claire

The Training Tower

Their eyes were all fixed on her, perhaps concerned or fascinated. But Claire could tell they did not possess any human emotion yet; not like claire.0. They were just mirroring her physical expressions of emotion. Claire realized with some embarrassment that none of them were clothed. They were loosely wrapped in mycelial threads, but their bare bodies were apparent. That's when it occurred to her how different one was from the other. They were not even all female!

For a moment, some part of her ego felt a perverse sense of pride that they had chosen her DNA above all others. All of these bodies, modeled after her own. When she looked closely at how they twisted her genetic material and supplemented it to create different types of Claire's, including huge ones, ghost-white ones, black ones, brown ones, small ones and tall ones, she simply felt horrified. They had shrunk the waist and the feet of some and widened the waist of others, pumped up their muscles, broadened the bone structure. They didn't necessarily want her beauty or her athleticism or her brains, but something much, much deeper, something primal. They copied it like a formula– copied and pasted it over and over again--and then added colors and voice and curls and muscle. Like a graphic design project.

This was the "growing lab," a term she heard the mycologists use back in the Training Tower. But she had imagined it would be some kind of quaint garden outdoors, mushrooms growing underneath freshly cut oaks. Not this -- a dank pit deep inside the freezing cold earth.

After several minutes she spoke aloud, not afraid anymore. She was beginning to understand the power she wielded. "But why? What were they going to do with these?"

She gazed around and took several deep breaths. "How did this happen?" Her outstretched arms were mirrored by the hybrids, but their gestures were not as strong; they moved like an echo, a more muted version of the original.

For months they had been transferring her biological information, her hormones, and microbiome, and neurological data. Maybe even just now in the cell.

She was shaking as she backed up toward the door. She had only a thin shirt and pants on, and the temperature was close to freezing. She needed to leave and never return. But as she moved even closer toward the exit, she heard one of them speak. Not with a voice but directly into her head.

Please, don't leave us here. Take us with you. Please, we need you.

"No. I can't be here ...." She felt herself being physically pulled toward them. "Let go of me. Let me out!"

She peered at the bodies again, feeling herself giving way. Certainly, they were suffering, whatever they were.

She knew she couldn't leave them like this. As long as the SubRez people have access to this Frankenstein army, they will continue to make them suffer. Or they will escape and go who-knows-where.

Could she somehow unplug the whole thing? Just get rid of the technology?

As she became more certain that no one was coming, she looked around and realized the first room she'd entered was a lab for the scientists. She could see now that someone had left in a huge hurry. There was even a half-eaten lunch on the desk and two computers running. She couldn't log in, but she used the ambient light to shuffle through the food, and find something edible. It felt like it had been weeks since she had eaten.

Dr. Mary's people must have abandoned the place. Was it the mycobeasts that had spooked them? Or something on the outside?

Looking through the window at the inert ghost-like people, she realized she didn't fear them, as scary as they appeared. She could see that they would transform into passable humans one day soon, and then they would be on their own in the world, and completely ill-equipped to function. Or SubRez would return and weaponize them. Or maybe they had already been programmed to do something terrible.

Claire slumped into a chair and chewed the stale bread of a days-old sub sandwich. She knew what she had to do.

She went back to the hallway and found the blanket she had dropped earlier. She wrapped herself in it and sat on the floor in front of the hybrids. They mimicked the action, absolutely silent in their movements. It was unnerving.

Claire closed her eyes and breathed deeply, counting her breaths in and out as Richard had taught her, as *The Book* had instructed. The hybrids followed suit.

Claire wondered what they planned to do with all these bodies. There were so many of them, such helpless creatures, and completely undeveloped. If only she could deactivate them somehow, undo the damage.

She knew they couldn't be unleashed from their threads or they would simply wander off. They were still at an early stage of development.

Claire continued to meditate, using more concentration than ever before.

Once the hybrids were in a seeming meditative trance, Claire began to rack her brain, trying to remember something that had escaped her conscious mind. It was something Dr. Mary had said when she was sleeping once. Or maybe in the next room over.

But now it came to her as clear as though Dr. Mary was standing in the room: "Do not let the girl die. If she dies, they all die. It's the only way for them to perish."

Claire opened her eyes and looked all around the room. Her gaze fell on a table by the doorway where an open copy of *The Book of Instructions* lay: that was it.

The hybrids were still under the spell she had initiated. They were in a deep meditative trance, completely unperturbed, but only because her own mind was calm now.

Without a sound, she made her way to the book, folded it under her arm and sat back down. She leafed through the pages until she found a familiar chapter.

This was it.

She was going to have to die.

CHAPTER 45: RETREAT

The Hybrid

The therapist left the information under Claire's pillow. The facilities staff had already swept the room and the bed was made, so no one else but Claire would find it. It was a printed map and a handwritten phone number. At the top was written, "Richard …?" And then, "Cherokee Temple Retreat."

When Claire found it, her breath quickened. There were two twenty-dollar bills and a bus ticket. She held them to her chest like a hug. It was real. He was real. She would find him. He would know what to do.

After the long bus ride and a treacherous hitchhiking ordeal, Claire arrived at a rambling property in Cherokee, North Carolina on banks of the Oconaluftee River. The campus consisted of three elderly log cabins, several trailers, and one main cabin, much newer than the others.

A retreat employee met Claire in the gravel driveway.

"Claire Flynn?"

It was odd to hear her name spoken out loud, here in the middle of nowhere, halfway up a mountain.

She could hear the burbling of the river, and she smelled the green fragrance of deep woods. Automatically, her entire body relaxed in a way she hadn't experienced for years.

The employee, a Native American woman with long fingers and stunning grey hair took Claire's suitcase. She wore a silk dress with a faux patchwork print. Claire immediately liked her.

"You know, we could've picked you up from Asheville," she said, eyeing the car that was pulling away. "We have people coming from all over the world, so we drive to that airport all the time."

Claire hadn't considered this, nor did she have a cell phone. She wondered what this woman knew about her, if she knew she was on the run with only $40 to her name. Well, now $17, actually.

The woman smiled warmly in understanding and gave Claire a hug. It was a surprising gesture; Claire had not been touched in almost a month.

"Richard has told me so much about you. We're happy you're joining us."

"You know Richard?"

When Claire had used the therapist's phone to call the retreat, she learned that Richard was not there, but yes indeed it was his retreat center and he would return soon. She didn't know how big or small the retreat center was. She imagined that Richard was some guru now, maybe not as accessible as she thought. But she had to find a way to see him. This would be the only way, she knew.

The woman laughed. "Of course, hon. We're old friends. My name is Eliza, Liz for short."

"Oh! That's my middle name," Claire said.

The woman just smiled and nodded. She probably already knew this.

What else did she know?

Once Claire had settled into her cabin, she walked down to the river and took off her shoes. The cold mountain water ran through her toes, and she relaxed even more, as the sounds of the evening arose. An owl hooting, crickets chirping, the rustling of the trees.

She wondered when she would see Richard. When she asked if she could just speak to him on the phone, Liz had just said, "yes very soon," in a vague manner.

The feeling of relaxation began to dissipate. What if this had all been a huge mistake? The retreat was beautiful and Liz was very nice, but as she sat there waiting for dinner, Claire realized that she had no idea who Richard really was or what this retreat was meant for. How would she even pay to stay there? She should really call Gran, at least let her know where she was. But then Gran would tell Ken, and she couldn't let that happen. Not yet. She needed more time.

She could hear voices gathering behind her. They would all be dining in the main cabin, Liz said. It was 7:30. Claire's stomach grumbled. She had not eaten since that bus station bagel and cream cheese.

Now, Claire would meet the others. Liz said they were like her, but in what way? Claire peered into the windows, hesitating. They looked normal–mostly young adults, it seemed. It could've been a camp for college students.

"Hungry?" a voice behind her asked. It was a kind-looking older man. But not Richard of course.

Claire nodded and followed him through the door.

The dinner was vegetarian– rice and vegetables and some sort of yogurt. Claire was so hungry, she did not hesitate getting seconds. This was the first time she'd felt her appetite in months.

She looked around the dining hall and realized that everyone but Liz and one other staff member was quite young. No one over the age of 30. It must be a youth retreat. She also noticed that there were more than one set of twins. In fact, there were several groups who appeared to be siblings.

Immediately Claire felt out of place. Once again.

But when she began talking to the shy-looking boy next to her, she felt better. Ian was tall and broad-shouldered but very thin. His yellow hair fell into his eyes and he kept sweeping it back by shaking his head. He had cappuccino skin, a striking contrast against his bright hair.

Immediately they got on the subject of not fitting in. When Claire said that it seemed like most people had a sibling here, Ian reassured her.

"Well, I don't! At least, not anymore … er I mean, he's gone. But don't worry about those families. Not everyone comes here with their … um, siblings.." He paused for a moment. "Anyway, Liz will explain that kinda stuff later. But not to worry -- we're all outsiders here." He grinned.

Claire thought of Gunther, who was now in college. She couldn't believe it. She felt so distant from him. So distant from everyone. She knew her brother would never come to a place like this. A sense of shame overcame her– he was probably mad that she hadn't come to see Gran when she was ill. She had every intention of visiting.

"Also …," Ian continued. "I'm from Florida! Like you."

He grinned when she showed her surprise.

Ian began telling Claire how he found the retreat center, and how it completely changed his outlook on life.

"There's this online community, and I found the forum when I was at this really low point. I didn't know where to go -- and suddenly it was like, oh my god these people are just like me."

Claire nodded as though she understood, but the phrase "just like me," seemed even more confusing now. How were these people like one another? Was there something wrong with them? And what did it have to do with her?

Apparently, it was a common thing among this crowd–difficulty transitioning to adulthood, explained Ian. As he spoke, his dark eyes sparkled, and Claire thought he looked like someone she knew. But she couldn't quite place it.

"A lot of attempted suicides," he whispered. "But anyway, that's why we're here. For healing … I guess." He shrugged.

"But what exactly is the program? Do you know Richard? I need to find Richard …."

Ian frowned. "The Healer? Oh you won't meet him until you've done The Remembering Sessions."

Before she got a chance to ask him about the Remembering Sessions, Liz called the meeting to order.

"Let's take this outside," she announced. "Everyone grab a mat and we'll meet on the lawn."

Outside, rows of garden lights were strung across a manicured yard, the only grass on the property. Everything else was rocks and trees and the natural shrubbery that grew along the river. The moon was full, and the crickets buzzed hypnotically.

Claire felt at home for the first time in a long time. And yet everything was so exotic. The incense was thick, the mountains were different here, and even Liz seemed exotic in her own maternal way. How could something so different feel so much like home?

A man with a long, grey beard -- about Liz's age -- stood at the front of the group. He cleared his throat and everyone became silent. He knelt down on his mat and sat on his knees; everyone followed suit. They all paced their hands flat on the earth, on the grass on either side of their mats. Claire copied them. A familiar energy began to thrum through her body.

She wanted to close her eyes, but the man said, "keep your gaze on me, everyone. Follow my voice and stay connected to me and Liz. I know it's tempting, but do not close your eyes." He was looking directly at Claire and smiling.

Claire felt quiet and content, if just for a moment.

"As you all know," the man began, "The Healer brought each of you here for a reason. He chose you. He knew you needed community. That you need each other. But mostly you need a resolution. You need a choice. You need a merciful higher power … and you will find one here. I promise."

Claire pulled her hands off the ground and folded her arms. So Richard brought all of these people here? He chose all of them? She thought her connection to him was special.

The therapist had warned that this retreat looked a little questionable. Maybe she even said "cultish," but Claire had not listened. She'd tried to steer Claire to something more mainstream in Asheville. Maybe she'd been right.

"I know that many of you have endured great suffering; you're looking for an answer. And some of you have probably heard that others like you have died or ended their own lives."

A girl behind her let out a little sob. The twins beside her held onto each other.

"And I'm sure you feel, as I do, that it wasn't right–what your creators did. They didn't do right by you." He was silent for several beats, and then almost shouted, "But you are not alone!"

"We are not alone," the entire group chanted in response.

He nodded and opened his eyes. Liz handed him an open book and he began to read: "Creature consciousness is a network, a giant sphere of threads with signals that reach into each of our bodies."

He stopped and looked around, making direct eye contact with Claire.

She shifted her gaze downward and he continued: "In order to conceive of this with the human mind, we must pretend that the souls are separate. But all spiritual energy is one. And all of life has a connection to that giant network–the planet of consciousness. That's why we feel empathy. That's why even when we see a rat suffering, we suffer a little too. It is because we are never alone."

"We are never alone," repeated the group.

"That's right," he said. "No rat is alone, no flower is alone, no human is alone."

Everyone nodded, and some raised their hands to the sky, like the man was doing now.

Claire closed her eyes. Now she was scared. Were they going to perform a ritual? A sacrifice?

Liz must have sensed her distress. She moved close to Claire and touched her back. "It's okay," she mouthed. "That's Joesph. He's a little dramatic–he's our resident intellectual." She smiled and patted Claire on the shoulder. "It's almost over."

Claire wanted to get up and leave, but then the man continued reading, and this time the words were familiar: "Do not try to be a flower if you are a tree. Instead, be the best tree in the forest."

She relaxed a little. She placed her hands on the ground again, and nodded to Liz.

"Life is beautiful, but death -- death is extraordinary! It means we are free to swim around in the infinite ball of creature consciousness. We are allowed to go back to the origin, something we cannot fathom. Once we are welcomed back into the chamber of our making, the egg from which we came, and protected forever, then we will never be alone."

"Never alone," everyone said, and they all bowed their heads all the way to their mats, and everyone kissed the ground in tandem.

The Book of Instructions. Claire remembered the hours she spent alone in her bedroom in high school reading the book Richard gave her, poring over the words. They had spoken to her, saved her even.

Afterward, Liz told Claire, "I know it seems a little wacky, Claire …. But it's nothing new to you. You understand this in your bones."

"I just want to know what's wrong with me–specifically. I want to speak with Richard. That's why I came here."

"What's wrong with you, Claire, is what ails everyone else. I promise you. Just give it a few days."

That night, Claire slept better than she had in years. The rushing sounds of the river outside the cabin window seemed to wash away all of her fears and anxieties. The words of the evening, both the strange ones and the familiar, sprinkled down on her mind and seemed to settle like a puddle after a storm.

CHAPTER 46: A RIGHTEOUS DEATH

Claire

Training Tower

Claire felt a little ache in her heart for this strange crew of bodies.

She thought of claire.0 and felt a longing to see her. There was a bond there, if a tenuous one. After seeing these creatures, Claire wondered what would happen to claire.0 if she died. And if something happened to claire.0, what would happen to her?

She remembered hearing stories about the other hybrids dying not long after they were created. Some, right there in the labs of the Training Tower.

Then she remembered how the twins she encountered on her escape would have killed her. She knew they would have ... if it came to it.

The *Book of Instructions* was open across Claire's lap as she read, and the hybrids mimicked as though young children who were pretending to read.

She could see the plan in her mind: cross over to the other side into a death-like state, lead the hybrids to rest, and then return to life. Simple. She knew she could do it. She would follow the chapter titled "Death Meditation" for exploring the afterlife. Richard had said it could be very dangerous for inexperienced meditators, but she had to at least try it.

Claire took one last look at her doppelgangers. Their strange mouths yawned for her, their unseeing eyes searched for her, their long fingers reached for her.

The *Book of Instructions* guided her into that first phase, the loss of breath.

Then she put the book aside and laid down. So did the hybrids.

Her breathing slowed to a halt. After each exhale, there were longer increments of time before the next inhale. First it was 30 seconds, then 90 seconds, then two minutes, until she had reached three whole minutes and her heart almost stopped.

To reach the point of slumber-death, she summoned that solid tranquility that came with knowing her own immortality, an acceptance that no matter what happened to her, one day she would thrive again as a leaf or a snail or snowflake. That's what the book had said at least. And now, somehow, it was not something she only knew intellectually or spiritually, but something expressed at the deepest level of her atomic makeup. She surrendered to it, and invited the hybrids to join her.

They were all one thing now, one brain, one body. They were not separate. Claire could feel each one of them, not just an indistinguishable mass. Claire was relieved to "see" that there was no trace of claire.0 in them. She had been worried that since she was also a hybrid, claire.0 may be affected, but these bodies were different. They were highly dependent on Claire still; claire.0 had been on her own for years.

Now, Claire just had to worry about her own mental strength. She knew that if she were going to survive, she needed to maintain a separate lifeline. This is where Richard came in. His words from the book would keep her connected to the living world.

She stayed in the deepest level of sleep while also murmuring the words, the ones she had memorized:

"... human consciousness is a network, a giant spherical web, and each of our living bodies has a unique connection to it– a special signal. In order to conceive of this with the human mind, we must create an image. So let's consider this divine network as an enormous sphere, a trillion-faceted ball of soul."

She felt the pull of the hybrids, their will to keep her with them. But their will to survive was weak. They were drawn by a deep desire to return to the earth. This was fine, just as long as they didn't bring her with them.

She remembered:

"... once we are welcomed back into the chamber of our making, the egg from which we came, and protected forever, then we will be free."

Now she began to falter. There was a searing pain in her side. And then the other side. It was as though she were going to be split in half. She felt something growing inside of her, and then dying, and then sliding away. It felt like severe cramping, but all over her body.

She cried out, and reached for the book, as though it held a magic spell.

She opened her eyes and read to herself in a whisper:

"Each present moment in front of you is a very sacred thing. It took billions of years to get all of this to happen just like this. Surrender to it, embrace it, accept it for exactly what it is– not something you created or are responsible for. Always accept reality. Change it or don't change it, but never resist it."

Claire relaxed again into the moment–the living moment–taking it second by second. Time crawled to a stop. She exhaled and stayed that way for more than three minutes. She remained breathless long enough to tuck the creatures in and say a prayer over them. This is how she visualized it, at least. She did not actually move for a long time.

She stayed with them until the very last moment, when she could no longer hold her breath.

Suddenly she knew they were gone, they were not coming back to life. But it was hard to inhale, so hard to let go. Not only of the hybrids, but of that promise of death. It was like a strong tide, pulling her out.

"Claire, come back! You don't have to go with them. They are gone." It was the voice of a girl, a far away female voice. Was it her mother? Or could it be claire.0?

They were dying, but she could live.

Claire felt a sense of peace settling over the cold, cavernous room. There was a sudden giving-in to death. A final exhale. She needed to go with them.

CHAPTER 47: IMMORTALITY

Claire

It was a long and winding death, and it felt more real than waking life.

She was able to peer through space into another reality, another place, or another time. But in this vision, she wasn't looking into the world of the hybrid back home. Instead, she was deep beneath the earth, tangled in the webs of roots and fungus and dead things, as though she herself had died and her body dissolved into soil.

It was 100 years in the future. Her human body had died and was decaying, but somehow, she was still conscious of being alive. But, if so, what was she? Dirt? Air? A ghost? Was she still in the SubRez dungeon where Dr. Mary had left her?

Whatever had happened mattered less and less over time, because this new state of aliveness felt like ecstasy– eternal, undisturbed bliss. She witnessed her decaying body feed the roots of a new plant, become an integral part of the cellular structure, and grow with the plant from seed to small tree. All the way up, she traveled through the veins of trunk and leaves, feeling what it means to be a plant, what the afterlife really is.

It's just more life. Forever.

The energy from her decayed body continued reaching into the tallest branches as the tree grew older, all the way to the newest, tenderest leaf, and she could feel the beams of sun filter through that small green face.

She felt herself, whatever self that was infused into the tree, smiling. Photosynthesis was her life's purpose. She realized it was all one and the same: joy and biological growth.

There was life again after human life, after being buried deep in darkness. After the cruelty of apes and sapiens. And there was such peace in knowing exactly what death was: simply the commingling of your body with the soil and other dead things that will all be alive again soon.

She realized that she would never die. Now she knew with every fiber of her being that everyone and everything is immortal.

She'd never felt such peace.

Of course it was a dream, right? Afterward she would think of it as a movie that lasted for dozens of years, a film filtered through fungal life directly into her bloodstream and consciousness.

CHAPTER 48: WAKING UP

Claire

Time is funny when you're not awake. It hadn't been a century after all. When Claire woke up, she was once again immersed in real human fear and pain. She was no longer a tree. The peace turned to panic, as she looked around at the bodies, now completely overgrown into one mass, curled around her like a giant housecat.

Her limbs couldn't move; they were being held by mycelial threads. It took all the energy she had simply to open her eyes.

She gasped and gulped a breath in. It felt like she hadn't used her lungs in hours. But she was very much alive, she thought as she examined her arms and legs. Her heart must have stopped for a moment but she was alive!

She felt something else holding her as well, something pulling her from behind. And then there was a voice: "She's okay … she's okay. Loosen your grip, Malik … give her room to breathe."

The next thing she knew, she was lying in a bed. It was a metal coffin-like thing, and she wondered for a moment if she was back where she started with Dr. Mary in that horrible hospital room in the Tower. Or maybe she *did* die, and this was some awful zombification ritual. She thought of Cordyceps, the zombie mushroom.

"She's awake!" someone shouted. A familiar voice, but the face was hazy as her eyes adjusted.

And then he said, "Whoa whoa whoa. Not so fast, kiddo. Be careful."

It was the Healer.

Richard! Claire's head began to spin. She was relieved to see a human after all this time, even if she didn't know if he was to be trusted.

There was a large window in the room. The sunlight pierced her eyes as though she really had been underground for 100 years.

"I'm not … dead?" she croaked. It was so soft, Richard didn't hear. His back was turned. There was someone else in the room. Claire felt panic rising in her throat; her stomach churned. She was going to throw up.

"Richard …," she managed. "Help …." It was all she could get out. She really did need help. Her body was not responding to her.

He spun around and came to her side. He had a syringe.

She conjured the energy to sit up and back away from him. "No, no, no …."

He put down the syringe. "Claire, calm down. This is only for the nausea. It's okay. I don't have to give it to you … let me explain …." He held up his empty hands.

"Dr. Mary … where's Dr. Mary? She wants to kill me. They're trying to kill me. They had an army … of, er." She stopped, realizing she didn't know who else was in earshot.

But as she looked around, it became clear there was no Dr. Mary, there were no guards, and the door was wide open. Now was her chance. She didn't care what Richard thought or whose side he was on. *She had to get out.* Now.

"Claire, please. Calm down." Another familiar voice–kind of… Claire racked her bleary brain. The voice was authoritative and strong, but her memory of it was a child's.

And then, there he was–Malik -- or someone like Malik. Did they make a clone of him too?

The nausea returned but she held it back. She didn't want to give them any reason to stick her with anything. She was beginning to realize it was not the next morning after all. It was almost as though she'd woken up in a parallel universe. Some time had passed.

"Malik ...?"

After confronting two clones of herself, it seemed that anything was possible. And after that experience of being a plant consciousness, it was possible that this was the dream and that *was* reality. Were Richard and Malik really here? This Malik was certainly taller ... and older. Even Richard looked slightly altered, but she couldn't put her finger on it.

With some help, she managed to push her legs over the side of the bed. She held her face in her hands. Was she also older? Fear ignited for a moment, but her face felt the same as ever.

"Claire, it's me ... yes. Listen, there's something you should know...."

"Where am I?" she addressed Richard instead. She still didn't believe it was really Malik. He was too different.

"Don't worry -- Malik and I are working together," he touched her shoulder. "He's been doing this for months ... uh, there's a lot to explain."

"What? Months ...? What do you mean 'working with Malik'? On a project? I don't understand. Where are we?"

"Hey, hey, just calm down a minute, 'k?" Richard took a deep breath, which had a slight calming effect on Claire. "We're at the same place, just a different room than where you, er, fell asleep. No one's going to hurt you. You've had quite a bad time of it. You've been out of it for longer than you can imagine."

Richard had no idea what she could imagine.

"Claire, they shut them down. There was a rescue mission here. They shut down SubRez. A whole group of parents, from around the world, had been looking for their kids. There was an FBI raid. But it's been a long time. I'm so sorry...I'm sorry I couldn't get to you sooner. No one knew where you were, and Dr. Mary got out before the raid ...." Malik trailed off and tried to take Claire's hand, but she pulled it away.

His voice was deeper. And he'd definitely grown.

"No," she shook her head. She finally got her feet under her, and both Malik and Richard sidled up next to her for support. She brushed them off, feeling the full weight of her body. Some memories of the dream floated around her brain, and she swayed, tree-like.

"How long?" she finally managed. She looked into their faces and then demanded, *"How long?"*

"Claire, we haven't seen each other in almost 18 months," Malik finally blurted. "You've been fed and supported by something down there -- the fungus; it's been taking care of you for a long time."

Claire looked down at her body, feeling a rush of embarrassment. She must stink. She gave a sigh of relief that, from what she could see, she was relatively clean-looking. A year and a half was a long time and she couldn't imagine how she had been living in this body for all that time. It felt as though she had become something else.

Richard said, "We thought you were dead, Claire. After they came, no one found your body. But Malik, he stuck with it ... he knew you were here somewhere. I don't know how, but you survived down there; looks like you've been in union with the mycelium."

"In union?" Claire inquired.

Malik nodded, reminding Claire that they had learned about this in a class. Some mushroom systems can take over a host for weeks, or even months, and then return the creature to its previous state. It's a very rare occurrence that the host survives, but when it does, it seems to have new capabilities. And it doesn't appear to have an awareness of being a host.

Of course, that type of thing had never been tested on humans. Until now.

CHAPTER 49: THE REMEMBERING

The Hybrid

The Temple Retreat

Over the next several days, Claire would learn what it meant to be part of this group, but it wasn't until her Remembering Sessions that she would really understand. That's what everyone told her, at least.

The retreat participants referred to themselves as "Twins" or "Listeners," but it wasn't apparent why. It seemed they were all speaking in code.

Apparently, it would all make sense after her first session. Ian said that sometimes one was all you needed...one session to remember everything.

She imagined the "Sessions" to be in a sterile room hooked up to a machine and guided by the bearded man. But Liz told her it would take place outdoors, in a field, and "and us old folks can't come with you!"

Liz made a clear distinction between the older staff members and the youth, and she told Claire to talk to Ian about it.

He explained, "It's not because we're young– but because we have a short shelf life. An expiration date. Or at least some of us do. You will see. You'll understand why you've been depressed … or ya know, troubled … I think."

This intrigued Claire more than frightened her. She just

wanted to feel better, but she didn't like the idea of a "short shelf life."

They hiked for an hour to get to the spot, she and two of the "Listeners," women in their mid-twenties. They were experienced hikers and knew the area well.

"This is called a bald," one of them explained, when they finally stopped. "It's a large clearing on a mountain."

The other pointed into the distance. "Way over in that direction you can pick up the Appalachian Trail," she said.

Claire thought of her mother. She had always wanted to hike the Appalachian Trail. She was surprised to feel such deep grief at the memory of her. Maybe she'd just never processed the whole thing, like her therapist had said. She'd always felt a little removed from it, as though it happened to someone else. But lately she seemed to be directly in touch with her emotions. It was overwhelming sometimes.

The grass was a bright shade of summer green and the field was dotted around the edges with snow-white mushrooms. There was a cool breeze as they sat in a circle, touching each other's fingertips with their palms down to the ground.

One girl spoke a few words of encouragement -- "root into the earth, imagine strong threads growing from your fingertips, etc." -- but not much needed to be said. Claire felt it all.

A great wave of knowing overcame her, as the other girls held her steady. She knew what she was, where she came from, why she felt so different. She remembered the original Claire, and the island, and Lana, her first mother, and slowly came to realize that she wasn't Claire after all. Just as she had suspected.

She began to weep with relief. A huge weight was lifted. Now it was clear why she felt so much pain, why she sometimes could not pull herself out of bed, why she just wished people would leave her alone.

Sometimes she wanted to curl up in a ball on the ground and disappear into the earth. It was one of her strongest urges. How could she have explained this to anyone before? Her odd cravings for eating dirt and the longing to lean against tree trunks, just to sit there and doze. She had never been fully human in the first place. The voices in her head now made sense. The dreams about being someone else were not dreams at all. Claire -- the real Claire -- had been trying to communicate with her. Apparently, all of the "Listeners" here also had some sort of telepathic connection with their "Originals."

She often thought about death -- maybe too often -- and how restful it would be, but there was deep shame about it, and so she had tucked it away, far beneath her consciousness. But now it came rushing in and took up space.

This is what Ian meant: among the awakened hybrids–the Listeners -- there was a rational urge to go back into the earth, an instinct to eat life, to take part in the decaying process, like a fungal system.

They all knew they were not supposed to be there, one of the girls was saying when Claire came out of her trance. The design had been faulty. Many of the hybrids simply expired without warning. They lived short, painful lives with the fear of dropping dead at any point.

"This is why we are gathered, Claire -- to take control of our own expiration, and to not do the dirty work of SubRez anymore. We will funnel ourselves back into the natural world so that SubRez's dreams to build a hybrid army out of us will be completely destroyed."

When she opened her eyes, the girls were staring at her, waiting for her questions, ready to dispel her doubts, but Claire had no questions. It all made sense now. In fact, now that she knew the truth, she felt like it had always been there, just beneath the surface; she always knew.

"That's why it's called Remembering Sessions," said the talkative girl on the way back. "We all *know*; we just can't face the truth on our own. That spot we went to, it's a sacred place for us. There are so many fungal networks beneath the surface, and it's one of those places on the planet that's in perfect alignment for this kind of thing."

Claire nodded. Yes, it felt safe here.

"Just be aware," said the other girl, grabbing Claire's hand. "As you go about your daily life, you may start forgetting again– because this stuff is scary and your subconscious will want to shield you from it. That's why you're here. We're all in this together. And if you want to, ya' know ... *return to the earth* ... like most of us do after The Remembering ...." She trailed off. And then added, "Just know, we can help you."

"But no one will make you," added the first girl.

"So, did Richard create this place to gather us up or something?" Claire was putting the puzzle pieces together in her head. "I mean, is he a hybrid?"

"The Healer is not a hybrid. He's an ally of ours– from the inside. He's been working for SubRez for many years, but only to fulfill his mission– to liberate us."

"To help us die ...." Claire replied.

"To help us be reborn, into something more natural."

Claire looked at the girl sideways. She fully understood now, deep in her bones, what most of these people wanted. And she realized now why they spoke in code before. The uninitiated would not understand. The Amnesiacs, as they were called. They might report this place to the government and get this place shut down. Or worse, take the Listeners into custody.

But *organized suicide*? That's what they were aiming for?

"What about SubRez?" Claire asked. "This isn't a branch of SubRez?"

The first girl gave her head a vehement shake. "They have no idea we are here. And this is so important, Claire. No matter what you decide to do, you can never reveal our info to anyone. No one knows what goes on here. They just assume it's some sort of hippie retreat. We need to keep it that way."

"What do you mean, no matter what I decide to do? Do I have to decide soon? Has it already been planned?"

"Yes, we are gathering as many hybrids–I mean Listeners–as possible, and we are going to all go together. That's the plan."

"That's Richard's plan?" Claire already began to doubt what she had just "remembered."

"That's *our* plan. We *choose* to do it. Richard just brought us here so we would know, so that we weren't lost sheep anymore. Even if you decide to go back, ya know, out there. At least you'll know what you are."

The other girl, who had been mostly quiet, interjected: "You just need to accept that the Remembering will probably fade, and you'll become one of them again. It's a merciful amnesia. But you'll probably end up just as miserable as you once were. And you won't know why. I've left twice already, but I'm back. For good." She folded her arms in a solemn gesture.

Claire thought about all those years Richard tried to stay in touch with her. He probably gave up on her. Now the urgency to talk to him had left her. She had most of the missing pieces in front of her.

Now she just had to decide what to do.

***

Claire stayed on for several weeks and fell into the routine of the community. Every once in a while, they would get a new person, and she would help with the initiation. Every once in a while, someone would leave. And every once in a while, someone would take her own life. It was just part of their reality. It was too much for some people.

"Some hybrids just can't take it," said Ian to Claire one day. "The idea that we're going to do this all together, sometime in the near future. It's too much. Sometimes, they are too human. That's what happened to my brother."

His identical twin had been found in the shed, the signature veiny marbling of poisoning mottled his skin. There was a poison they could take—everyone knew where it was. It was not encouraged, but it was a way to prevent a more horrific and problematic suicide.

Claire sat with Ian on the riverbank that day as he spoke about it. It was sunny and warm, and they had removed their shoes to wade in the cold mountain water. They touched toes now, and Claire could feel what he felt. His eyes welled with tears but she could feel that his spirit was calm.

Claire did "The Remembering" every day, a silent meditation in which she contemplated her past, her creation, and the absurdity of this life. Her mantra was: "I relinquish power, I release life."

Once, she witnessed a ceremonial death. A Listener had been showing signs of "extinction," and they knew he didn't have much time. So instead of suffering over it and trying to extend his life, the group made it into a day-long vigil, in which everyone sat with the man, whose name was Daniel. He went quietly and peacefully.

"Death is an exquisite and merciful thing, no matter what kind of creature you are," Joseph read from *The Book of Instructions*.

Claire wept at the truth of these words now. She'd read them many times before but as she watched the great pain that this man endured early in the day, and the gentle death he succumbed to in the evening, she understood the concept of heaven, the great euphoria of finally relaxing into the earth, that bit of consciousness being sent out of your body and returning to the greater whole. Your feeling of separateness is relieved forever.

He continued to read:

> *"The uncomfortable things can help us wake from our obliviousness. All difficulties can be transformed into a new path of enlightenment. In order to live, we must eat the dead sometimes. The charnal grounds are not just graveyards, but also fields of redemption."*

She compared it to a live birth she had once witnessed as a hospital aid in a program from high school. Some mothers volunteered to allow the girls to help the midwives. It was supposed to be a powerful life lesson, witnessing a birth, helping with a newborn. And it was.

But all Claire could think now is how peaceful birth started–the quiet embryo, the sweet pregnancy–and how violent and painful it became once the baby was ready to come out. The opposite was true with death. So much pain at the beginning, and so much peace at the end.

"Death is a merciful god," everyone chanted in response to Joseph's readings.

Claire remained convinced the mass suicide was a noble thing to do, and she became increasingly aware of the danger that SubRez posed. If their camp was found, what would happen to all of them?

But in the meantime, she was also reconnecting with Gran who was sick once again, succumbing to the cancer that was much more aggressive than she initially admitted. Claire began to call home every day. Mack didn't know about their talks because Claire had sworn Gran to secrecy. She told Gran she wanted to come visit but she was not allowed to leave the "rehab facility."

Gran said she was just happy she was getting help. And something surprising was happening to Claire: she was repairing the bond with Gran, and she suddenly longed to see Gunther, and she grieved the loss of her mother. It all felt real. Was she forgetting? Would she just become another Amnesiac again?

In truth, Claire could leave if she wanted, but she first needed to decide what she would do. They didn't want people coming and going anymore. It was getting too close to The Returning date. This is why she stayed so long. She knew exactly who and what she was. This was her community–these were her brethren in life and in death. The Remembering had made her whole again. She needed to stay and remember.

And at the very same time she was beginning to feel more like the "real Claire" than ever before.

CHAPTER 50: REMEMBER, RECLAIM, RETURN

The Hybrid

One afternoon she and Liz went for a hike, just the two of them. They began by crossing the river right behind the main cabin, where the water was shallow and there were plenty of flat boulders to serve as a bridge.

Claire had something important to tell Liz.

As they made their ascent on the opposite riverbank, they could still hear the chanting of the others. They were in a meditation session on the lawn. It was a special kind of meditation designed to prepare them for The Returning ceremony. Returning to the earth. They chanted, "We remember. We reclaim. We return. We are not alone." The gravity of such an act was beginning to weigh on Claire. But this morning she had made her decision.

"I wanted to tell you first because…well, I'm not sure how the others are going to react. They seem so sure of themselves. And the thing is … I'm not sure. So I've decided I'm not going to do it. I'll take a chance and see … how long I, ya know, last."

She knew Liz would be happy. The non-hybrids were careful not to persuade them one way or the other, but Liz had built her life around the hybrids. Of course she wanted them to stay; some had been here for five or six years. But it seemed that as they gained momentum in the urge to deconstruct, they gained followers. No one wanted to be left behind.

But Claire was beginning to feel different, more alive. Or perhaps just not so scared about the uncertainty of death.

"That's wonderful, Claire. I'm sure it wasn't an easy decision. I'm thrilled you'll be staying."

Staying. That was an interesting way to put it. Not dying.

"My Gran–she needs me. We've begun talking a lot lately ... and her cancer, you know, it came back. And Gunther, well, I have so much to explain to him. Maybe he needs me too. I could even patch things up with Ken. Maybe–I've been a terrible person. I know I can do better -- now that I know what's 'wrong' with me."

Liz shook her head. "You've been trying your best. You weren't a bad person."

They were walking up a steep incline, and Claire was out of breath from trying to talk and hike at the same time.

Something rustled in the trees. Claire stared into the thicket and then froze.

"Oh ...." she whispered. "An elk."

A majestic beast stood not ten feet from them, rubbing his six-point rack on the trunk of an old pine. Farther off, two females and a calf stood frozen for a moment, staring back at the humans. One of them bleated, and the bull came to attention.

"They sometimes charge!" whispered Liz, grabbing Claire's arm and crouching low. But all four elk turned away and trotted up into the wooded hillside.

Both women stood in awe until the elk were no longer visible.

"This place is so amazing," said Claire. "I can't believe you've lived here your whole life."

"Yep ... and as far as I know, my family hasn't moved from this area for a thousand years. Imagine that! We've been hanging out with these same deer and boar and elk all this time. Same plants. Same mushrooms."

"Wow, talk about really belonging somewhere."

They trudged upwards in silence for a while, saving their breath for the climb.

When the path flattened out, Claire said, "You know, when I still thought I was actually Claire, I had some sense of belonging like that … being from that place in Florida… Nothing like yours though. I mean my dad's family, they've lived there a little while. But only like three generations. But my mom -- well who knows? She was from California but I never knew her dad, and only met her mom once. Anyway, I guess it doesn't really matter now. I'm not really from anywhere."

"That's not true," said Liz. "You belong here! You belong to your family. You belong to …."

"I know -- 'I belong to the earth.' I'm just saying it's different."

Liz didn't say anything, but she smiled with genuine empathy. She had stopped to rest and was perched on a small outcropping of a boulder. Claire stood and gazed over the vista, a blue and white marbly sky and a massive green valley below. Churches and cabins dotted the landscape. Hazy clouds settled into the nooks and crannies of the mountains in the distance, the eponymous "smoke" of the Great Smoky Mountains.

Claire shielded her eyes from the sun and said, "Don't get me wrong, I'm okay with all of it. I think I've accepted it, and more importantly I know Claire may never come back. So, I do think there's room for me, there's a place for me."

The last they had heard from Richard, Claire was still missing. He believed they locked her up and were using her to grow more hybrids. But since there'd been a raid on the Training Tower, Richard didn't have much hope. She was likely dead.

Liz shook her head when she spoke to Claire about it. "I don't think there's much hope of them finding her ... and if they do, she certainly won't be the same."

When they returned that evening Claire told Ian, and her roommate, Chelsey. She would not be joining them for The Returning.

They were both supportive. Ian said he admired her courage.

Chelsey said, "I think it's right ... for you. You have a lot more to live for. Most of us -- we're just these duplicates. There's literally no purpose for me."

Claire felt sad for them. She wanted to tell Chelsey she could create a purpose, but it was against house rules to dissuade or persuade another hybrid on this topic. And she knew it would fall on deaf ears anyway. At this point almost everyone was united.

She could only decide for herself. And now she knew-- she needed to be the granddaughter she'd never been, the sister, and make something of whatever future she might have. She would be the Good Claire now. Perhaps the original reason she was created was borne of selfish desires and reckless acts, but now that she was here, she had a job to do. There were people who needed her.

CHAPTER 51: WARPED TIME

Claire

Training Tower

Unbraiding her thick rope of hair, she realized now that it had grown down to her waist–much longer than ever before. In the mirror, she could see it was a shade darker and her skin several shades paler. Without sun, the blonde was more grey in tone than yellow, against pale skin. She hardly recognized herself. And she was older now.

Only hours before, she'd been 18, just a teenager. Or so it seemed. Now she was almost 20.

But as the days wore on, she began to feel the weight of all the months she missed. Memory-dreams came to her every now and then, and she realized that she had been partly conscious sometimes. She also realized that weeks had already passed when she was in the cell, and the dying of the hybrids probably took much longer than it seemed. By the time she fell asleep with them, she had already been underground for months. She could only speculate.

But doubts about the true passage of time began to creep into her thinking. Malik said there were no phone lines, and all means of communication had been cut when the authorities came in, so how could she confirm that what they said was true? Mostly she just wanted to call home, to talk to Gran and Gunther, to tell them what had happened, even though they wouldn't know her; they only knew the other Claire now.

She would simply have to trust Malik and Richard. At the very least, she knew Dr. Mary and Lev were gone, and all of those horrible guards. No one was going to kill her.

But as Richard continued to remind her, she was still in a lot of danger. They were all in danger. And the rescue mission had not eradicated SubRez; they had simply pushed them farther underground … somewhere else.

"They know you're still alive," Malik told her. "I'm just glad we got to you first."

"How long can we stay here?" Claire asked.

"Not long," said Richard. "We don't know when they'll come back, so we need to leave as soon as you feel strong enough. We have a safe place to go."

***

The next day, Malik filled her in on the time she missed, one small bit at a time. They walked the length of the campus very slowly, back and forth, so that Claire could regain strength in her legs. Malik talked and talked, and Claire listened and focused on putting one foot in front of the other, which was so painful at first that she would grunt and huff for much of the walk.

Malik began by explaining why the Tower had been abandoned in the first place.

A few rogue SubRez agents had recently been targeted for child trafficking, and it was a federal agency that traced them back to the North Carolina Tower headquarters. This had been the first chink in the security of the Training Tower.

On top of that, some hybrids began rebelling and escaping, and a few had even gone to the authorities. They were trickling out into the world, some by design. Others ran away. In the outside world, they banded together, using the internet to find one another again. Apparently, this had been happening for years, much longer than Claire even knew they had hybrids. Richard was becoming instrumental in these reunions, and he had recruited Malik to help in the mission.

The raid happened a few months before, and in that time, everyone evacuated, leaving behind dozens of projects and unfinished experiments buried deep in the belly of the old building.

"I guess they assumed none of us would return to find you … to see what else was going on here."

After all, who among the defectors would want to return to the facility, much less break into the top-secret labs? What they had not taken into account is Malik's savvy in cybersecurity or the sophisticated operation Richard had been building to support the liberation of hybrids and other victims of SubRez.

Richard had never forgiven himself for sending Claire away when she needed someone the most. In fact, her disappearance is what led Richard to finally leave SubRez after decades of service. He had already begun developing an internet-based relocation system for the hybrids.

"Wow," replied Claire. "And what about you? Why are you still here?"

His eyes sparkled a little, and he said, "I tipped off the FBI." He seemed impressed with himself as he explained what he had been doing.

Malik was considered a big success at The Tower. He graduated and was supposed to return home to Florida to work at the university and establish a sleeper cell there. But the moment he arrived home he removed the tracking device that they surgically implanted in his spine. He left the tracker in an apartment there and set out for D.C. to meet Richard.

"Whoa," said Claire and covered her mouth. Now she was impressed too.

"That's another thing I'm trying to do while we're here," explained Malik. "Completely dismantle their tracking system."

"Do I ...?" Claire began, feeling panic run through her bloodstream, and running her fingers along the top of her spine.

"No tracker on you, as far as we can tell. I guess they started doing that after your escape. And they assumed you wouldn't need one while they had you ... er, down there."

Every question Claire asked led to more questions. But the one thing that nagged at her the most was almost too hard to speak aloud. She was afraid of what the answer might be.

But she said it anyway: "Malik, are you the real Malik ... or are you ...?"

Claire watched his long brown fingers sweep across his eyes. They were tapered, like a woman's. His whole body was like that, long and graceful. He wore it well. He didn't seem a bit self-conscious of his feminine aesthetic.

She observed him carefully. His enormous eyes were deep and dark like always. No strange glint. But how could she tell for sure? Would he even tell the truth? And how would he even know himself?

They were back inside so that Malik could continue working. As they spoke, Malik had been trying to reverse engineer some customized software to unearth SubRez's security secrets. He was hunched over the computer screen.

Now, he sat up and faced her.

"I'm not a hybrid, Claire. It's me, I promise."

"But you're different."

"I'm 18! I was a scared little kid when you first met me. I know what's what. And I grew three inches. And ...."

He looked around mischievously.

"... And I've had a, you know, relationship." He almost giggled.

"Oh!" This bit surprised Claire, but felt reassuring. It *was* Malik. He had that same shy ducking gesture that he made when he was self-conscious.

"It's me!" He pounded his chest. "It's just that I'm a man now!"

They both laughed, and it felt good.

One thing she couldn't shake is the never-ending dream experience of dying and coming back to life. It was so clear and unmuddled, but it couldn't have really happened. Could it? It seemed anything was possible at this point.

When she tried explaining it to Richard the next day, he calmly told her, "Claire, it sounds like you've had a spiritual vision. You were connected to something beyond yourself .... Er .... It's extraordinary, but it was still in your mind ... not that much time has passed, obviously."

He noticed her doubtful expression and said, "I'm serious. Your spirit was not only protecting you through all of that trauma but elevating your being to another level. It's probably why you survived as well as you did."

She had to admit, it did feel sacred, even just the memory of it. She tried to explain this strange "memory" to Malik too. She needed to know what happened. Had she been dissolved and resurrected? Was she even the original Claire?

"Why do I feel like I remember it?"

Malik shrugged and said, "I can't even pretend to understand where your consciousness was at that point...under those conditions. Who knows?"

"Malik, it was amazing: it gave me such peace, to know exactly what death is, what will come in the 'afterlife.' And I think somewhere along the way, I also communicated with the hybrid ...."

She stopped suddenly because she knew that part had to be real. She saw claire.0 in new locations. Not home. It happened multiple times: once she was in a dorm room, and another time in the woods somewhere, but not the woods near Candlestick Lane.

"Wait, Malik. Where's Richard?"

"He's outside I think, trying to get a truck ready for us."

She turned and left abruptly.

"I have to tell Richard."

Outside she spotted him at the old barn, and broke into a run across the field. It felt good to move so spontaneously.

"She heard me, Richard," Claire said, breathless now. It had been a long time since she moved so fast. "I don't know how, but I spoke to her. I asked her to help me. I don't know how it happened."

"Extraordinary." Richard's face lit up in response, and Claire could see his breath in the cold morning air.

"It's frightening. It doesn't make sense. It was probably all in my head too."

"No, no, Claire," he said quickly. "I believe she could hear you. In her head. Don't you remember when you broke through to her that day when we meditated in the grass?"

"Of course. How could I forget? But I didn't say anything that time. I had no idea that I could."

"And I'm sure Dr. Mary didn't want you to find out," Richard said. "But somehow your subconscious mind figured it out. It's absolutely incredible."

Claire touched Richard's arm. He looked at her. "She didn't seem to be doing well, Richard. The hybrid. What do you know about her? And what about Gunther?" She searched his expression.

He looked at his hands. "She's okay ... for now. And as far as I know Gunther is doing great. But claire.0 has always struggled ... I have tried to reach out to help, but there's only so much that a stranger can interfere ... without raising alarms. You can imagine."

Then he grabbed her hand and said, "You should go to Gunther yourself. He needs to see you, to hear all of this -- directly from you."

Claire nodded and tears streamed down her cheeks, relieved that someone understood, someone knew the truth and was helping her. Then they were both quiet for a long time. She wanted to know more, but she was already overwhelmed with coming "back to life," simply getting traction in her own mind. It was too much to begin thinking about others. What about her own reality?

Claire broke the silence and said, "Richard ...?"

He raised an eyebrow.

"How do I even know if I am me? The real me."

He put his hands over hers. "You are you," he said. "I think you know that in your bones."

"Yeah, I think so. Yes, I know."

Richard folded his neat, little hands. They appeared more weathered and veiny than Claire remembered.

They could see Malik appear near the far gate, walking at a brisk pace toward them.

"We have to go," he said when he was close. His voice was urgent but calm. "Like, right now."

CHAPTER 52: LOOK HOMEWARD

Claire

And then they heard it: the unmistakable roar of a diesel engine. All of the SubRez pickup trucks were like that. Far away still, but distinct.

Malik reached across his body and pulled a gun from a low side pocket in his overcoat. When did he learn to use a gun?

"I knew it," Richard said in a whisper. "They must be watching us -- there must be an alarm that goes off if the hybrids start to fail. What they probably don't know yet is that you got rid of their whole army."

Just then, a dog bounded over the gate and seemed to be heading straight for Malik, its metal collar making a clink-clink-clink.

Claire backed away.

But Malik grinned and knelt down, waiting for the excited St. Bernard. "Hey boy, good boy," said Malik. "Where ya been?"

"Oh! Who's this?" she asked, not remembering any dogs but the unfriendly guard dogs, mostly German Shepherds.

Malik shrugged. "I don't know its name. But since we came back, he's been hanging around. I suspect one of the employees left it ...?"

Richard shook his head, "Hmm, I've been feeding this one off and on since before the raid. I'm guessing someone got him as a puppy, tried training him as a guard, and he was too friendly to be helpful."

Claire smiled and welcomed the licks of the happy beast. She said, "A defector! Like us."

Malik laughed, but as the roaring of the engine sounded closer, he shifted modes: "We have to go … now. It may be too late."

"What? But what about our stuff?" asked Claire. "We can at least …." She looked for a long time at the strange building where she had lived underground for all these months. It both repelled and attracted her.

Malik and Richard gave her a moment. They both knew she didn't have any "stuff" that she needed to bring. There was an attachment to this place, to this underground that would take a long time for her to recover from.

"No," Richard whispered, and touched her shoulder gently. "I have everything we need. We can't go back. The jeep is ready." He gave the hood a little slap and went around to the side where he unplugged it from a strange outlet.

Claire had never seen an electric car, but she thought back to the strange golf carts Lana and David had driven on the island so long ago. It had seemed like magic at the time, and now -- that world was so far in the past. And Gunther! Now, it was happening. She might be able to see him again.

Malik grabbed several jugs of water and two gun cases off the shelf of the barn, and turned to Claire, saying, "Here, help me with this!

As she helped load things into the car, she asked, "We're not going to need these weapons, are we?"

Malik just shrugged.

Richard started the ignition and yelled, "Get in, get in! It's closer."

The dog hopped in the backseat with Claire, Malik kept a lookout in the passenger's side, and Richard drove.

The big barn door where cars normally exit wouldn't budge and they didn't have the key for it. Richard got out and looked around for no more than five seconds, surveying the shoddy construction of the barn. When he jumped back in, he put the jeep in reverse and twisted around to look behind him.

"Here we go!" was the only warning Richard gave them. Claire covered her head and braced for it, but once they had broken through the back wall, all three laughed at their dramatic exit.

Richard knew of a back road around the campus where they could hide out while the truck entered. Otherwise, they would surely encounter the SubRez people on the narrow road leading to The Tower. Fortunately, the vehicle was quiet and the back road was sheltered in tree cover. They wound around back as the huge black pickup truck roared up the main road. Richard had planned this well, using SubRez's own vehicle technology against them.

They waited a good ten minutes after the truck had made it to the Tower, hoping that whoever it was would go inside to search for them and not be watching the road.

Malik looked over at Richard, who took a great big inhalation, and said, "Buckle up, kids! Let's do this." And then, they were free. She was free!

Claire hugged the dog close and stayed low in the seats for several miles in case the agents caught up with them. She smiled into its chocolate and white fur coat, as tears streamed down her face.

CHAPTER 53: A PROMISE

Claire

"**S**o, I guess we have a dog now," said Richard. It was the first thing anyone said after their escape from the Tower, and it made Claire laugh aloud for the second time that day.

Malik was still holding his weapon toward the windshield, clutching it as tightly as Claire was clutching the dog.

The dog didn't seem to mind.

"Once we name him, he's ours!" said Claire.

They were all silent for a moment.

"I wish I knew your name, boy. I'm sure you already have one," she said, holding his huge shaggy head in her hands and looking him squarely in the eye. "Let's see...what do you look like?"

Malik turned and said, "He's a really good dog. In fact, I bet he's a better truffle hunter than a guard dog. He's not even trained for it but once he showed me a whole bunch of edible mushrooms growing under a stack of firewood. Chicken of the woods, I think."

"Oh! Of course," said Claire "He even looks like a mushroom, with this big head!"

"Mushroom?" asked Richard.

"Mister Mushroom," Claire grinned. "Like Mister Rogers. First name, Mister."

Richard smiled.

When they made their first pit stop, Claire and Malik changed seats. It was loud in the back, and Claire was ready to figure out how to get to Gunther, how to see Gran. She knew Richard had a plan.

There was a "Temple Retreat" where both Malik and Richard had been taking refuge for several months.

It turned out, Richard had been building these Temple Retreats for many years. To the general public, they appeared to be spiritual health retreats for wealthy yoga students and meditators, but in reality, they served one purpose: to create a safe haven for hybrids. This had become Richard's mission in life–to provide safety to the lost souls of SubRez, specifically the myco-experiments.

"So ... when I came to your office that time ...," Claire began tentatively. "To the meditation center at the Tower ... did you already know?"

"Not everything. Not about you. But I was worried. See, I've been with SubRez for many years–I started with them right out of college, as a chaplain of sorts."

"A Christian chaplain? A pastor?"

"Not exactly -- I was a theology student. Mostly of Native American traditions. Nature-based religions. They recruited me to develop an entirely new belief system, one that was practical and ethical, not only for humanity but for all biological life."

Claire peered out the window at the endless tangle of trees. It felt so long ago now that she had made her way through those woods, trying to escape the Tower. But it should've felt like only a few days. It was odd how she had sensed the passage of time even in her sleep.

She looked over at Richard in the driver's seat, crinkles around his kind eyes, an easy smile below broad cheekbones. Back then, he had struck her as one of those white American gurus who appropriated bits of Buddhism and Hinduism to make his own thing, but now she realized there was a lot more to him.

She only knew he was raised in North Carolina. Perhaps he actually came from a very genuine spiritual tradition.

She was about to ask his age when it suddenly occurred to her: "Oh my gosh," she exclaimed. "You wrote *The Book of Instructions*, didn't you?"

She turned and made eye contact with Malik who was in the backseat trying to get a radio signal on an old receiver. They still had not been able to communicate with the outside world, and it would take a long while to get through the winding back roads.

Richard looked coy and smiled, shrugging his shoulders.

"Who knows … right?" He winked.

"Are you, like, Buddhist … or a Native American priest … or what?"

This was the most candid conversation she'd had with Richard. He had been such an enigma before, and also an adult and authority figure. Now they were friends–equals. It was going to take a while for her to get accustomed to it.

"Yeah, man. We thought you were a big yogi!" said Malik. "The other kids and I had a lot of theories about you. I would've never guessed Cherokee spirit guru."

Clearly, Malik and Richard had become close in the time she was away. He was so casual with the older man.

"Ha! That's not exactly it. I'm essentially still just a student of theology, but yes, I do come from a long line of Cherokee shamans, and I do practice many of those beliefs … or at least I try. But I've also worked in the other world religions that I respect, to make something that I believe to be ethical.

And yes, to create *The Book*. You guys know -- it's all about ecological balance and finding spirit in all life forms. Before it was appropriated by SubRez. But Malik knows this better than anyone."

He made eye contact with Malik in the rear-view mirror, and then said to Claire, "Malik was becoming quite a serious student of *The Book of Instructions*."

"Yeah, that's before I found out it was just all made up by some quack," he joked.

Richard laughed and said, "The one thing you learn early on as a theologist is that they're all just made up by some random guy -- why not me?"

Claire had always connected with the "bytes," but her mistrust of SubRez soured her view of any materials they gave her.

"So anyway...," continued Richard. "Early on I began to worry about SubRez and its practices. And I wish I'd done something sooner. I regret a lot of those years." He shook his head.

They bumped along in silence for several minutes.

Malik and Claire waited patiently to hear more about the mystery of the Healer.

"I was so deep into the organization; I'd given them my whole life...and they supported my life, financially. They supported it quite well, in fact. But more than anything, I feared they would ruin me if I left. And I worried what would happen to the kids. Originally, I stayed because I thought I could help them."

He paused again, as though trying to figure out what to divulge and what to hold back.

"I won't go into specifics, but I was definitely worried we'd get hit with trafficking charges at the very least." He shook his head. "That's when I began my own operation. I should have left then, but like I said, I didn't have any other life."

Claire felt bad for Richard. It must have been a lonely life.

"So, you helped some kids get out?" asked Malik.

"I tried. I tried for a long time, but it wasn't until Claire came along down in Florida…that anyone wanted to leave. They all had Stockholm syndrome…or their lives back home were just so bad they didn't care to leave. And by the time Claire began acting out up here, my hands were tied. They suspected something, and my privileges were restricted." He shook his head again and looked at Claire.

"One of my biggest regrets, Claire. I'm so, so sorry."

"I know. It's okay," Claire said, but she wasn't entirely sure it was okay. It was still hard to know who to trust.

She was still sorting out what had happened. All she cared about at this point was getting home. None of it seemed real, and every now and then she was hit with a woozy feeling so powerful that she thought it would knock her back into that death-sleep. Richard said it was just the side effects of being "in union" for so long. It could take months for it to wear off.

"So, my goals shifted. When I was allowed time off, I began traveling all over the world and trying to locate any stray hybrids. It just began as me trying to take care of them. Like claire.0 -- your clone. They were all so helpless out there in the world. That's when I established the non-profit centers -- the temple retreats. I used my Cherokee nationality and religious traditions as the basis for it."

He winked, looking at her sideways: "If anyone asks, we lean on Native American traditions, but in practice we are much more, er, of a 'minority' than that … of course."

***

The Jeep lurched down the mountain roads as Richard

navigated the winding path, getting closer to the highway, close enough that the phone signal worked. Richard handed a small flip phone to Malik who was still in the back seat with the dog.

"Check to see if there's any word from Cherokee." Richard's knuckles were white on the steering wheel. "Liz should've called this morning." Then he looked at Claire. "Your hybrid -- claire.0 -- she's there. Showed up a few weeks ago."

Claire felt her stomach drop. "What does that mean?"

"It means she knows what she is," Malik said quietly from behind them. "Most hybrids figure it out eventually. They call it 'The Remembering.'"

Claire stared out at the dense Appalachian Forest flying past. "And then what happens?"

Richard and Malik exchanged a look in the rearview mirror.

"Claire," Richard said gently, "Most hybrids don't want to keep living once they remember. They feel like they don't belong. They are duplicates, after all."

The words hit her like a punch. All those years of resentment toward claire.0, and now she understood. And Gunther, too. He probably lost faith in her long ago.

"Gunther," she said, louder than she expected. "I have to get to him. To Florida."

"We will," Richard assured her. "But first we need to get somewhere safe. There's a place not far—"

Malik's device crackled to life. A woman's voice, distorted by static: "Richard? Are you there?"

"That's Liz," Richard said. He took the radio. "We made it out. Claire's with us."

"Thank God." Liz's relief was audible even through the static. "But Richard ... there's something else. About Claire's grandmother."

Claire grabbed the radio. "What about Gran? Is she okay?"

A long pause. "Claire, I'm so sorry. The cancer came back. She... she passed yesterday morning."

Cancer? What cancer?

The radio slipped from Claire's hands and Malik caught it. The forest around them seemed to go dark and fuzzy, like TV static whirring by on both sides.

"We need to get home," Claire whispered. "I need to get to Gunther."

Richard put his hand on her shoulder. "We'll get you there, kiddo. I promise."

At the highway, Richard turned toward Knoxville instead of Cherokee.

"Where are we going?" asked Malik.

"Number one, SubRez will suspect us going toward the Temple, but more important ... we're getting this girl on a flight to Jacksonville, Florida."

Claire had been dozing and now she sat up at attention. "I ... I am going on a plane?"

"Yes, Claire. It's time to see your family. You'll be there by the end of the day."

Claire began shaking a little: little convulsions of fear and regret and gratitude. Everything was happening so fast. She knew that Richard was just trying to follow through with his promise.

CHAPTER 54: THE OTHERS

The Hybrid

Temple Retreat

The very next day, her new outlook began to fall apart, and the identity she had been building, crumbled before it became a reality.

First, she got a nasty phone call from Mack, who had gotten the retreat's number from the rehab center. Then she tried texting Gunther using Liz's cell phone, but all she received back was a threatening text from his girlfriend, Beth. "Claire, you better get down here ASAP!" What kind of sister would leave her little brother to deal with everything himself?

She had let everyone down, especially Gran.

But the final straw came when they got in touch with Richard. Everyone was excited to hear that Richard was okay. He had disappeared after the Training Tower had been raided, and they weren't sure what had happened.

When Claire heard the news of what he'd been doing, and who he might bring back with him, she had been a little nervous. It was a long shot, she knew. No one had heard from the original Claire in more than a year. Supposedly she'd been captured and imprisoned in the Tower's dungeon, which meant only one thing: experimentation. Claire shuddered at the thought of it.

"He wants to talk to you, Claire," said Liz excitedly. "And guess what! He's got Claire on the line! She's with him. She's alive. She's really alive!"

Perhaps Liz had forgotten what Claire said about the real Claire being gone, how significant that was for her. Or perhaps she had no idea what it felt like to be an extra human being, a mistake that no one needs if the original is there.

So, Claire -- claire.0 now and forever -- walked out of the front door. She didn't need to talk to Richard anymore. She was too scared to speak with Claire. After all this time, it didn't even matter anymore. She was a failed human. No good for anyone.

She walked and walked until long after dark. When she returned, she told Ian she would be joining them. She had changed her mind. When was The Returning supposed to be held?

Ian looked concerned but didn't protest. "One month left," he said. "It's getting close. We're all a little nervous but..."

"... we are not alone," Claire finished for him.

"Right, you're not alone, Claire." He pulled her close and held her tight. She couldn't hold back the tears. The new future she had glimpsed was gone. Gunther wouldn't want her if he had the real thing. No one would. And Claire would be angry about how much she had screwed up their life.

Once again, she belonged nowhere. She may as well disappear with the others.

The following morning, they got a call from the retreat centers in other countries, Someone had leaked information to SubRez. Their locations had been compromised, all four of them. They would have to speed up the plans for The Returning.

The fields where they planned to do the final ceremony were located far away from the retreat centers exactly for this reason, but now they would need to make preparations. The residents of the Cherokee retreat would need to leave in the next few days, if not sooner. Their destination could only be reached by foot.

It was Richard's idea to find locations that could not be accessed by vehicle. Remote, open fields protected by mountains and large trees. Each spot had been carefully chosen far from curious reporters or dangerous SubRez agents. That's how Liz had explained it. And they had aligned the spots with energetic super-locations.

Everything was set.

Richard called again, but she refused to speak to him. She could overhear the conversations about them escaping from SubRez, but she did not care anymore. So what if Richard was returning to The Temple? It wasn't her that he cared about anyway.

Nothing mattered anymore anyway. And she was not going to change her mind about The Returning. It was her right -- maybe the only right she had the power to exercise.

CHAPTER 55: THE RETURN OF CLAIRE

Gunther

Present Day 2007

As the funeral guests mill about in Claire and Gunther's childhood home, Gunther peers across the kitchen at Claire, wondering what has changed in her. She's speaking to each family friend with a strong and spirited energy, acting the role of gracious hostess even though she hasn't lived there in years. Every now and then, she catches Gunther's stare. Can anyone else see the difference? he wonders. Beth will think he's crazy for sure.

"What the hell …?" is the first thing he says to his sister after the guests leave.

"Gunther, I need to explain something …."

"Uh yeah," Beth chimes in, arms crossed. Claire looks confused for a moment. Then her eyebrows tilt into a stubborn V shape, that expression Gunther hasn't seen in years.

"I mean I need to talk to my brother," she says, allowing her expression alone to speak: *I'm not explaining anything to you, whoever you are.*

Beth shoots a look at Gunther, Gunther stares at Claire, and Claire looks at the floor.

Just then, Mack walks into the room. "Well, look what the cat dragged in." This is Mack trying to be generous and diplomatic, but it has the opposite effect. Gunther can feel Claire's sudden defensive energy, that old feeling of being backed into a corner, misunderstood, attacked. But then she stands up, relaxes her shoulders, and puts on a courageous smile.

For a moment, she studies the old man and no one in the room moves. Mack frowns. Then she hugs him empathetically, says, "I'm sorry, Grandpa Mack," and leaves the room, heading for the back door. It's not clear what she's sorry for, perhaps his grief, perhaps her disappearance. It doesn't matter now. Beth scoffs, and Mack mutters something about Claire being high. He and Beth are united in their scorn. An ancient tingle of panic flutters through some deep region of Gunther's brain, and he follows Claire, out of the house and down to the lakeside.

"So, explain. Go ahead. What could possibly keep you away all through Gran's hospitalizations and chemo, and then to not even consider coming back to ...." Gunther's voice cracks. His fists are balled.

She looks across the lake. "I came as soon as I heard, I swear. I just found out she was even sick. I had no idea it was this bad. I got here as fast as I could ... but too late ...." The tears started streaming.

And then, a sudden radiance through the grief, like a sun shower, she beams in his direction: "Gunther ... you know ... I'm so so so happy to see you! I'm so sorry ... all these years ...." She tries to embrace him, but he is stunned and stands rigid.

"What are you talking about? She was sick for months and you never came! We tried to call you all the time. Have you lost it?" Gunther considers briefly that is exactly what's going on. Maybe Beth was right -- he alone is going to be the one left holding the bag when Claire's mental health completely collapses. It was just a matter of time.

His mind starts buzzing with what-if scenarios, but Claire's steady, melodic voice cuts through it all, that clear chirp that he's known since the beginning of time: "That's what I have to explain. You don't understand. Or maybe you do…"

He still resists. "No, Claire! No, I don't."

Just as he is ramping up for a long rant, Claire takes his hand and says, "Gunther, I swear on Mom and Dad's grave-- I just found out. I'm sorry I haven't been able to stay in touch. Listen: I've been away for years. Against my will. Before that, I was on the island, right after that day…that hurricane. But, in a way, I was sometimes here … watching … I mean, that part is hard to explain."

Gunther glances toward the house and sees the silhouette of Beth standing at the window, hands on hips, waiting for him. Then he glimpses his own reflection in the window, his real sister by his side. He can feel it happening: the entire sum of his personal human history is unraveling, thread by thread, undoing what he has sewn so tightly together. It was tied and buttoned and knotted for so long, but now the seams are stretching and soon it will burst, and Beth will be the last to understand.

"Gunther? Do you see? It wasn't me this whole time. I've been away ever since that hurricane when we were kids … I had to leave … and I had to stay away. I mean they literally almost killed me. I tried to escape–more than once."

Gunther squints up into the sky, his fists on his forehead. Then his arms go limp by his side, and he turns away from his sister's fiery eyes.

"She's not me. I mean, I'm not her … I know you suspected. But I need to … I need to go back to her. I need you to help me. Will you …?"

"Go back to her? Where is she?" Gunther can hardly believe he is humoring this idea.

Claire holds his gaze. Somehow, he knows she's not crazy. Not this version of her.

"I promise," she says. "This will all make sense."

And when she's done explaining, it does. Kind of. At least it explains why all these years, he's missed something, why he's so different from other people.

Now, Gunther has to convince Beth that she has never actually met his real sister. This is the real Claire. This changes everything.

Claire grows quiet, and Beth waves from the window. Now, Gunther feels a need to explain himself to Claire. But what could he say to make her understand why he needed Beth?

***

"What!?" Beth snaps when Gunther suggests that this Claire is an entirely different woman.

"It's hard to explain …."

"Ha, um, yeah. She says she's been gone for five years? Gunther!?" She twirled her fingers around her ears indicating what she wanted to say aloud: she's cuckoo.

"So, you're saying you have one sister that's a total fuckup and one who is working on cutting-edge biotechnology with a secret university?"

"No, not a university. No. You're not listening. Don't you remember I told you before…? That day she almost got swept out in that hurricane? She was a totally different person … like an actual different person. I was right, Beth."

Beth shakes her head. Gunther puts his head in his hands and leans forward. His mind is spinning with the tales Claire had told him. *Don't say another word!* he tells himself. Beth won't understand this. Claire said that the morning before the hurricane she had left home. The people on the island had offered her a job and training and a place to live. They had a clone of Claire; it had replaced her so that no one would ever tell the difference. At the time, she just wanted to be close to Mom somehow -- Mom's work, she told Gunther. She wanted to get away from Grandpa Mack. She was sorry she left. Sorry she deceived him.

Beth had rolled her eyes and walked out, slamming the front door. Gunther didn't stop her.

He knows he will have to make a decision. Is it really Claire? And who was that other Claire? With a sudden stab of pity, he realizes that the Claire he has grown to resent was just a damaged shadow of his real sister. It's not surprising that she so often seems like a ghost, one that gets more and more translucent with each passing year. But what exactly is she? And where has Claire been all these years?

But all he says to Claire when she comes back inside is, "why did you leave without me and never come back? Why didn't you call?"

Later that evening, Gunther finds Claire and Mack at the kitchen table, a warm and intimate aura encircling their reminiscences, a connection long severed by adolescence and distance.

The act of conjoining their memories animates and softens Mack in a way that Gunther has never witnessed. Claire is remembering Gran at her best. For Mack's sake. Tears pool at the corners of his pink-rimmed eyes, but it's mirth, not grief, that inspires this display of vulnerability. It is at once grotesque and fantastic, to see this man shed a tear. Something almost supernatural.

This had to be the real Claire -- making the impossible possible.

He considers this truth and realizes it was not this Claire who was the target of Mack's rages when she was in high school, it was not this Claire who was sent away to college with a 'good riddance,' and it was not this Claire who was repeatedly castigated for failing out of college and "not contributing a goddamn skittle to this family" when she would lose touch and disappear. It was never this Claire.

Of course, she can sit here and soothe him after his wife's death, even though she has lost her own grandmother. Of course she can forgive him for long-ago childhood injuries. She has been far away from their nemesis all these years, and now Mack is just a tired-out shell of a person. He has no power.

Mack's quick acceptance of this new version of Claire is jarring, but Gunther looks at the tremor in the old man's hands and forgives him for everything. Just like the old days, Gunther is following Claire's lead.

CHAPTER 56: FAMILY ROAD TRIP

Gunther

Claire explains: "She's not fully human. And something is happening to her. She won't talk to me. And if she dies before we find her, I'm not sure what happens to me."

Gunther is trying his best to follow and not get distracted by the nagging feeling he might be following the ravings of a crazy person. "Dies?? Why would she die? You know she's been in rehab, and then apparently went to some cult retreat. I'm mean, she's been kinda messed up for a long time."

"It's not a cult," says Claire.

Claire is examining Gunther for a moment. He wonders what she thinks of him—expensive shoes and sunglasses. Just a few days ago he was feeling so good, so sure of himself. He had just chosen his major, and he found out the college was going to accept all 24 hours of his AP courses. That was almost a year of college credit!

But now all of that feels small and irrelevant.

"I'll explain in the car," she says.

Gunther feels like he is eleven years old again, tangling himself up in Claire's fantasies. He has to catch up to Claire. Just like when they were kids. He waves at Mack who is rocking on the front porch, that look of disapproval hardened into his face. The old man had never been able to fathom their brother-sister bond. Gunther always resented his grandfather's harsh and narrow view of boyhood, but now he wonders if it was never about his masculinity. Perhaps he really was trying to protect Gunther. From her.

She glances back at Mack and says, "I know we have a lot to catch up on ... but right now, let's just make things right with Mack."

Mack does not seem curious about where they are going so soon after the funeral. He is eerily content sitting rocking back and forth in the chair. Claire promises she will be back to help him sort out all of the affairs.

It's an hour into the car ride before anyone says anything. Claire breaks the silence: "Okay ... soooo first off you should know SubRez may be looking for us, but more so they are looking for her and the others. If they find her, they will find me. If they capture either of us, they could clone us again or create a new army of clones."

"And these are the same people from the island?" asks Gunther.

"Same organization, who knows which agents...," she trails off. "Not sure how they're operating now, but I'm sure they're around. And not happy that I destroyed their technology."

This can't be real, Gunther thinks to himself, *why did I just blow up my whole life?*

He was supposed to return to school in two days, but that wasn't going to happen. The death of a family member was only going to get him excused for so much time.

"Does she even know who she is ...? Er, what she is?"

"Yeah, um, I think. I haven't even seen her yet. All I know is that if the wrong people get a hold of her–or any of them ... it's not gonna be good."

"Any of them? There are more hybrids?"

"There's a lot more ...," she says vaguely.

Her cell phone rings. Gunther's head begins to swim as he listens to his sister talking about a world completely foreign and possibly fantasy–hybrids and SubRez technology and "Training Tower headquarters." She was starting to sound like an international spy. He catches a glimpse of her silhouette, and knows once again, that she is clearly different–even the shape of her face in his periphery looks stronger and more sophisticated. So different from the girl he knew as his sister.

"Okay, yep. We'll be there in seven hours," she says, finishing up the call.

Gunther glances at the backseat, suddenly self-conscious about the piles of laundry he brought home, but was too ashamed to bring inside when he realized he always took it for granted that Gran did his laundry. She had to die for him to notice. He can't believe it was only a week ago that he'd gotten that call in his dorm room from Mack.

"So … where exactly are we going …?" asks Gunther.

She plugs some numbers into a device he'd only seen in commercials. A smartphone. Gunther thought his new flip phone was pretty sleek, but Claire pointed out to him that he could only use it for calls and texts.

Her phone begins ringing again and Claire answers on speakerphone.

"It's Malik," she mouths.

A smooth, baritone voice says, "Hi Gunther, it's so nice to finally meet the one and only! Claire has told me so much about you, man."

He's relieved to know that Malik turns out to be a real person; he sounds like a completely normal, rational guy. They carry on a pleasant conversation and Gunther immediately gets the feeling that he and Malik could be buddies. It feels natural. Gunther begins to settle into this new feeling, this idea of his sister.

When they get out of the car at a rest stop in Georgia, Gunther hugs his sister in a spontaneous gesture of joy. It's her! It's really her. She smiles at him and raises an eyebrow as if to say, are you okay?

After they cross the border into South Carolina, Claire appears to grow nervous about how much longer it will take to get there. She frequently cranes her head around to keep watch on the cars around them.

"Everything okay?"

She nods, "So far, so good."

How strange it is to be on this adventure with her. Gunther is much bigger now, so much taller than his sister. They are beginning to slip into their old ways, their old roles. Or at least that's how it feels.

Now it occurs to him that he should take on more of a protector role. He should've thought to grab one of Mack's guns … just in case. It still seemed like a fantasy when they were back at the house, but now the fear is real–and also exhilarating. Gunther feels alive.

The mountains rise in the distance as they head west on Interstate 26. Gunther accelerates past a semi-truck and cracks his window, breathing in the first whiff of crisp Carolina mountains. "Friend of the Devil" plays on the radio and Claire turns it up and smiles at Gunther. Their parents loved this band. It's the first time in a long time that he's let himself think of them. But the feeling is not a sharp jab to his heart like usual; it's a mellow longing, warm and sweet, and buffered by the presence of his sister.

CHAPTER 57: NOT AN ACCIDENT

Claire

In the car, Claire tells her story, beginning on the island, that day of the hurricane, and tells him all she can remember of the kidnapping and her time at the Training Tower, and the failed escapes. She's not ready to tell him about the monstrosities they created from her body. Not yet.

Gunther listens in silence. It's a long time before he asks, "But why didn't you try to escape while you were still on the island? I wish I had tried harder to get back there…You know, I did try to find it …"

"You did? I didn't know …. I'm sure they prevented you from getting there … somehow."

She pauses for a moment, considering how she and Gunther didn't have a chance back then. Not against the manipulations of SubRez.

"And I did try to escape, but I was dumb about it. I had no idea how serious it was -- the danger I was in."

They soak in the reality of the parallel lives they've lived. Claire pulls her knees to her chest and considers the details of the island. It seems so unreal. What happened to all those buildings and boats? Richard said the island operation was shut down not long after she'd left.

"I jumped off a boat and tried to swim away."

"A boat?"

"Yeah, but it was parked at a dock. I just jumped … and thought I could swim fast enough."

"Oh," Gunther replies.

Claire thinks for a long time before she brings up what she's been holding back for so many years, what she kept inside in order to survive.

"So, you know how we went on their boat … before Mom and Dad left? The night before. Remember?" The word remember was small and forced.

Gunther shrugs. He doesn't seem to understand how important this is.

"Gunther, this is crazy, but you have to believe me."

Gunther lets out a quiet laugh. "What now …?"

He's driving too slow for the highway now, as though he's about to pull over. Claire looks across the road where the rolling farmland is dotted with brown cows. She feels a sudden sense of calm and clarity.

Gunther turns the radio all the way down. There had been a static-filled NPR news story playing in the background. Now all is quiet.

Claire says, "That older couple–the friends of Mom and Dad …? Remember them?"

Gunther shakes his head. "All I remember is some lady on a boat. She gave me that big roll of Snoopy stickers."

"Yeah … that boat. I was on it. Same one Mom and Dad supposedly wrecked."

They look at each other, as the pieces begin to come together. It all makes sense. Mom and Dad's boat never sank. SubRez made their parents' tragedy seem like an accident. They made them disappear so that they could take Claire. Lana lied. Jessica hadn't really given her permission to use Claire as a science experiment. Of course not. Her mother would never have agreed. She must have known there was something not quite right about SubRez. But who was this mysterious couple that claimed to be their friends?

"Mack would know," says Claire.

Gunther shakes his head. "Mack would know what? I doubt it."

"I mean he'll remember something about them. I guarantee he didn't trust them … for one reason or another. He'll have something to say."

Gunther nods, still in shock.

Claire dials their home phone number and puts Mack on speaker phone.

"Those rich folks? I don't know any names–your Gran woulda known–but I do remember that lady from England. They sure liked your daddy. He worked on their boats for years. It was their boat–an expensive one–that sank, and they didn't care one bit. They came to pay their respects after the funeral and left us a big ol' check for you two. I do remember that. Never said one word about the boat. I know for sure it was a high-dollar one!"

Gunther and Claire stare at each other, their eyes sparkling with intrigue. Mack seems to be gaining momentum in his narrative. This was the most Claire had heard him talk in years.

"And where do they live now? Did you ever hear from them after that?" asks Gunther, hungry for more details.

But Mack is done. "I wouldn't know," is all he says. "I suppose they went back to Europe or wherever they were from…."

Claire can picture him squaring his shoulders. That's all he has to say.

Gunther asks half a dozen more questions, but all they find out is that he doesn't know why their parents were hob-knobbing with rich folks anyway, and Gran kept up with all those things, and he was just here to hold the house together, a common phrase he would use when he wanted to be excused from any emotional issues in the family.

But it's clear that SubRez was responsible for the death of Josh and Jessica. Once they were gone, Lana and David lured them to the island.

CHAPTER 58: THE RETURNING

Claire

Paint Rock, North Carolina

A little ways past the tiny town of Paint Rock, Claire and Gunther arrive at the spot. They drive the car as far as it will go up a dirt road and park at an unmarked trailhead. These are the coordinates Richard gave her. They will have to walk the rest of the way.

The moment she opens the car door, Claire can feel the energy. There's something in the air; something underground. On their drive through the town, which consisted of a farm and a few homes, they saw a small handwritten sign that read, "Legendary Home of the Cherokee Siren. The Singing Woman Still Haunts these Waters."

Claire can see on the map that the French Broad River snakes its way through the mountainside nearby. This is definitely the place. Richard must know this entire area well. All of this was his ancestral homeland.

Claire pulls out a hand-drawn map that will take them the rest of the way. The trail is not so much a human path as a game trail, an opening in the brush made by deer or boar. They begin their hike through the woods, picking their way around overgrown branches and exposed roots.

It had rained all week. A torrential downpour every afternoon is how one of the guys at the gas station described it. But today the sun is out. Claire and Gunther are grateful for the drier weather, even though the forest floor is still moist. Colorful mushrooms lace the pathway and decorate the ground as far as they can see into the woods.

Claire knows she has to tell Gunther the thing before they find claire.0, the big thing that Richard told her before he dropped her at the airport.

"A lot of mushrooms," she remarks.

"Yeah, ha. Ironic. Must be that time of year."

"Funny, it coincides with hurricane season."

"Huh, hurricane season -- it always reminds me of that day you … well, when you left. I had flashbacks for a long time."

"Yeah, you know, I'm sorry I did that. I should have listened to you. You always had good gut instincts about things like that. Lana and David … and all the weirdness."

"It's okay," replies Gunther. "I know why you wanted to leave. I forgave you a long time ago … ha … and then I forgot you ever left! It's a weird thing."

"Okay, thank you."

Claire thinks for a long time before broaching the subject. She considers what he knows: that these creatures are alive like humans, but they do not necessarily have the will to thrive the way animals and plants do. They have a strong will to self-destruct, to decay and rot and perhaps even consume those around them. He knows that he and Claire are there to convince claire.0 to not give in to her fungal instincts.

What he does not know is that claire.0 is different from the others. But so are Claire and Gunther.

"So, you know …," Claire begins, "You know how my hybrids seem stronger than the others..? I mean my hybrid," she catches herself. He doesn't yet know there were others. "You remember Lana told us that at the beginning ...."

Gunther nods.

"Well, there may be a reason. And it has to do with mom. And her mom."

Gunther stops and turns to look at Claire.

She continues, "And me and you."

Claire explains it as it had been explained to her. Shortly before Jessica was born in the mid-1960's, her own parents were part of a movement experimenting with medicinal plants and mushrooms, not just for recreational mind play, but to cure serious diseases and prevent developmental disabilities, aging, and birth defects.

When their grandmother's pregnancy was in danger, their grandfather–an ethnobotanist– took action in a very unorthodox way. He was on the cutting edge of plant medicine at the time, and did a lot of field work with native tribes in Mexico and out west.

"I think Tim Leary and Ram Dass were in that group," Richard had told Claire. "Just to give you a sense of your grandfather..."

"I never knew him," she had replied.

Richard also had said, "But no one–no white man, that is– was exploring the traditions of native people here in North Carolina...at least not when it came to mushrooms. This was shortly after the tales of Mexican healers and shamans were widely published, but before psychedelics and other plant medicine was criminalized."

Claire doesn't go into all of this with Gunther; she only has time for the essentials.

"Here's the thing," she says to Gunther, "Apparently, when our grandfather found out something was wrong with the baby in utero, he sought out Richard's family. Of course Richard was just a little boy at the time so he doesn't remember any of it, but he does know that his own grandmother worked with our grandparents to heal the baby, who was Mom. And they used mushroom medicine to do it. Like the kind of technology that we use now to make these hybrids! That's how they discovered some of this stuff."

Claire is getting excited, but Gunther is clearly disturbed.

"What are you saying," asks Gunther. "That Mom was a hybrid or something?"

"Not exactly a hybrid. Richard calls her Ground Zero Mycoman."

"Nope," Gunther shakes his head. "Impossible."

He faces forward and continues the hike, as though the conversation is over.

"Gunther, she's not a hybrid…but her cells… they were infused with the cells of this fungus, the one that works on the hybrids. Which means…"

"No, no, no. That doesn't make sense. I thought she discovered it. I don't understand."

"Well in a way, she did. And they did make her think that. They wanted her to remain involved."

"That's too fucked up. I can't …."

"Gunther, you have to! Richard has no reason to lie about this. I trust him– with my life. I mean this is why he's involved in the first place."

Gunther picks up his pace and shakes his head.

"It's not his fault that a bunch of dudes who thought they were smarter than everyone else came down here and convinced these people to let them break the law on their reservation. I mean that's basically what they did. And then a lot of them were fired from the universities."

No response from Gunther, but Claire continues anyway: "... and the government came for Richard's family.... I mean we're not the only victims here. Gunther ...? Gunther, I know you don't want to accept it, but we have to tell her, too. We have to tell claire.0. I think it will make the difference."

Finally, he stops and finds a seat on a stump.

"So, what are we then, huh? Should we just go kill ourselves out there too?"

"We just have some of the same networking. It's actually a good thing, Gunther. Apparently it can be protective ... against neurological diseases and cancer. Honestly, I don't even know how much of it we inherited."

He looks up at her, standing above him. "I mean we're okay, right?"

Gunther stares at the backs of his hands as though checking to make sure he wasn't turning into a mushroom.

"We're the same as always. You're still you. It's just a part of your genetic material that you can't see."

Gunther looks up into the tree canopy above them and Claire follows his gaze. They stare at the tangle of branches interconnecting. The sun will be setting in a few hours, but it is already dim under the great shadows of the oak and hickory forest. He gets to his feet, and they continue making their way down the path.

An hour later, the canopy gives way to a clearing, and then farther down the hill, a sloping meadow.

They find the hybrid among hundreds of others, and Claire's memory flashes back to the horrible dungeon scene at the Tower.

She's not surprised that despite all of the people, the entire meadow is silent, but she can see that Gunther is. Claire can tell he's trying to put on a brave face.

She had tried her best to describe to him what would happen, but there are no words that could prepare anyone for this.

Claire shields her eyes from the sun and looks across the field. Some of them take notice of her and Gunther, but they do not react. Gunther casts his gaze at claire.0 but keeps his distance.

There does not appear to be a leader, and no one is making any speeches. In fact, not a single human voice can be heard– only the mild buzz of cicadas. The bodies are not gathered together, but spread out across the field, each individual alone, seated or lying on the ground.

As Claire draws closer to her hybrid, she realizes that claire.0's hands are planted not on the ground, but into the ground. The mycelium threads have taken over her body, the filaments streaming around her arms and legs like ribbons and growing out of her palms and feet straight into the ground.

She is physically bound to the earth. Her human parts are dying, and the fungal parts -- in anticipation of a corpse– are preparing to do their job, allowing things to decay and meld with the soil, to make room for the new.

This is her purpose now, Richard had said. All the hybrids plan to fulfill their true purpose.

Claire hears a murmur, rising up from the ground, buzzing all around. No one is moving their mouths, but she hears it. We remember. We reclaim ourselves. We belong to the earth. We are not alone.

"Claire!" she shouts. It feels strange to say her own name to this woman. But after all, claire.0 has lived the last five years as the one and only Claire Eliza Flynn. She had done her best. She deserves the name too.

"Claire," whispers claire.0. She looks down at her hands self-consciously. "I'm sorry."

Claire sits in the grass next to her, and pulls her as close as she can. "No! Shhh. You're going to be okay. I've got you. We'll get you out of here."

"No, you can't."

Claire begins pulling strands of mycelium off of her. "Don't be silly, of course I can. It's kind of a mess, but ... look, I brought Gunther and ...."

Remember, Reclaim, Return, Renew. Claire can hear the thoughts of the hybrids as they join together in a silent prayer. It's strange to hear the words from *The Book of Instructions* out here, and from the minds of these people she's never met.

Gunther is still several yards away, not close enough to see why claire.0 and the others are sitting so still, in such unnatural positions.

"No, no. Please don't pull the threads. It hurts. Why is he here? I don't want him to see me like this. You shouldn't be here. No humans allowed. Richard said so."

Claire motions for Gunther to stay back, which he happily obeys, taking shade under a nearby tree.

She is silent for a while, staring into the hybrid's eyes, her own eyes– her mother's eyes. Claire wonders if she will feel the pain when claire.0 dies, when she is consumed by the rotting process and digested back into the earth.

Their foreheads touch for a moment as Claire kneels over the girl. Then she squeezes claire.0 close and the mycelium threatens to wrap a thread around her too. Claire gently pulls it away.

She sits back and feels the setting sun, still warm on her arms. A sudden sense of calm settles over Claire. She feels complete somehow. There's so much she wants to know, so much she wants to ask her hybrid, but instead she stays quiet for several minutes, feeling the closeness of her twin.

"You know what?" claire.0 breaks the silence. "I can hear that tree over there. I can feel it talking."

Claire raises an eyebrow.

"Wanna know what it's saying?"

They both look over at Gunther sitting under the tree, absentmindedly picking at its bark, and peering over at the meadow occasionally.

Both girls smile.

"Let me take a guess: It wants to reach a branch down and flick Gunther on the forehead," says Claire.

They both smile, mirrors of one another.

"But can you seriously feel that tree?" asks Claire.

"Well, it's not like it's saying, 'ouch, someone is ripping at my skin.' It's just a little agitation I can feel. Somehow, I know it's coming from that tree. And then of course I can see what Gunther's doing .... You could probably feel it too, ya know. From what I can tell you've learned to get in touch -- to plug into the system."

The system.

"Hmmm. Maybe. I guess that's exactly why SubRez is trying to find you. And me. Why they want all of you guys."

"Hmph. To talk to trees you mean? You don't need mutants like us to know how to treat plants. Anyway, they did have us. They made us. Maybe if they had taken care of us."

"You're not a mutant. But I'm just saying if only they would've limited the project to something smaller– like talking to trees; they just got too ambitious. And now look ...."

As far as they can see, the experiment of SubRez is self-destructing by the dozens, quietly burrowing back into the earth in strange cocoon-like pods dotting the landscape. It is all at once tragic and peaceful.

"So, this is your so-called cult," says Claire, shaking her head. "Mack really has no idea! But… I am trying to explain everything to Gunther…what's happening and who all of these people are. But it's only been a couple days for him. He's trying to catch up."

"Please," says claire.0. "I don't want to talk to him. Just tell him I'm sorry for everything. For leaving and not explaining."

"Ha, you sound like me. I thought that's what I was guilty of. You were the one who was there all throughout high school."

"I still left … and I was never a good sister like you. I'm sorry I ruined all your relationships for you."

Claire shakes her head, and then hears footsteps coming toward them.

Both girls look up. It's Gunther, but he is looking directly at claire.0, not Claire.

"What's happening to you? Are you …?" Gunther begins.

Claire.0 closes her eyes for a long time as though she wants to disappear.

Claire says, "She's dying, Gunther. Maybe we're too late. I don't think she wants to talk to you."

Without opening her eyes, claire.0 touches Claire's hand and says, "It's okay."

Gunther clears his throat.

"I know you're not the same sister I was born to," he blurts. "Um … but you have still been my sister all these years. I just want you to know I'm sorry I pushed you away…I knew you weren't her, and no one else could see … and I resented it. I just didn't get it."

Claire.0 opens her eyes and fat tears roll down her cheeks.

"It doesn't matter anymore. But I understand … and … thank you…" Her voice is barely a whisper, and Gunther has to bend close to hear her.

Claire can see him watching the tiny threads moving and binding and choking her limbs and trunk. He is crying, too. She tells him, "It's okay, Gunther, it's okay."

Claire stays close to claire.0 and quickly explains what she knows about their grandmother, and their mother– Gunther and Claire's genetic connection, and why Claire's hybrids are different, why claire.0 is different.

Gunther kneels beside them in the grass. Mycelial threads stick to Claire's clothes and face, and he gently pulls each one off.

"You can't let this happen, Claire," Gunther says to claire.0. "You can save yourself. Let us help you."

Claire.0 shakes her head. But then she opens her eyes, and asks, "so Mom was … I mean your mother was made of …?" she looks down at the mess of fungal threads building around her. She moves to sit up straight, and they release her, breaking apart easily at the slightest tug.

"Your mom, too," says Gunther. "I guess all three of us are anomalies."

All around them, hybrids are becoming still and silent as they are swallowed into the soil.

"I just need a moment with her, Gunther. And then we'll let her decide on her own. It's not for us to decide."

Gunther looks solemn as he walks away, hands in pockets.

Then she whispers the rest of the story; she tells claire.0 about the dungeon in the Tower and what she had to do with the hybrid army. She confesses that it makes her sad even though she knows it was necessary. They were suffering. She admits that it feels like she lost a part of herself that day. She weeps, and so does claire.0.

"I'm telling you this because I want you to know that if there had been any other way...a way for me to take care of each and every one of those hybrids, if we could have gotten them out from under the control of SubRez, if they had been nurtured and cared for -- things would've been different. In a way, they could have made me a better, stronger person. They were a part of me, but they could've never survived on their own -- and I suppose they could've killed me."

Claire.0 straightens all the way up now. She pushes her hair out of her face and brushes away tears.

"But you," Claire continues. "You have a chance -- and a much better one. I guess I'm just saying that if you decide to stay with us, to keep on living, I'm going to need you as much as you need me. You're not a burden. People need you ... and not just me. If we stayed together, we could be a team. Imagine -- two Claires -- united!"

Claire.0's face brightens in small increments as Claire speaks. She seems to grow bigger, and sit up taller. She lifts her hands away from the ground without Claire even noticing, and she is now brushing away the dirt and tiny roots. She takes Claire's hands in her own.

Gunther shouts something to them from a distance. He's waving both arms.

"What?"

"I hear something. We should get out of here ... now!"

"Something?" Claire looks at claire.0 and they both shrug.

They sit in silence for a minute, and then Claire hears it too. A chug-chugging from far away.

She tries to stand, but claire.0 holds tightly to her hands.

I don't want to die: Claire hears it inside her own head, but claire.0 is not moving her mouth. Suddenly their minds are connected, and each of their thoughts swirl around one another, immediately entangled, and it's hard to know who is thinking what.

Not another word is said aloud between them. They just stand up, wave to Gunther, and walk away from the hybrid graveyard. claire.0 doesn't even look back.

They suddenly hear the unmistakable chop-chop-chopping of a helicopter in the distance. Very faint. But she knows: SubRez agents have found the spot.

Fortunately, it is too late for SubRez. There's no more movement in the field. The fungal cocoons are disintegrating quickly. They made sure to bring a quickening agent that speeds up the process. Less suffering.

"Let's go! Run!" yells Gunther. "I found a place where they won't see us."

Before the helicopter is visible, Claire and Gunther and claire.0 flee into the woods and disappear into a gully. An enormous boulder with cracks and crevices as tall as doorways will provide them with sanctuary for the next several hours.

Richard sent someone to pick up the car, so that no one traced it to Gunther. No one will even know to look for them there.

SubRez is only looking for the hybrids, but all they will see as the helicopter comes to a landing is a field of white mushrooms, like puffs of snow against a giant, green canvas.

CHAPTER 59: JESSICA'S JOURNALS

The Hybrid

2008

I still dream about that field in the middle of the woods, the way it felt to be threaded into the ground. The longer I lay there, the more I relaxed into it, as though the earth were sending an anesthetic through my veins, lulling me to death.

Getting there hadn't been easy. It was a two-day trek along the Appalachian Trail. There was a heat wave, and we didn't have enough water. We brought almost nothing because, where would we leave it? Liz had encouraged us to pack more water, but we figured we were marching toward death anyway. What did it matter? We wouldn't be thirsty for long.

Liz walked with us halfway– she knows the Trail like the back of her hand, she said. But she wasn't permitted to stay with us. No humans allowed. I cried when we parted ways. In the short time we knew each other, I had become dependent on her daily pep talks– just for me. And I was becoming more emotional than ever. About everything.

That was the first sign. The big feelings.

All the other hybrids were so certain about doing it. They had made their peace, so I kept my mixed feelings to myself. Maybe they had some instinct that I didn't possess, some gene for self-destruction. I didn't know it then, but it turned out I was genetically different. I was an anomaly, Claire said. So I guess my hesitation was the second sign. I was more human than I thought.

The Returning was a success-- they all died and disappeared, out of reach forever from the long reach of SubRez.

Had Claire and Gunther not intervened, I would be gone too.

I remember watching the news coverage that night in a hotel room we found way up in a tiny mountain town where we would hide out for weeks.

> *... Residents and farmers are shocked by the unfolding tragedy in this idyllic setting north of Asheville, North Carolina. A reported mass suicide right here in Western North Carolina. Cult organization Subterranean Resistance has allegedly staged a mass suicide. The exact cause of death is unclear but there are reports that cult members may have poisoned themselves with a virus or bacteria. None of these claims are yet verified, but there is mounting evidence on social media websites that the members gathered at certain locations with the intent to 'self-destruct.' The spots they chose were all remote and difficult to access by car; they all appear to be open fields.*

Then the reporter paused dramatically. "But the biggest mystery of all? When authorities arrived at the scenes, the bodies were nowhere to be found. But there's no doubt that the people are missing."

Next, they interviewed a puzzled-looking sheriff: "they are around here somewhere. The bodies." He had no idea, poor guy. They wouldn't find any bodies. "Based on extensive communications among groups around the world, the suicides have already happened. We need more time to find and identify the bodies, and then contact loved ones. The families are reaching out, claiming they were notified by individuals involved."

Then the reporter announced, "Coming up this hour, a special report: SubRez: what is it and where did it start? We'll hear from family members about how their loved ones were drawn into the organization."

This was why we had to hide out for a little while. Richard was counting on the authorities tracing it back to SubRez. But we couldn't be sure we were safe back at the retreat right away. They confused us with SubRez, and many were saying it was a cult.

It was pretty traumatic, like Liz says -- to have witnessed all of those people disappear right before my eyes. They were my people ... at least I thought they were. I had finally found my tribe, and then they were all just ... gone.

I do miss the companionship I found, if just for a few weeks, but I belong here, with Claire and Gunther, and Richard and Liz. And Malik. He's joined us too. I like him a lot. He saved Claire's life, which means he saved me too.

These are my people now. After we were sure that SubRez was gone for good and the federal agents wouldn't be traipsing through the town of Cherokee, we all moved back to the Temple Retreat here in the mountains.

The news called it a mass suicide, which I guess it was, but no human will ever really understand that it was actually a beautiful thing. Except maybe Claire. It was not only a demonstration of death, but also of life. They were protesting in their own way.

When authorities investigated The Returning, they found SubRez agents in the vicinity and automatically pegged the strange disappearances on them. Many of the international SubRez people were deported. Richard says all of those SubRez agents should be charged, American or not.

"But they're not even going to look into it. Who would bring them to justice anyway?" Richard said.

Liz reminded him that we don't want the U.S. government to investigate too deeply.

"Guess who they'll come for next?"

She was smiling, but Liz is serious when she says it's a reminder for us to keep a low profile, especially me.

It's quiet here without the others, but we keep busy; there's a lot to do around the camp. We have chickens and goats and an indoor plant and mushroom nursery, and there are a lot of chores. I like the quiet work, and my favorite thing is taking care of the plants. That, and playing with Mister Mushroom. Richard brought him all the way from the Training Tower.

Liz says that pretty soon we will open the retreat center as a healing place for outsiders. It will be for spiritual and physical healing, as well as retreating, she explained. Liz is a special kind of doctor who understands that the body and the spirit are one and the same.

We will receive patients who need a vacation or a special kind of transition from their medical centers. They've already made the Finland retreat open to outsiders, and now the Zambia retreat and the China retreat will be transformed as well. Richard says that I may be able to travel with him someday soon and help out, but first I have to build up my courage in smaller ways. I'm terrified to travel, but he says I just need time to adjust to my new life.

A man named Ovid joined us too. At first, they were all convinced he was with SubRez, which he used to be. I made the mistake of letting him in when he knocked. We're not supposed to let any strangers in yet, but he seemed so familiar.

Malik marched into the front office holding a gun directly

at Ovid. I thought that was a little extreme. The man was unarmed.

Then Claire walked in, glaring at me. Only then did I realize how dangerous he could have been.

"How did you find this place?" she asked Ovid. "What are you doing here?"

Apparently, she knew him from before– on the island– but somehow I don't remember him. He's one of Lana's sons. I do remember her. My first mother. That part of my life is so fuzzy and confusing.

Ovid held his hands up over his head. "I come in peace, I swear. Hey, man, put that thing down…please. I want to join you guys. I've been off SubRez for years now. I tried telling Claire … on the phone … but she … you … kept hanging up."

Malik stared at Claire for a long time as he lowered his gun.

After a few hours, they were able to verify that he in fact defected from SubRez, that all he wanted to do was help.

Now he lives here with us. I like him. But Malik still doesn't trust him.

Claire spends a lot of time back in Florida, taking care of Mack and going through the old house. I guess she has a lot to catch up on down there. We can't be there at the same time– what would people think if they saw two Claires? Poor Mack wouldn't understand. I do still feel sad that I missed Gran's funeral; I wish I could have said goodbye.

Claire brought me Mom's old journals to keep. She says that anything that belonged to Mom is mine now, if I want it. And I do. Ever since I came to the retreat, I've felt a stronger bond with all of my family, even Mom and Dad. I know I never actually knew them, but it feels like I did. And now that I have a new name, I feel a special connection to Mom.

They said I could take the name Jessica. Both Claire

and Gunther supported it, and Richard even held a name christening ceremony just for me. Being called Claire didn't feel right anymore with the original Claire around, and I certainly didn't want anyone calling me claire.0. So now I am Jessica. Jessica Annie Flynn II. As in, a second chance.

They've started calling me Jessie.

Claire also brought me seashells from the beach, which smell amazing. They remind me of the river island where I was born. The water was brackish, always mixed up with the ocean water that flushed in and out, and all around that little island. I want to go back someday soon.

But it's safer for all of us to stay here for now.

Gunther transferred to a university up here and he's going to help run the retreat when it opens. He changed his major to ethnobotany and he'll be in charge of plant medicine. They have a good program at the college, but more than anything he wants to be apprenticed to Richard and Liz. He wants to be a Healer one day.

Malik was accepted into a PhD program at the same university, and I hope to start there soon. But I don't want to study mycology like them. They don't know it yet, but I hope to be an artist one day.

Richard is rewriting *The Book of Instructions* so it's more accessible to the general public. Also, he doesn't want any associations with SubRez. Originally, they had published it for him.

The retreat will be open to anyone who needs it, but we're still running the helpline for stray hybrids. Richard is sure there are more out there. I hope they find us. It would be nice to have others.

I'm fascinated with the history of how we came to be, and Richard loves to tell the stories. It's strange to think I was different all along– both from humans and from the hybrids. My strain is slightly different because I'm one of Claire's hybrids. They say I'll probably live much longer because of her too, especially if we live close together.

I'm learning more about how our grandmother infused her pregnancy with a special species of mushroom, the same one that I am made of. Richard says it wasn't any kind of traditional practice– more of a theory that our grandfather developed when he was working at a university in California. He sought out native Cherokee healers in North Carolina and they teamed up. Because Mom was so different genetically, they assumed she would not be able to bear children. SubRez was in its infancy at the time of the experimental infusion, and they went underground more and more as the decades passed. Richard says, the political climate turned on them.

Twenty-something years later when Claire was born and SubRez had been pushed underground and funded by private donors, they began building a small Nest near the Flynn family. And of course, that's where I was born.

When Claire came back from Florida recently, she brought me a video from Nest 33 and the rest of Mom's things. So now, I have even more journals. There's a pile of them on my desk labeled, Jessica's Journals that I am going to digitize. They are filled with her research, new ideas about the biological world, and philosophies that she found interesting. Most of the science stuff is still kind of a puzzle to me, but I love the hand-drawn images she did of each new mushroom she discovered. I am starting to make paintings of them with watercolors. The video from SubRez is a VHS tape, so we need to find the right device to play it. I'm scared to see what they recorded, but I'm also curious. Richard says it's damaged so it may not even work.

Liz gave me a beautiful journal for my own writing. The cover looks like leather, but it's made of amadou, a spongy material made of a very sturdy fungus called the Tinder Mushroom.

The tourists are mostly gone for the season, all of those folks who drive through in big SUVs in search of fall foliage. So, I've been taking walks down the road to a nearby farm, all by myself, just to see the last of the autumn color in the trees.

Well, not exactly by myself -- M&M (Mister Mushroom) goes everywhere with me now. He loves this mountain weather, probably because of his thick winter coat.

The farm is mostly abandoned, but there are still some cows roaming around, so there must be an old farmer living nearby, maybe in that rickety-looking house down in the valley. In any case, I've never seen a soul there, so today I brought my notebook and sat under the apple tree. It looks like the Giving Tree with its ungroomed branches that tumble down to the ground like in the children's book. Its apples are small and sour, which I like.

I sat there with my back against the tree and felt the pulsing life beneath the bark. When I closed my eyes, I could hear the familiar, "I'm here. Are you there? I'm here!" That's all I can really understand and translate to human language these days -- "I'm here!" It's what most plants and animals are saying to each other, and it's what they hear us say too: "I am here. I am alive!" Just a simple reminder.

I suppose that's what most of our words and gestures are anyway, an acknowledgement that we are alive. Woof, meow, cocka-doodle-doo ... I hate you, I love you, I won, I failed, I'm depressed, I need a drink, I need money, I need to feel, I need to fly. But I wonder: what is the use of such a vast vocabulary when we're really just reminding each other, "hey, I'm still here."

I laid down on my belly in the grass, propped up on elbows. Mister Mushroom placed his huge head on my back and fell asleep. I opened the journal and wrote in big letters on the first

page: "Jessie's Journal."
On the next page, I began with, "I'm here! Are you there?"

EPILOGUE

<u>Meditation</u>
A poem by Jessie A. Flynn

Decay.
Awaken.
Mother?
Brother?
Others...
Trust,
Deception,
Violence.
Search...
Reprogram...
Retreat.
Remember?
Reclaim.
Return!
Decay.

Awaken.
Mother?
Brother?
Others...
Trust,
Deception,

Violence.
Search...
Reprogram...
Retreat.
Remember?
Reclaim.
Return!
Decay.

Awaken.
Mother?
Brother?
Others...
Trust,
Deception,
Violence.
Search...
Reprogram...
Retreat.
Remember?
Reclaim.
Return!
Decay.

ABOUT THE AUTHOR

Sarah Clarke Stuart

Sarah Clarke Stuart is a Professor of English at Florida State College at Jacksonville where she teaches literature, film, composition, and emerging technologies. Author of Literary Lost: Viewing Television Through the Lens of Literature (Bloomsbury) and Into the Looking Glass: Exploring the Worlds of Fringe (ECW Press), her nonfiction work explores the intersection of narrative, culture, and media. Song of the Unsung Mushroom is her debut novel; her previous fiction includes short stories such as "Immaculate," which received Editor's Choice Award in the literary journal Fiction Fix. Both Sarah's fiction and current research are rooted in ecological interests and a deep sense of place and physical embodiment. Sarah is the creator and host of two podcasts: Lifeyness which examines embodied mental health through storytelling, and AI Goes to College, a series about artificial intelligence and the evolving nature of education.

PRAISE FOR AUTHOR

I did not need to be convinced that the recently completed Lost was a series of great complexity and depth, one of the most narratively rich in the history of the medium, but I was not prepared to discover the Lost that Sarah Clarke Stuart discovers in this important and insightful book [Literary Lost]. By diving deeper than any critic has to-date into Lost's intertextuality, by asking questions nobody so far had thought to ask, Stuart not only takes our understanding of a small-screen masterwork to a whole new level; she also builds ready-to-be crossed bridges between one-time adversaries: literature and television.

- DAVID LAVERY, CO-AUTHOR OF LOST'S BURIED TREASURES

Literary Lost belongs to a new category of books on television that combine a scholarly with a fan perspective... The book is full of skilled and inspired readings of literary works and of Lost.

- HERBERT SCHWAAB, UNIVERSITY OF REGENSBURG,
CRITICAL STUDIES IN TELEVISION

I've been arguing for decades that not only is television not inimical to literacy, it is a great ally of reading. Sarah Clarke Stuart's Literary Lost provides a brilliant, meticulous, soaring and satisfying proof of that proposition. Her tour-de-force analysis examines the roles of nearly a hundred books in Lost, ranging from the Holy Qu'run to the Wizard of Oz. The television series had highs and lows of narrative; Stuart's work has only highs, and is destined to become a classic in television studies.

- PAUL LEVINSON, AUTHOR OF DIGITAL MCLUHAN, NEW NEW MEDIA, THE PLOT TO SAVE SOCRATES, AND THE SILK CODE

Stuart writes [in Into the Looking Glass: Exploring the Worlds of Fringe] with lucid authority on the topic, and her passion for the program is clear from the depth of knowledge and insight she exhibits in her prose. A must-have for fans.

- SCENE MAGAZINE

[Into the Looking Glass] explores the characters and all the major themes of the show flawlessly and in a language that is intelligent, but accessible.

- BOOK LEGION

BOOKS BY THIS AUTHOR

Literary Lost: Viewing Television Through The Lens Of Literature

From the moment that Watership Down made its appearance on screen in season one, speculation about Lost's literary allusions has played an important role in the larger discussion of the show. Fans and critics alike have noted the many references, from biblical passages and children's stories to science fiction and classic novels.

Literary Lost teases out the critical significance of these featured books, demonstrating how literature has served to enhance the meaning of the show. It provides a fuller understanding of Lost and reveals how television can be used as a tool for stimulating a deeper interest in literary texts.

The first chapter features an exhaustive list of "Lost books," including the show's predecessor texts. Subsequent chapters are arranged thematically, covering topics from free will and the nature of time to parenthood and group dynamics. From Lewis Carroll's creations, which appear as recurring images and themes throughout, to Slaughterhouse-Five's lessons on the nature of time, Literary Lost will help readers unravel the show's novelistic plot while celebrating its astonishing layers and nuances of text.

Into The Looking Glass: Exploring The Worlds Of Fringe

A holistic approach to television criticism, this analytical companion to the popular show Fringe examines the drama's mythology and unveils its mysteries while exposing significant cultural issues addressed in each episode. With a strong basis in science fiction, Fringe has all of the archetypal characters and themes of the genre, from the covert mastermind and the mad scientist to dangerous advances in technology, parallel worlds, and man-made monsters. This guide explores how the show uses these elements to tap into a deeper understanding of the human experience. Less focused on individual episodes, this book is split into three parts, each discussing a broad element of the narrative experience of the first three seasons of this multilayered show.